M.C. HUTSON

Slow Cooked Feelings

Messy Love With A Side Of Drama

ISBN: 9781738253869

Slow Cooked Feelings

Cover Design: Miblart

Character Art: Masha Grimm

*Dedicating this book to pillow princesses 'cause
the internet be trolling y'all too hard*

NOTE FOR READERS

- This book is written in Canadian English.
- In Canada, Thanksgiving is held on the second Monday in October.
- This book contains characters struggling with depression/mental health challenges, profanity, homophobia, drug use and abuse, explicit sex scenes, and reference to sexual assault (off the page).
- To get updates on what I'm working on, sign up for my newsletter by visiting: **mchutson.com**

NOÉMIE'S PLAYLIST

- Perfect Stranger (FKA twigs)
- Faded (Alan Walker)
- Fantasy (Dean Gouws)
- Mind Is a Prison (Alec Benjamin)
- Memories (Yungblud & Willow)
- Drew Barrymore (SZA)
- My Immortal (Evanescence)
- All That I've Got (The Used)
- Feels (Kiiara)
- No Love (August Alsina ft. Nicki Minaj)
- What Would You Do (Joel Corry, David Guetta & Bryson Tiller)
- LOVE. (Kendrick Lamar ft. Zacari)
- Intoxicated (Harricane & HUG-Z)
- The Motto (Tiësto & Ava Max)
- Heart to Break (Kim Petras)

- How We Party (R3HAB & VINAI)
- São Paulo (The Weeknd & Anitta)
- Young & Foolish (Loud Luxury ft. charlieonnafriday)
- Messy (Lola Young)

ONE

There's no way this is going to work. My gaze darts over to the security at the door, and my heart hammers in my ears. For the millionth time, I stare down at the card.

I don't look anything like the woman in the photo. Her hair is frizzy and dull. She's got crow's feet and laugh lines around her mouth. Her lips are way too thin. She's supposed to be twenty-five but looks way older.

I lean towards my sister and whisper, "Can we go? They're not gonna let me in."

Antoinette rolls her eyes. "Merde, Noémie—chill out. You're worrying for nothing."

"I look nothing like her."

"We aren't leaving," she says. "You know how much this means to me."

I do know. My sister is obsessed with anything RuPaul and everything drag. Months ago, when she found out that her favourite comedy queen, Rita Bitch, was coming to Toronto, she immediately bought two tickets—one for herself and the other for her girlfriend. But she broke up with Arlene a week ago.

Antoinette begged our older brother to go with her first, but Claude refused. I was the second option. She didn't ask but demanded that I tag along. I said yes. I always say yes to Antoinette.

There's a big problem with my sister's plan. I'm eighteen. If we were in our native province of Quebec, it'd be fine. However, in Ontario, the legal age to do anything fun is nineteen. Antoinette's solution: a fake ID.

But I don't even look related to the woman in picture. And if I get caught, will I be turned away? Or will the authorities be called? Will our father be called? The unknown scares me, and I'd rather bolt than find out.

If our father ever finds out that we are trying to attend a queer event … it'll be our funerals. It doesn't matter that Antoinette is twenty—a grown woman in her own right. We still live under his roof. He will not approve. And that's putting it lightly.

The night air bites, but I hug my upper body because my stomach is wrecked with knots. Cold sweat beads and rolls down my spine.

We are next in line to enter the venue. Antoinette nudges me forward. I'm so nervous that I trip as I walk up to the security guard. He's as tall as he is wide. He wears a black toque and an even darker expression. My hand shakes as I hand over the plastic card.

He looks down at the card, and then back up at me. I suck in a breath and send up a silent prayer to God. It probably isn't right to pray at this moment. Lying is a sin. Homosexuality is a sin. We shouldn't be here. Our father is going to kill us.

The security guard says something, but I don't catch it. "Huh?" I blink.

"I need to look in your purse," he says, handing me back the faux licence.

I pocket it and dumbly blink again. "Oh, yeah—sure," I mumble, opening my St. Laurent chain wallet.

Clicking on a flashlight, he quickly beams a light down the narrow cavity. A moment later, he's holding open a door that is completely covered in Rita Bitch advertisements. I can't quite believe that it worked.

The nervous coils in my belly unspool as I step into the club. Lady Gaga's voice and the catchy melody vibrate against my skin.

I survey the area. It's dark, chaotic, and narrow. Neon-pink, electric-blue, and vivid-green graffiti is scrawled all over matte-black walls. The vibe is giving grungy back alley —all it's missing is a dumpster. There's so much trash strewn on the creaking wooden floors. My nose wrinkles when I step in something sticky. Towards the back of the space, there is a tiny stage with fraying red curtains where the crowd packs tightest.

A hand on my shoulder makes me jump. "See? I told you that you were worrying for nothing," Antoinette says.

Turning, I frown at my sister. "We got lucky."

She snorts. "You seriously need to learn how to relax, Noémie. You're so uptight. C'mon, let's get a drink. You need it." Grabbing my hand, she drags us over to the bar and puts in an order for two shots of tequila.

The bartender is a muscly woman with a purple mohawk and a face peppered with piercings. Her black nail polish is chipped. I wonder when she last washed her hands. With a sloppy flourish, she fills two plastic shot glasses, topping them both with a lime wedge.

Antoinette pushes a crisp twenty down on the counter and tells the bartender to keep the change. She sprinkles salt on the back of her hand, licks it off, downs her shot, and bites down on the lime. The ritual is effortless for her—like it's second nature. Perhaps it is.

My sister is in university now, studying business at Western. From what I've heard, the students party hard there. If Antoinette's big into the party scene, I wouldn't know though. She only talks to me when she wants something or to vent.

Antoinette likes to tell me that we're not friends. I wish we were. That's part of the reason I didn't make a fuss about coming out tonight. Sure, I might not be as beautiful as she is. I might not be as stylish. I might not be as confident. But maybe by rebelling a bit she'll start to see me differently. Doubtful, but a girl can dream.

Antoinette feels a lot of resentment towards me. Claude does too. They hate that I'm Hugo's favourite. It's obvious that our father favours me—mostly because he says it all the time. He's constantly praising my skills in the kitchen. He loves that I've expressed a desire to follow in his footsteps and become a great chef one day. Honestly, if my siblings showed any interest in cooking, Hugo would probably stop acting like I'm the only child who matters.

"What are you waiting for? Drink up," Antoinette orders, bumping my shoulder.

I reach for the plastic shot glass and just go for it. I wince as the alcohol burns down my throat, eating the lining of my stomach. I decide against chasing it with the lime wedge—this bar just doesn't look that clean, and I'm not trying to get hepatitis.

Setting down the empty plastic cup, I wonder how anyone can like tequila.

Antoinette grins at me. "Like it?"

"Yes."

"You're such a bad liar," she says with a chuckle before taking my hand. She's tugs on my arm like it's a fridge door she's trying to open. "Come, let's try to get a spot near the front."

My sister drags us towards the stage. She pushes through the crowd, weaving through groups of friends and couples. Even with the loud music, I hear a few curses sent our way. Antoinette doesn't care if she's pissing people off, she wants a good view of Rita. I mutter apologies as we worm through the crowd.

When we are close enough to the front, she drops my hand. "Would it kill you to try and pretend that you want to be here?"

I bite my lip. "I do want to be here."

Antoinette rolls her eyes. "Merde, quit frowning so much."

"I'm not."

"Whatever." My sister reaches into her pocket and pulls out her phone. The glow of the bright screen lights up her beautiful face. *Great, she's decided to ignore me.*

Sometimes, I despise her.

Compared to Antoinette, I'm underbaked. She's every colour in the rainbow, while I'm muted grey. I spent hours deciding on what I would wear tonight. A complete waste of time. Beside her, I look like I'm cosplaying being a woman in my dark high-waisted jeans, champagne camisole, and leather jacket. Before we snuck out of the house, my sister eyed my outfit with what I can only describe as mild repulsion.

Antoinette's style is loud, sexy, and bordering on obnoxious. It gives dyke, and our parents do not approve. I doubt it's ever crossed their minds that their eldest daughter is gay, but they still tend to grit their teeth almost every time she walks into a room.

If I had to guess, there's maybe eighty people in the bar. Amongst them all, Antoinette stands out. Not surprising. She's the best part of a cinnamon roll—the frosted gooey centre. Everyone else is dry edges, the parts you eat only because it's there. Here I am hoping that, one day, some of my sister's icing will drip on me.

Tonight Antoinette wears distressed low-rise Balenciaga jeans, styled with a chunky black belt and a thick gold buckle. She wears a studded leather harness over a black cropped turtleneck—only my sister can pull off wearing a harness without it looking weird. Her top layer is an oversized grey and green plaid shirt with orange stitching. Rings stack all her fingers. Three pendant necklaces of varying lengths decorate her elegant neck.

I love her shoes the most—they are the black Chrome Hearts × Rick Owens Geobasket collab. I want to get myself a pair, but I know the moment I do, Antoinette will make a fuss. Emulation doesn't please, it irritates her. "You can't just wear what I wear and expect it to work," she told me one too many times. "Be authentic for once."

If I knew how to dress, I wouldn't try to copy her. She should be flattered.

I'm most envious of the bag she carries tonight—an orange Hermes Clemence Birkin. Our grandparents gifted it to her when she started her first semester of university. When I finally figure out where I want to go for post-secondary—I'm taking a year off to decide—they better get me one too. I want a more palatable colour though. Orange might look good on me, but I find it abrasive. It's impossible to tone down. Impossible to ignore. Maybe that's why it's my sister's favourite colour.

Antoinette is still on her phone, texting. I grit my teeth. I'm bothered that she's pretending I'm not here. Like she wasn't the one who demanded that I join her tonight.

Staring down at the thin Cartier watch on my wrist, I wonder if I have enough time to use the washroom. Rita's set starts in five minutes. I really have to pee, but will I even be able to go? If the facilities are as clean as the main space, I might not be able to. Public washrooms have always been the bane of my existence. Flushing a toilet isn't rocket science, and I'd say the same thing about not pissing all over the seat. Seriously, people are disgusting.

I lean in towards Antoinette's ear. "I have to pee."

"Hold it," she says, her gaze snapping to my face. "Rita's going to start."

I bite my lip. "Don't think I can."

"Câlisse. Whatever. Go." My sister dismisses me with a wave of her hand.

It'd be nice if she'd come with me. Not wanting to stoke her ire, I keep the thought to myself.

I push through the crowd, apologizing as I go. The stairs that lead down to the washrooms are warped and rickety. I have to touch the gross banister to guarantee I won't fall. The air in the basement is thick and smells like the establishment has a problem with sewage.

It's an all genders washroom—the first one I've ever seen in real life. A man wearing a pink cowboy hat emerges from a stall the moment I walk in. Am I a bigot for being a little weirded out? He pays no attention to me, and I feel stupid for feeling uneasy. Times are changing; I need to get with the program.

I walk into the nearest unoccupied stall, and I'm pleasantly surprised to find that the toilet bowl is empty and the crooked seat isn't speckled with piss. Definitely isn't what I'm used to, but it will do.

Pulling down my jeans, I hover over the bowl. I'm about to pee when the sound of a woman's moans, a few stalls over, puts me on high alert.

"Fuck—yes," she says.

I go still. My jaw clenches. There are people fucking in the washroom—gross. Sounds like a UTI waiting to happen.

I try to block the sounds out. I try to pee. But I can't. The woman's whimpering gets louder. "Oh my gawd, yes … yes, I'm so close," she cries. "Fuck, Jay, don't stop."

Exhaling a deep breath, I squeeze my eyes shut and conjure images of waterfalls and streams and running faucets. I think about how water sounds. I think about rain. I think about ocean waves crashing against the shore. I start to pee.

I flush the toilet at the same time there's a bang, and the woman screams out, "Fuck!"

Exiting the stall, I rush over to the sink. The first soap dispenser is empty, so I scramble to the second one at the far end. All I want is to get out of there and back upstairs.

I'm vigorously lathering my hands when a stall door opens. Curiosity makes me look up in the mirror. A blond woman in loose-fitting clothing stumbles out, sniffs, and wipes her nose. Her face is flushed, and she's grinning wide enough to make me think she just won the lottery. She's really cute—Antoinette's type.

When a second person exits the stall, I don't know why, but the world hits a red light. Everything stops. My mind blanks as I stare dumbly at them. I stop registering the sensation of cool water running on my hands.

At first, I think they are the prettiest man I've ever seen, then I notice the swell of breasts beneath their black button-down shirt. Her skin is honey brown. Her jaw is strong. Her posture is relaxed. I start wondering if her curly black hair is as soft as it looks. She's tall and lean like a model—she could very well be. At least, she's got the air of one—cool and detached. Her beautiful face is a blank canvas revealing nothing. How can she look so unaffected—like she hadn't just been fucking in a public washroom?

Other questions pop in my head. What is her name? Why is she here at this drag bar? Is she the type to laugh at crude comedy? I find it hard to imagine her cackling at Rita's quick barbs and sick jokes.

Our eyes meet briefly in the mirror, and my stomach turns over. I feel off balance, bordering on sick. Perhaps the tequila didn't sit well with me.

Cheeks burning, I shut off the water and leave. For some reason, my heart races. The stairs seem even more precarious as I climb them.

Rita Bitch is on stage, mic in hand. Everyone is laughing at something the queen just said, but I don't catch it. I can't focus on anything as I thread my way through the crowd. The image of the tall stranger sears my mind.

Antoinette doesn't acknowledge my return. She's grinning up at the stage. I try to pay attention, but all I can think about is the tall woman. It's frustrating. I don't understand why the world feels tilted and hot. Must be the tequila. I'm never drinking that shit again.

Minutes go by, and I'm still unable to focus on anything. So I stop trying. I give in, letting my brain take me back to that moment downstairs. Just thinking about her—the brief moment our gazes connected—makes my chest tight.

It doesn't make sense. I'm not attracted to women. Sometimes, I think I'm not attracted to anyone. At least, I've never had crushes the same way my friends do. I've never felt that kind of tug for someone else—that kind of obsession love songs drone on and on about.

Definitely, I'm not like Antoinette. I'm a good Catholic girl with a boyfriend my father approves of. A boyfriend who is already talking about our future together—a future I don't want. There's something cagey about picturing forever with Travis, even if we're perfect for each other. He's so handsome. He comes from a good family of bankers. He looks good on my arm. I tell Travis that I love him, but the truth is that I don't. Or perhaps I do. Perhaps everyone lies, and love isn't as overwhelming a feeling as I've been led to believe.

Staring up at the stage, I attempt to concentrate on the words coming out of Rita's mouth. Nothing registers.

My gaze drifts, scanning the room until I find her. Somehow, she got a spot nearer to the stage than Antoinette. The blond chick hugs her around the waist.

My jaw clenches. I don't know how long I'm staring at them, but it's long enough that Antoinette takes notice. She nudges me in the side.

I glare at her. "What?"

My sister glares right back. "What the fuck are you looking at?"

"They were fucking in the washroom," I say, cocking my head in the direction of the women. "I almost couldn't go."

"They're a hot couple," Antoinette says. "Wonder if they'd be down for a third. Even if studs don't do it for me, I'd get in on that."

Stud? What's a stud? "TMI," I say. "I don't think they're a couple."

"You've always been a prude." My sister snorts. "And what makes you so sure they aren't together?"

"The blond chick seems a little desperate for attention," I say. "Looks to me like the other woman wants nothing to do with her." There's bite to my tone, and it doesn't go unnoticed.

Antoinette's gaze drills into me. Her stare tells me that I've crossed a line—like reheating salmon in the microwave. I'm not sure what line that is.

I direct my attention to the stage. My sister does too. Rita says something about never trying bath salts again. The room erupts with laughter.

My eyes drift back to the black woman. She isn't laughing like everyone else is. I wonder if I could make her laugh. I wonder what her laugh sounds like. I wonder what her voice sounds like. I wonder if she comes here often. I wonder how old she is. I wonder and wonder. I have so many questions.

Antoinette jabs me between the ribs. Her grey eyes grill me. "You're so pathetic," she says. "I like girls, so now you like them too? Give me a fucking break. Quit hanging out in my shadow and build your own life."

My mouth drops open, and my eyes start to sting. I don't know what to say. Why is Antoinette attacking me like this?

My sister pokes me hard in the shoulder. "You aren't a lesbian."

"I never said I was." I rub my shoulder. The area is tender. I'm probably going to bruise.

"You're nothing like me, Noémie."

Suddenly, there's applause all around us. The audience claps, and there are a few whistles. Rita's set just ended, and Antoinette's anger bumps up a few levels when she realizes that she missed the last bit. I char under the heat of her gaze.

"You realize that you ruined the show for me," she snaps. "I fucking hate you sometimes. Let's just go."

Antoinette turns and pushes through the crowd. I follow after her.

Outside is cold, but the chill doesn't numb the slap of my sister's words. It's not the first time Antoinette's said that she hates me, but for some reason the statement hurts more tonight than it ever has.

My sister pulls out her phone to order an Uber. I want to talk to her—clear the air. I don't want her mad at me. But I'm not sure where to even begin.

"Antoinette! Noémie!" A familiar voice calls out to us.

I freeze. My blood runs cold.

Both my sister and I turn slowly towards the caller. It's Henri—our father's butler. The only explanation for his presence is that he was sent to find us. Fuck!

Henri's face is somber—not good. He opens the back passenger door to my father's silver Bentley as we shuffle towards him.

My sister glowers as she slides into the back seat.

Before I hop in, I try and fail at smiling at Henri. "How mad is my father?"

Henri doesn't respond. The butler's silence tells me everything I need to know.

The drive to our family home in the Bridle Path is spent in a suffocating hush. Antoinette doesn't look at me. I wish she would. We should try to come up with an explanation together. We need to get our stories straight to bear the brunt of Hugo's anger better.

But my sister shuts down any attempt on my part to stir

up conversation. Probably because she's still pissed at me. I wish she would talk to me. I wish she didn't hate me.

When we get home, Henri guides us through the grand entrance and towards my father's office.

Both our parents are inside. My mother sits on a chaise longue, wringing her delicate hands. It's the only sign signalling her inner turmoil. Hélène's beautiful features are blank. If she wanted to frown, I doubt she could with all the Botox she pumps into her face.

My father, on the other hand, is a bubbling pot of rage. Anger steams off him like a hot dish just removed from the oven. Hugo's face is red. His grey-blue eyes are wild flames that lick over my skin, making me shudder.

He takes a large gulp of his cognac before slamming the crystal glass down on his desk.

Both Antoinette and I flinch. He barks at Henri to leave. The butler obeys, shutting the door behind him.

My father begins to pace, cursing and lashing out at us in French. He calls us ungrateful. He tells us our behaviour is unacceptable. He shouts that we are stains on his good image. Finally, he asks for an explanation for why we would ever visit a cesspool of sin.

I open my mouth to say something, but Antoinette beats me to it, "Papa … je suis lesbienne," she says. Tears stream from her grey eyes.

I want to go to her and take her hand, but the piercing look my father lances our way stops me.

My father grabs the crystal glass from off his desk and hurls it at the fireplace. The glass smashes, splintering into a million little pieces. His breaths heave as he knocks over a table lamp. He kicks his chair, making it turn over onto its side.

Hélène just watches. I wish she would say something to calm him down. Can't she see how his behaviour is hurting her daughter? Can't she see how much pain he is causing Antoinette? With every curse and insult sent my sister's way, she becomes smaller, hunching in on herself. Watching Antoinette wither isn't right. Antoinette isn't meant to be small.

Hélène says nothing. Her gaze drops to her lap as Hugo continues to scream and destroy things.

Rounding his desk, Hugo stomps towards Antoinette and shoves a beefy finger in her face. His eyes glint with a hate I've only seen when he speaks about Prime Minister Trudeau. "Dégage d'ici câlisse!"

"Get the fuck out," he said. Antoinette does just that. She flees the office in tears.

I turn to follow after her, but my father grabs my wrist. His grip is tight. "Ne me dis pas que tu es lesbienne aussi."

When I confirm that I'm not a lesbian too, he releases me. I rub my sore wrist and stare at the wide-open door. I decide not to go after my sister. I tell myself that I'll console her in the morning.

Unfortunately, I never get the chance.

There's a call to the house around 4:00 a.m. Antoinette was hit by a car. Her condition is critical. They are operating on her. They're not sure she will make it.

TWO

Eight Years Later

"It's Wednesday, let's get dressed," I say, looking into the camera with a forced smile. "Starting today with a simple pair of dark jeans." I hold up the denim for a moment and then step out of the frame to slide them on.

Next, I toss on a ribbed white crop top from Michael Kors and stuff my arms through a vintage oversized tangerine blazer. Opting for a more casual look, I cuff the sleeves up to my elbow.

I present two pairs of shoes to the camera. The first are orange stilettos from Bottega Veneta. The second are textured black Valentino boots with stud detailing. Even though I already know that I'm going with the heels, I make a show of deciding.

I style the look with some jewellery—a couple gold

bangles, large hoop earrings, and a pendant necklace from Tiffany & Co. And to complete the look, I need a purse. "Today's a Birkin day," I announce, reaching for the black bag my grandparents bought me, a little over a year ago, when I graduated from culinary school.

I hold a pose for a hot second and then tap the red button on my phone to stop recording.

Before leaving my bedroom, I eye myself in the mirror and look over at Céline. The Yorkshire terrier stares up at me with large black eyes from the bed. "What would Antoinette think?"

When my dog yawns, I sigh. "You're right. She'd say I'm trying too hard." The outfit looks good. Way too good for my daily itinerary. My shift at the restaurant starts in about an hour, and I'll have to take it all off.

But it's all worth it. I can't wait for *her* to see me. It's always the highlight of my day.

The doorbell rings, and I frown. I don't remember ordering anything, and I'm not expecting a visitor.

Céline jumps off the bed. She begins barking like crazy. Her nails scratch against the door.

"Tais-toi," I say, but the dog doesn't listen. I've tried to train her to not get so excited at any little sound, but she is stubborn.

Hurrying down the staircase, I lift Céline into my arms before opening the front door. Cara stands on the landing holding two coffee cups.

"Morning," my girlfriend says, beaming brightly. "Wow, you look amazing." She leans forward to kiss me.

I take a step back. "What are you doing here?" Cara's

disrupting my weekday morning routine, and I'm not pleased. She knows how committed I am to ritual. She shouldn't be here.

"I was in the area," Cara says, grinning. "I thought I could drive you to work."

"I have my own car. I can drive myself," I say flatly.

She bites her lip. "I know, but I've been out of town for a while, and I … I just thought it'd be nice to see you."

Cara is a model, and she travels around the world for work. For the most part, we get along well enough. I like how good we look together, but I hate how clingy she is. We don't need to spend every waking hour together when she's back in Toronto.

I want to tell her as much, but I'm not in the mood to fight. Actually, I just don't have time to argue. My shift starts soon, and I still need to go to the coffee shop. To not have Hot Barista see me when I put so much thought into my outfit would be a tragedy. "Fine, let's go," I grumble.

"I got you coffee," Cara says, lifting the cup in her right hand.

I roll my eyes. "You know I hate Starbucks."

"Since when?" Cara lifts a brow.

"Since forever," I say, setting Céline down. "Let's just go."

I slip into the passenger side of her Porsche and buckle up. Cara slides into the driver's seat. Her hands grip the steering wheel tightly as she reverses out of my driveway and takes off down the street. She's annoyed, but I don't care. She shouldn't have interrupted my routine.

I pull down the car's visor and check my face in the mirror. My makeup looks good, but I decide to add an extra coat of lip gloss. "You can drop me in front of Grind That Bean," I say.

"For real?" Cara snaps, glaring at me. "Is that why you're so dolled up—to put on a show for Hot Barista?"

"I love it when you get jealous over nothing," I say, dropping the tube of gloss into my purse.

"It's not nothing," Cara says. "I've seen the way you look at her. I don't like it."

Cara and I went into the coffee shop once together. In that short time, I'm not sure how she managed to clock that I have the hots for Jordan. But whatever, it is what it is. And I'm sure Cara must fancy at least one of her model colleagues.

Snorting, I say nothing more and turn my gaze out the window. Crushes are harmless like a pinch of cayenne added to a recipe. A little spice never hurt anyone. Cara is being ridiculous.

Hot Barista is a fantasy. She's always been that to me, ever since the first time I saw her all those years ago. I'd never act on my feelings, and that's what matters. We're from two different worlds. There's probably nothing me and Hot Barista would ever have in common. Cara and I are better suited.

When Cara pulls up to the curb a couple of store fronts down from the coffee shop, she leans forward in her seat to kiss me.

I'm quick to put up a hand to stop her. "What are you doing? Someone might see," I chide. It's not paranoia. It's the truth. My work is only a block away. The last thing I need is a co-worker seeing me lock lips with a woman. Just the thought of the questions that would stir unsettles me.

Also, we're in the Financial District, where more than a few of my father's business associates work. If word ever reached my father that I was in a relationship with a woman … well, I can kiss my dreams goodbye.

Hugo and I have a deal. If I can prove that I can work in a restaurant for a couple of years and then get an MBA from a reputable university, he'll completely fund my first restaurant venture. I want my own restaurant more than anything. I want it more than Cara. I want it more than love.

So I can't fuck up. I can't disappoint my father. I have to be perfect in his eyes.

Sighing, Cara slumps in her seat. She sulks in a bad way— like a toddler who's being forced to eat veggies. I hate it when she gets like this.

When we first started dating about two years ago, I told her how it'd have to be between us: no public displays of affection, no social media posts announcing relationship milestones, and no celebrating the holidays together.

Back then, she'd been okay with it. She told me that I was worth it. More and more, I'm starting to think she's regretting the deal she struck.

"Look, how about you come over later for dinner," I say, trying to lighten her mood. "You can choose what we order in."

"I can't. I got a thing," she says.

"Okay. How about tomorrow night?"

She shakes her head. "I'm booked up for the rest of the week."

A silence yawns between us. I stare at her side profile. She's purposefully not looking at me.

My gaze darts to the clock on the dash. I need to get going. My shift starts soon. Sighing, I open the door and step outside. "Okay, well, text me later and we can plan something," I say.

Cara is still refusing to look at me. "Sure," she mumbles.

Annoyed by her curtness, I shut the door harder than I probably should without saying goodbye. Cara takes off down the road. I grit my teeth as I watch her go.

Morning off to a bad start, I'm scowling when I step into the coffee shop.

My mood sours further when I see just how busy it is. The line is almost at the door. My shift starts in thirty minutes, and I like to be at least fifteen minutes early to give myself enough time to get ready.

The clock is not on my side. Joining the queue is out of the question. I step to the side and enter my order through the mobile app.

Grind That Bean isn't a conventional coffee shop. It isn't cozy vibes and slow jazz music. The colour scheme is a loud purple and chrome, and the harsh fluorescent lighting makes my skin look horrible. The aesthetic shouldn't work, especially not in Toronto's financial district. But surprisingly, it does. The place is always buzzing, and I'm not sure why. In my opinion, the coffee is mediocre—perhaps only a grade above Starbucks. Best coffee in the city, hands down, is Mos Mos, and there's one right around the corner. But I'm not here for the coffee.

My gaze wanders past the dozens of waiting customers

towards the espresso machine. When I see her, my pulse quickens.

Jordan is tall and lean and beautiful as ever, but this morning there are dark circles under her eyes. Her movements are off and her brows are pinched. Usually, she's so cool and relaxed. I wonder what happened to throw her off her game.

A man in a cheap suit and a woman in a horrendous frilly blouse begin spatting. Jordan stares at them blankly. She seems frozen, unsure what to do—it's so not like her. There's a part of me that wants to stride up to the shouting customers and tell them to shut up. Of course, I can't do that. Well, I could … but I won't.

The assistant manager bails Jordan out. I know his name is Wayne because all the coffee shop staff wear tags listing their names and positions. Wayne approaches Cheap Suit and Ugly Blouse with a smile. I don't catch what he says, but the quarrelling ceases.

A moment later, Jordan stares out into the crowd and our eyes meet. She stares at me like I'm her favourite meal. My heart beats hard in my chest and my skin buzzes, but I school my features. It wouldn't do to let her know how much she affects me. It wouldn't do to get her hopes up. After all, I'm taken. And part of the fantasy is keeping her in the dark.

I dream about her a lot. Sometimes I'm eighteen again and we're back at the club, but I'm the one she's fucking in the stall. In the dream it's sexy. In reality, I can't imagine anything being less so. I can't imagine ever being so turned on that I'd want to be fucked in a germ-infested public restroom.

When I first stumbled into Grind That Bean, a little over a year ago, I nearly had an panic attack when I saw her behind the counter. Jordan was a reminder of the worst night of my life. At the same time, she was the one who first made me realize that I can feel attraction.

Men don't do it for me. Most women don't either. I have a distinct type—Cara sometimes fits the bill when she dresses more masculine. Butchy women, the kind who look like they can throw me around and dominate me, they turn my knees to jelly.

I think I resent Jordan a little for making me realize that I'm not straight. But perhaps I should be grateful. If I hadn't met her, maybe I would be engaged to Travis—my first boyfriend whom Hugo loved like a son. My father keeps pestering me, asking when I'm going to find another fine man. My excuse for the last few years has been that I'm working on myself and my career.

I know it's only a matter of time before Hugo starts trying to set me up with the sons of his friends. Cara will definitely not like me going on dates with men to save face. It might be the tipping point for our relationship.

"Noémie," Jordan calls out.

Blinking away my thoughts, I go to the counter to pick up my order. Hot Barista watches me intently, and I light up inside. I always want her eyes fixed on me. Only me.

Lifting my cup, I take a sip. And I'm not sure why I do it, but I wrinkle my nose despite the drink being passable. I really don't have time for games this morning, but I've already started. I have to commit. I can't back away now.

"Excuse me, you got my order wrong," I say, waving for her to come back to the pickup counter.

Jordan frowns at me. "What's wrong with it?" She folds her arms over her chest.

Our heads are only about a couple of feet apart. This close, I can see just how perfect her skin is without a hint of makeup. She's got the longest eyelashes and the smallest black freckle underneath her right eye.

Every time I see her, I can't help but think that it's a shame she languishes behind an espresso machine, and the purple uniform is doing nothing for her.

Androgynous faces and bodies have been all the rage for years now. Jordan needs to be scouted for editorial. I could see her in photoshoot spreads or walking runways for brands like Maison Margiela. But maybe it's too late for her. Despite her youthfulness, the fashion industry is fickle. Jordan's in her early thirties. I know this because her Facebook account isn't private, and her information is out there for anyone to see.

I also know that she has a BFA and that she's a Cancer. So we aren't compatible at all if astrology means anything. Cancers are far too emotional and sensitive, and they're resistant to change. As a Gemini, I'm logical, independent, and I like to think I'm adaptable. Some would call Geminis chaotic or evil. But we're just misunderstood.

Setting down my drink, I push it towards her. "It's way too sweet," I say, answering her question with a smile. "I find your tone abrasive. There's no reason for you to get defensive."

I don't know why I'm trying to pick a fight with her this

morning when it's obviously the last thing she needs. The woman looks like she hasn't slept for days. Okay, that's a lie. I do know why—I want to prolong our interaction. I want to make her feel something for me in this moment, even if it's annoyance.

I get what I want. Jordan's hands drop to her sides and ball into fists. Her mouth sets in a tight line. She eyes the cup, and I'm thinking she's going to argue with me. An argument would be fun. She doesn't though. Instead, she says flatly, "I'm so sorry. I'll remake your order right away."

"Merci," I say, a little disappointed she gave in so easily.

About two minutes later, she drops off a new drink and doesn't spare me a second glance. Irritated, I grab it and take a sip. The first drink was better, but I don't have time to make any more complaints.

I leave the coffee shop and head to work.

THREE

Ten minutes early, but still somehow late for my shift. I'm rushing to get ready—I hate rushing. I'm warring to remove the white crop top without smudging my makeup when I start mentally dragging myself. Story of my life—I'm pathetic. So much time and effort put into looking this good just for Hot Barista to objectify me for half a second. And now I have to take it all off, trading designer for the cotton-polyester blend uniform and slip-resistant shoes. It's tragic, like pineapple on pizza. Just once, it would be nice if Jordan said something to me besides the standard customer service babble. Like, I know she thinks I'm hot. Would it kill her to compliment me?

I really should quit going to Grind That Bean, but I'm addicted to the high I get when her eyes devour me. She's my weekday morning fix. I need her more than caffeine. Maybe Cara has a right to be jealous.

Grabbing my knife kit, I shut my locker and hurry out of the staff change room and up the stairs.

It's 9:00 a.m., and the kitchen is starting to hum to life. Sally turns on the intake hoods, and suddenly the whirring of exhaust fans drowns out most sounds.

Sally is the sauté chef, and she reports directly to Thompson, the sous chef. She's my direct competition. I'm gunning for her position. It's only a matter of time before I usurp her, and I would have done so not because of my looks, but because I'm faster and more precise than her. Sally fucks up a lot. I don't.

A little over a year ago, when I started working at Chez Avignon as a commis chef, Sally instantly went on the attack, bad mouthing me every chance she got. At first, I thought she didn't like me purely based on the fact that I come from money. I figured that she saw a rich white girl who couldn't cut it in such a fast-paced and high-pressure work environment. But when I proved myself and was promoted to entremetier, I realized that my work ethic wasn't the reason for her scorn.

Sally hates me because I'm beautiful. She hates me because she's in love with Thompson, and our sous chef would sell his soul just to slip the tip inside me. But I wouldn't swap spit with Thompson for a vintage Chanel dress, which is really saying something. There are few things in the world that I love more than vintage designer clothing.

Yeah, Sally can go fuck herself. I'm not here to make friends anyways. I'm here to learn from the best, and Ricard is one of the most highly regarded executive chefs in the country.

Once I've put in my time and learned enough, I'll be one step closer to my goal: having my own restaurant.

After clocking in and greeting Thompson, I head over to my station. There's a prep list clipped to the rack above the stainless-steel counter.

The first part of my day is mundane. I spend most of my time washing, peeling, chopping and pre-cooking vegetables. Usually, I finish checking off everything on the list early, but the bundle of leeks we received from the supplier are exceptionally gritty, so it takes longer than I would like to get them ready.

Besides the clanking of pans, sizzling of oil, and shutting of oven doors, the kitchen is mostly quiet. Other than Thompson checking in on me every now and then, no one approaches me to talk. Partly, that's because of Sally and her smear campaign against me. But also, Chef Ricard is not a fan of his workers schmoozing.

By the time 3:00 p.m. rolls in, I've completed my prep and organized and tidied my station to Ricard's standards. It's family mealtime.

I grab an elegantly plated crepe stuffed with salmon, capers, crème fraiche, and sautéed spinach. I'm famished, and it's delicious.

As the team eats, Thompson leans against the bar and begins running through the details of tonight's dinner service. "We're looking at sixty covers to start the evening," he announces. "There's a birthday at table forty-six at seven fifteen. We have a large group of twelve at eight thirty. And we have a VIP dropping in at nine. Last service, there was an inconsistency of the sears on the fish, and Ricard is looking for perfection. So, Alain, if you need help on your station, please ask."

Sitting across from me, I watch as Alain's face reddens. I'm thinking they should put me on fish. It's one of the hardest stations, and I want to prove myself to chef.

Dinner service starts promptly at 4:30 p.m. We open our doors, and as customers begin filtering in, the dynamic shifts. The previous calm dissolves as Ricard shouts off the first ticket.

Only an hour into service, my feet are crying, and I'm sweating profusely. Hell is probably cooler than the Chez Avignon kitchen. It's loud and chaotic, but I know the strongest steel is forged in fire. If I can make it here, I can make it anywhere. If I can make it here, I will be able to run my own restaurant one day.

Chef Ricard demands the best from us, and his fiery temperament makes Gordon Ramsey look like a teddy bear. It's rare that I make a mistake, but I always get anxious when I send anything up to the pass for his review.

When I was still a commis chef, I almost cried the first time he screamed at me for forgetting to salt the boiling water for the potatoes. I'd felt like such an idiot, but I never repeated that mistake.

It's a little past 10:30 p.m when I clock out and change back into my stylish civilian clothes. I step through the back door and see Thompson smoking outside. He beams at me, and his gaze slides down my body. Holding out a pack of cigarettes, he asks, "Want one?"

Smoking has never been my thing—I've always preferred pills and alcohol. I shake my head. "No, I'm good."

Sally shoots out of the back door just then and scowls at me. I scowl right back and check my phone to see the status of my UberX. I'm annoyed that I can't just drive home. I should have insisted on driving myself to work instead of getting a lift from Cara.

"My ride is here," I announce. "See you tomorrow."

Thompson waves goodbye to me. Sally doesn't.

Walking down the narrow alley towards the street, I find my UberX and slide into the back seat, sighing out my exhaustion.

When I get home, the first thing I do is swap my heels for runners and take Céline out for a short walk around the block. During the day, there's a dog walker who swings by to take care of her needs. Sometimes, she's even brought to the off-leash park.

I know Céline hates the long hours I spend away from home, but it can't be helped. My dream is well within my reach if I work hard enough.

I'm dying of hunger, but I'm never in the mood to cook after a shift. I order pizza. While I wait for the delivery, I take a shower, washing off the sweat and grease of the day. As the hot water pelts against my skin, I think about Cara and how she drove off in a huff. She hasn't texted me all day. Usually she texts me often. She'll send me pics of her on set or of her meals. She'll send me kissy-face selfies along with messages like, *thinking of you*. She'll send me TikToks or Reels she thinks I'll enjoy.

Cara must be really annoyed with me. It's not normal for her to be this silent. I'll have to find a way to make it up to her. Sighing, I turn off the water and get out of the shower.

I'm blow-drying my hair when the doorbell rings. As always, Céline starts making a fuss, barking and whining.

I hurry down three flights of stairs—my bedroom is in the loft on the upper tier of my Victorian townhouse. My father gifted me the home when I graduated from Le Cordon Bleu. It's nicer than the home he purchased for Claude. Despite all the deals my brother has brokered for Hugo, I'm still his favourite. It makes Hugo happy that I'm following in his footsteps. Before he turned to business, starting his Poutine Heaven franchise empire, he was a chef.

As a kid, I bonded with my father in the kitchen. He taught me that spices are more aromatic when toasted or when tempered in hot oil. He taught me how to hold a knife and make quick, precise cuts. He taught me how to break down poultry and how to debone a fish.

For the longest time, Hugo had been my idol and the centre of my entire universe. But then, Poutine Heaven took off. Money started to pour in as more and more restaurants opened. I began to see my father less and less. His absence fractured our family unit, and then Antoinette got into her accident and we completely broke apart.

Hugo's been trying to make amends in his own way. Claude and I want for nothing. Unfortunately, all the money and gifts in the world won't buy back my brother's forgiveness.

Me, I don't know how to feel about my father. It's hard to hate him. Yes, he's to blame. He'd been the one who'd screamed at Antoinette, ordering her to get the fuck out of his sight. But I didn't run after her—I should have. If I had gone after her … maybe things would be different. Maybe she would still be here.

Forcing my thoughts away, I open the front door.

A pimply faced man with greasy hair sticking out from a baseball cap stands outside on the landing. He stares a little too long at me. His gaze drops to my chest.

"My eyes are up here," I snap.

He blinks rapidly and has the audacity to look embarrassed as he struggles to remove my pizza from an insulated bag.

I dismiss the option to tip and tap my credit card on the machine. Grabbing my pizza, I slam the door in his face.

Céline's nails rap against the wood floors as she follows me to the living room. I drop my dinner on the coffee table and collapse into the sofa. It feels so good to sit. It doesn't feel good to be alone.

My house is far too big and empty. I wish Cara was here with me, filling the space with her breath and warmth and voice. Most times, I just feel so overwhelmingly lonely. It doesn't matter that I work with people all day. It doesn't matter that I have tens of thousands of followers. At the end of the day, when I get home, there's no one to talk to. No one to vent to. No one who really understands me.

There are a lot of friends I've had to cut off over the years, and those I still keep in touch with either live abroad or travel for work. They have full lives, and I fear intruding on their time.

I switch on the TV and start up the next episode of Love Is Blind because I'm in the mood to watch something brain numbing.

My Tuscan pesto pizza is horrible. The crust is barely cooked through, and it's drowning in pesto sauce. I can only stomach a single slice.

I check my phone. Cara still hasn't messaged me, so I decide to be the bigger person and shoot her off a message.

NOÉMIE, 11:46 P.M.

Hey

Instantly, three dots pop up on the screen, but they quickly fade. I bite my lip, waiting for a reply. Fifteen minutes pass. I call, but I'm directed to voicemail. What the hell kind of game is Cara playing? I text her again.

NOÉMIE, 12:04 A.M.

Call me

She doesn't.

FOUR

The next morning when I strut into Grind That Bean, I'm one minor inconvenience away from throwing a kid-cracked-out-on-sugar tantrum. I scan the area, searching for Jordan. Hot Barista isn't around. Frowning, I grit my teeth.

Cara's still ignoring me, and I think the only thing that might levy my spirits is Jordan's eyes on me. I'm very fuckable this morning—I'd do me. Considering I'm generally not into redheads or feminine women, that's really saying something.

My look is very much Antoinette inspired—high-waisted jeans, a black Prada cami top with a leather harness overtop, layers of gold necklaces, and stacks of rings. My sunglasses are thick frames from Chanel, and I decided to carry a vintage Prada bag.

It's probably one of the most queer-coded outfits I've put together in a long while. I want Hot Barista panting when she sees me. But she still isn't around when I place my order with the stammering blond woman at the register. Her name tag identifies her as Corrine. She's a fairly new face. I never noticed before how much I hate her asymmetrical hair bob. Whoever talked the girl into getting bangs needs to be sentenced to death by guillotine.

When Corrine blurts out the total for my drink, I dig through my purse for my wallet. I tap my credit card and motion to move towards the pickup counter.

Corrine clears her throat. "Sorry … miss."

Why is she speaking to me? "What?" I glare at the woman. She flinches.

"It declined." Corrine lifts the card reader for me to see.

"C'est quoi ce bordel," I curse. Pinning the girl with a death stare, I remove a second card from my wallet and tap on the terminal. I'm shocked when I'm greeted with another declined message.

There's no way my father forgot to pay the credit statement on time. So what the fuck is this? The café's payment system is broken. Hot Barista is MIA. And Cara is ignoring me. It's taking every ounce of willpower not to lose my shit on Corrine with the horrible bob.

Like a bad omen, my phone starts buzzing. Claude's name lights up my screen. My brother almost never calls me. I step to the side of the register and indicate with a brisk hand gesture that Corrine should service another customer. I accept the call and raise the phone to my ear.

"So … Hugo knows about Cara," Claude says.

The universe pauses. Suddenly, my anger flips to dread. All the blood drains from my face, pooling to my stomach where it sits heavy like a twenty-course meal. Lightheaded and slightly off balance, I brace against the counter.

"Noémie, are you there? Did you hear me?"

I close my eyes and take a deep breath. "Oui—yes, I heard you."

When I open my eyes, all the staff behind the counter are watching me. Why are they staring? Don't they have work to do? It's a good thing Jordan isn't around. I can't imagine what expression is on my face, but I know it isn't good. Why am I even thinking about her? She's the least of my worries.

Letting out a groan of frustration, I rush out of the shop and hightail it to my car. "Esti de câlice de tabarnak!" I shout into the receiver. "How the fuck did he find out?"

Claude is quiet for a beat. "I might have … accidentally made it slip."

"Putain!" I throw myself into the driver seat and slam the door. "How the fuck did you manage that?"

"You know how that man aggravates me. We were arguing about—I can't even remember what. But I was angry, and I wasn't thinking. I'm so sorry. I didn't mean—"

I hang up on my brother. I can't hear anymore. My gut knots so tightly that I want to vomit. The world spins. It's hard to breathe. The car is suddenly too hot. The car's cabin closes in on me. I'm dying.

No, not dying. I'm having a panic attack. I haven't had one in a long time, but there was once a time when I couldn't go a single day without suffering a complete meltdown. After Antoinette's death, I began having them. At one point they got so bad that I finally caved and let my brother talk me into therapy.

Talking to a specialist helped. I was taught breathing techniques to regain control.

Now I try to implement them, inhaling deeply through my nose for a count of four, holding my breath for another four seconds and then exhaling through my mouth just as slowly. I repeat the process over and over. I try to ground myself by focusing on the external. I identify five things I can see, four things I can touch, three things I can hear, and two things I can smell.

All in all, it takes me thirty full minutes to calm the fuck down.

My shift starts in ten minutes, but I can't think about work. When I finally put my car into drive, I head north—the opposite direction from the restaurant.

Hugo knows about Cara. If I don't face his wrath now, I might never find it in myself to. I'd rather pour alcohol on this wound now instead of letting it fester. I'm hoping that I'll be able to find a way to salvage my relationship with my father. Maybe I can talk him down or spin my relationship with Cara into something else—a mistake, a dalliance.

If I can't … I can kiss my dreams goodbye.

Before I know it, I'm at the gate leading to my father's mansion. It's a grand home with a symmetrical façade, large Corinthian columns, and tall rectangular windows. The surrounding landscape is formal, with a tasteful arrangement of trees and shrubbery.

The mechanized door opens, and I speed up the winding road flanked by high, neatly trimmed hedges. I park in the roundabout driveway.

My pulse pounds in my ears as I rush up to the front

door. It opens before I get a chance to pop in my key. Henri looks at me with an expression that is meant to be reassuring. Clearly, he knows what's up. There's not much the butler doesn't know.

"Where's my father?" I ask.

Henri shuts the door. "He's in the study."

"Thank you," I say, turning to walk down the long hall.

"Noémie," Henri says.

I stop and look at him.

"If you need someone to talk to … I'm always here," he offers.

I smile at him. It wavers. My entire body vibrates from a fusion of colliding emotions, and it's hard to keep upright. The walls close in on me. I think about fleeing.

Do I really need to have this conversation with Hugo? What is keeping me from retreating? I can just run on my own terms. There's more than enough money in my bank account. I earn enough in dividends and interest to continue to live out my days in comfort since I don't have a mortgage or many expenses. I'd likely have to curb my shopping though. No more heavy bidding on vintage designer clothes and handbags. The prospect is horrifying.

Biting my lip, I stare down the hall. I can just barely make out the door to my father's office.

Breathe. Just breathe. I try to stand a little taller. I will not run away. I have a dream, and I need my father's money. I need to smooth things over with him. How hard can it be? I'm his favourite.

My heels clack on the polished marble floors as I advance

towards hell. When I knock on the door to the study, my palms are slick with sweat.

Behind the door, Hugo calls me by name to enter. I wonder how he knew I'd arrived. Has he been watching the camera footage?

I enter.

My father doesn't rise from his seat. His blue-grey eyes bore holes into me as he reaches for his glass of cognac and raises the rim to his lips. He doesn't say anything. It's just us in the space. The quiet is suffocating, and I'm chocking on nothing.

I inch closer to his desk and clear my throat. "Papa …"

Hugo holds up a hand and winces as if in pain. "Ça me rend malade de te regarder," he mutters.

Just looking at me makes him sick—his words fillet me like a chef's knife. "Really, because you think I'm in a relationship with a woman you can't look at me?" I say. My father favours French. I speak in English to knock him off centre. It's a tactic Claude and I often utilize.

Hugo sighs and rubs his temple with a hand. I was expecting anger from him. I was expecting him to lash out the same way he had all those years ago at Antoinette. Instead, he looks more tired than I've ever seen him.

Silence settles over the room again. The only thing I hear is the blood pounding in my head.

"You wanted to hurt me," he says. "Congratulations, Noémie, you have succeeded."

I swallow. "Papa—"

"I don't want to hear it." He holds up a hand. "I've heard enough, and I'm sick. Two years you've been making a mockery of me behind my back, philandering with a … woman. But it ends now."

My heart sinks like a rock thrown in a pond, because I know what he's saying. I will have to break up with Cara, and it's the last thing I want to do. Yes, our relationship isn't perfect, but I love her. She's my best friend—the person who peppers my days with text messages and photos and links to funny videos. She's my biggest fan and confidant.

But if that's the price for my dreams … I'll do it. "Okay," I say, my eyes stinging. "I'll never see her again."

My father snorts. "I've already seen to it that you won't."

I blink. "What?"

"I spoke with that woman—Caralyn. She was here last night. I wrote her a cheque for fifty thousand dollars." My father sits back in his chair and steeples his fingers. "She took the money in exchange for never seeing you again and keeping her silence."

His words hit like a cast-iron pan to the face. I stagger back. "You didn't … she didn't."

"I did, and she did," he confirms. "And now we can put this scandal behind us and move forward. My business partner, Monsieur Martin, has a son a few years older than you …"

Shaking my head, I massage my forehead. My skull pounds. If I was in a better frame of mind, if I could think, if my heart wasn't breaking … maybe I would have been okay with going along with my father's plan. But I can't focus, and I say no.

Red colours Hugo's face. "You're not in a position to say

no." He bangs a fist on his desk. "If you ever want anything from me, you will do as I say."

"Then I don't want anything!"

Our gazes collide. It surprises me that I hold his, unblinking. The moment stretches out like dough until Hugo cuts through it. "Câllise!" He swears, clenching his teeth. "You are not Antoinette. You are not a …" My father doesn't finish the sentence.

I'm not. At least, I haven't claimed a label. My sexuality is something I don't think about. I'm not straight, and that's all I need to know.

Whatever expression my father sees on my face, he doesn't like it. "We're done—this discussion is over," he shouts. "Quitter ma vue!"

For a moment, I just stand there. But then my feet unstick, and I do as my father orders. I leave.

How I managed the walk back to my car and drive home is a miracle. Tears blur my vision. I'm jittery, and I'm not sure how my heart pumps blood to my organs when it's a shredded block of cheese.

Cara chose money over me. I thought she loved me, but she never really did.

The conversation with Hugo replays over and over in my mind as I slug my way up the flights of stairs to my bedroom and crash down onto my mattress.

FIVE

If Antoinette could see me now, I know she'd hate me. What do I have to really complain about? I have my health. I am alive, free to go wherever I please. But I haven't done much of anything in the days and then weeks that followed my argument with Hugo. The only time I leave my bed is to feed Céline or take her out. Only when my hunger pangs are too noticeable to ignore do I order takeout. My room is littered with to-go fast food boxes and containers. Usually, I detest any kind of mess, but I can't be bothered to care.

I got fired. One shift. I missed one shift and Ricard dropped me. It was Thompson who rang me up with the news—Chef couldn't be bothered. I'm not surprised; I've always just been a number to him. He often told those of us on the line that we were easily replaceable. Sally must be ecstatic, and I fucking hate that.

Even before Hugo found out about Cara, work held me together like a roux. Without a job, I'm just a broken sauce. I don't take my antidepressants. I don't work out. I don't make videos. I don't cook.

I've thrown my entire routine out the window, allowing myself to crawl back into the same pit I fell in after Antoinette's funeral. The pit is safe and familiar. It's a place without anxiety. I'm just a heavy mass that sleeps and sleeps and sleeps.

All those years ago, Claude kept bugging me. He kept yapping that I needed to get up. But whenever I did, panic gripped me so tightly that I couldn't breathe.

Therapy saved me. I was finally able to crawl out of my hole, but I wasn't the same. Living felt like a burden. Even simple tasks were too much. I was diagnosed with depression and prescribed antidepressants.

The first pills I was given made me feel like a zombie and gave me the worst brain zaps. Then I was put on a different drug that fucked up my sleep and made me slightly suicidal. The third mood stabilizer did absolutely nothing after three months.

For awhile, I felt like a lab rat. Everything was trial and error. The whole process was frustrating, but my doctor finally landed on the right pharmaceutical to fix my chemical imbalance.

I hate being medicated. I hate that I need a prescription to feel somewhat normal, but I've gotten used to it. Just as I've gotten used to my regular visits with my psychologist.

Rebecca Dunlop is a darling. She listens and never judges. At least, she's given no physical indications of judgements—even when I say the wildest things or confess to thoughts or behaviours that would be condemned in polite society.

There are a few topics I refuse to talk to her about. I'm happy Rebecca doesn't push me. Overall, I like talking to her.

I know I should schedule an appointment with her, but my phone is dead. Reaching to put the device on the wireless charger just seems like too much work. Besides, I already know what Rebecca will say. She'll tell me that I need to start taking my meds again. She'll tell me that I need to stick to a routine. She'll tell me that I need to focus on self-acceptance and work on figuring out who I am. She'll tell me that I should join a support group. And at the more recent visits, she's recommended that I consider getting a roommate in response to my confession of feeling helplessly lonely. Blah, blah, blah …

I feel like I know what ingredients can build happiness, but the recipe eludes me. Or maybe that's just what I tell myself to avoid thinking about it. There's a lot I don't want to think about. On a deep level, I always knew Cara and I weren't right for each other. Did I ever examine why? No. Am I questioning everything now? A little. But I refuse to go deeper than wondering if I'm unlovable. Clearly, my ex never loved me. She wouldn't have taken Hugo's money if she did. Fuck her.

Céline suddenly sits up right in the bed. Her ears twitch, and then she hops off the mattress, scrambling for the door. She begins to bark.

Scowling, I sit up. "Tais-toi," I order.

The dog doesn't listen. If anything, she starts barking louder, and I soon understand why. There's a creak. Someone is coming up the stairs.

I grip my sheets tight to my chest. I'm not expecting

someone. Is it a robber? That would be just my luck. Some creepy man in a Scream mask is going to stab me repeatedly and defile my body. My murder will be broadcasted to the masses. Will my mother cry when she's interviewed for the evening news? Probably not. The cold bitch only sniffled when Antoinette's casket was lowered into the ground.

When the door to my bedroom opens, I suck in a breath.

The big light is flipped on, and I wince. Claude stands in the threshold. Céline pounces happily on his leg—the traitor. Hissing at my brother, I throw the sheet over my head and curl back up into a ball.

"Merde, it's a fucking mess in here," he says. "When's the last time you opened a window?"

"How did you get in? Ugh … go away."

"I have a key," Claude replies. To my annoyance, he doesn't go away. I hear him throwing the curtains to the side and opening a window. "It's been forever since one of your cringey dress-up videos popped on my feed. You know, I've been calling you for weeks. Why didn't you answer? I was freaking out."

"And you're just coming to check on me now?" I snort. "Yeah, sounds like you were really worried."

"I wasn't in the country. I was busy opening the new international stores in the U.K. and the U.S. I just got back to Toronto late last night," he explains. "Why didn't you answer your phone?"

"It's dead." I exhale a deep breath of frustration. This conversation is exhausting. I just want to go back to sleep. I close my eyes with the intention of doing just that when my duvet is ripped off of me. "What the fuck!" I glare at

Claude. The cool air filtering through the window makes me shiver.

"What the fuck indeed. You stink," he says. "When's the last time you showered?"

I grit my teeth. "Go away."

"No, I'm not going anywhere, but you're going to the shower—maintenant."

"You can't tell me what to do."

"True, but I promise to make your life a living hell until you get out of bed." As if to prove his point, he leaps up onto my mattress and begins to bounce. He's a grown-ass man in a tailored Armani suit jumping on my bed. I hope he falls off and bumps his head.

"You're going to break my bed frame," I growl.

The bastard smiles at me. "Get the fuck up, princess."

"Fine!" With a groan, I roll out of bed and stand. "Happy?"

Claude stops jumping. "Not quite. Go shower and get dressed. We're going out."

"I'm not going anywhere."

"Yes, you are. I'm taking you away from this pigsty," he says, hopping off the mattress. "I've made us reservations at Lee. I know how much you love that Singapore slaw. Don't bother denying it."

I do love Susur Lee's signature dish. It's perfect in every way, boasting twenty-four ingredients that, when combined, create a refreshing and unique blend of flavours and textures. But I'm not in the headspace to go anywhere. I'm not hungry.

"I'm not going anywhere," I repeat.

An hour later, I slide into Claude's Ferrari and cross my arms disapprovingly. Hugo bought the sports car for my brother as a gift for completing his MBA program. Claude now works for my father, selling and assisting with the opening of Poutine Heaven franchises globally. My brother is very good at brokering deals. He's made a lot of money for Hugo, and in so doing, he's raked in millions for himself.

I know it's only a matter of time before he splits from our father and starts up his own venture. Claude hates working under Hugo's thumb.

I really don't want to be going out, but Claude pretty much dragged me into the shower. He's always been persistent that way. I'm usually good at getting what I want. My brother's better at it—more stubborn. The only way to get him off my back is to do what he wants, but the wick of my temper is burning down to its explosive end.

He's the reason I'm in this predicament. He yapped his big fat mouth to Hugo, and … Cara took the money.

A lump forms in my throat. I feel the prickle of tears in my eyes. "I can't do this," I say, reaching for the handle.

Claude locks the door with the press of a button, trapping me. "Too late now, we're going," he says. "We're going to have fun tonight. We're going to eat good food and bitch about our tyrant father."

I don't say anything. I stare out the window.

Claude pulls out of my driveway. He talks. I don't listen.

When we arrive at Lee, we're led to our table. The restaurant's aesthetic is sleek, contemporary, and sophisticated. The artwork and fine detailing is Asian inspired. The lighting is dim and intimate.

I can't be bothered to look at the menu, but I request the most expensive bottle of French white wine.

My brother peruses the menu and orders a slaw, lobster dumplings, spicy shrimp cheung fun, char sui barbeque duck with Peking garnish, and a rack of roast lamb. It's a lot of food for two people.

The wine arrives, and the waiter pours a conservative amount in my glass. I finish it off fast and pour myself another.

Claude watches me from across the table with his lips pressed firmly together. I dare him with a look to say something about me drinking too much. If he so much as makes a peep, I will blow up on him.

When our first appetizer arrives, my brother attempts to strike up another conversation. He reaches for a dumpling with his chopsticks and says, "I heard that you quit Chez Avignon."

I don't correct him. I don't tell him that I was fired. It's embarrassing, and I'll take that secret with me to the grave.

I pop a dumpling in my mouth and chew. My mind registers that it's delightful, but it's like there's a film coating my tongue, preventing me from fully distinguishing its taste.

Moments later, the slaw is brought over. It's a beautiful tower of julienned vegetables, crispy fried taro, and vermicelli. The waiter begins explaining the edible building blocks of the stack as he begins to systematically tear it apart with two large forks. Soon, all that's left is a colourful mash.

Waiter gone, I nibble a bit at the slaw and then fill my glass to its brim with wine.

Claude exhales a loud breath. Tossing his napkin onto the table, he rises out his seat. "I'm going to the restroom. Don't take off."

I roll my eyes at him.

The rest of dinner is just as awkward. I shut down all attempts a discussion. The way I see things, I'm well within my right to hate my brother. He outted me to our father, and now he's expecting me to pretend like I'm okay. Fuck him.

When I slip back into the passenger seat of the Ferrari, I'm well and truly drunk, and the pin that had been holding back the brunt of my anger is gone.

"Putain, je te déteste," I explode on my brother as he pulls out of the underground parking lot. "You fucking ruined everything. You know that right?"

His grip tightens on the wheel. "I didn't mean to out you to our father."

I snort. "I don't fucking believe you."

He glares at me. "Noémie, I would never do anything to purposefully hurt you, and you know that. It was a mistake, and I'm—"

"You wanted to hurt him, so you said the one thing that you knew would piss him off more than anything."

"Noémie, I'm sorry."

"Fuck you, and fuck your apology!" I shout. "Do you know what he did? Do you know he paid Cara never to see me again?"

"Yes, but it sounds like he did you a favour," Claude murmurs.

"What?!"

"If she took the money, it's sounds like Hugo did you a favour," my brother repeats.

Hellfire consumes my vision. Before I can even register what I'm doing, I'm hitting him. I shove and pummel my fists against his arm and shoulder.

"Stop it! You're going to get us in an accident."

I don't stop. I hit him harder.

My brother screeches to a halt at a curb, and I jerk forward in my seat. "Are you done?" he snaps.

I scowl at him. Before he can lock the door on me, I throw it open, stumble out of the car and slam it shut.

My brother zips down the window. "Get back in the car!"

"No." I fold my arms defiantly across my heaving chest. Claude looks like he's about to storm out of the vehicle and drag me back inside.

I spin away, strutting away fast in my heels. He'll have to throw me over his shoulder and carry me back kicking and screaming. I don't care if I make a scene. I don't care about anything anymore. I don't look over my shoulder to see if he's coming after me. I just walk faster.

Looking straight ahead, I see a familiar face, and the anger clouding my vision immediately recedes. Our eyes meet. My mind goes offline.

Then my brain is screaming because no, she can't be here. I don't want her to see me like this. I'm a fucking mess. For weeks I've allowed myself to waste away. Time in bed, eating nothing but junk, has impacted my figure. I'm far less toned.

The strapless orange dress I threw on doesn't fit the way it used to, and just when I'm thinking things can't get any worse, my heel catches.

I stumble forward.

Hot Barista catches me before I fall, and for the first time, there's no counter between us. She's touching me. Her hands are on my bare shoulders, but I feel it all over. For weeks, I was an empty vessel. Now, liquid fire runs through my veins. She lets go too soon, and the embers start to die.

We're standing close. Jordan smells like cigarettes and vanilla cologne. She's out of her uniform. She wears a nondescript black blazer and black-collared button-down shirt that has way too many buttons undone. Too much of her chest is on display, making it impossible not to stare. Her honey-brown skin looks like it'd taste sweeter than caramel. I have an urge to lick her. We are way too close for comfort.

I manage to pull my gaze away when I hear the growl of my brother's sports car. Turning my head, I watch him speed off.

I sigh and rub my temples. Why'd Claude have to barge into my home? Why'd he have to drag me out of the house? Why'd he have to run his big mouth to our father and upend my entire world?

My thoughts turn to Cara, and my heart aches. I loved her. I trusted her. I was duped. She made me think that she would always stick it out. Yes, I was difficult, but she made me feel like I was worth it. Fuck her.

"Fight with your boyfriend?" Jordan asks, pulling me from my thoughts.

I glare at her. I'm annoyed she assumes I have a boyfriend and decide not to answer.

Being this near to her makes my head spin. I take a step back and open my Chanel clutch. I remove my phone. Of course, it's dead. "Tabarnak!" I curse. With Claude rushing me to get ready, the time it took me to shower and get dressed barely recharged the battery. Fuck Apple and their shitty batteries. I should switch to Android.

"You know, a thank-you would be nice," she says. There's an edge to her tone.

My gaze snaps up from the black mirror. I stare into her eyes. They are so dark brown, they almost look black. I hate that she isn't looking at me the way she normally does. Instead of desire, all that's reflected back at me is exasperation. The weight of her stare feels like a scale adding up my faults, and it's been a long time since I've felt so insecure. It's like I'm an awkward teenager again. I'm dressed up for the drag bar but look like I'm cosplaying the role of a grown woman.

"And what exactly would I be thanking you for?" I say.

She frowns. "Stopping you from faceplanting."

There's a retort on my tongue, but before I can say it, a group of drunk men stagger around a corner. When they see us, the catcalling begins. A few lewd gestures are directed our way. One of them acts out giving a blowjob. Men can be so crude sometimes, it's a wonder women put up with them at all.

Jordan steps between me and them. She straightens and stares them down like she's daring them to come at her. Her bravado is stupid. Sure she's tall and athletic, but she'd probably only be able to land a single punch before they took her down. Still, her gesture makes me all the more hot for her. Cara wouldn't have done that. My ex would have used me as a shield.

There isn't an escalation. The men are gone as fast as they came.

Jordan turns to face me. Her gaze drops to my purse, which I realize I'm clutching tightly to my chest. I shiver. It has nothing to do with the cold. My body still remembers her brief touch and hums for more.

If I asked Hot Barista to come home with me would she? Internally, I cringe at the question. It'd be a bad idea to explore anything with her. We're way too different, and the last thing I need is to get involved with someone. I'm not in the right headspace. I need to see Rebecca and work on building myself back up. Then again, what's the point? My dreams are swirling down the toilet. I'll never be able to open a restaurant without my father's backing.

"Where are you headed?" Jordan asks.

I blink. "Home."

"Are you going to call a Lyft or Uber? I can wait with you," she says, like it's not a big deal. I like that she's offering.

"My phone is dead, so no, I won't be calling a Lyft," I reply. "But I don't live far. I can walk." It's a lie. I live too far to make the trek in heels. I'll be jumping in the first cab I can hail, but she doesn't need to know that.

"I don't think you should walk home alone," she says.

I resist snorting. What right does she think she has to tell me what I should or shouldn't be doing? "It's a good thing I don't need your permission," I mutter, deciding that I need to end this interaction before I do something I regret. The longer I stay in her air space, the more I feel like landing on a proposition.

It's getting harder and harder not to stare. I've wanted her from the moment I first saw her at that stupid drag bar. Now I'm single, and she's here, and there's nothing between us, and she's gallant and gorgeous. But she isn't looking at me like she wants me. And that hurts.

I walk away from her, gritting my teeth. I head east down Richmond.

Just ahead, I see an orange cab. I'm about to lift my hand to wave it down when I notice Jordan behind me. Are we headed in the same direction or is she following me? I let the cab pass and walk a few more blocks, determining that she is indeed following me.

If she was anyone else, I would be annoyed or perhaps fearful. But she isn't anyone else. She's the woman I've been fantasizing about for years, and I get a sick thrill knowing that she's stalking me, making sure I get home safe. Or at least, I have every reason to believe her intentions are good willed. She just seems like that type of person—a good person. We are definitely very different.

As we make the forty-five-minute trek to my home from the Entertainment District, I barely notice how my shoes pinch my feet. My mind's too preoccupied to register pain.

With Hot Barista only paces behind me, I let my imagination run wilder with every step. I see us getting to my home. She follows me up to my front door. Her chest presses against my back as I slide my key into the lock. "What are you, some kind of sick stalker?" I say.

She grabs me by my waist and pulls me flush against her, making me gasp. Her body is both hard and soft. "Is it really stalking if you want it?" she whispers in my ear.

I think about the feel of her breath on my skin. I think about her full lips on my neck. I think about her tugging up my dress and fucking me hard against the door. I think about her fingers curling inside me, stretching me. I replay the scene over and over.

My panties are soaked by the time we reach my Victorian home in Yorkville. It's a miracle I can walk at all. My kneecaps feel like Jell-O. I'm aching between my thighs.

I climb the short flight of stairs leading up to my door, and naturally, nothing I fantasized about plays out. Turning, I look at Jordan. She stands on the empty sidewalk. The streetlamp illuminates her beautiful face. She looks incredibly irritated, which tickles me for some reason.

I consider whether I should invite her inside. Merde, I want her inside me.

Shaking my head, I push my key into the lock and push through the door.

Instantly, I'm greeted by nails clipping against the floor. Céline barks and twirls at my feet. Picking her up, I go to the window and stare out over the street. Jordan is gone.

I take Céline out to the backyard to do her business and then rush up to my bedroom. Stripping, I grab my vibrator and get myself off thinking about what I wished had happened tonight. For the first time in weeks, I don't want to retreat back to my safe space. I feel alive.

SIX

The stupid curtains are still open, and I'm awoken by the heat of sunlight on my face. It's 6:00 a.m.—close to the time I was used to waking. I've always been an early riser, but it's been weeks since I've roused before midday.

With a groan, I roll onto my stomach and cover my head with my sheets. I have every intention of diving back into my pit and sleeping the day away. Surprisingly, I'm unable to drift back off.

My body feels like it weighs double its mass, but yesterday I was ten times heavier. I'm lighter. The fog in my head is less hazy. Has the hurricane passed or am I the eye of the storm? Is today the day? Am I ready to move on and piece myself back together?

Emerging from the cocoon of my bedsheets, I turn my head and stare at my beside drawer for a full minute.

I sigh and pull it open. I remove the orange hued plastic bottle that holds my antidepressants. I shake two out, and it's only once I've tossed them in my mouth that I realize I have no water to wash them down. The bitter coating dissolves on my tongue, saturating my mouth with an awful taste. I dash downstairs to the kitchen, where I fill a glass with purified water and chug it back.

I slam the glass down on the counter and wipe my mouth with the back of my hand. Céline yawns at me, and then her little paws scrape against my shins.

Bending, I scratch her head. My dog leans into my touch. "I'm so sorry that I've been such a bad mommy. I promise to do better," I say, realizing that I mean it. I am ready to make the climb out of my hole.

After taking Céline out to the backyard and feeding her breakfast, I toss my phone on its charging stand and take a seat at my desk. I shoot off an email to Rebecca, my therapist, on my MacBook.

From my closet, I remove a pair of yoga pants and a sports bra. I pull them on and descend to the home gym in my basement after another visit to the kitchen where I fill up my water bottle.

I workout for two gruelling hours. My lungs burn as I push myself to run 5K on the treadmill. I don't know why I'm set on doing such a long stretch—usually I only run 2K and then focus on strength training.

Maybe I think have something to prove. Or maybe it's as simple as hating the way my body looks now. There's no nice way to say it—last night, I looked horrible. Hot Barista didn't check me out, and I'm mortified.

Gritting my teeth, I push myself to run harder and faster. By the time I finally hit my target, my legs tremble fiercely. I dial the machine down to a walk, reach for my water, and take a long swig.

I decide to work my upper body next, training my shoulders, arms, and chest. I can't lift as much weight, but I haven't lost much strength. That's a win, I guess.

It's quarter to nine when I set down the weights and stretch. Staring at my reflection from all angles, I decide that I look okay. I'm a little less toned and a little thicker around my midsection, but I don't totally hate what I see.

For most of my life, I'd been quite chubby. Possibly because of my love for butter and good food. Antoinette, Claude, and my mother used to tease me relentlessly about my weight, but I'd been unwilling to go on a diet. So I picked up playing sports in high school and got a personal trainer.

By the tenth grade, I had a body that drove Antoinette crazy with envy, and I always wore the skimpiest swimsuits when we vacationed just to show off. I'd offered to coach my sister at one point, thinking time in the gym might bring us closer together. She refused to take me up on the offer.

Thoughts of my sister bring back the thick head fog. Suddenly, I feel very exhausted. I sit on a bench and wait for the mist to clear. It doesn't. So I stay rooted to the seat until Céline's persistent whining forces me to stand and make the journey back upstairs.

Céline doesn't like the basement. She refuses to climb down the stairs. She's weird like that.

I shower, change into some loose-fitting clothes, and scowl at the state of my bedroom. I don't think I have the energy to tidy. My bed is calling to me. Maybe I'm not ready to be a person yet.

My phone rings. Sighing, I walk over to the charging stand and grab it. Felix is calling me. He never calls me. I wonder what he wants.

"Hello," I say.

"Finally! Do you know how long I've been trying to get a hold of you? I've sent you a billion messages. Why are you ignoring me?"

I pinch my forehead. "I'm sorry."

The line goes quiet for a moment. "I don't think I've ever heard you apologize for anything. Are you okay? What happened?" There's genuine concern in his tone.

"It's a long story … you probably don't want to hear it." Felix is my best friend, and he definitely would want to hear about it. He's always hated Cara. He'll be happy about our breakup, but I'm not ready to talk about her or what happened with my father.

Perhaps after I've spoken to Rebecca I'll be in a better place to speak about it.

"I'm home in Toronto for business, and I was calling because I was thinking we should go out tonight," he says, changing the topic.

"Not in the mood to party."

"Ugh … you're no fun." I just know he's pouting. "If I beg will that change your mind?"

"No, I don't think it will," I say.

"Well, I want to see you. It's been so long—too long. And I'm only here for another day before I fly out to Dubai," he says. "What if I come over for dinner and you cook me that lamb dish I like?"

"You say that like I have a rack of lamb sitting in my

fridge."

"Buy one," he says. "I'll stop by around six thirty. It's a date."

Before I can utter a rebuttal, the line goes dead. I frown down at my phone. I'm tempted to call him back and make up an excuse for why now is not a good time, but I do want to see him.

Since Felix is coming over, I have to tidy. There's a high chance he will make his way upstairs to my bedroom. He's always stealing items from my closet. He likes to say that he's just borrowing things, but to this day he's yet to return my Tom Ford sunglasses. I wish the cheap bastard would buy his own shit. Heaven knows he can afford it.

I clear my room of the takeout containers, make my bed, and push the button on my app to start up the Roomba. My housekeeper kept the rest of the house in order, which I'm grateful for. Gigi does an amazing job, but I refused to let her come near my bedroom for the last few weeks.

My fridge is empty, so I make a trip to the Whole Foods a few blocks away. Felix is out of luck, I had a nibble of lamb last night at Lee's. I'm not having it for a second day in a row. Also, I don't have the energy to make anything super over the top.

As I scrutinize the produce section, the carrots call to me. They're so bright, and the stems are a rich leafy green. I bag up a bunch and throw them in my cart. Potatoes, fresh thyme, and mushrooms make their way into the cart next. I still have no idea what's on the menu, but then I see a selection of black truffles for sale, and I'm reminded of Wolfgang Puck's famous chicken pot pie.

It's an easy dish to make. Not much prep, especially if I buy frozen puff pastry. Decision made, I grab the truffles and head over to the meat section to get a chicken.

Back at home, I unpack my grocery haul, pull my long auburn hair up into a ponytail, and tie on my apron.

I get to work prepping the vegetables and then move on to deboning the whole chicken to use the remains for the broth. The weight of my chef knife feels good in my hand. I fall into a flow, and for the first time in weeks, I feel almost normal.

At the last minute, I decide against using the frozen pastry dough. There's more than enough time to laminate my own puff pastry, and the rest of the elements of the dish are easy to put together.

Around 6:00 p.m., the pies are in the oven and I've put all the dirty utensils and bowls into the dishwasher. I select a bottle of Condrieu wine from my collection, place it in the chiller and set the table.

I'm just finishing arranging the forks when the doorbell chimes. Céline rouses and charges off the couch. Who does she think she's protecting? She's like eight pounds, and most of her bulk is hair. I really need to do better about training her.

Opening the front door, a genuine smile blooms across my face when I see Felix.

"Hey," he says, pulling me into a hug the moment the door shuts behind him. An odd feeling comes over me. I didn't know how much I needed this—to be held by someone who cares about me.

My eyes burn, and I sniffle.

"Noémie ..." Felix says. Taking a step back, he looks at me. "Is everything okay?"

I wipe my eyes and stare up at the ceiling in an attempt to push back my threatening tears. "I ... I'm good," I say, clearing my throat. "It's just really good to see you."

"Bullshit. Don't lie to me."

"I need to check on dinner," I deflect, turning to walk back to the kitchen.

Felix grabs my hand, stopping me. "Noémie, what's going on?"

I yank my hand away. "I'm not ready to talk about it."

His lips press together, but he doesn't push me for information, which I'm thankful for.

Felix is a handsome man with his shaggy brown hair and icy blue eyes. He's got the type of chiselled features most women swoon over.

We met at a dark time in my life. A time when I thought I needed to live life to the fullest because my sister couldn't. Back then, I thought living meant partying—hard. I'd just turned twenty-one. To celebrate, my friends and I booked first-class flights to Vegas. It was on the plane that I met Felix and his buddies. Upon discovering that we were all staying at the Venetian, our groups merged.

Vegas had been an eye-opening trip for me. Before Vegas, I still was under the impression that I was incapable of feeling attraction for anyone. I'd had many casual hook ups with men that always left a bad taste in my mouth. I started experimenting with women to test the waters and discovered that I preferred their company. But I never experienced that spark—that attraction everyone kept talking about.

That all changed when I met Tamara in Vegas. I'd been drawn to her from the moment I first saw her standing by the blackjack table. I liked the way her shoulders filled out her perfectly tailored navy power suit. I liked her short clipped hair. I liked the way she exuded confidence.

She was much older than me—almost forty. I can't recall exactly how we started talking. But I found myself ditching the group to have drinks with Tamara at the bar. One thing led to another, and then I was in her hotel room and her mouth was all over me. She'd been a possessive lover. A dominant lover. And the first woman I actually wanted to put my hands on, but Tamara was having none of that. In the end, I think I preferred it that way. I liked being directed. I liked being tied down. I liked that my pleasure gave her pleasure. There was no expectation that I reciprocate.

We spent two whole days together, and for the first time ever, I understood the feelings behind love songs. Two days was all it took to make me hooked on her. Naive as I was, I thought she felt the same. She didn't. On the day she had to check out from the hotel, I asked to exchange numbers. I think I would have followed her across the world if she would have let me. I was so smitten.

But with a few words, Tamara crushed a future together. "It's best if we don't," she had said.

To say that I was devastated would be an understatement. For weeks after, I couldn't stop thinking about her, and I spent the rest of the trip in the worst mood. My temper was so bad that no one wanted to be around me. Everyone, but Felix, began to chirp that I was a negative Nancy.

So Felix was the only person I confided in. "Sounds like

you can't do casual if you actually like someone," he'd said after I told him.

He was right about that. If I really want someone, I can't do casual. I'm not good at letting go when I want someone.

Felix hangs up his jacket and follows me into the main room. "Dinner smells amazing," he says.

"Don't get too excited. I didn't cook lamb."

My friend frowns. "What did you make?"

"Chicken pot pie."

He rolls his eyes dramatically. "I guess it'll do."

I roll my eyes right back at him and remove the pies from the oven. I'm happy with how they turned out. The puff pastry formed an impressive golden dome over the individual ramekins. I made six, so there's enough for seconds or thirds if Felix's appetite is up to it.

I place a ramekin on a plate and carry it over to Felix, who sits at one of the set places. "Oh, wow, it looks amazing," he says.

"Who knows, you might like it better than the lamb." My tone is dry.

"Doubtful."

Snorting, I walk back over to the kitchen to grab myself a pie.

Before I sit down, I crack open the bottle of wine and pour us each a glass.

Felix carves a hole into the dome with his knife. Steam rises from the opening. "So ... you really don't want to talk about it?"

I fiddle with the stem of my glass and grit my teeth. I

wonder if I should tell him. I don't want to, but maybe venting will help.

"Like, you don't have to tell me, but I'm here to listen," he says, reaching over and squeezing my hand.

A sigh escapes my lips. "Cara and I broke up."

"Oh … I'm so sorry to hear that," he says, not sounding sorry at all. He never got along with Cara. Felix always thought she was wrong for me, but when I pressed for him to pinpoint what exactly about her he didn't like, he could never give me a straight answer.

I take a long sip from my wine glass and stare down at my plate. The pot pie looks delicious, but my stomach is knotted and unsettled. I drink more wine.

"So are you going to tell me what happened or …"

I decide to tell him everything. Felix is so engrossed by what I have to say that he drops his fork and forgets about his dinner.

I'm crying over my plate before I can get it all out. Somehow, I speak past the painful lump in my throat.

Felix leaves his seat and hugs me. I tremble in his arms. "I knew I always hated that bitch," he says. "You deserve better. You deserve someone who will treat you like the princess you are and worships the ground you walk on."

Felix is being a bit much, but I appreciate the sentiment. I'm not sure why his words make me think of Jordan. Suddenly, she takes up all the space in my mind. I remember how she caught me. I remember how she put herself between me and the group of rowdy men. I remember how she walked me home.

Felix pats and rubs my back. "If I ever see Cara again, I will kill her," he vows.

"Always so dramatic." I wipe my eyes and sniff. "Your food's getting cold."

My friend stares at his plate, and then back at me. He goes back to his chair, grabs his fork and digs in. "Fuck, this is so good."

I arch a brow. "Better than the lamb?"

"Nope, but it's close. Aren't you going to eat?"

I should. I need to hit my macros, especially after my intense workout session earlier in the day. But I'm not hungry. There's a heavy stone sitting in my stomach. I try to wash it down with wine, draining my glass.

Felix finishes his pie and asks for more. I've nibbled through a quarter of my dinner by the time he finishes his second serving. We talk about light topics as we eat—the weather, sports, and the stock market. Felix tells me that I should invest in more bitcoin because the price is going to soar soon. I nod politely because I'm his friend and that's what friends do—feign interest. Frankly, I don't care about crypto.

Both Felix and my brother are obsessed with anything blockchain related. I've done my research, and I still don't think I know enough to get what the big deal is. It's never wise to make an investment unless you know all your risks. At least, that's a lesson my grandfather drilled into my head. "The first rule about money is don't lose it," he likes to ramble. "And the second rule is to not forget the first." I'm pretty sure my grandfather thinks we don't know he stole his lines from Buffett.

Felix has moved on to talking about the applications of artificial intelligence and a new startup that's using large language learning models to develop software. The whole thing goes over my head. "I'm thinking about acquiring a majority stake," he states. "I think I'll double my investment easily. I'm actually in Toronto because I had a meeting with the founder yesterday."

I nod and try to smile. "Sounds like fun."

He frowns. "You couldn't care less, could you?"

"Yup."

Felix chuckles. "Sorry, I probably shouldn't have prattled on so much about business."

"It's okay."

"So … it's been over a month since your breakup with Cara," he says, changing the topic. "When do you think you'll be ready to hit up the dating apps?"

My nose wrinkles with distaste. "I will die before I ever make an online dating profile."

"Everyone uses the apps these days. That's how people meet now."

I think about Jordan again. Does she have a Tinder profile? Is she on one of the countless apps searching for love? Does she list the qualities she's looking for in a part-ner? Would I check off any of her boxes?

"Dating is the last thing I'm thinking about right now," I say.

"I don't believe that—not for a second," he says. "You hate being alone. Your vanity demands that you have someone pampering you with compliments."

He's not wrong about that. I have a big ego that likes to be stroked constantly. "I don't need to be in a relationship for that."

"You don't care for casual, so something's got to give," he says.

I sigh.

A wide grin spreads across his face. "So how about it—let's make you a dating profile on Bumble."

"No."

"Come on, it's fun, and the best way to get over someone is to get under someone else."

I think about Jordan on top of me. Her weight pressing me down into the mattress. Her mouth on my neck. Her hands digging in my hair. I drink more wine.

"Wait. Why are you blushing?" Felix asks. "Is there someone you're interested in? Already?"

"Shut up."

"Oh my God, there is … Who is she? Do I know her?"

Felix does know her. Well, he knows of her. The day I stumbled into Grind That Bean for the first time and saw Hot Barista behind the espresso machine, I text-vomited everything to him once my gay panic subsided.

His response had been that I should figure out if Hot Barista is single and dump Cara if she is. After that, I made sure never to bring Jordan up to him again.

But I'm not dating Cara anymore. So it's fine if we talk about Jordan now. "Remember how I told you about my first real crush …"

Felix's eyes widen. "The Hot Barista?"

Nodding, I feel the tug of a smile on my lips. "Yeah …

ummm she and I sort of bumped into each other in the wild Friday night."

My friend's mouth drops open. "Don't tell me you hooked up with her. Noémie, I'm so proud of you. How was it?"

I snort. "I didn't hook up with her. I was drunk, and she just sort of walked me home."

"Really, that's all she did?" He waggles his eyebrows suggestively.

"Yes." Biting my lip, I tell Felix everything that happened Friday night. I don't leave anything out.

"So you didn't even thank her."

I roll my eyes at him. "As I said, I wasn't looking my best, and she … she makes me nervous."

"You need to thank her," he says.

I sigh. "I don't see the point."

"The point is that she's hot. So go to the coffee shop, tell her thank-you, and ask her out."

I almost choke on a mouthful of wine. Coughing, I say, "I'm not going to ask her out. She might not even be single."

"That's easily verifiable," he says, pulling out his phone. "What's her last name. I know you know it."

I know Jordan's last name, but I'm not telling Felix. I'm not going to the coffee shop. Merde, there's no way in hell I'm going to ask Hot Barista out.

SEVEN

I want to throw up. The butterflies in my stomach flit around like they're high on acid. I'm not sure how Felix convinced me this is a good idea. I don't know why I'm here.

Turning, I look at my Tesla parked across the street. It isn't too late to bolt. I don't have to do this.

Biting my lip, I stare into the coffee shop window. I don't see Jordan behind the counter. She wasn't here the last time I dropped by—the day my world went to shit. Perhaps she doesn't even work at Grind That Bean anymore.

My reflection in the window is what makes me decide to go inside. I look good—really good. I'm wearing a Chrome Hearts biker jacket, distressed black jeans from Diesel, and my favourite pair of chunky black Jimmy Choo boots. My orange messenger bag was custom made in Italy and perfectly matches the shade of polish on my nails. A black beret sits on my auburn hair that I pulled up into a tight bun.

The overall look is chic, and I'm hoping it reads as … not

straight. I even went for a more natural look with my makeup as I figured full glam reads hetero.

If Hot Barista is working, I want her to see me. I want her to eat me up with her eyes the way she usually does. I want to feel desired. And, maybe, I'm hoping that she might be the one to ask me out. Because I don't think I can do it.

I'd say that over the years, I've trained myself to go after what I want. And for the most part, I'm comfortable being direct. But Jordan is someone who has always felt out of reach. For so long, she's just been a woman in my dreams—a fantasy. There's something scary about changing the status quo.

I walk into the shop, and my heart leaps into my throat. Jordan isn't at the counter. The assistant manager, Wayne, smiles up at me. He's a short Filipino man who is prettier than most women.

Turning, I look away from him and lower my Ray-Ban sunglasses down the bridge of my nose, surveying the area. My gaze narrows when I see her, and then the panic dials back up.

Our eyes meet. My pulse hammers in my ears. My skin buzzes as I cross the shop, walking over to her.

"May I sit?" I ask, stopping next to the table. I'm annoyed that her expression is blank. She's barely looking at me, and I spent so much time fretting over my outfit this morning—for her! Was I so repulsive on Friday night that she no longer finds me attractive? Ugh.

I drag the stool out from under the table before she can answer my question.

"Yeah, sure," she mutters, dropping a stack of papers onto the table.

There are dark circles under Jordan's dark-brown eyes. I wonder why she's been looking so fatigued lately. But even her exhaustion doesn't detract from her beauty. Somehow, she's both handsome and pretty. I like that her short curly hair is always neatly clipped with a high fade. I probably think about her hair too much—an embarrassing number of times. Frankly, she pre-occupies too much storage in my mind.

A counter usually separates us. Now it's a table. I wish it wasn't there. I want to sit beside her. I want to feel the brush of her leg against mine, even if it's just for a second.

I realize that I'm staring at her, so I busy myself by removing my bag, setting it down on the vacant seat beside me. Next, I take off my sunglasses and hook them onto a pocket near the lapel of my jacket.

An awkward silence settles around us. All I can hear is my heart thumping in my chest. It's so loud. I hope Jordan can't hear it. I hope she can't see how anxious I am. I try to school my features.

She crosses her arms. "So …"

"So … I just wanted to say thank-you for walking me home Friday night." My fingers drum on the tabletop. I stop.

"I didn't think you recognized me," she says.

What? I blink my confusion. How could she ever think that? A flush of heat crawls up my neck and burns my ears. "I come here all the time. Of course I recognized you."

Jordan winces, and I scold myself for the harshness of my

tone. Fuck, this conversation is not going well. Merde, if only there was a rewind button. I'd like to start over.

"Okay. You're welcome," she says flatly. "If that's all you had to say, I'm kind of busy." She nods at the heap of papers on the table. I read the header on the top document. It's a resumé.

"You're hiring?" I ask. It's such a dumb thing to ask. Why am I asking dumb questions?

"Yeah."

"I want to apply," I blurt, not quite believing that the words came from my mouth. Why did I say that? Do I want to even work here? Unconsciously, maybe I do. I like making coffee, I'm out of a job, and I'm trying to settle back into some sort of routine. Though maybe it's the prospect of seeing more of Jordan that tempts me.

But what if she's hiring for the night shift, or even worse —weekends? Frowning, I reason that it's doubtful she's hiring for the evening roster. It always seems like they're understaffed in the day. Still, working at a coffee shop won't get me any closer to my end goal. I need to work in a restaurant and learn the trade. Then again, my dreams are dead. At least for now. Without my father's financial backing and connections, it will be impossible to open the restaurant I've envisioned.

So perhaps I should throw in the towel for the next little while as I consider my next real move. What's the harm in being a barista for a quick minute? Purple is so not my colour though. The uniform would look hideous on me. It's the last thing I want Jordan to see me in.

Jordan's chuckle disrupts my volleying thoughts. "You want to work here?"

"Why is that funny?" My lips press tightly together. She doesn't think I could cut it as a barista? Little does she know, I could do the job with my eyes closed. I'm used to working under gruelling and mind-numbing conditions. My attention to detail is immaculate. I'm an excellent employee. "Why wouldn't I want to work here? It's not far from where I live, and I'm more than qualified. I've been working in the hospitality industry since before I can even remember. Also, I recently graduated from Le Cordon Bleu in Ottawa, where I received my Grand Diplôme."

Jordan blinks with surprise. "Le Cordon Bleu—I think you're a bit overqualified for a barista job," she states. Her brown eyes sparkle with amusement, almost like she doesn't believe I've worked a day in my life. I kind of hate her for it. She continues, saying, "I don't know much about culinary school, but isn't Le Cordon Bleu a big deal? Wouldn't you rather work in one of those fancy restaurants where they plate food with tweezers?"

She's being condescending, and it's on the tip of my tongue to tell her that I had a job like that, but I don't say it. The moment I do, she'll ask why I don't still work there, and that's not a conversation I want to have.

Folding my arms over my chest, I lean back a bit in my seat. I've determined that I will be working at Grind That Bean. I want to see the look on Hot Barista's face when I show her that I can operate an espresso machine and make coffee way better than anyone in her shop. Most of her team can't steam milk to save their lives. They overstretch it, introducing way too much air and far too quickly, resulting in a foam that's thick and frothy instead of velvety smooth. Frankly, it's inedible. They're lucky I hadn't complained more about the quality of their drinks.

I learned from the best. Before I dated Cara, I was in a relationship with an older butch who was a coffee connoisseur. It had been a very unsatisfying relationship. The moment Jess and I became serious, she became an entirely different person in the bedroom. And maybe I'm a little backwards in my thinking, but if I'm dating a butch woman, I have expectations of being taken care of. Like, I want to be the pillow princess—not the other way around.

Just thinking about Jess annoys me. She was such a waste of my time.

Sighing, I try to land on what I'll say next to Jordan. I think I know how to steer this conversation where I want it to go. "Here's the thing—are you familiar with Poutine Heaven?" I ask.

"Yeah, I think so," she says. "It's the fast-food chain with the founder who hates gay people?"

My jaw clenches. "My father doesn't hate gay people. He just thinks they're confused."

Jordan snorts. "And what do you think? Do you think the gays are confused?"

I open my mouth to tell her that, of course, I don't think 'the gays are confused' because I'm not straight. But I know the moment I do, she'll grill me about my label. I don't have one. Lesbian doesn't feel right—like I'd be appropriating a title that doesn't fit. Antoinette was a lesbian—loud and proud. I am not like her.

I'm pretty sure I'm not bisexual. Kissing men always felt like swapping spit, and I don't like having sex with them. I don't like the queer label, because when I think queer, the image that forms in my head is a woman with short hair dyed in a shade of purple or some other pastel colour. Gay is a term I associate with men.

I don't have a label because I don't feel like dissecting my attraction. It's not something I think about even when Rebecca tries to get me to reflect on it. She says it's important, but I don't want to and I'm stubborn. It's not a conversation I want to have with myself. I'm not straight—that's enough for me to know, and it's really not anyone else's business.

Jordan's staring at me. She's waiting for an answer. "I … I'm an ally," I reply to get her off my back. Her expression tells me she isn't convinced, so I repeat more confidently, "I'm an ally."

She rolls her eyes slightly. "Okay, so your daddy owns Poutine Heaven. I'm even more confused why you'd want to work here."

I bite my lip. What I have to say next will be hard to say, and I'm just hoping I can get the words out without falling apart. "The plan was that my father would help me open my own restaurant, but a few weeks ago he cut me off. So I just need a job to help tide me over until he cools down." It's a partial lie. I don't need money, but I do need a job. Work and being busy keeps me sane. Too much free time makes me crawl into bed or leads me to fill my time with other harmful behaviours.

I got the itch yesterday to reach out to the old gang—my

party friends. Getting back with that crowd wouldn't be good. I'd be swept back up in the fast lifestyle. It'd be a huge setback. The regression might be fun, for a time, but I'm so over the days of waking up with my head pressed against the toilet bowl and the bathroom reeking of vomit. And drugs aren't what they used to be. They're cut with only God knows what these days.

I think about my friend Patrice, the way her body convulsed when she overdosed. That could have been me. It's not how I want to go.

"The way I see things, it makes no sense to hire you," Jordan says, pulling me free from my thoughts. "I need someone I can depend on, and you're a flight risk. The moment your daddy forgives you, I'm down an employee."

"My father is stubborn. It's unlikely he'll be forgiving me anytime soon." And it's the truth. He might never forgive me. The knowledge weighs heavy in my chest.

"Your background is in food and restaurants. I think coffee is outside of your niche," she says.

Why is she being so difficult? "Coffee is one of my hobbies, and I'm not interested in working in a restaurant that isn't my own," I counter. "Look, if you are looking for someone you can depend on, I'm super dependable. I'll work whatever hours you want. I'm a fast learner. I'm a team player. Just give me a chance and I'll show you." I shoot her a challenging look and hope it doesn't read as desperate—because I'm not desperate. Far from it. I don't need this job. I just want to rub it in Jordan's face when I disprove all the false beliefs she has about me.

She strokes her chin and shakes her head. Finally, she

sighs. "Fine, I'll take a chance on you. But I'll need you to fill out an application and your references will need to check out."

"Merci infiniment!" Surprisingly, the news delights me. I'm so delighted about getting my way that I hop from my stool and hug her.

I'm hugging Hot Barista. My heart thumps like a ticker timing down to explode. Hot Barista feels so good. Soft, but also firm. She's so warm, and her uniform smells clean like fabric softener. If moments could be pulled like noodles, I'd try to extend this experience for as long as possible, cataloguing every fine detail. But moments are more like ice cream. They're meant to melt away at the first taste.

I drop my arms from her and take a step back. "I'm sorry," I say. "The last few weeks have just been really rough, and I'm just so grateful and excited to start." I don't think it's a lie.

Jordan nods, the expression on her face is unreadable. She gracefully slides off her stool, grabbing the stack of resumés. "Wait here," she orders. "I'm going to grab an application for you."

"Okay." I say, smiling so wide that she must think I'm a lunatic. Merde, I sure am acting like one. I came to the coffee shop intending to apologize and to flirt my way into getting Jordan to maybe ask me out. My mission failed miserably. When I tell Felix about this, I just know his belly will split with laughter. He'll call me hopeless. I probably am.

EIGHT

Fifteen minutes early for my first shift, and I'm already regretting every life decision that brought me here. My stomach feels like I chugged an entire two-litre bottle of coke and chased it with a pack of Mentos. Staring at my reflection in the coffee shop window, I tell myself that I don't look that hideous. But the large purple shirt swallows me—I look like a kid going to camp. I'm just missing a backpack.

Seriously, how much hairspray did I inhale the other day? Applying to work at Grind That Bean is probably the stupidest decision I've ever made, and I have made a lot of dumb decisions in my life. Like the year I had a little too much fun with molly and thought it'd be a good idea to go surfing in the Pacific when I can't surf. Yes, this is dumber than that. At least then I looked hot almost drowning.

I don't do party drugs anymore. The pandemic put a pause on my fast lifestyle of popping pills and chasing shots with lines of cocaine. However, when the Covid restrictions let up, I threw myself back into it all harder than ever. Patrice overdosing is what scared me enough to want to make a change. I started taking my mental health seriously and increased my sessions with my therapist. I enrolled in culinary school, and the rest is history.

Sometimes I'm still haunted by the sound of Patrice's gurgled gasps and the way her eyes rolled to the back of her head as she convulsed. She's lucky Sophie had Naloxone in her purse. It's hard not to think—that could have been me.

The road to recovery meant cutting a lot of people from my life. I miss the old gang. The world's a little less lonely when you're suffering with others who are just as fucked up. I wonder how Patrice is doing. Last I saw, she moved to Sydney with her boyfriend. Every now and then, I see her posts in my feed. A brush with death hadn't been enough to chase her off the rave scene. Patrice still lives on the edge.

Wayne turns a corner, staring down at his phone. When he looks up and sees me, his face scrunches like he's smelled something foul. What's his deal? He doesn't know me. How can he hate me already? I'm not having it.

"Is that your natural expression, or are you practising for a horror movie?" I say with a bright smile.

Wayne's mouth drops open, and his perfectly plucked eyebrows pinch together. He's probably not used to anyone calling him out on his shit, but I think I know his type. If I'm right, the key to his heart is being cattier than he could ever dream of being.

"Oh, sweetheart," he says with a roll of his pretty brown eyes. "Your attitude needs a serious makeover. Right now, it's serving before and not in a cute way."

Crossing my arms, I arch a brow. "Really, that's the best you've got? Why did I expect more from you?"

He chuckles. "Gurrrl, it's your first day and you're trying to come for me. You know I can get you fired like this." He snaps his fingers.

"Yeah, you're not going to get me fired," I say. "Not when I'm the best friend you've always wanted."

He snorts. "How do you figure that?"

"Maybe I'm a fortune teller, or maybe I just wager that it's not as fun reading customer outfits with any of the other Grind That Bean staff."

"Hmmm … so you're a betting woman?"

I shrug. "If the payoff is worth it, sure."

"Interesting," he says. "What's your star sign?"

"Gemini."

He nods. "I won't lie. You've got me curious, but I'm not shopping for besties at this time."

A notification goes off, and I recognize the distinct sound —Grindr. I only know it because of Felix.

Wayne's gaze drops to his phone. I stand beside him and look over his shoulder. "He's cute, but you could do better," I say.

Wayne looks up at me and laughs. "I could."

"Dancing videos?" Both Wayne and I jump at the sound of Jordan's voice. She walks towards us, stopping when she reaches the coffee shop's front doors.

While I was bantering with Wayne, my unease washed away. It's all back now. My stomach revolts as if I swallowed expired sushi. It's irrational how nervous Jordan makes me, and it's not helping that she looks sexier than I've ever seen her. Meanwhile I look like a high schooler with the way the purple shirt renders my body amorphous.

This morning, Hot Barista sports a black jean jacket and a formfitting black tank underneath. Her khaki pants ride low enough that the white-and-black band of her Joe Boxer briefs show—I love a woman in boxers. A pair of shiny Doc Martin boots completes her outfit.

She carries a beat-up motorcycle helmet by its chin strap. My gaze darts across the road. I see her bike—it's impossible to miss. The deathtrap is a green so vibrant it almost hurts to look at it. I wonder why she chose that colour. Doesn't seem her vibe. Jordan's not loud and flashy.

It's kind of hot that she rides, but motorcycles terrify me. Driving in general kind of does. I think, after Antoinette's accident, I became aware of my fragility—at least where vehicles are concerned.

"Grindr," Wayne says, answering her question. He slips his phone into a front pocket.

"Only a week ago you were telling me that you were done with that app," Jordan says. "Thought you were looking for something real, something more than just a hookup."

Wayne rolls his eyes. "I've decided to do both: look for something real while also hooking up."

She snorts. "You aren't good with casual. You get too attached."

Me too. I think. Wayne pouts.

Jordan doesn't look at me. I've grown accustomed to her staring at me over the past year. But it's like I'm invisible to her now. I'm a drunk mess around her once, and now she doesn't want me. I hate it. And I hate that this goddamn shirt is too big. I should've never applied for this stupid job. I should quit now while my pride is still somewhat intact.

Finally, her gaze shifts away from Wayne. Our eyes meet briefly, and I melt. "Morning, Jordan," I say softly, too softly. Is that even my voice? Merde.

Jordan doesn't say anything. Instead, she gives me a curt nod. She slides her key into the lock, opening the doors to the coffee shop and disappearing inside.

Wayne drills me with a look, eyeing me like I'm a puzzle he's figuring out.

I scrunch my face. "What?" When he doesn't immediately respond, I yank open the door and step through.

The coffee shop is dark until Wayne slaps on the lights.

Jordan glances at me and cocks her head towards the seating section. "You can start by taking down the stools," she says brusquely.

Isn't she going to show me around before barking orders? I want to ask her if she has a problem with me. She's acting like she does. Whatever. I walk away from her and begin taking down the stupid stools.

Jordan and Wayne round the counter, vanishing to the back.

I've finished my task by the time Jordan returns to the front. I go to her. She's filling the register with cash and coins. Done, she slams the money drawer shut and puts space between us like I've got the plague or some other communicable disease.

I grit my teeth. What the hell is her problem? First, she ignores me. Now, she's actively going out of her way to avoid me.

Wayne shuffles out of the back and ties on his apron.

"Can you show Noémie how to work the ovens?" Jordans asks. "And then show her how to operate the till?"

I don't need to be shown how to operate ovens. I know how ovens work. I'm not interested in playing cashier. "You're not going to show me how to make drinks?"

Jordan exhales an exaggerated breath. "If you're still here in a month, you'll be taught how to work the espresso machine."

Oh, so that's how it's going to be? I cross my arms. She doesn't think I'll last a month. It's exactly as I thought. Jordan believes I'm some spoilt rich brat who doesn't know how to work hard. In a way, she's just like Sally.

I'll show her. Grind That Bean might be a busy shop, but it isn't a fraction as intense of a work atmosphere as Chez Avignon. If I can handle being yelled at by Ricard, I can put up with anything.

"You got a problem with that?" she asks.

"Kind of," I say, deciding to be honest. I'm not interested in taking customer orders. "I want to make drinks."

"Well, you're not going to," she says. "Wayne will show you how to enter orders, and that's that."

There's a part of me that wants to debate more—plead my case. I'm pretty sure I can pull a better espresso shot than she can, but I don't want to come off as too difficult, so I walk over to the ovens where Wayne stands. The devil is grinning ear to ear. "Problem in paradise?" he asks.

"What are you even talking about?"

"I'm on to you, Noémie. I think I know what you're about."

I have no idea what Wayne is implying. I stare at him blankly.

His gaze darts over my shoulder and then he's smirking again. "Morning, Jordan," he says, in a soft demure tone. The bastard is mocking me. Worse, he's realized I have a thing for Jordan. *Merde!*

I grit my teeth.

Wayne chuckles. "I can't quite believe it—you're just like the dozens of other women who come in here peacocking for Jay's attention." He sighs loudly. "Why did I expect better from you?"

I blink. Did I hear him right? Did he just say that Jordan's got dozens of admirers who frequent the coffee shop to see her? I clench my fists. The thought of other women coming in here and flaunting themselves at Jordan stirs a hot pot of emotions in me. Does Jordan check them out too?

I look over my shoulder to make sure Jordan's not within earshot. She isn't—thank God. "I've never peacocked for anyone's attention," I whisper.

He snorts. "Sure."

"It's really not like that."

"Yeah, I don't believe you," he says. "But let me give you some advice. Steer clear of Jordan if you know what's good for you."

"Well, it's a good thing I'm not interested in her," I lie.

"Hey, why are you guys standing around?" Jordan calls out. "We're opening soon. Get the pastries in the oven, give Noémie a quick tour of the shop, and then show her how to operate the register."

Five minutes before the coffee shop is set to open,

Corrine with the horrible bob shows up. Instantly, I can tell that Wayne doesn't like her. So when she greets me with a smile, I give a dirty look in return. Frankly, I couldn't care less if she thinks I'm a bitch. I've picked a side. I want Wayne to like me.

The morning rush is hectic. At first, I'm slow at inputting orders on the POS, but I've always been a fast learner, and I figure it out. Also, it doesn't hurt that there aren't a lot of items on the menu and customers keep ordering the same shit—ice coffee, café lattes, tea …

While I find my rhythm, Corrine keeps fucking up on drinks. I can see why Wayne hates her now. She's kind of useless. There are a ton of customer complaints. *Serves Jordan right.* She should have let me work on the espresso machine with her. I'm pretty sure that, despite it being my first day, I could've done a far better job than Corrine.

Around 11:00 a.m., things get less chaotic. Fewer and fewer people trickle through the doors. Jordan's still barely looking at me, and I can't stop staring in her direction.

Wayne catches me staring. "Man, you've got it bad," he whispers.

"Shut up. You've no idea what you're talking about," I retort, keeping my voice low.

"I don't need to be a rocket scientist to know that you've got it bad for Jay. Your heart eyes are sickening," he says. "I'm surprised I didn't pick up on it before."

Jordan leaves her spot at the espresso machine and walks over to the register where Wayne and I stand. She glances at me for barely a second and turns to Wayne. "Show her how to restock supplies."

"Sure thing, boss." He gestures for me to follow him.

We go to the back. Wayne throws open a door leading to the stockroom. He points at the shelves. "Basically, almost anything you'll need is somewhere in here. If you notice cups or lids are getting low out front, you come back here and grab some more."

I nod.

We exit the stock room and cross the narrow space. Wayne opens another door that steps into a walk-in fridge that's ten times smaller than the one at Chez Avignon. "In here we keep the milk, produce, and deli meats, and that shelf at the bottom is reserved for staff. So if you bring a lunch that needs to be kept cool, you can put it there." When I just nod, his lips press together. He crosses his arms. "Why are you here?"

"I'm here to work."

"Yeah, but why are you *really* here? Jay says your daddy cut you off and you need the paycheque, but I'm not gullible like she is," he says. "I sense you have an ulterior motive."

I don't like how perceptive he is, and it's hard to think of a response while he scrutinizes me. "I need work," I admit. "After my father cut me off, I sort of went to a dark place, and I quit my job at Chez Avignon—"

"Chez Avignon! You worked there? I've always wanted to go. I've heard the food is amazing, but it's impossible to get a reservation," he frowns. "Wait. Why would you need to work there if your family is so rich?"

"Mainly to learn. Chef Ricard is one of the highest regarded chefs in the country. I want to open my own restaurant one day," I say, a little surprised I'm revealing so much. But at the same time, I think I really do want Wayne to like me. He reminds me of Felix. I continue saying, "Working—keeping to a routine—is important. It keeps my mind busy enough that I can't focus on the shit that weighs me down."

Wayne doesn't say anything for a beat. The hum of the fridge's condenser is the only sound filling the space. "So you're not here because of Jay?"

I roll my eyes. "No," I say. "But I don't think there's any sense in denying that I'm attracted to her. Why should I steer clear of her?"

"Jay's got a track record of breaking hearts—she doesn't do relationships. So if that's what you're after … if that's why you're really here, abort your mission now."

My jaw clenches. "I just told you that my interest in Jordan has nothing to do with me being here."

"I think it does."

"Well, you're wrong," I say. "I'm not looking to pursue anything with her."

"Good, I'd hate to see her steamroll your heart."

"You say that like there's a possibility of that ever happening."

Wayne leans against a shelf. "If you're lying to me, and the actual reason you're here is to tie her down, that's exactly what will happen."

I snort. "If I wanted her, I could have her," I say. It's my pride talking. The way Jordan's been acting around me lately —like she wants absolutely nothing to do with me—makes me believe Wayne's right.

The bastard smiles. "How about we bet on it?"

"Bet on what?"

"You tying Jay down," he replies, arching a brow. "Personally, I think that's why you're working here. You have a little crush, and you want to get close to Jay. And I think you have no chance in hell. That woman will never settle down with anyone."

"I'm not going to bet on this."

He sighs. "I thought you were a betting woman? But I guess you see the writing on the wall. You know I'd win," he says, pushing against the fridge's door and stepping out of it.

I follow after him. "No, you wouldn't win."

He stops walking and looks at me. "Let's bet on it then."

"Fine. What are the terms?" I cross my arms.

Frowning, he taps his chin as he thinks. "If I win, I get anything I want from your closet."

I guess it wasn't only Jordan eyeing my outfits over the last year. "Fine, and if I win …" Unfortunately, I don't know Wayne well enough to pick a punishment he will hate. "I need some time to figure out what I get. Give me a week."

"No. I'll give you until Wednesday," he says.

"Thursday."

"Deal." Wayne extends a hand. I take it, and the deal is struck. "I can't wait to claim my prize," he says.

"Yeah, that's not going to happen. I always get what I want."

"Not with this," Wayne says. "And when I win, you'll have to give me anything I want from your closet. Jay will—" His mouth snaps shut.

"Jay will what?" I hear Jordan ask.

Heat crawls up my neck and face. How much did she

overhear? I turn to look at her. She's standing near the shelves that house the flavoured syrups.

"Jay will what?" she asks again.

Wayne sighs. "Noémie thinks she can sweet talk you into letting her operate the espresso machine this week, and I bet her that she couldn't." The lie falls from his lips easily, and I'm thankful for his quick thinking.

Jordan glares at him. "You're supposed to be training her. Quit messing around."

"You're such a micromanager," Wayne says.

She rolls her eyes and shakes her head. "Just get back to work. Seriously."

Back out front, Wayne and I iron out the rest of the details of the bet when we're sure no one is listening.

The rules are simple: he can't let on to Jordan that I'm interested in her or women in general. I can't sleep with her unless she confesses her love for me. If he wins, he can select almost anything from my closet—I made it very clear that my Birkins and my jewellery are off limits, which he wasn't happy about. And finally, I got Wayne to agree that there isn't going to be a time limit.

I had to really push for that last item, and I'm glad Wayne conceded because I've no intention of taking this bet seriously. I'm not going to bother trying to seduce Jordan.

The whole thing is juvenile and stupid, but there is a positive to the madness: Wayne has to keep his big mouth shut. Which gives me time to figure out what the hell I'm doing with my life before I quit Grind That Bean. I don't intend to stay here for long.

NINE

My first work week flies by. The coffee shop is pretty busy, but it's nowhere near as stressful as Chez Avignon. In the slow hours, I chat with Wayne. Sometimes I'll talk with Kevin Wong. He's handsome in a conventional way, and he's studying to become an engineer. I can tell he likes me. His face gets all red if I stare at him too long, and if I ask him to do something—like clean tables so I don't have to—he jumps to do it.

Corrine with the horrible bob—I'm ignoring her. Stacie isn't that interesting, and she smells like cat dander, so I don't go out of my way to speak to her. And Jordan … she's still avoiding me.

It's so frustrating because I want to get to know her. I want to figure her out like a secret recipe. I want to know what makes her laugh. I want to know what she does in her spare time besides partying and screwing women. According to Wayne, that's all she does, but he's probably exaggerating.

After my shift on Friday, I see Rebecca. My psychologist is a middle-aged woman with a warm disposition. Every time I see her, it looks like more strands of silver replace the blond real estate on her head. Soon, she will be completely grey, but I think it will suit her. She gets more beautiful each year. Her eyes are the kind of light blue that you can get lost in, and I think it's a shame she hides them behind thick black-frame glasses, especially since they aren't designer. With the amount of money she charges per session, I know she can afford a pair of Ray-Ban's.

Rebecca's office is cozy despite its drab beige design and sparse furnishings, but I think it's her presence that makes the atmosphere so welcoming.

I take my seat across from her on the comfy beige couch and cross my legs. Rebecca smiles at me. "It's been awhile. It's so nice to see you, Noémie," she says. "How have you been?"

I bite my lip. "To be honest … not so good."

Rebecca leans back in her chair. "Why's that?"

A sigh escapes my lips. "My father found out about Cara."

"Oh … and how did he take the news?"

"As good as you can guess," I reply. My chest feels heavy as I remember my argument with Hugo. I tell Rebecca everything, and she listens like she cares. I believe she cares, which makes it easier to get the words out. But it's still difficult. By the time I finish recounting my fight with Hugo, I'm crying. Feels like I'm always crying lately.

Rebecca holds out a box of tissues. I take one and dab my eyes.

"Thank you for sharing, Noémie," she says. "It's understandable to feel hurt and betrayed by the people you care about. What have you been doing to cope?"

"Honestly, I fell back into my hole for a while," I admit. "I quit my job and laid up in bed for weeks."

Rebecca nods. "And how are you feeling now? Are you taking your medication?"

"Yes, I'm taking it now. I stopped for a few weeks, but I'm trying to bounce back."

"You look like you're doing good," she says. "What are you doing to keep busy now that you aren't working?"

"Actually, I got a new job."

"That's good, and where are you working?"

"Grind That Bean. It's a coffee shop in the Financial District," I say.

Rebecca's eyes narrow on me. "Is this the coffee shop that I'm thinking of?"

Heat burns up my neck. I shouldn't have been so descriptive. I'm not sure I want to talk about Jordan right now. In prior sessions, Rebecca recommended I cease my visits to the coffee shop. She said that I needed to be more considerate of Cara's feelings. Well, I'm glad I didn't listen. Fuck Cara.

"Yes, it is," I admit.

Rebecca steeples her hands and adjusts in her seat. "Do you think it's a good idea for you to be working there?"

"Probably not," I reply, deciding that I will not be mentioning the bet I made with Wayne. It's not that I plan on never telling her. I likely will tell her, but not now while the ink is still drying. Besides, I'm not taking the bet seriously, so what does it even matter? "But I do think the change of scenery is good for me. The restaurant was very stressful, and you know how I feel about being cooped up in my big empty house with nothing to do."

"About that … have you given thought to my previous suggestion?" Rebecca asks.

"Yes, and I'm not interested in getting a roommate," I say. "The last thing I need is a stranger in my home, making a mess." Yes, I'd rather suffer loneliness than put up with someone who I might not even get along with. Not to mention that Toronto recently updated its tenant laws. It's almost impossible to evict someone nowadays.

"It was only a suggestion," Rebecca says. "One of many that I've made."

"I'm not interested in joining any support groups or clubs," I say.

"Yes, I know," Rebecca says. "But I understand that you're lonely, and that you've felt this way for some time. The only cure for loneliness is connection. As always, all I ask is that you consider my advice."

On Monday, when I show up for my shift, Jordan's still treating me like I'm invisible. Wayne thinks it's hilarious. "You're simping so hard for Jay. It's only a matter of time before I'm raiding your closet," he says with a chuckle.

My jaw clenches. "I'm not simping."

"If it quacks like a duck and looks like a duck, it's simping."

Rolling my eyes, I grab a bottle of vanilla syrup and return out front. I exchange the empty bottle for the filled one and take my post at the register. It grates on my nerves that Jordan is keeping her word, refusing to let me anywhere near the espresso machine. How am I supposed to shove it in her face that I make excellent drinks if she keeps me on cash?

A customer in an expensive and perfectly tailored business suit walks up to the counter. I try to feign politeness with a smile, but my lips refuse to curve. That doesn't stop the man from grinning at me. His blue eyes give me a once over.

"How can I help you?" I ask flatly.

"How about you tell me your name, beautiful?" He says.

I'm unable to stop my eyes from rolling. "It's on my name tag."

He chuckles. "So it is — Noomi." His attempt at saying my name isn't even close.

When my family lived in Québec, everyone knew how to say my name. Then, we moved to Toronto, and everyone couldn't get the pronunciation right—teachers, students, and even my friends. So I started getting my English pals to call me Naomi, like Naomi Campbell. Now only my family and my friends from Montreal call me by my given name.

"I'll have a cold brew coffee, and a ham and Swiss croissant," the man says.

I enter his order. He pulls out his wallet and removes a

crisp fifty-dollar bill from a stack of money. I take it and give him his change. The man arches a bushy brow and puts all the money I just handed him in the tip jar. If he's trying to impress me, he's failing. He's not the first patron to do this. Wayne's been ecstatic about the increase in tips.

Before moving away to the pickup counter, he slides me a business card and winks. *Who the fuck winks these days?* "Give me a call, beautiful. I'll show you a good time."

When he's gone, I grab the card. I'm about to tear it in two and toss it in the trash when I see Jordan staring at me. Her mouth is a thin line, and she's frowning. I pocket the card. Her frown deepens, and I'm pleased about it. I have no problems letting her think I'd go out with a man twice my age.

On a Thursday, just after three in the afternoon, the coffee shop is quiet. There are only a few customers in the seating area. I'm at my post at the register, and Kevin is blabbing to me about a show he just finished watching about people who get their memories wiped at work. I can't remember the name of the show because I'm only half paying attention. While Kevin talks, the other portion of my focus is directed at Jordan.

She's leaning against a counter and glaring at a laughing Wayne. I wish I could hear their conversation, but the rock music playing overhead is loud enough that I can't. Sometimes I can't catch customer orders.

Jordan does a lot of glaring. She seems to be in a perpetual bad mood lately. According to everyone, it's not normal. There's speculation that she's pissed about her best friend moving to Vancouver.

When Wayne bursts out into another fit of laughter, I nudge Kevin and cock my head towards the managers. "Let's see what's so funny."

He gives me one of his puppy dog smiles. "Sure."

We walk over to Wayne and Jordan.

"What's so funny?" Kevin asks.

Jordan shoots Wayne a look of warning.

Wayne wipes tears from his eyes as he continues to cackle.

"I was just telling Wayne about this apartment I went to see over the weekend. The property manager wants nineteen hundred dollars for a three-hundred-and-sixty-square-foot bachelor pad," Jordan says, folding her arms.

"Doesn't sound funny to me—just sad," Kevin says.

Jordan's gaze darts from me to Kevin, and she frowns. "Kevin, go wipe down the tables." Her sharp tone makes him wince.

"I wiped them down twenty minutes ago," I say.

Jordan turns her head and surveys the seating area. "They still look dirty. Just go and wipe them down."

Wayne starts to hoot again, and he slaps his knee. He knows something I don't know, and I'm going to find out what it is.

Kevin exchanges a look with me and shrugs. He moves away from our group and grabs the spray bottle and cloth. Wayne is the next person to leave. Shaking his head, he snatches up a sleeve of cups from off the counter and walks over to the espresso machine. And just like that, for the first time since my first day, I'm alone with Jordan.

A fire lights in my stomach, warming me all over. I catch

myself almost stepping towards her. I want to be near her. I want to lean beside her and have our shoulders brush. I just want her. Hopefully she can't read me so easily.

Jordan must know the effect she has on women. Wayne had been right—I've seen for myself how some female customers preen in front of her, making fools of themselves. Sure, I used to dress up before my daily visit to the coffee shop, but I never made my intentions obvious. I never complimented Jordan or teased my hair. I never leaned over the counter in a shirt with a low neckline. I never let my gaze linger on her too long. Frankly, I always acted disinterested. I didn't want her to know that I was interested.

"So you're apartment hunting?" I ask, trying to start a conversation.

"Sort of," she says with a sigh. "I either need to find myself a new roommate or find a new place."

Is this the actual cause for her foul mood? The renters market in Toronto is brutal. I've heard enough staff at Chez Avignon complaining about it to know.

Jordan motions to turn away from me. I stop her with another question. "What kind of place are you looking for?"

"Something affordable," she says. "If I'm lucky, close to work."

Makes sense. A very stupid thought pops up in my mind. Seems like all my ideas are dumb lately. Despite the fact that Grind That Bean is growing on me, I should never have applied to work here. I want to be a chef. I want to open a restaurant. Me working here is like putting my life plans on hold.

Jordan's looking at me funny. I can't read her expression,

but it's not angry for once. Her eyes are so dark they look like black holes, and I'm being sucked in.

The stupid thought resurfaces, and I blame Rebecca. The only reason it's even coming up is because of our last conversation. *"The only cure for loneliness is connection,"* she's said more than a handful of times. I'm not keen on having a roommate, someone occupying my personal space. But at the same time, I can think of no other person I'd rather connect with.

Jordan has lived rent free in my mind for years, and I can't help wondering if it is coincidence or fate at play. When I really consider all the steps that had to have happened for me to get here, it does seem like I've been guided to make this proposal. Of all the people I could've bumped into when I stormed out of Claude's car, it was her. And now she needs a roommate while Rebecca insists I consider getting one. I'm pretty sure my therapist wouldn't approve of Hot Barista being my housemate, but I've made my decision.

My body buzzes. I rock back on my heels to expel some of the nervous energy. "I've been thinking that it might make sense to rent out one of the rooms in my home … I could use the money," I lie.

Jordan blinks at me. Her brows squish together in confusion as a thick wall of silence slams between us. I hate every moment of it. Why isn't she saying anything? I know she has a problem with me. She's been a dick since my first shift. I wish she would say something.

Annoyance overtakes my nervousness. Angling my chin high, my teeth mash together. "Forget it," I say, crossing my arms. "It'd probably be weird right? Living together? I'm your employee, but I just thought it makes sense. You need a place, and I've got a spare room."

Jordan blinks at me again, and then finally says, "Actually, I wouldn't mind seeing it. Unless you think it'd be too weird."

TEN

Jordan is going to be here in an hour, and I can't decide on an outfit. Part of me wants to go full glam. I miss the way she used to eat me up with her eyes. Now, she doesn't even nibble. I blame the hideous Grind That Bean uniform. It erases all my sex appeal. No one can tell I have boobs under all the loose purple fabric; it's tragic, like scuffing a new pair of Louboutins.

The hangers click on the metal rod. I push through my inventory of blouses, dresses, and sweaters. I bite my lip. Why is this so hard?

I want to look good, but effortlessly good—like how Zendaya pulls off activewear. I settle on Netflix-itinerary-chic: a pair of grey Roots sweatpants and one of my favourite shirts. It's white with a giant collar that falls off my right shoulder. My tits look great in it.

Eyeing myself in the mirror, I decide I look okay. My makeup's on point. My ponytail is on point. But … I'm still not sure. Maybe it's too laid back. But I don't want it to look like I'm trying …

The doorbell rings. Immediately, Céline starts making a fuss.

I look down at my watch and can't believe how quickly the time flew by. Staring at my closet, I wonder if I have enough time to swap my sweats for jeans. Sighing, I decide I don't.

Heart hammering in my ears, I rush down the stairs. I blow out a breath and then another. I open the door.

Jordan stands on the opposite side. My heart swoops low in my chest. She wears a worn leather jacket and a black tank top tucked into baggy jeans. She carries her bike helmet by its chin strap.

Our eyes meet, and I forget to breathe. The world narrows to the space between us, and I think about Jordan closing the gap. I think about her pushing me up against the wall and kissing me until my knees buckle. I think about her hips pressing into me.

She looks away just when my cheeks begin burning from the thoughts. Her gaze veers, landing on her green motor-bike parked in the driveway.

I clear my throat and force myself to smile when I say, "Hey." Stepping back into the foyer, I wave for her to come inside.

Jordan doesn't smile back. Her face is blank. I would kill to know what's on her mind.

Céline yips at my heels and paws my calves. Jordan flinches when she gets barked at.

Is she scared of dogs? If she doesn't like dogs that might be a deal breaker. Cara hadn't cared much for Céline, and the feeling had been mutual. That should have been a red flag.

"Tais-toi, Céline," I say, scooping up her squirming little body. "She doesn't bite. Normally, she's very quiet, but visitors make her excited. She's just saying hi," I ramble, unable to help it because Hot Barista is in my home. It's kind of surreal.

Jordan just nods. She slips out of her black Air Force 1's and frowns when her socks touch the ground. "Heated floors?" she asks.

"Yeah, all throughout the house." I scratch Céline's head to get her to relax.

Jordan clears her throat. "Fancy."

"Just wait until you see the kitchen," I say, moving out of the foyer. Beginning our tour, I point at a room opposite the staircase. "That's the sitting room. It's good for collecting dust."

Her eyes dart around, absorbing the details of the space. I wonder what she thinks of the home. My style leans pretty modern—neutral colours and minimal clutter. Cara called my house cold. "Only your kitchen and bedroom have personality," she told me on more than a few occasions. "Don't you get bored of staring at all the blank walls?" I grit my teeth at the memory. Fuck Cara.

Jordan says nothing as we walk down the hallway, passing the formal dining room. Will the entire tour be like this, me pointing at things and her just nodding? She always struck me as the strong silent type, but the whole point of getting a roommate was to have someone to talk to, someone to connect with. Jordan never talks. At least, she doesn't talk to me. Are we even compatible?

We enter the main space. It's an open layout. Natural light pours in from giant windows overlooking the quaint backyard fitted with a canopied deck, grilling station, and hot tub. If Jordan moves in, I wonder if she'll ever join me in the tub. My mind conjures an image of her in Billabong board shorts and a bikini top. I think about our thighs touching under the water.

The thoughts warm my skin. I know I'm blushing, so I turn away. I put some distance between us. While Jordan surveys the living room, I park myself in the kitchen. For a second, I consider gulping down ice water to cool off.

Jordan turns. Her brown eyes go wide when they land on the kitchen. It's on the tip of my tongue to ask her what she thinks about it. I designed the space myself, selecting the large white marble slab for the island and countertops. I spent hours online, searching for the right hardware to go with the sage cabinet doors and drawers. I landed on classic gold handles. The fixtures and the range hood are also gold. My pride and joy is my custom Lacanche gas stove.

Jordan swaggers up to the kitchen island, setting down her helmet. Her gaze narrows on the espresso machine. Figures Hot Barista would be interested in it —it's a La Marzocco. It's not a novice machine. I bet she's wondering if I know how to operate it. Maybe now is my opportunity to rub my coffee skills in her face. "Would you like a coffee?" I ask.

"Sure."

"What kind of drink would you like?"

She pulls out a stool and sits down at the island. "How about a latte?"

"Sure." I set Céline down on the floor. She shakes violently and yawns before taking off for the couch.

I feel Jordan's eyes on me as I work and feel the same excited nervous energy I felt when Chef Ricard looked over my shoulder as I prepped. I want so badly to impress her, just like I had wanted to impress him.

I weigh out nineteen grams of coffee beans and spritz them with water to prevent static during the grind. Toasty notes of coffee season the air as the beans get pulverized. Before tamping, I whisk the grounds with a WDT tool to ensure even distribution and prevent channelling. After tamping, I toss on a puck screen before twisting the portafilter in place and pressing a button to begin the extraction.

The machine hums as the water forces its way through the grounds. The double-walled glass fills. The golden emulsion is capped with a gorgeous layer of crema.

I pull a carton of full fat milk from the fridge and proceed to steam it. This is where I can truly show off. The espresso machine squeals as I bring the milk up to the perfect temperature. After tapping the stainless-steel jug on the counter a few times, I methodically pour it out, forming a swan out of the foam the way Jess taught me. Sure, Jess had been a lazy lay, but she'd been good for something.

Setting down the completed drink. I smirk when Jordan stares down with wide eyes. Her mouth opens slightly, revealing her amazement. She's impressed. She's probably wondering where I learned how to do latte art. She's probably thinking that she should have put me on drinks at the shop. I can't wait to gloat.

"Thanks," she says, lifting the cup to her lips. Her eyes close when she takes her first sip. Clearly, she's enjoying it. That knowledge fills me with contentment. There's a special bliss in watching someone savour what I've made. And Jordan's not an unknown diner, which makes the feeling more intense.

"C'est bon?" I ask, needing the verbal confirmation.

Jordan blinks her confusion.

"I asked if it's good."

"It's excellent." She licks her lips.

For a beat, I'm staring at her mouth. I force myself to look away and divert my attention to my nails, pretending to inspect them.

"Why didn't you tell me that you knew how to work an espresso machine?" she asks. Annoyance is thick in her tone.

How dare she be annoyed with me? Folding my arms, I lean against the counter. "Before you hired me, I told you that coffee is one of my hobbies."

She nods. "Yeah, you did." I wait for her to say something else, but she doesn't.

My jaw clenches. "And I've been trying to talk to you about it, but you literally go out of your way to ignore me at work," I say. "Do you have a problem with me?"

"I don't have a problem with you. I haven't been ignoring you."

What a load of bullshit. I roll my eyes. "If you say so."

"I do." Her fingers drum against the double-walled glass

of the coffee cup, and then she sighs. "Look, starting your next shift, I'll put you on drinks."

She better. Corrine with the horrible bob is the absolute worst on the espresso machine, and I'm sick of gross men making passes at me, thinking that leaving big tips will land them a date. And while I have no expectations of anything happening between me and Jordan, it would be nice to get closer, to work beside her.

When Jordan finishes her drink, we continue our tour. I show her the gym in the basement, and then we head upstairs. I show her the largest guest room, and her eyes go wide when I open the walk-in closet. They go wider when I open another door that leads to the ensuite bathroom.

"Is this the primary bedroom?" she asks.

Her astonishment makes me chuckle. "No. I told you, this is the guest suite. My bedroom is on the third floor."

"I didn't know guest suites had ensuite bathrooms," she says.

Her confession makes me laugh, but it also makes me a little sad. Even with my family drama, I know I have things really good. I grew up wanting for nothing except the acceptance of my sister and father. Not everyone can say that. I wonder about Jordan's life—where she grew up and what her childhood home looked like. From Wayne, I understand she's from the east side—Scarborough. I've never had a reason to travel to that part of the city. It's foreign territory.

"So you like it?" I ask.

"Yeah, it's great," she says, shrugging. "But I don't think I can afford it."

I frown. "What makes you think that?"

She gestures at the room. "You have to know what a space like this could go for on the market."

"Yes," I admit. When Rebecca first proposed the preposterous idea of finding myself a roommate, I looked into the going rates. There would be a bidding war if I listed the room for 2,500 dollars a month. "But I'm not keen on living with a stranger."

"Aren't I a stranger?" Jordan says. "You don't know anything about me."

I don't say the truth, —that I want to get to know her. A lot of the time, me and the truth are estranged. "I know you're the type of person who doesn't let drunk girls walk home alone," I say. "I know that Wayne thinks the world of you, and I trust his judgement."

"Doesn't change the fact that I can't afford to live here."

Why is she fighting this? Seriously, I'm here doing her a favour, and she's trying to convince me to find another renter. It should be the other way around. I'm still not even sure I want to live with someone. Being alone isn't so bad. Whenever I get weighed down by the feeling, I can always hold on to Céline while I blubber or drink or go to sleep. There are other options. Unfortunately, Rebecca doesn't think I cope well.

"You don't even know what I'm asking for it," I say.

"And what are you asking for it?"

What can you afford is the question on the tip of my tongue. But I can't ask that. "What are you paying in rent now?" I ask instead.

"Twelve hundred," she replies, shoving her hands down

her pockets and slouching a bit. "I can afford as much as fifteen hundred, but even that is pushing it for me."

I consider what she told me. Technically, she could live here for free. I don't need her money, but it'd be weird to make such a generous offer. Especially since she thinks I'm down on my luck and need the cash.

The way I see it, I have two choices. I can tell her that fifteen hundred is not enough, leaving me roommate free and her having to continue her search. Or I can propose an amount in her budget. The possibility of rooming together makes my heart race. But do I really want a roommate?

My brows knit together as I think about it. What is the worst thing that could happen? I guess there are a lot a worst-case scenarios. Jordan might be a slob, but she doesn't strike me as one. She keeps herself very neat, and I see the way she runs the coffee shop. If there's even a single boot print on the floor, she's ordering someone to grab the mop.

I decide that I want to do Hot Barista a solid. I'm due to do a good deed. Who knows, maybe karma will repay me. Maybe Jordan will quit being such a grouch and open up to me. Maybe we'll fall madly in love and live out the rest of our days happy and having mind-blowing sex. But perhaps that's too much of a stretch. Is happiness real? A long time ago, I determined it's an achievement as out of reach as the stars.

And how can I expect to be happy now, when my dreams have been crushed. Hugo wants nothing to do with me. I might never open a restaurant.

Pushing away my thoughts, I ask, "Would you be open to renting the room for thirteen hundred?"

"You can get more than double that if you rent to someone else," she rebuts.

Merde, she's so annoying. "Seriously, why are you fighting this? I already told you that I'm not interested in living with a stranger. Besides, I am not hurting that bad for money now that I'm working. Thirteen hundred is more than enough to cover the utilities, which is why I'm looking for a roommate in the first place."

"Don't you think it'd be weird—living together?"

"Because you're my boss?"

"Yes."

I toss my ponytail over my shoulder. "No, not really. This house has more than enough space for the two of us."

Jordan stares at the floor. She bites down on her lower lip. I'm jealous of her teeth. What I'd give to feel her lips on mine.

She looks at me, and my stomach turns over. "Thirteen hundred?"

I clear my throat. "Yeah."

Nodding, she diverts her gaze and scratches the back of her ear. "Okay." She grins, but it's tight. It doesn't reach her eyes. I don't think I've ever seen her light up with a smile. There's always been a heaviness around Jordan—a melancholy that calls to me, mimicking my own. I wonder what trauma she carries with her. I wonder if she will ever tell me. I wonder if we will ever be friends … or something more.

ELEVEN

My pulse spikes when the truck pulls into my driveway. Jordan sits behind the wheel. The passenger door pops open and a slender woman hops out—Amari. Jordan said her sister would be helping her move in.

I step away from the window and head for the front door. Céline heard the vehicle and she's posted herself in the foyer. I scoop her up before she starts making a fuss.

Before stepping outside, I check myself out in the full-length mirror hanging on the wall across from me. I'm trying today, sporting a full face of makeup and orange romper I purchased at Harrods while on a trip to London. My accessories include a gold chain belt from Louis Vuitton and matching gold hoops from the same line. I'm probably over-dressed, but it's been a while since Jordan's seen me glammed up. My confidence needs a boost. I want her to drool over me the way I drooled over Zendaya's custom

Erdem Fall 2024 dress. Without hesitation or regret, I would rob a Girl Scout to have that floral and hand-painted gown.

I step through the front door and descend the short flight of stairs.

The sisters are glaring at each other, and I catch the tail of their conversation. "You always think the worst of me," Amari says curtly.

Jordan mutters something, but I can't catch her words. Today she's wearing a loose-fitting black Adidas track suit. Asides from the Grind That Bean Uniform, I've never seen her in a colour other than black. I think it's a shame. Sure, she could probably wear a cardboard box and look good, but I think emerald or cornflower blue would pop on her.

When I reach Amari, I hold out a hand and smile. "Hi," I say. "You must be Jordan's sister. I'm Noémie—I work at the coffee shop with her."

Jordan's sister shakes my hand firmly. "Yes, I'm Amari. I must say your home is absolutely stunning," she says, all acidity gone from her tone. She looks a lot like Jordan, but they also seem like opposite sides of the same coin. They are both very attractive, tall, and lean, but Amari is feminine presenting. Her makeup is applied flawlessly and her long microbraids are styled up in a tight bun.

"And who is this adorable guy?" Amari coos.

"Her name is Céline," I answer. My eyes go to Jordan, who stands rigid with a full trash bag slung over a shoulder. I assume it's filled with her clothes. "Do you need help unloading the truck?"

"No," Jordan says, at the same time Amari says, "Yes." She

shoots her sister a dark look that Amari returns. "I don't have a lot to unpack," Jordan adds.

Amari folds her arms. "If she's offering to help, why not let her?" The tension between the two siblings is palpable. I'm reminded how Claude and Antoinette used to bicker.

Tomorrow is the anniversary of the accident. A chord of sadness resonates in my bones, but I don't let my grief show on my face or in my voice when I say, "It's no bother. Let me just put Céline down."

Jordan was right, she doesn't have a lot of stuff. Even with Amari disappearing to the washroom for twenty minutes, we empty the truck in three trips. We don't talk as we cart boxes and bags up the stairs to the guest room. The silence is kind of awkward.

"Do you want help unpacking?" I carefully set down the box I'm holding.

Jordan's brows furrow. "Ummm … no," she says, shaking her head. "I don't have a lot of stuff, but thanks for helping me unload the truck. I appreciate it." And for the first time since she arrived, she looks at me. Like, she's really looking at me. Like old times. Like before my father found out about Cara. Before she walked me home. Before she hired me.

Her gaze slowly scans my body from the bottom up before coming to rest on my face. There's nothing platonic about the glint in her eyes. It's a relief to know she still finds me hot. My skin warms with the knowledge. The rush I get feels better than a high. I never want to come down.

"I'm back," Amari says, ruining the moment. "Need help bringing anything else up?"

Jordan looks off to the side and scratches the back of her

neck. "Nope … no thanks to you. We emptied Uncle West-on's truck."

Amari rolls her eyes at Jordan. Her expression softens when she looks at me. "Thank you, Noémie, for helping."

I shrug. "Happy to help." A quiet falls over the room. I take that as my cue to leave since Jordan made it clear that she doesn't want anymore assistance. "It was good meeting you, Amari."

Jordan's sister smiles at me. "Likewise."

When I leave, I'm still feeling the aftereffects of Jordan's intense gaze. I'm giddy. Suddenly, I'm a lot less worried about this roommate situation.

I decide to burn off my restless energy, but an hour of cardio and strength training only pumps me up more. I take a shower, rinsing the sweat from my body. I change into a more comfortable outfit—yoga pants and an oversized Thom Browne cardigan.

Falling onto my mattress, I stare up at my ceiling. My nerves feel like sparklers. I'm so awake and hot all over. Hot Barista is my roommate. She's one floor beneath me. My fantasy is manifesting into a reality I never imagined, and I can't wait to see how this plays out. There's a possibility that nothing will happen between us. There's also a possibility that something might. It's a gamble, but I'm excited to see where the dice land. I could hit the jackpot. I could get the woman I've coveted for years. Or I could get nothing.

What will living together be like? Will she keep to herself and stay holed up in her room all the time? My nose scrunches with distaste. I don't like the idea of Jordan ignoring me at both work and at home.

I think about my bet with Wayne. What started out as a stupid game now seems like something to prove. There's no way I will sleep with Jordan unless we are in a relationship. She's not someone I'd want a casual fling with. If we do anything, it's because we're together. Period.

I think about what Wayne told me on my first day on the job. He said Jordan's got a track record for breaking hearts. Later, when he found out that Jordan was moving in with me, he broke down into a fit of laughter and said, "Gurrrrl, you really are that desperate."

I gritted my teeth. "I'm not."

"You're going to cave faster than a city suffering a level nine earthquake." Sobering, he wiped his eyes. "But seriously, I'm starting to like you. And while I really do want one of your fancy purses, I'd hate to see you hurt. Moving in with Jay is a bad idea. You can't seduce your way into her heart."

"I have no plans to."

He sighed. "Look, it isn't too late to change your mind. Tell Jordan that something came up and the room isn't available."

"But … she needs a place."

"And she will find one. She's a big girl and can take care of herself," Wayne said. "I don't think moving in together is a good idea."

"I'm not going to retract my offer for her to live with me."

"Then it's your funeral, and my advantage," he said, shrugging. "Want to up the stakes? I say you don't last a month before you sleep with her."

"Fuck you." Glaring at him, I stormed out of the stockroom.

There's a part of me that worries Wayne's right, and I've never wanted anyone as much as I want Jordan. Wanting her wrecks my logic, but the cracks in my reality aren't as sharp when she's near. Wanting is insanity.

Exhaling a loud breath, I wonder if there really isn't a way for me to be the exception. If there's a key to Jordan's heart, I'd like to find it.

My father confessed, on many occasions, that my mother fell for him the moment he presented her with a plate of seared scallops on a bed of mushroom risotto. Thinking of him makes my chest ache. After everything, I still love Hugo. I miss him. I miss his approval and praise. I miss the future he promised me—a restaurant of my own. Once, I was his favourite. Now, I'm just a stain on his reputation.

I push thoughts of my father away and sit up. I know what I can do to spend the rest of my nervous energy. Jordan must be hungry after a day of moving and unpacking. I will make her something.

TWELVE

The timer goes off, and I roll off the couch. Stuffing my hands into a pair of orange mitts, I open the oven door and remove the heavy braising pot. It smells delicious, and I'm hungry.

I nudge the oven door closed with my hip, set the pot down on a trivet, and toss my gloves to the side. When I look up, I see Jordan. My breath hitches. I can't find my voice, so I smile. She doesn't smile back. Instead, her gaze wanders over to the set table.

Jordan ditched the Adidas track suit for skinny jeans and a black-collared shirt that she opted to leave all the top buttons undone. It's evident she's not wearing a bra. Her small perky tits are on display for anyone to see, and I stare. My pulse drums. Want for her pools in my core.

Oh, this is dangerous. She's only been here a few hours, and I'm already feeling my willpower crumble. All I want to do is touch her.

"You're going to cave faster than a city suffering a level nine earthquake." Wayne's words repeat in my mind, and my resolve strengthens. Wayne can go fuck himself. I'm not a teenager with crazy hormones. I can control myself.

Jordan clears her throat. "Expecting company?"

"No. Why do you ask?"

She looks at me and frowns.

Why is she frowning? "Is everything okay?"

"Yeah," she says. "There are two place settings. Is one for Céline?"

I chuckle. "She's spoiled, but not that spoiled. I figured you'd be hungry after moving. But no pressure to join me," I say. "Looks like you're heading out." I'm not happy that she's going out.

The entire time I prepared dinner, I daydreamed about our first night living together. First, we'd eat dinner, polishing off the bottle of wine. After dinner, we'd settle on the couch and talk about anything and everything. Jordan tells me that she's never met a girl like me. She confesses to having a secret crush on me. She leans in to kiss me. Naturally, I stop her. I tell her I don't do casual hook ups. Then, feigning tiredness, I make to retreat to my bedroom. But just as I rise, Jordan grabs my wrist. Pulling me onto her lap, she says breathlessly, "When it comes to you, I don't want casual."

From there, the images in my head got really wild. I got so caught up in the erotic movie playing out in my head that I almost cut myself while chopping herbs.

"I have time to eat," Jordan says, snapping me back to now.

"Have a seat." I muster up a smile that I'm not feeling. "I'll bring you a plate." Sure, I'm glad she's going to eat with me, but I'm disappointed she has plans that don't involve me. Is she going out on a date? My stomach twists.

Jordan sits down at the table, and I work on plating the food. I made one of my favourite dishes, beef bourguignon with a side of crusty bread. It's the perfect comfort meal, rich and packed with flavour.

I garnish the dish with a sprig of thyme, wipe down the sides of the dish, and set the wide-rimmed bowl down in front of her. Jordan mutters a thanks as she scrutinizes the dish. She's incredibly hard to read. I can't tell if she's impressed or revolted by the meal. Some people are picky eaters. Fingers crossed that Jordan isn't because I have all the time in the world now to experiment in the kitchen, but food doesn't taste like much when I'm alone at the table.

I return to the kitchen, grabbing my plate and the basket of bread. As I slide into my seat, my heart gallops in my chest. Jordan still hasn't touched her food. She fiddles with the end of her knife.

Biting my lip, I reach for the wine and pour us both a glass. I take a sip of my wine and watch Jordan. "Do you not like beef bourguignon?"

"Thought it'd be rude of me to just dig in," she says.

Oh, so she was waiting for me. Relief spreads over my chest like wings. "Take a bite. I want to know what you think." Anxious, I swallow back some more wine. I hope she likes it.

Jordan stabs a piece of meat with her fork and pops it in her mouth. Her eyes close as she chews. She makes a sound that's close enough to a moan, and my arousal is instant.

Heat burns up my neck, and I know my blush will be noticeable. Merde.

"Fuck, this is so good."

"Glad you like it." I drink more wine, hoping it will douse the fire burning in my stomach.

We eat mostly in silence. We barely look at each other. The clinking of metal against porcelain acts as an awkward symphony. Thankfully, the alcohol starts to hit, making me relax somewhat.

After Jordan wipes her bowl clean with a piece of bread, she sits back in her chair and reaches for her wine glass. She'll be leaving soon. I don't want her to go.

"So where are you off to?" I ask.

"Going to a party in the Village."

"Alone?"

"Nah, with a friend," she replies.

Good, it's not a date. If she was off to meet some random, I'm not sure how I'd react. It never bothered me when men or women flirted with Cara right in front of me. But the moment a female customer smiles at Jordan, I see red. The few times Jordan returned their smiles made me feral.

Is she really as bad as Wayne says? It's hard to imagine Jordan breaking hearts. She's so soft spoken and reserved. Aren't womanizers supposed to be boisterous narcissists?

"Wayne says you don't date," I blurt. "Why is that? I'm sure there are plenty of women who'd want to date you."

Jordan blinks at me. For many moments, she doesn't say anything. Finally, she shrugs. "Relationships just aren't for me," she says flatly. "I get bored easily."

Her response plays over in my head, hollowing me out. I

pour myself another glass of wine. "Oh, okay, makes sense." My tone is tart, and I hope she doesn't read into why that may be.

Jordan's phone buzzes. Her chair scrapes against the floor as she rises to her feet. "I'm so sorry, but I have to get going. Thanks for the meal, it was delicious."

She bends to pick up her plate, but I wave her hand away. "Don't worry about clearing the table. I can do it." If she's going to leave, I'd rather she just go.

"You sure?"

I nod. "Yes. Have fun tonight." I don't look at her as she makes her exit. The front door creaks open and clicks shut. I take a long sip of wine and stare down at my half-eaten plate. The appetite I worked up earlier is gone.

I finish off the bottle of wine and then aggressively clean up. After slamming the dishwasher shut and jabbing the button to start the cycle, I sink into the couch and consider opening another bottle of wine. I decide against it. Tomorrow is a monumental day—the anniversary of Antoinette's passing. I'm not going to visit my sister hungover. She deserves better.

Sighing, it crosses my mind that perhaps there's a logical reason for me being so on edge tonight. Maybe it has nothing to do with Jordan and everything to do with me not wanting to be alone tonight—the eve of the worst day of my life.

I curl up on the couch. My eyes burn as my head fills with memories of Antoinette—my beautiful, sassy, confident sister. Sorrow lulls me to sleep.

Céline's barking wakes me up. Blinking, I sit up and rub my eyes.

"Shhh, Céline," I hear Jordan say.

A woman's giggle puts me on high alert. It's soft and feminine. There's no way it came from Jordan. Anger washes over me. *No, Jordan wouldn't bring a stranger into my house.*

But she did. I get the confirmation when I hear a woman say, "Fuck, I want you so bad."

Storming up from the couch, I have the mind to shout at them both—give Jordan a piece of my mind. However, I lose the ability to speak when I see them together. A sour taste fills my mouth. My stomach flips over. Their pressed bodies and lips disgust me, but I can't look away.

The woman is tall, thin, and somewhat pretty. Jordan pulls away, grabbing her hand and tugging her towards the staircase.

My pulse hammers as I seethe. Wayne was right. Jordan really is that bad. One night. She's been here one night, and already she's bringing women over.

Céline bounds back to the main room and hops up onto the couch. She assesses me with her large beady eyes and yawns. She can sense my dark mood brewing.

I check the time on my phone. It's just past 4:00 a.m. My body is tired, but my mind is wide awake.

THIRTEEN

Antoinette St. Pierre, 1996–2016, the tombstone reads. The grass is wet from morning dew, but I still kneel. Placing the bouquet of flowers in the holder, I stare at the stone for a long time and give myself permission to feel the weight of the grief I keep buried.

Tears run from my eyes. I don't try holding them back. I let them fall.

"I … I should have gone after you," I say with a sniffle. "If … I had, maybe you would still be here. You should still be here."

There's no response. Of course, there isn't. There never is.

Sniffling again, I wipe my eyes. I decide that the orange lilies I brought aren't sitting right in the holder and rearrange them. Orange was Antoinette's favourite colour. A lot of people think it's mine too, but it's not. I just like to surround myself with the colour because it reminds me of her. I'm so scared of forgetting her. Antoinette deserves to be remembered, but it's a fine line I walk. I know I'm not her. I know I can never be her. However, sometimes, when I look in the mirror, I see her.

I spend over an hour at the cemetery. It's still early, so the drive back into the city isn't so bad.

When I get home, the first thing I notice is the pair of Vans that were kicked off by the front door. I see red. That bitch is still in my home. Gritting my teeth, I unzip my Prada boots and stomp up the stairs.

I have every intention of causing a scene, banging on the door and shouting obscenities in French. Jordan has some fucking nerve.

My breaths come heavy when I reach Jordan's bedroom door. I lift a fist. I'm about to start pounding. I hesitate upon hearing the moaning on the other side.

Putain—they're still at it? Everything in my stomach curdles. In the wave of sickness, my sanity returns. I realize that making a scene won't do anything but hurt me. I don't want Jordan flinging open the door undressed in a panic. I don't want to see the naked woman on her bed. I don't want to see anything.

I can yell at Jordan later. Once I've reduced my rage to a simmer. Once I've settled on exactly what I want to say.

I back away, steering myself towards the ascending staircase. Céline follows me up to my bedroom. Picking her up, I hold her tight against my chest and collapse onto my bed.

Too many emotions swirl in my head, and for the second time that day I'm crying, and it's so stupid. I have no claim on Jordan. She isn't mine. She can fuck whoever she wants—just not under my roof.

I try to burn off my temper in the gym, but nothing's going right. The treadmill is making a clicking noise, and even with my headphones blasting Charli XCX, I hear it. I can't ignore the sound. If anything, it gets louder with every stride.

Hopping off the machine, I kick it a little too hard and hurt my foot. "Merde!" Wincing, I double over.

I try lifting weights next, but why does everything feel so heavy? Ditching the dumbbells, I decide to work on my core, but boat pose burns more than usual. Everything just fucking hurts. But maybe I should feel grateful for the pain. Feeling means I'm still alive—I could be dead. I could be Antoinette.

I'm crying again. I'm a blubbering mess. I hate it.

My phone buzzes. I look down at the screen and see a text from Wayne.

WAYNE, 10:12 A.M.

Can I collect my prize? Or did you manage to last the night?

Clenching my jaw, I sit down on a bench, wipe my eyes, and message him back.

NOÉMIE, 10:12 A.M.

Fuck U

Bet is still on. And I'm more determined than ever to not lose.

WAYNE, 10:12 A.M.

Shiiiit, more determined? Why????

Biting my lip, I contemplate whether I want to tell him. I decide that I do. I need an outlet. I need to vent to someone.

NOÉMIE, 10:13 A.M.

Jordan went out last night and brought someone home with her!!!!!!!!

Can u fucking believe that?

She didn't think to ask if it was ok!

If she's this inconsiderate I prob want nothing to do with her TBH

WAYNE, 10:14 A.M.

LMFAO. That girl gets around.

Told U

I don't want to acknowledge his statement, so I click off my screen and head upstairs to the kitchen. Grabbing a protein shaker out the cupboard, I mix myself a drink. The protein powder tastes exceptionally chalky this morning.

Jordan walks into the kitchen. When she sees me, she grins. "Good morning."

Something about seeing the satisfied expression on her stupid beautiful face blows my top. I slam my bottle on the counter.

Jordan flinches. "Did I do something?"

Like she doesn't know. She has to know that what she did was not okay. She should have asked me if it was okay to bring someone over. I can't look at her. Turning, I yank open a cabinet and reach for my vitamins.

"Can you tell me what's wrong?"

I whirl on her. "Esti de câlice de tabarnak, c'est pas possible d'être cave de même!" I stab a finger in her direction. "What's wrong? What's wrong is that I'm not running a brothel. I don't want random women in my home!"

"Look, I'm sorry," she says, having the audacity to look like a kicked puppy. "I didn't think—"

"Maybe you should start."

"I won't do it again."

"Yeah, whatever." Rolling my eyes, I storm out of the kitchen. I can't look at her right now. Everything is too fresh and raw.

Jordan makes it hard to stay angry at her, and I want nothing more than to hold on to my rage. When I'm pissed at her, I don't want to sleep with her. And I really, really don't want to sleep with her. Well, I do. But only if it means we are together. I'm not interested in being just another number to her tally. I might be unlovable, but I still deserve better.

With every day that passes at home and at work, she makes it impossible to stay mad. She lets me get away with being a total bitch and borderline insubordinate. Chef Ricard would've fired me earlier if I acted even a percentage as bad at the restaurant.

Jordan's also been actively trying to talk to me, which is new. The urge to engage in casual conversation strikes hardest at home. She spends hours curled on the couch on her iPad with a stylus in hand. I know she's drawing. I asked Wayne about it, but he's clueless.

I want to know what she's sketching. I want to see it. I want to know if she's any good. If she's a crappy artist, I'll likely be less attracted to her. Incompetence is undesirable. Competence is sexy. It'd be nice to find something about Jordan that I don't like. There's too much about her that does it for me, and it's unnerving.

I thought Jordan would be like my ex around Céline. Cara hadn't cared for my baby, and the feeling had been mutual. But Jordan went from looking terrified of Céline to becoming my dog's newest best friend. Only yesterday, I found Céline curled up on Jordan's lap as she worked on her iPad. My heart just about collapsed.

Now, it's Friday, and Jordan's sitting in her usual perch, sketching away. She's so engrossed in what she's doing that she doesn't notice me staring. I watch her for a while—too long. I lose track of just how long. I probably could stare at her forever and never get bored.

My eyes keep going to her hands. Her skin is smooth and unblemished. The fingers curled around the pen are long and slender. She's got perfect nail beds. The night she walked me home, she caught me. For a short time, I felt her hand on my shoulder. The brief contact had been electric, lighting me up. I'd donate my favourite vintage Mugler dress to make Jordan mine. If she was mine, she could touch me in all the ways I've dreamt about.

"What are you always doing on your iPad?" I finally ask.

Startled, Jordan drops her stylus. It falls in the crease between the couch arm and seat cushion.

"Nothing," she says, clicking the button on the tablet. The screen goes black and she sets it face down on her lap. She looks at me blankly. I wish I could decipher her better. Jordan's too tough a safe to crack.

"Seems like it's something," I say, crossing the room.

Jordan keeps silent.

"Digital art?" I probe.

Her jaw flexes. "Yes, I like to draw," she confirms. Her tone is curt. Whatever she's working on, she's very protective about it. I'm even more curious to see it, so I'm annoyed when she says, "But don't bother asking to see it. I'm not comfortable sharing."

Naturally, I want to poke some more. But we're on thin ice. Ever since Saturday morning, I've been a total and utter bitch to her. It's a wonder she hasn't snapped at me yet. Her patience for my bullshit is impressive.

When I nod instead of pushing for an explanation, Jordan's whole body seems to relax.

"Wayne mentioned once that you have a degree in fine arts," I say, sitting down on the thick armrest on the opposite end of the couch. Although, I already knew about her degree thanks to Facebook.

Jordan neither confirms nor denies it. She just stares at me like she's waiting for something.

I guess, if I were in her place, I'd want an apology—I'd want rationale for the bratty attitude. I decide to give her one. I probably owe it to her at this point. "The beginning of

October is always hard for me," I tell her. "I know that I've been really bitchy these past few days, and I shouldn't have taken my anger out on you."

"You had every reason to be upset," she says with a shrug. "I should have asked you if it was okay to bring someone over."

"Yeah, you should have," I agree. "I would have told you that it wouldn't be okay. I don't want strange people in my home."

"Fair enough," she says. "Am I allowed to have friends over?"

"I don't know. Maybe if I meet them first. I don't really trust anyone, even people I know. So having people I don't know in my space makes me uncomfortable."

She nods. "I get and respect that."

"Do you though?" I ask. Cara never did. She was always trying to get me to host parties. She was always trying to get me to post videos of us together. She was always trying to get me to do things together in a public forum, where anyone could snap a photo of us. Back when we were together, nothing scared me more than having our relationship uncovered.

None of that matters anymore. My secret's out, but I still haven't made peace with it.

I look at Jordan and our eyes meet. My chest grows warm and fuzzy. It crosses my mind that brown eyes are so under-rated. Hers are so dark that I can get lost in them. I'm a little jealous of her eyelashes. The girl's not even wearing mascara, and they're so thick and long.

"Yes," Jordan says, replying to my question.

Tension crackles between us. I wonder if she feels it. I wonder if she can sense how much I want her. I wonder what her reaction would be if I closed the distance between us.

I will not do that, of course. Jordan is danger wrapped in a pretty package, and I know what it feels like to be burnt.

I look away first and stand. "I am going to warm some leftover butter chicken. Do you want some? It's one of my favourite dishes to make, and it usually tastes better the next day."

"Yeah, sure," she says quickly. Her face brightens, and for a second, she looks like an entirely different person. Lighter.

We eat dinner. I pair the meal with a crisp Riesling. Jordan demolishes her plate and asks for seconds. I like that she has a healthy appetite and relationship with food. It's hard not to compare her to Cara, who counted calories like how my brother tracks the price of Bitcoin.

A ball of dread forms in my stomach as we finish eating. It's Friday night, which means Jordan might be going out. I don't want her to go.

"Any plans tonight?" I ask.

"No," she replies, shaking her head.

The ball unspools, and I perk up. "Do you want to watch something on Netflix?"

Jordan blinks like she can't believe I asked. "Was there something you wanted to watch?"

"No," I say. "But I am down to watch anything that isn't a rom-com."

She arches a brow. "You don't like rom-coms?"

"You're telling me that you do?" I take a sip from my glass.

"I definitely do not watch *How to Lose a Guy in Ten Days* at least once a year."

I choke on my wine as I laugh. "Oh my God—you don't."

"I really don't see what's so funny," she says with amusement.

"You just don't look like someone who would watch a movie like that," I reply. She really doesn't. She comes across as someone who'd be into superhero movies or indie flicks.

"In my defence, Kate Hudson is a total babe in that movie," she says.

"And Matthew McConaughey isn't too bad himself," I state out of habit. It's something I've always done, playing up being straight to throw people off. It's a habit I need to break. Jordan thinks I'm straight. I've led her to believe so, and I know I will have to come clean soon. But that time isn't now. The chill between us is just starting to defrost. I don't want to ruin the moment.

Jordan volunteers to tidy up, but I'm not sure I trust her to do it right. What if she's one of those people who packs the dishwasher all wrong, and so specks of food remain on the dishes after the cycle?

I tell Jordan that I can clean up. She doesn't look happy about it, but she doesn't argue with me.

Twenty minutes later, I'm finished. I drop down on the couch right beside her. Our thighs touch, and I thrill in the feeling of being so close to her. Tonight, she isn't going out. Tonight, I will pretend she's mine.

FOURTEEN

It's Monday, but the coffee shop is closed for Thanksgiving. A normal person would be happy about having the day off, but with almost everything shut down, I'm not sure how to pass the time. And I guess I'm a little butt hurt about not being with my family.

After the incident with Antoinette, my father made it a point to be present for special occasions. Unlike Claude, I always looked forward to holidays because Hugo usually cooked. I was always expected to help out, which made me happy. Holidays always felt like old times—the times before Poutine Heaven operations consumed every minute on my father's calendar.

Working in the kitchen with my father is probably one of my favourite things in the world. I've learned more from him than anyone. It makes me sad that we might never cook together again.

The doorbell rings. Growling, Céline scrambles for the front door.

Setting down my coffee cup, I slide off the stool and exit the main room. My eye roll is immediate when I open the door.

Claude smiles at me. "Bon matin, Noémie."

I don't smile back.

My brother pushes his way into the foyer, and Céline excitedly barks and paws his legs. Claude smiles down at her, but then directs his focus on me.

I shut the door with a little too much force and cross my arms. "You know I hate it when you just show up without texting first," I say.

"You're looking better," he says, disregarding my statement. "Have you been taking your medication?"

I snort. His question doesn't deserve a response. My brother isn't my keeper. "Why are you here?"

"Our mother wants you to come to dinner," he replies.

"She does? She tell you that?" I arch a brow.

My brother's jaw works as he contemplates an answer. "No, she didn't, but she didn't have to say it. She's worried about you. She misses you."

"She knows my number. She could always call me," I snap. My skin buzzes with anger. It's just like Hélène to get Claude to do her dirty work. The woman has no backbone.

"Noémie, our mother isn't doing well," he says softly. "She really does miss you."

"I don't care!"

"How can you not care? She's your mother."

"The way you feel about Hugo is how I feel about Hélène," I say with a huff.

Claude glowers at me. "I don't get how you can forgive him after what he did."

"Hélène is just as responsible!"

"No, she's not!"

"Yes, she is!" I clap back. I hate how much of a mama's boy he is. "You weren't there. I was!"

"Merde! Hugo is a monster!" My brother shakes his head. His fists ball at his sides. "Why do you care so much about what he thinks?"

I'm about to answer when I notice movement—Jordan is standing on the third step from the bottom of the stairs. My heart skips a beat. How much did she hear?

Claude turns his head, following my gaze.

"She's my roommate," I blurt, not wanting my brother to get the wrong idea.

"Roommate," he repeats.

"We also work together. Her name is Jordan." I pin my brother with a hard look. He better not say anything to make Jordan uncomfortable. He better not mention Cara. My pulse hammers in my ears.

Jordan descends the last few steps. She walks towards the foyer, extending a hand. "Nice to meet you."

My brother's grey eyes narrow on her. With her short curly hair and androgynous features, it's very obvious that Jordan is gay. I can tell that Claude's mind is calculating whether me and Jordan are an item. Ugh … he's so fucking annoying. Why'd he have to show up? I woke up in a mood, and him darkening my doorstep is only putting me in a worse mindset.

"Jordan," he says, shaking the offered hand. "I'm Claude—"

"My brother," I chirp, shooting him a glare.

"Nice to meet you, Claude," Jordan says, dropping his hand.

My brother smirks. "You should bring her to Thanksgiving dinner."

Great, he's determined that Jordan and I are together. My lips press together. "Like I said, I'm not going to dinner unless I'm invited." Bending, I scoop up Céline. She's been yapping the entire time, and her barking is starting to give me a headache.

Claude gives me a dose of side eye. "We both know Hugo's not going to do that, but you know our mother wants you there. She misses you."

"Then she should be the one asking me to come, not you," I say, hating that he's making me repeat myself in front of Jordan.

Releasing an exaggerated sigh, Claude says, "Can't say I didn't try." He looks down at his watch and makes a face that tells me he's late for something. When he turns for the door, relief floods my system. "It was a pleasure meeting you, Jordan," he says, giving her a final once over before throwing the front door open and stepping through it.

Needing confirmation that he is actually leaving, I go over to the window and peek through the blinds. I watch my brother slide into his Ferrari and reverse out of the driveway.

When he's gone, a wash of emotions overrides my system. The heaviness I woke up with sits on my lungs. It feels like I'm suffocating. Why'd he have to come here and stir up feelings that I wanted to keep settled?

My eyes burn and my body sags. Sliding down to the floor, I hug Céline and bury my face in her hair. I take a couple deep breaths, trying to push back the tears.

I hear footsteps and look up. Jordan stares at me with a tenderness that makes me want to unravel. It's the last thing I want to do in front of her. I hate that she's seeing me like this. I want to tough it up. I want to stand up straight and shake it off. But I feel so small.

Céline squirms out of the cage of my arms. She shakes violently and takes off down the hall. Without her warmth to comfort me, I hug my knees.

Jordan drops down to the floor. She mirrors me, hugging her own knees. Our shoulders brush. She smells like soap. Water drips from her hair onto the collar of her shirt. She must have just hopped out the shower.

"Do you want to talk about it?" she asks.

When I shake my head, she doesn't press for an answer. I'm grateful for it.

She sits with me. For once, the silence doesn't feel awkward. It feels right. It feels like, on some level, she understands without me having to say anything.

I rest my head on her shoulder. Jordan doesn't pull away. The load on my chest lightens, and I can breathe better. She smells good. My nose picks up notes of vanilla. I wonder what body wash she uses.

My mouth moves before I even realize what I'm doing.

"Claude hates our father so much," I confess, "and he's always looking for ways to punish him. I'm so sick of it."

Jordan's brows draw together. "Don't you hate your dad for cutting you off?"

I should hate Hugo. For some reason I don't, while I can't find it in myself to forgive Hélène. "No, he has his reasons," is all I say.

Jordan nods.

Another hush ferments between us, and my mind wanders back to my fight with Claude. What did he mean when he said our mother wasn't doing well? She hasn't been well for a very long time. Is she worse? Is she drinking more than usual? As her daughter, I should care. Why don't I care? What does that say about me? I bite down on my lower lip.

"So you're not celebrating Thanksgiving with your family," Jordan says. "Did you want to join my family dinner?"

Lifting my head from her shoulder, my lips curve into a slight smile. I do want to go. Not only will it be a distraction, but it'd mean I'd get to spend more time with her. It'd be nice to learn more about this woman who's lived rent free in my mind for so long. I want to learn everything about her.

"Sure, if it won't be too weird," I reply.

FIFTEEN

I'm probably fussing over my outfit a little too much. But I'll be meeting Jordan's family—her mother—and I need to make a good impression.

After trying on several outfits, I settle on a knit dress from Balmain. With its squared neckline and cream textured fabric, I think it suggests subtle sophistication without trying too hard. The selection of my accessories is a lot easier: Hermès gold buckled belt and my favourite fire opal stud earrings—the stones are cut to look like maple leaves. Not wanting to come off as flashy, I omit rings, donning a simple Cartier watch and thin gold necklace.

The reflection in the mirror pleases me. I look hot, but the ensemble is something Hugo would approve of—something I could wear to Mass. Which is what I am going for. I understand Jordan's mom is quite religious.

Blowing out a breath, I exit my bedroom and rush downstairs. Jordan said dinner started at five, and I don't want us to be late because I took too long getting ready.

I see Jordan before I reach the bottom. My heart stutters. I catch myself almost stumbling down the last steps.

Jordan doesn't witness my blunder. Thank God. She's focused on her phone as she leans against a wall. The glow of the screen illuminates her handsome face. I wonder if she's messaging someone. Hopefully not that girl she brought over here.

When I clear my throat, she looks up at me. Her eyes go wide. I take it as a good sign, but I want verbal confirmation that she likes what she sees. "How do I look?"

She stands straighter and puts away her phone. "Nice."

I frown. Nice is not the compliment I was looking for. But I guess she'd never say that I look like a virgin she wants to ravish, which is what I want to hear. "So that's what you're wearing?" I guess it shouldn't surprise me that she's wearing sweatpants and an oversized hoodie, but it's a special occasion. Why couldn't she have put on one of her button-down shirts?

Jordan shrugs. "Thanksgiving is casual where I'm from."

"Okay," I say. "Well, I'm going to just grab a bottle of wine and then we can go."

"You don't need to bring anything."

"Where I'm from, it's rude to show up empty handed to dinner."

Jordan sighs, but says nothing more.

At quarter to four, we climb into my car. I sync my phone up to the Bluetooth. It's as I'm backing out of the driveway that my anxiety cranks up a level. I'm going to see where

Jordan grew up. I'm going to meet her mother. This is kind of a big deal.

Even knowing Jordan doesn't date seriously, I wonder if she has ever introduced a girlfriend to her mother? How does Paulette feel about her daughter being a lesbian? Obviously, better than mine. But considering that religion is a huge pillar in her life, how accepting can she really be?

"Aren't you a little too young for this music?" Jordan asks.

My playlist is a blend of EDM and hits from the early 2000s—music before my time. Music that aired on the radio when Jordan was in high school. More than half the songs were Antoinette's favourites. Listening to them makes me feel closer to her. Right now, "All That I've Got" by The Used is playing. Before that it was "Lithium" by Evanescence.

"The Used was my sister's favourite band," I explain, clearing my throat. It's dry and tight. "And she had an unhealthy obsession with Amy Lee."

"She has great taste in music," Jordan says.

"Yeah, she did," I whisper.

Jordan's quick to say, "I'm so sorry." She sounds like she means it. Like she's truly sorry. Like she understands to a degree most can't and never will.

"Don't worry, it's okay," I say quickly, even though it really isn't okay. "She died years ago …"

"That doesn't mean it doesn't still hurt," Jordan says before adding softly, "The hole of your grief might get smaller with time, but it never goes away."

Her words carry the weight of someone who knows loss. Sorrow salts her syllables. How big is her hole? My sister's death crashed into my heart like an asteroid, and I don't think a lifetime can shrink the crater.

"Isn't that the truth," I say, my fingers drumming on the steering wheel. "October fifth was the anniversary of the … the incident. Antoinette got hit by a car. When that date rolls around, it's like I feel everything all over again. If that even makes sense." It surprises me that I'm opening up about this. I rarely talked about Antoinette with my exes. Cara doesn't even know the whole story.

"It does." A moment passes, and then Jordan fills the space with her own confession. "My father overdosed three years ago around Christmas, and I can't find it in myself to feel merry around that time."

"I guess we have something in common," I manage to say around the thick ball forming in my throat.

"Guess so," she murmurs gently.

"Were you close with your dad?"

"It's complicated." She goes quiet for a beat. "Before my parents divorced, my dad was always around. He was the one who picked Amari and I up from school and made us dinner. My mom's a nurse, so she's always worked crazy hours. After the divorce, my grandmother moved in, and my dad's visits became more infrequent with time."

"That sucks, I'm sorry," I say. My heart goes out to young Jordan. I think about reaching over to squeeze her knee, but I'm not sure how'd she react. Only a few days ago we weren't talking. In many ways, we are still strangers.

"It's okay. It is what it is." She sighs. "What's the deal with your parents? Why'd your dad cut you off?"

I stiffen. I'm not ready to talk about what happened with

Hugo. By asking about her parents, I opened myself up to this question. I can't not answer. "There's nothing much to say. My family is dysfunctional. It's always been that way, even before my sister passed," I say, choosing my words carefully. "My father has expectations of me and Claude, and if we don't fall in line … it's a problem. And even if my mother doesn't agree with him, she always takes his side."

"I hate that for you."

"It's okay. It is what it is," I say, parroting her earlier words.

Not wanting to say anything more on the subject of my family, I turn the dial up on the music. Jordan understands the signal. We don't speak for the rest of the drive.

Arriving at the apartment complex, I reverse into a visitor parking space. Getting out of the car, I scan the large orange brick building. It's in rough condition. The grey balconies are caked with rust. Some windows are boarded up and even more have air-conditioning units sticking out of them.

The asphalt of the parking lot is cracked and pebbled with sinkholes. Somewhere in the distance, rap music booms. There's a weight to the atmosphere that makes me want to hug my purse close to my body, but I could be imagining it. If it's bias, does that make me a racist?

Jordan stands at the hood of my Tesla, staring at the building too. There's a despondent glint in her eyes. She's tense. Her hands ball by her sides.

"You okay?" I ask.

She blinks and turns to look at me. "Yeah, I'm good." She

scratches the back of her neck. "Maybe, I'm a little embarrassed. This isn't Yorkville."

I'm irritated that her words somewhat reflect my unease. "I know what you think of me, Jordan, but I'm not a rich white girl who expects everyone I interact with to come from money. I would never judge my friends for where they come from," I say. It's not a complete lie. Some of my friends aren't rich.

A smile breaks out across Jordan's face. It's a true smile, and the brightness of it lights me up on the inside. I can't stop myself from smiling back. We share a moment, wrapped in each other's gazes.

Jordan looks away first. She cocks her head towards the entrance and starts walking towards the building. I follow.

All my words were bullshit, but I'm committed to not letting Jordan see how apprehensive I am as we cross the lobby that reeks of marijuana. The elevator is dark and claustrophobic. The ride up is jerky. When the doors finally open, I hold back from exhaling a breath of relief.

When I'm not in a funk, I'm quite the germaphobe, or maybe the right word is snob. I hate mess. I hate dirt. I hate odours. The hallway we walk down is all those things. I smell cat piss and stale cigarette smoke. The colour of the carpet leads me to believe it hasn't seen a vacuum in ages. There are three garbage bags strewn outside of the disposal room. I make a point of not scrunching my nose in disgust. This is where Jordan grew up, and I literally just gave a speech about not passing judgement.

It's kind of eye opening, seeing how some folks live. I feel a little guilty knowing how different my world is from Jordan's.

She stops at a door. Lifting her hand, Jordan hesitates before knocking.

I adjust my hold on the wine bottle and try to ignore the way my stomach flips over. The seconds we wait, standing in the hallway, seem like an eternity.

When the door opens, I plaster on my warmest smile. A woman sticks her head out. I assume it's Jordan's mother. The resemblance is strong. It's easy to see where Jordan gets her good looks from.

Paulette Alexander doesn't look a day over forty, and unlike my mother, her features aren't frozen by Botox. She wears a modest indigo kaftan. Her hair is hidden underneath a satin bonnet featuring an eye-catching motif of red, green, yellow, and black geometric shapes. Even without a hint of makeup, Paulette is stunning. Only the sagging skin at her neck and the fine lines under her brown eyes give away her age.

Paulette's eyes narrow on me for a moment. "You didn't tell me you were bringing a friend," she says dryly.

Jordan looks blankly at her mother and doesn't say anything.

Stepping back, Paulette swings the door open wide, and we shuffle inside.

The apartment smells much better than the hallway. Cooked food fragrances the air. I recognize some of the scents—like sautéed onions. The spicy notes are foreign to me, but not unpleasant.

I understand Jordan is Jamaican. Asides from a beef patty

I ate once, my palate isn't familiar with the cuisine. I'm excited to try it. I hope I like it. If I do, I'll make a point of trying to make some of Jordan's favourites.

Jordan's mother closes the door, and she's back to scrutinizing us. Her eyes pinball between me and her daughter. Her gaze is intense. My grip on the wine bottle tightens.

Jordan clears her throat. "This is Noémie … my roommate."

"Very nice to meet you, Ms. Alexander," I say, increasing the voltage on my smile. Not thinking, I greet Paulette the way I'm used to doing, leaning in and air kissing both her cheeks.

When Jordan's mother visibly stiffens, I realize my error. The heat of my embarrassment rushes up my neck and spreads over my face.

"She's French," Jordan says, shrugging.

Paulette's brows pinch. "French," her mother repeats.

I hold out the bottle of wine, and now I'm grinning so wide that my cheeks hurt. "For you. It's a Bordeaux—pairs well with beef and lamb."

Paulette accepts my offering, sticking the bottle under her arm. "Thank you, Noémie," she says, her voice softening the slightest bit. "Make yourself comfortable. Dinner will be ready soon." She leaves us without another word, disappearing behind a green, yellow, and black beaded curtain that I assume leads to the kitchen.

Biting down on my lower lip, I look at Jordan. "That could have gone over better. I'm sorry."

Jordan shrugs again. "Don't worry about it. I should have warned you about my mother. She isn't always the most welcoming." She holds out a hand. "Give me your coat, I'll hang it up."

Nodding, I remove my jacket. Our fingers brush when I hand it over. The brief contact is electric, but Jordan doesn't seem to notice the spark.

Turning her back on me, she puts our coats away in the closet. I busy myself with unzipping my boots.

The walls in the living room are a bold colour choice—canary yellow. Knickknacks like giant cat figurines and large dark furniture cramp the space, but there's something cozy about the aesthetic. The room feels lived in. It feels warm from memories I can only guess at.

An oak China cabinet, filled with an assortment of plates, bowls, and cups, towers over the TV stand. My gaze lands on the picture frames lined next to the television. Many of the photos feature Jordan and Amari as children. They were very cute, but it's odd seeing Jordan with long plaited hair and wearing dresses.

I want to ask her about it or maybe tease her, but I'm not sure how she'd respond, so I don't.

Jordan drops down into a three-seater couch. It's red, and the fabric is corduroy. There's a matching love seat on the other side.

Sitting down beside her, I cross my legs and catch Jordan checking me out. Her gaze trails up from my calves up to my thighs. Does she even realize how obvious she is sometimes? Not that I mind. I love it when she looks at me. I always want her eyes on me.

Jordan stares down at her lap and clears her throat. "So, I know I said dinner starts at five, but … it never does."

"That's fine," I say.

She scratches the back of her ear and her leg bounces. I'm starting to learn her tells. She's nervous. Part of me hopes I'm the reason. "If you're hungry, I'm pretty sure the soup's ready," she says. "I can get you a cup. Have you had Jamaican yellow soup before? It's pretty good."

"No, I haven't tried it before," I say, "but I'm good for now." I don't want her to go. I want her to stay here beside me with our shoulders brushing.

She nods. "Okay."

I wait for Jordan to say something else, but she doesn't. In the absence of conversation, my ears tune into the smooth reggae playing from the speakers. I don't know the song. I can't understand most of the words, but the rhythm is relaxing.

I go back to scanning the room. A wall with more than a dozen sketches and paintings draws my attention. All of them are quite good, but there are some that are far better than others, as if the artist got better over time. One in particular is an almost photo realistic portrait of Paulette comprised of mixed media—newspaper clippings, beading, paint, and thick impasto. The colours are bright and bold, almost reminiscent of a Basquiat, but unabstracted.

Are they Jordan's works? My pulse speeds up. "Artist in the family?"

"Sorry, what'd you say?" Jordan's brows draw together.

"Artist in the family?" I repeat, cocking my chin towards the collection of sketches and paintings.

Jordan's teeth mash together. Before she answers, someone says, "Yes, my Jordan is so talented."

Turning in my seat, I see an older woman with kind brown eyes and a warm smile.

Jordan bolts to her feet and enfolds the woman in a hug. I stand too.

"This is my roommate, Noémie," Jordan says, pulling away. "Noémie, meet Grandma Janet."

Having learned from my encounter with Jordan's mother, I extend my hand in greeting. "Very nice to meet you. I have to say, before today, I didn't know just how talented your granddaughter is. Jordan refuses to show me her drawings."

Jordan side eyes me.

"It's nice to finally meet one of Jordan's friends," her grandmother says, clapping me on the back. "Oh, let me get you some soup. It will do your belly good." She leaves and returns moments later with two steaming Styrofoam cups brimming with soup.

Not wanting to be rude, I thank Jordan's grandmother and take the cup despite not being hungry.

From the kitchen, Paulette calls out for Janet. Jordan's grandmother yells something back that I think is English, but I can't be quite sure. She tuts her irritation. "Better go and see what she wants."

When her grandmother disappears behind the beaded curtain, I head for the art display. I sense Jordan's presence at my back. My fingers fiddle with the plastic spoon in the cup.

"You are really talented," I murmur.

Jordan doesn't say anything, and I guess that's to be expected. I think I'm starting to understand her. I think Jordan's silences say a lot. Right now, my guess is that Jordan isn't saying anything because she's self-conscious about her art—art that she obviously puts so much of herself into.

I hope the day comes when she gets comfortable showing me what she's working on.

Lifting the spoon to my lips, I take a small sip. "Ah, c'est délicieux," I say, meaning it. Frankly, I'm surprised how much I like it. The broth is flavourful and balanced. Taking another sip, I close my eyes and try to discern the ingredients. There's definitely thyme and allspice, but I'm not sure if the base is squash or pumpkin. "I will have to ask for the recipe."

Jordan snorts. "I'm not sure my mother will give it to you."

I roll my eyes at her. "I can be very persuasive."

"Is that so?" She arches a brow.

"I usually get my way," I shoot back with a smirk. Where Jordan's concerned, it'd be nice to get my way. I like her. I want her to like me enough to ditch her fuckboi routine. But if Wayne's right about her, that might be impossible.

Doesn't she get tired of it—fucking around? Nothing made me feel emptier than sleeping with women I didn't care about. Most of them I wasn't even attracted to. Sex is always better when there is a real connection. Jordan must know that.

She opens her mouth to say something, but just then the apartment door swings open. Amari walks inside toting a box of Popeyes chicken. Following closely behind her is a beautiful woman with legs for days and long, neat dreadlocks. She's rocking a black Canada Goose puffer jacket and tan Timberlands—it's giving Toronto starter pack.

Jordan's attention immediately goes to the woman, and her jaw sets. I can read the room. Obviously, there is history between them. As curious as I am, part of me doesn't want to know.

Without saying anything, Jordan turns her back on the newcomer. Without saying anything to me, she storms out of the living room, exiting through a door leading out to the balcony.

Amari smiles at me, but it doesn't reach her eyes. "Hello," she greets.

"Hi," I answer back.

The woman at Amari's side stares me down like I just stole her lunch. "Who's this?" she asks, nudging Jordan's sister.

"Noémie," Amari replies. "Jordan's new roommate."

"Roommate," the woman repeats flatly. Her lips press together.

I wait for her to introduce herself. When she doesn't, I set down my cup of soup on a lamp table and say, "I'm going to check on Jordan."

I head for the balcony door.

SIXTEEN

The heavy door whines and clatters shut behind me. Out on the balcony, the wind makes a mess of my hair. Pushing strands back, I approach Jordan.

She's on the far side, leaning her elbows on the rusting railing. She doesn't turn or acknowledge me. She's somewhere else, deep in her mind.

"You okay?" I ask, coming to stop beside her.

Jordan doesn't say anything. She sucks hard on a cigarette. The end glows red. I know she's trying to quit. It says a lot that she's out here smoking.

"You know you can talk to me." I nudge her gently.

Jordan turns and looks at me. There's a question in her eyes. She's probably assessing whether she can talk to me. I want her to. I want her to open up to me again, like she did in the car. I want to pull her back to the present.

She sighs. "There's nothing to talk about."

"I'm not buying that, but if you don't want to talk about

it, I get it. Lord knows there's a lot I refuse to talk about." I hold out my hand, gesturing for the cigarette. It's been ages since I last smoked. The habit never gripped me the same way pills and blow did. Now I just drink. Maybe too much, but I'm nowhere near as bad as Hélène. I will never be like her.

Jordan passes the dart over. Her eyes don't leave my face as I take a drag. The smoke warms my lungs. I exhale a cloud and hand her back the cigarette.

Jordan stares down at the filter where my lip gloss left a mark. She taps ash over the railing before popping the cigarette back in her mouth and sucking hard. The tip burns down. "I wasn't expecting to see Samira," she reveals.

I fold my arms over my chest. "The woman with your sister?"

She nods slowly. "Yeah."

I preferred it when the beautiful stranger didn't have a name. Now I know it, and there's a weight to how Jordan said it. "You guys have history?" I ask. I don't think I want to know their story, but I'm also too curious for my own good.

"You can say that," Jordan replies, drumming her fingers on the railing. "She's that person for me, you know? The person I can't shake—like a piece of me will always belong to her."

And there it is—the real reason Jordan doesn't date. Like every other lesbian on the planet, she's hung up on an ex. Her heart belongs to someone else. My own frosts over. I have to smother the cold chuckle that threatens to burst from my lips.

"So you're in love with her." I almost wince at the sharpness in my voice. Fuck, I couldn't sound more jealous.

Jordan doesn't seem to notice. She shakes her head. "No, not anymore."

I don't believe her for a second. She might believe she's over Samira, but that woman takes up prime real estate in her mind. If Jordan really didn't care, she wouldn't have ran out of the apartment. If Jordan wasn't still in love with her, she'd be open to moving on with someone else.

Jordan turns and props her back against the railing. "It's more like, when I look at her, I remember," she says softly. "And sometimes I wish things were different ... that I was different."

I wait for her to explain some more, but she doesn't. She's leaving me hanging, and I'm left wondering what about her she wishes was different. Sure, she's a little grumpy and a little closed off, but that's part of her appeal. Physically, everything about her does it for me. I don't think I'd change anything about her. Then again, there's still a lot about her I don't know.

"I get that. My ex did a number on me—turned my life upside down. Looking back, I wish I could have done things differently too," I say. "But maybe things are supposed to happen the way they happen. Maybe we have to go through the tough shit to appreciate something good when it comes along." I'm not quite sure if what I'm saying makes sense. It might be complete bullshit, but I'd like to believe that everything that brought us to this place—to this moment—isn't coincidence. All those years ago, Jordan captivated my teenaged heart, and now we are living and working together.

Maybe I've been manifesting our future together. But Samira is a roadblock, and I'm not sure I want to compete. I'm a sore loser.

"Is this a recent ex?" Jordan asks, stamping out the cigarette in an ashtray.

I blink away my thoughts. "Yes."

"What'd he do?"

"I'd rather not talk about it," I say, gritting my teeth. I shouldn't be irritated that she's assuming my ex is a "he," but I am. One day, I will have to set Jordan straight, but I'm not up for that discussion today. My feelings are still too raw. When I'm sure I can talk about what Cara did without dissolving into a puddle of tears, I might say something.

Thankfully, Jordan doesn't press for information.

"We should probably head back inside," I say. The chill outside is getting to me, and I don't even want to guess what my hair looks like.

She nods.

When we step back inside the warmth of the apartment, there are three new arrivals. One is an older gentleman with hair going grey at his temples and brown eyes as warm as Grandma Janet's. The youngest sports a pair of thick-framed glasses and has a nervous disposition. He's handsome—they all are. But the last man is striking. He's the type of man Felix would slobber over. He's tall and built like a football player with neat cornrows and a neatly trimmed goatee. I don't like the way he looks at me, undressing me with his eyes.

Jordan greets the older man with a fist bump. I learn he's her Uncle Weston and that the other two are her cousins.

The man with the goatee grins and cocks his head in my direction. "Who's your friend?"

"Noémie," Jordan answers quickly.

"And she's with you?" he asks, arching a brow.

Jordan drills him with a hard look.

"Nah, they're just roommates," Amari says, popping out of nowhere. Jordan's ex—Samira—is standing just a pace behind her. She's much prettier up close. I hate it. Why does she have to be here? I pray my face doesn't give my irritation away, but I can feel heat on my cheeks.

"Nice to meet you, Noémie." The words snap my attention away from Samira. There's a large hand in front of me. I shake it and look up to meet the tall man's eyes. They're dark like Jordan's but lack her tenderness. "I'm Ezra," he says.

"Nice to meet you too," I mutter just as Jordan announces she needs to use the washroom. And just like that, she's gone, leaving my side. Again.

I notice Amari whispering something in Samira's ear. The two women laugh.

The younger man presents his hand to me next. "Samuel," he says, flashing a jittery smile.

"It's lovely meeting you, Samuel." I return a smile and shake his hand. It's sweaty. I wipe my hand discreetly on my dress.

Things get more uncomfortable from there. Samira disappears from Amari's side, and I become the focus of Jordan's sister's attention. She announces to everyone that I'm Hugo St. Pierre's daughter. She tells everyone that I put Jordan up in a luxurious room in my Yorkville home.

"I didn't put her up," I say, trying to maintain a polite tone. "We're roommates."

Jordan's uncle extracts himself from the conversation and moves to sit down in the smaller of the two corduroy couches.

"Yorkville's got that bougie flex, styll," Samuel says, sounding a little more confident. "No lie, I hit up Poutine Heaven whenever I'm marved—that Blessed Brisket poutine is top tier. I'd ride for it."

Ezra claps his brother on the back and chuckles. "No mans are riding for Poutine Heaven."

"True, true," Amari says. "Samuel's gassing it up too much. But the fries are bomb."

Their slang is unfamiliar, and I have no idea what they are talking about.

Paulette calls out that dinner is ready, but Jordan's relatives don't seem to care. I'm more interesting than food apparently. A flurry of questions are tossed my way. Jordan left me to the wolves.

Ezra asks me what I do for fun. Amari asks if I have discounts for Poutine Heaven. Samuel asks if he can get some coupons too.

I ignore Ezra, I tell Amari and Samuel that I can ask my brother for some coupon codes, and then I announce that I need to use the washroom and slip away.

I head towards the hallway Jordan disappeared down. I'm not sure which door leads to the bathroom, but Jordan's bound to exit soon. I lean against a wall and rub my temples.

Muffled voices reach my ears. Straightening, my gaze narrows on the door directly across from me. While I can't make out the words, I recognize the first voice as Jordan's. The second … is Samira's.

Heart hammering, my hands ball into fists. Jordan left me to be with Samira. My anger sizzles like oil in a hot pan. The door swings open and Jordan rushes out. She almost collides with me.

Forcing down my rage, I say evenly. "There you are. Dinner's ready."

Samira steps out of the bathroom and exaggerates adjusting her dress. The woman wants me to know that they'd been fooling around. But I'd already guessed as much. I almost tell her that there's no need for theatrics. It's a good thing I don't. Saying anything would just play into her hand. If Samira thinks I'm going to act out and make a scene over this … She can fuck off.

"It's not what it looks like," Jordan says. She scratches the back of her neck.

Her lie leaves a bad taste in my mouth. I need a moment to consolidate my feelings. "Sorry, I have to pee." I slide between Jordan and her ex, shutting the bathroom door behind me.

I glare at the reflection staring back at me in the medicine cabinet mirror. My hair is a fucking mess. I work on fixing it, but my efforts are fruitless without a brush. Fucking wind.

I pace the tiny space, and then reach into my bag for my phone. I shoot off a text to Wayne.

NOÉMIE, 7:15 P.M.

What do you know about Samira?

His reply comes moments later.

WAYNE, 7:16 P.M.

She's Jordan's ex from forever ago.

It was a bad break up. Very on and off, from what I've heard.

Why are you asking?????

NOÉMIE, 7:16 P.M.

Jordan invited me to celebrate Thanksgiving with her family.

Samira's here.

WAYNE, 7:17 P.M.

Not surprising. Amari and Samira are besties.

I grit my teeth at that bit of information. If Amari and Samira are tight, that means Jordan's ex will always be around—always tempting her. Is that a situation I'd want to put myself in? I decide that it isn't. Yes, I might like Jordan—a lot. But the woman is everything Wayne warned me about. Last thing I need is her kind of drama in my life.

I'm so fucking stupid. What had I been thinking? Applying to work at the coffee shop was a dumb idea. At least, it's easily rectifiable—I can quit anytime. But on a whim, I opened my home to Jordan, and I can't ask her to move out. Okay, I can, but I know I won't. Where would she go? I'm not that heartless.

Also, in spite of everything, I'm not sure I want her to go. Merde. This crush is making me insane. It's making me ignore all her red flags and hope for an outcome that will likely ruin me.

I stare back at my reflection and will myself to calm the fuck down. A minute goes by, and then another. I don't settle, but dinner is ready. I don't want people questioning why I'm taking so long in the bathroom. I don't want Jordan thinking I'm taking a shit.

Exhaling a deep breath, I try to ground myself. I count five flowers on the yellow shower curtain. I count four beads of water that drip from the faucet. I hear the fan, and the murmurs of voices beyond the door. I smell the lavender Glade deodorizer that sits on the top of the toilet tank. I breathe and breathe.

At last, the racing in my head and in my chest stops. I exit the bathroom.

In the main room, everyone is gathered around the table. Everything laid out on the spread is foreign to me. I don't see turkey, stuffing, cranberry sauce or any other traditional dishes. Not a big deal. The food smells good, and I'm open to trying new things.

I take my place at Jordan's side. She spares me a quick look, and I hope my face lies better than my heart does. Her grandmother begins blessing the food. Like the good Catholic girl I'm supposed to be, I close my eyes for the prayer, but I tune out the words. All I see in my mind's eye is Samira righting her dress. Over and over.

Before I know it, we're all saying amen. Opening my eyes, Samira's pretty face fills the crosshairs of my gaze. She smiles at me. I shoot her a glare, but my attack does nothing. Her smile widens to the point where she flashes teeth. Fuck her.

A line forms to grab food. Jordan points at dishes and

tells me what's what—curry goat, oxtail, jerk chicken, rice and peas, steamed fish, and fried plantain. I take a little of everything, piling my paper plate.

All the seats are taken, so Jordan and I have to eat standing. It's uncomfortable and awkward, and the way my luck is going, I'm sure to get food on my dress.

I'm not that hungry. My stomach's already filled with loss. I can't stop sneaking looks at Jordan's ex. I loathe how perfect her body is. Even if I doubled the number of squats and lunges I do each week, there's no way I'd manage to have her thighs. She's got the genes for great curves and ass. I hate how chummy she is with Amari. I hate the way they laugh together on the couch. I hate that a piece of Jordan will always belong to her.

I begin stuffing my mouth because I don't want to speak to Jordan. The food is quite good—maybe a tad too spicy, but the blend of spices and textures are complex and interesting. I especially like the oxtail. The meat is tender, and the savoury gravy pairs well with the rice. I will have to ask for the recipe.

"Is it good?" Jordan asks. She looks at me expectantly, like my opinion matters.

Nodding, I focus on my plate.

Having finished eating, Ezra approaches the wall where we stand. He leans in close to me. "So what do you do for work, Noémie? And how do you know my cousin?"

Instinct makes me want to roll my eyes and tell him to go away, but Jordan beats me to it. The side eye she deals him is a little extreme, especially for her. I deduce she doesn't like her cousin too much and decide to keep him around.

"I work at the coffee shop with Jordan," I say with a smile.

"Interesting … aren't you, like, rich? What are you doing serving coffee?"

"My father's rich," I correct, because it's true. I'm not rich. I might have more than most people, but I'm not my brother. I'm not my father. I don't have access to millions of dollars. If I did, I'd be opening a restaurant—my restaurant. "What's wrong with serving coffee?"

Ezra holds up his hands defensively and chuckles. "Oh, there's nothing wrong with serving coffee, it's just that …" His gaze scans over me appreciatively, and he licks his lips. "I was just expecting you to say you're a model or something."

My responding laugh is a little too loud even for my ears, but Jordan's grunt of annoyance makes it worth it. "No, I'm not a model. A girl can dream, but I'm not tall enough," I say. I don't add that my face isn't interesting enough for editorial. A lot of people are misinformed about the fashion industry. They think any hot person can be a model. Not true. Hot people book commercial gigs. High fashion demands intrigue—a special look that I don't possess.

Ezra and I continue to chat, and Jordan gets more and more aggravated. She doesn't even try to hide her frustration. Her teeth mash together, and she huffs and puffs. She really hates the guy. One day, I'll ask her why, but for now her frustration fills me with glee.

I play up my interest in Ezra. I flirt with him, touching his arm here and there. I laugh at his stupid jokes.

When Jordan finally storms off to the balcony, I'm way too pleased with myself. I don't follow her.

I'm not pursuing anything romantic with Jordan. Like ink drying on a contract, it's been decided. She's back to being a fantasy—someone I'll only enjoy at the darkest hour when I lay beneath my crisp sheets. At least, that's what I tell myself. Consistently. Over and over.

The mantra is easy to forget at work. We just work so well together. We are more in sync than the line at Chez Avignon. We crank out orders at record speed. There are practically no complaints.

"Wow," Jordan says one day after an unusually busy shift. "You crushed it today."

"Yeah, I did," I say. "Bet you're kicking yourself for not putting me on drinks the moment I started."

Jordan rolls her eyes. "I knew complimenting you would be a poor life choice."

"Take that back," I say, nudging her lightly with my elbow.

"Would it really kill you to say that you were wrong about me?"

When she chuckles, my insides melt like butter on warm toast. Jordan's laughs are rare. It's my mission to make her laugh more.

"It just might," she says. Our gazes hold. Her dark eyes sparkle like champagne, and all I want to do is lean in and take a sip. But I remember where we are. I remember that I'm not pursuing anything romantic with her. I take a step back.

Jordan clears her throat. "I have to hang around to do some paperwork, so you should head home without me." She leaves my side.

When I turn, I see Wayne. "It's only a matter of time before I collect my designer bag," he says walking around the counter.

I snort.

Wayne blows me a kiss and exits the coffee shop.

The evening shift staff start gathering in the front, tying on their purple aprons. Not wanting to fraternize, I go to the seating area and drop down on a stool. Sure, Jordan told me to head home without her, but I decide to wait.

The next few weeks fly by in a blur. I find that I enjoy serving coffee. It's the kind of fast-paced work that I easily get absorbed in. Only time I break flow is when there's an accidental brush of my arm against Jordan's. Or the couple times our fingers graze when reaching for a cup at the same time. In such instances, the world stills and everything goes blank. But the feeling lasts a second. I recover quickly, and Jordan never seems to notice. I'm lucky she's so clueless.

In the dead hours, I chat with Wayne when there's nothing to fill or clean. He's slowly solidifying himself as a real friend, and I don't have many of those. I'm thankful he doesn't bring up the bet often.

Jordan and I slip into a sort of weekday routine. We leave work together, and I drive us home, where I zip downstairs to the gym.

I've started doubling my leg days, but I don't think I have the genetic makeup to get thighs like Samira. It's kind of demotivating.

When I finish my work out, it's always to find Jordan settled on the couch with her iPad. She's so secretive about her work, but I'm sure she'll show me someday. I'm wearing down her defences. I can tell because she's talking a lot more. Over dinner, the small details she shares about herself I drink down like wine.

Before Jordan moved in, I rarely used my fancy kitchen. It's a sad truth, but Cara always preferred to eat out, and I always got home so late from shifts at Chez Avignon. After cooking all day in the restaurant, the last thing I wanted to do was busy myself behind the stove, and it felt wrong to fuss over a meal that I'd be eating alone.

Jordan's company gives me a reason to cook and try out new recipes. It's nice to have her in my line of vision as I weigh and measure, chop and dice, sauté and boil. I think I fell a little out of love with cooking when I worked in the industry, but I'm finding my passion again.

On the Tuesday following Thanksgiving, I made seared salmon with a side of sautéed peppers, shaved fennel, preserved lemon, parsley, and olives. The next night, I prepared fresh pasta and a slightly modified version of Marcella Hazan's Bolognese meat sauce. Jordan liked it so much she asked for seconds.

At the restaurant, I got subtle pleasure from the glimpses of diners enjoying the fruits of my labours. The gratification I get watching Jordan eat is on another level. She's very vocal with her appreciation. Her satisfied groans make me blush. Sometimes she raps her fist on the wood of the table after a first bite.

She tells me that she never knew food could taste so good. She tells me that I'm the best cook she's ever known. She tells me I should open a restaurant.

I record everything to memory, playing her words back in my head when I'm alone in my room. The moments before I fall asleep, I convince myself that it's okay to edit my recollections because it's just a fantasy. Instead of watching Netflix after dinner—which is what actually happens—Jordan forces me against the kitchen island. She kisses me all over and undresses me. She kneels and spreads my legs. She tells me she never knew a woman could taste so good. She tells me I'm the best she's ever had. She tells me she wants no one else.

I pretend it's her mouth on me instead of a vibrator, and when I'm coming the fantasy feels like it's enough. But then I roll over and the empty space in my bed mocks me.

I don't like being alone. The time I have with Jordan fills me up, but only halfway. And it's annoying because Rebecca told me that I would feel better if I got a roommate and made deeper connections. Okay, that's not exactly what she said, but I'm still irritated because some nights I feel emptier than ever. And it doesn't matter how much I text with Wayne or Felix. The only time I'm not weighing my happiness on a scale is when I'm with Jordan, and that scares me.

"Why did you study art?" I ask her on a Wednesday night while we are eating stir-fried noodles with grilled prawns.

"I was really into comics as a kid—Spider-Man, The Hulk, Teenage Mutant Ninja Turtles, Wonder Woman …" she answers. "My dad got me into it. He had a huge collection, and even though my mother didn't approve, he let me read them. Maybe around eight, I got it into my head that I wanted to make my own comic, and I picked up drawing. I thought studying art in post secondary would help me hone my craft, but …"

"But what?"

She shrugs. "Not really sure school did anything but leave me with a huge debt to pay."

Her confession makes me feel slightly guilty—makes me realize again just how different our worlds are. The cost of tuition is not something I ever had to worry about.

"I never got into comics. My sister was really into them though," I say, taking a sip of a 2021 Sauvignon Blanc from Chenonceaux. "So is that what you're up to on your iPad—a comic?"

Jordan's silence tells me everything I need to know. I consider pressing her, asking when she'll show me. But I remember how her teeth mashed together at her mother's apartment when I spotted her paintings and sketches. I decide to drop it.

Another night, after I finish my workout and shower, I'm surprised to see that Jordan's not on the couch. Instead, she's on the floor with Céline. She holds a fistful of treats and is trying to get the dog to perform for her. The tableau fills me with a sensation I can't name.

I'm about to tell Jordan that she shouldn't waste her breath, that Céline is set in her ways. The dog won't roll over for anything—not even steak can tempt her. I've tried.

But just as I'm opening my mouth, Céline does the unthinkable: she flips onto her back. My jaw hangs open.

Jordan notices me standing at the entrance to the main room. "Hey."

"How'd you get her to do that?" My eyes narrow on my dog—the betrayer.

Shrugging, Jordan hands Céline a treat and scratches her head. "I looked up how to do it on YouTube."

I frown. "I've tried to get her to do things, but she refuses."

"Yeah, she's pretty stubborn. We've been at it for awhile now, but she's gotten with the program."

I kneel beside them on the rug. "Do it again."

"So bossy."

I roll my eyes. "Just do it." I need to know it wasn't a fluke. If it isn't, maybe Jordan can work on getting Céline to stay quiet when she hears the doorbell.

"Okay," Jordan says, holding out a treat. She commands Céline to lie down. To my utter amazement, the order is obeyed. The dog's head turns, following the treat Jordan moves over her shoulder, and then ... she rolls over.

"Mon dieu! She did it!" I say, grabbing Jordan's forearm. "Give me one, I want to try."

Jordan hands me a beef liver scrap, but when I issue the

same directions, Céline stares at me for a hot second before yawning. Defeated, I toss the dog the treat and rub her head. "Why won't she do it?"

"You reward her bad behaviour, that's why."

I pout. "I do not."

"Yes, you do," Jordan says. "She disobeyed you, and you gave in. Try it a few more times, but don't give her anything until she rolls."

It takes a few attempts on my part, but Céline finally rolls over for me. When she does, I shower her with a fistful of treats. "You're such a good girl," I coo, picking her up and kissing her forehead.

Chuckling, Jordan rises and shakes her head.

"What?"

"Céline has you wrapped around her paw and she knows it," she says. "It should be the other way around. Put some of your sass to use and show her who's boss. You'll be able to get her to do anything."

Staring up at Jordan, I wonder if the same could be said about her. Is there anything I could dangle in front of her to get her to want me too?

EIGHTEEN

Halloween is the best. It's that time of the year where everyone tries to be hot and spooky but usually fail at both. I can read a costume to filth and no one thinks anything of it; they assume I'm joking and laugh it off. I'm never joking.

I love everything horror. I love dressing up and pretending to be someone else. I love decorating the house and carving pumpkins. And oddly enough, I've got a soft spot for kids. Handing out candy while admiring their costumes gives me a sliver of happiness. It makes me imagine a future where I am on the other side of the door—a mom with a daughter dressed up as Elsa. If I ever have children, I'll give them what I never got—a mother. I won't disappear behind hired help and empty promises.

For the last few years, with school and then working in the restaurant, I couldn't celebrate the way I wanted to, but this year is different. I have the time, and I'm excited. I'm even thinking about getting a fog generator, which I'm sure will piss off my snobby neighbours. I couldn't care less if they want to complain.

About a week before Halloween, Wayne and I go shopping for the season. He's far less enthused, but when I tell him of my plans to get Jordan to dress up, he perks up.

"I'd kill to see Jordan in a costume," he says. "There's a part of me that wants to bet that you won't get her to do it, but …"

Tossing three foam tombstones into the cart, I stare him down. "But what?"

Wayne grits his teeth. "Nothing."

"Spill it, Wayne." I cross my arms.

His lips press together defiantly.

Skirting around the cart, I poke him. "Spill it."

"Ouch, I'm delicate," he exclaims, rubbing his arm.

"You're such a diva. That wasn't even hard." I roll my eyes. "Seriously, you can't just leave me on a cliffhanger and expect me to move on."

He sighs loudly. "Fine. I was going to say that I think I'd lose that bet. If anyone is going to get Jay to wear a silly costume, it's you," he says. "Happy?"

I grin. "Ecstatic."

We walk down another aisle where I find some pumpkin banners and orange fairy lights, which I toss in the cart.

Wayne eyes me with curiosity.

I halt in my tracks. "What?"

"I don't think you looked at a single price tag," he says. When I frown, he adds. "You don't shop like you're hurting for money. You're so full of shit, Noémie, you're overflowing.

Drop the act already. Admit Jay's the only reason you're working at the coffee shop."

"There is no act," I say. "We've been over this already. I quit my job at Chez Avignon, and I needed a new job. I need to work because I go to a dark place when I'm not busy. So no, Jordan isn't the only reason I applied."

"But she is *a reason?*" Wayne arches a brow.

My jaw clenches.

"I knew it," he says with a shrug. "And your offer to let her live with you … I doubt you needed her rent money. Just admit it."

I grip the shopping cart handle tighter. "You're so annoying."

"Jay's my friend—I'm looking out for her," he says.

"Bullshit, you're not looking out for anyone."

"You're wrong about that," Wayne says. "I care about Jay a lot. The girl is almost family to me."

I snort. "Sure she is."

"She is," Wayne states firmly. His expression becomes more serious than I've ever seen it. "Actually, I've been thinking … about our bet. At first it seemed harmless, but now you two are living together and … I don't want to see Jay get hurt."

"Hurt?" I repeat, confused. "You told me that she'd be the one to steamroll *my* heart."

"I consider you a friend too, and I don't want to see you hurt either." He pauses, and his perfect brows knit together. "Things are just really messy now. I think you should come clean—tell Jay how you feel."

Every cell in my body cringes. "Absolutely not. That's the worst thing I could ever do … if I had feelings."

"You do have feelings," he retorts. "And while I really can't believe I'm saying this … I think Jay might like you too."

His words make my heart trip and fall into a river. It flails in my chest. "How do you figure that?"

"Don't tell me that you haven't noticed the way she barks at Kevin whenever he's near you."

Yes, I'd noticed, but … "That doesn't mean anything."

"She's jealous. Jay doesn't get jealous," Wayne says. "At least, I've never seen her jealous before. It means something. Just consider what I'm saying—being honest might save you two a lot of grief."

I do consider what Wayne is saying. The entire drive back home, it's all I can think about.

Pulling into the garage, I remove my haul from the trunk and struggle not to drop anything as I ascend the tiny staircase. I'm fiddling to find the right key when the front door opens.

Jordan stands in the frame, cradling Céline in one arm. She smiles at me, and my lungs suddenly feel way too small. "Hey," she says. "Need help?"

Before I find my voice, Jordan reaches over and takes one of the larger bags from me. Our hands brush during the exchange. I tremble.

She moves back, making room for me to enter. I step inside, set down my bags, and bend to unzip my Fendi ankle boots.

Jordan puts Céline on the ground. My dog immediately rushes over to me and claws my legs. I scratch her head.

"Looks like you bought out the entire Spirit Halloween," Jordan comments.

Whether she's teasing or being sarcastic, I can't tell. Her face is blank, totally unreadable. "I love Halloween," I say with a shrug.

Jordan nods.

For a few moments, we just stand in the foyer staring at each other. My pulse spikes. *Tell Jay how you feel.* Wayne's words haunt me.

"If you're hungry, I ordered pizza," Jordan says, breaking the silence. "It'll arrive soon."

"What kind?"

"Hawaiian."

I make a face. "Pineapple doesn't belong on pizza."

"Who made you the pizza czar?" Jordan says. Her tone is dry, but there is the slightest curve of her lips that hints she's joking.

"I'm just doing my civic duty," I say, crossing my arms. "It's a crusty job, but someone's gotta do it."

Jordan snorts out a laugh. Her whole face changes, softening with amusement. "That was so bad, don't quit your day job."

I love it when she laughs. "I don't plan to," I say, realizing that I mean it. Grind That Bean may not be a Michelin-star restaurant, but I don't mind the work. I like that it keeps me busy. I like that I get to work with Jordan. I like gossiping with Wayne.

The experience is totally different from Chez Avignon. Sure, I'm not working under a world-renowned chef, but it's almost better. With my new schedule, I can hone my skills the way I want, experimenting with food and recipes in a way that feels true to me.

I might not have my father's money. I might not have my highly regarded position under Chef Ricard. But maybe I can pave a new path to reach my dream.

Hope blossoms in my chest for the first time since the blow up with my father. It's possible to get everything I want; the road will just be bumpier. It's about time I planned for it.

Jordan and I cart my bags into the main area. It doesn't escape my notice that the air smells like the curtains caught on fire. There's also a draft. A window is open, letting in fresh air. "You burn something?" I ask.

"Ummm … yeah," Jordan says. She scratches the back of her ear. "I tried to cook dinner for us, but there's a reason my mother never let me anywhere near the stove."

Gaze travelling over to the kitchen, I observe that it doesn't look like Jordan followed a recipe straight into chaos. Actually, the area looks cleaner than we left it this morning. The faucet and counter tops gleam. The rangehood even looks like it's been dusted. Gigi only swings by on Monday to tidy while Jordan and I are at work, so it's not the housekeeper's doing.

Of course, Jordan would make a mess and overcompensate. Compared to her, I'm the slob. She even packs the dishwasher better than I do.

"I ordered pizza," she reminds me.

"Yeah, but it's Hawaiian."

"Just pick off the pineapple," she says.

"It shouldn't be there in the first place."

Jordan rubs a hand over her jaw and sighs. When she mutters, "I can't get anything right," I mentally kick myself. She was trying to do something nice for me, and here I am being difficult.

"What were you trying to cook?" I ask.

"Mac and cheese," she replies. "But before you get on my ass, not from the box."

The doorbell rings, and Céline goes crazy. Jordan rushes off to answer the door. She comes back in the room carrying a large orange box. I've never liked Pizza Pizza, but I hold back my comment about the crust tasting like cardboard.

I grab some plates. We sit at the island. Jordan miserably bites into a slice and chews. I pick off the pineapple and follow her lead. The pizza makes my taste buds want to self-destruct, but it's edible.

"I have a really great mac and cheese recipe," I say, filling the silence. "If you want, I can show how to make it tomorrow night."

Jordan swivels her stool to face me. Her knee knocks against mine. "I'd like that."

"It's a date," I say. Feeling my cheeks heat, I angle my face away from her and stare down at my plate. I clear my throat. "Not going out tonight?" It's Friday, so I figured she'd be going out. The main reason I asked Wayne to hang after work was to keep my mind busy and off Jordan and her whereabouts. But it's a little after nine now, and she's dressed down in black sweats. She doesn't look ready to go anywhere.

"Nah, I have to take my bike into the shop, so I have to be

conservative with my paycheque this weekend," she says. "So you're stuck with me tonight."

"I'm down to put a dent into *The Haunting of Hill House* if you're up to it," I say, trying my best to sound nonchalant. I'm super glad she's not going out. I don't like the idea of her partying with other women, dancing with other women, kissing other women …

She shrugs. "Sounds like a plan."

Jordan offers to help me decorate the house. While we're arranging the faux tombstones on the front lawn, she confesses that she's never carved a pumpkin before. So naturally, that afternoon I pick up two large ones from the store.

It's while we're carving the pumpkins in the kitchen that I bring up the topic of dressing up for Halloween.

"Nope, I don't do costumes." She stabs her knife into the orange flesh.

"Think of the children," I say.

"Children?" She makes a face and shudders.

"Trick-or-treaters," I clarify. "You can't hand out candy in sweatpants."

She arches a brow. "So now I'm handing out candy?"

"It'll be fun," I say sweetly. When she doesn't say anything, I bat my eyelashes at her and say, "Pleaaase."

Jordan shakes her head and drops her gaze to her lap. Just

when I'm sure she's going to say no, she sighs and says, "Okay, fine."

I kill the squeal that wants to escape my throat and return my focus to my pumpkin.

Where it takes me under an hour to scoop out the guts and carve out two eyes, a nose and a smile, Jordan spends more than double the time trying to get the details of the jack-o'-lantern just right. The end product is the most picture-perfect carved pumpkin I've seen someone make without a stencil, but Jordan's not happy with it. "The grin is crooked," she says.

Tilting my head, I try to see what she sees. "Looks straight to me."

Jordan grits her teeth. "It's not."

Again, I look at her pumpkin. I can't see the flaw.

Later that day, I show her how to make mac and cheese. Jordan's culinary skills start and end with boiling water. I play the role of head chef, and she's a confused intern. I get a kick out ordering her around. But there's something kind of romantic about imparting wisdom. She leans in close when I tell her that some spices are more aromatic after being tempered in hot oil or, in this case, butter. When she holds the knife stiff and awkwardly, I step behind her, directing her into the right position. It's kind of unreal, being this close to her. My palm rests lightly against the back of her hand. I fight off the urge to brush my thumb over her skin.

"You're going to want to hold it like this. And you're going to want to tuck your fingers and use you knuckles as a guide," I say, my voice sounding strange to my ears. Jordan doesn't seem to notice, and that's good. I probably will listen to Wayne and fess up to my feelings soon, but not yet. I'm not ready to risk losing this connection.

NINETEEN

"I look so stupid," Jordan grumbles.

Tonight, I'm Princess Peach, and she's Super Mario. I dig the bristly moustache, blue overalls, and signature red cap on her. I've always been into role-play. If only I could drag her up to my bedroom and re-enact being rescued from Bowser's Castle. I have some cuffs and chains, but Jordan's off limits. Call me dramatic, but I think I'd literally die if we hooked up and the next day she pretended like it never happened.

"You look adorable," I say, pinching her cheek. I'm not quite sure when I started being touchy with her, but I can't stop. Now, whenever we watch TV, I rest my head on Jordan's shoulder. Whenever I want to show her something, I grab her hand. It's dangerous territory. I know I'm testing my luck.

Jordan swats my hand away from her face and scowls. "I can't believe I let you talk me into this."

"You're doing it for the kids," I remind her. "You didn't tell me what you think of my costume. How do I look?" I spin slowly for her and take some pleasure in how her stare lingers at my pushed up boobs. Pink might not be my colour, but I'm doing Princess Peach justice. I've made the character look the part of a woman instead of a little girl. My waist is snatched in the custom corset I ordered. The flowing pink skirt parts down the middle to show off my legs.

Jordan scratches the back of her neck and diverts her gaze. "You look good for someone who looks like Pepto Bismol threw up on them."

My mouth drops open, and I shove her lightly. "You're the worst."

Jordan chuckles and drops down into the couch. Turning on her iPad, she fiddles with the white stylus. I know she's waiting for me to leave. She won't start drawing until she's sure I'm out of range to see what she's working on. I really wish she'd just show me.

Around 6:00 p.m. I'm in the kitchen reheating leftovers when the doorbell rings for the first time. Céline starts barking and bolts out of the room.

Jordan rises from her seat. "I can get it."

I make to follow after her out of the room. The flash of her tablet's screen stops me. I look down at the image on the display, and my heart stumbles. *Is that me?*

I drop down on the couch and grab the device. My fingers trace the cartoon face, the auburn hair, the pouty mouth. Where my eyes are grey, the character's eyes are green. She's also got a mole above her upper lip. But her resemblance to me is still uncanny.

Jay might like you too. Wayne's words play over in my head, like they have since he first sputtered them. Is this depiction of me evidence that my feelings are reciprocated?

Needing to learn more, I scroll to the start of the story and start reading. The main character of the comic is a woman name Zara. She looks similar to Jordan, with her short black hair and androgynous features. But her clothes are more feminine than anything Jordan would be caught wearing.

I quickly deduce that this isn't the first volume of the comic Jordan is working on because I feel like I've been dropped in the middle of the story. I'm lacking background. Still, I'm sucked into the narrative.

From what I've gathered, it centres around an assassin, Zara, who is trying to sabotage evidence that points to her being responsible for a string of murders in the city. The artwork is vivid and highly detailed. The sexual tension between Zara and Detective Pamela Cross—the woman who looks like me—is palpable.

Time loses meaning as I get absorbed into the dark world Jordan created. A sadness grips my heart as I read. The story is unapologetically gay. Antoinette would have loved it. My sister had been a little too obsessed with comics, manga, and anime. She would have killed to read something like this.

I startle when someone barks, "What are you doing?"

The tablet slips from my fingers and drops to my lap. I stare up at Jordan who looms in the archway with her fists clenched. She stomps over to me and rips the tablet off my lap. She points a finger at me. "What the actual fuck—you had no business going through my shit!"

I don't get what she's so angry about. Yes, I know she's sensitive about her art, but her intention has to be to get published one day. Her comic is way too good to not get picked up. Jordan needs to get used to people looking.

I try to tell her as much. "Je m'en fous. I don't get why you're so pissed."

"I'm pissed because you know—you know that I didn't want you to see ..." Jordan sighs and paces a bit.

My crown topples when I shake my head. I fix it before saying, "Look, I'm sorry if I made you upset. I guess I shouldn't have looked." I rise off the couch and go to her. "I really don't get what the big deal is. Why do you insist on hiding your work? I read about two chapters and it's so fucking good. You're so talented, Jordan. You're doing a disservice not sharing your art with the world." I reach for her hand, and she pulls it back like I burned her.

Jordan glares at me. Contemplating my words, I bite down on my lip. Her gaze falls to my mouth. We're standing really close. A rush of heat spreads throughout my body. Suddenly, I'm hot all over. I swallow, but my throat is dry. *Tell her how you feel.*

No, now's not the right time. We are arguing, but ... perhaps I will tell her later. For the first time, honesty doesn't feel as risky. I think Pamela looking like me means something—it's more of a sign than hints of jealousy towards Kevin. But now's not the time; I need Jordan's boiling anger to drop to a simmer.

She needs to understand that me seeing her comic isn't the end of the world. Frankly, it's probably a good thing—I have connections in the industry. Okay, it's a single connection, but François Lafontaine has sold millions of comics, and he's Claude's best friend. François is also possibly the sweetest man I know. He'd definitely help Jordan out if I reached out.

The doorbell rings. I blink away my thoughts and head for the front door. I'm expecting Jordan to follow me, but she doesn't. She storms up the stairs. My heart sinks.

I go to Jordan's room when I'm sure there'll be no more trick-or-treaters and knock on her door. "Jordan, can we talk?"

It takes her a moment to answer. "Yeah, sure."

I step inside. My gaze sweeps over the space. Jordan keeps it very clean.

She's out of her Mario costume and in her signature sweats. She sits on her bed with her legs stretched out on the mattress and her back resting against the headboard.

I take a seat on the edge of the bed and turn to face her. "Look, I've been thinking, and I'm sorry that I snooped."

She snorts. "You don't sound sorry."

"Well, I am sorry. Clearly, I overstepped, even though I don't get what the big deal is."

"I draw for myself, nobody else," she snaps, crossing her arms.

Her response makes me frown. "And why is that?"

Jordan stays quiet. She shuts her eyes tightly, and her

head knocks back against the headboard. When she stares back at me her dark eyes glimmer.

"Jordan?" I whisper, touching her leg.

She moves so my hand drops back down to the mattress. "Why do you even care?" she asks.

Because I care about you. That's the answer, but it's too bold a statement to say aloud. I consider what I can admit. What could I possibly say to dissolve her anger when she's vulnerable and defensive? Maybe the solution is to be vulnerable myself.

"You know … Antoinette was really into comics and manga," I say. "She was gay—I don't think I told you. And you know how my father is …"

Jordan says nothing.

I clear my throat and continue, "My sister used to complain so much, and Claude was so annoyed. I don't remember being annoyed, but I didn't get her constant need to talk my ear off about the lack of queer representation or feeling forced to stay in the closet. She whined so much about having to hide her *L Word* DVDs and Batwoman comics." My throat constricts as the memories wash over me. My eyes burn, and I stare down at my wringing hands. "I'd give anything to hear her complain again."

Sensing my sadness, Jordan scoots down the bed. Suddenly, we sit side by side. Our thighs touch. She places a hand on top of mine and squeezes. She locks eyes with me.

"I'm sorry that I looked at your artwork. I didn't mean to, I swear," I say. "It's just that the display was on, and I glimpsed an image of two women holding hands, and I was reminded of Antoinette's obsession with Batwoman. And I just …" It's not a complete lie. Most of it is the truth.

Jordan's still not saying anything, but she doesn't look angry anymore.

I release a deep breath. "You're so talented, Jordan, and the world needs more stories like yours. There aren't enough."

Jordan blinks, and she looks at me in a way I haven't seen before. There's a softness to her stare. She looks at me like I matter.

If I told her the truth, if I put all my cards on the table, what would she say? Would she say anything?

Tell Jay how you feel. Jay might like you too. The words "I like you" itch my tongue and want to escape my mouth. My heart begins to pound in my ears as I really consider telling her. It'll either be a huge mistake or the beginning of something I've wanted for years. But am I even ready for that, for another relationship, after what happened with Cara? And Jordan's clearly not over her ex.

Is the risk worth it? The ache in my chest tells me it is.

Jordan's phone vibrates. We both look down at the screen. There's a message from Audrina. I understand that she is Jordan's fuck buddy. According to Wayne, the woman is obsessed with Jordan and can't take a hint.

Am I just as pathetic as she is? My body stiffens like a cutting board when I read the text.

AUDRINA, 8:47 P.M.

Heading home around 10pm

Want to come over tonight?

> I'd love for you to tear my nurse
> costume off with your teeth

"I didn't know you were still talking to Audrina," I say. There's a harsh edge to my tone. I force myself to soften it when I add, "At least … Wayne mentioned something about her being crazy and not being able to take a hint."

Jordan turns her phone over face down on the mattress. "You really are such a snoop," she says with a grin.

"I guess I am." The room suddenly feels cold and way too small, like the walls are closing in on me. I feel like a fool. I'd just been about to tell Jordan that I liked her. Possibly the stupidest thing I could do. Jordan isn't a check engine light, she's a massive red flag. She's a car crash waiting to happen. I refuse to be wrecked. I refuse to be like Audrina.

Jordan's heart belongs to Samira, so we can be friends—never lovers. It doesn't matter how much I burn for her.

"It's been a day. I'm going to sleep." I stand and make to leave her room.

"You don't want to finish watching *The Haunting of Hill House?*" she asks.

We only have one episode left. We decided to save it for tonight. But this exchange drained me. I'm wilted from reality, and I just want to crawl under my sheets and forget that moments ago Jordan looked at me like I mattered.

I don't matter to her—at least, not in the way I want.

TWENTY

Wayne is getting on my last nerve. Any chance he gets, he pesters me about coming clean to Jordan. Worried that he'd go behind my back and tell her everything, I paid for his silence. I dragged his ass to Holt Renfrew at Yorkdale and bribed him with a Loewe tote bag and a eyeshadow palette from Yves Saint Laurent. With the purchases came an avalanche of questions I've heard before. How can I afford it? When will I admit that I don't need Jordan's rent money? What do I think will happen when Jordan finds out I've been lying to her?

It was all too much, and I was on my period. I wound up crying about everything to Wayne on the drive back home.

So now the nosy bastard knows about Cara and what happened with my father. He knows that I have some money. He knows bits and pieces about my sister. He knows even more about my depression and need for a strict routine. He knows that it was my therapist who suggested I get a roommate. He knows that Jordan is the woman who first made me realize that I wasn't straight. Everything—I told him everything.

At the time, it felt good to vent. Wayne seemed to be understanding. But now he is back on my ass about being honest with Jordan. He says that he's worried about me. He says I should come clean before it becomes impossible—before it's too late.

Wayne doesn't get it—that it might already be too late. Jordan and I are in a good place. We are friends, and if I told her that I'm not straight … I reckon she'd jump to the conclusion that I'm only telling her because I like her. And she wouldn't be wrong. I don't want her to know that I like her like that. I fear it'd be the beginning of our end, and I'm growing fond of her company. I'd rather have her friendship than nothing at all.

Now, I can feel Wayne scowling at my back. We're at the Christmas Market in the Distillery District. Despite being negative a million degrees, the market is more packed than an unopened bag of rice.

Jordan walks beside me. We're holding hands—our gloved fingers interlocking. It's almost easy to forget how painful the harsh wind is when her proximity torches my insides.

Jordan's wearing a black puffer jacket zipped up to her chin, dark-washed jeans, and Timberland boots. A black toque covers her ears. She looks more like a pretty young man than a woman.

It's a quarter past seven at night and the historic site sparkles. Millions of lights hang over our heads and encase art sculptures. The towering fifty-foot tree sparkles in the main square. I pull away from Jordan to snap a few pics. Wayne and I take a place in line to get an unobstructed photo in front of it.

When it's our turn, I toss my phone to Wayne and drag Jordan to the base of the tree. She's frowning.

"Smile," I say, tugging on her arm.

Jordan's lips turn up the slightest bit. I clutch her arm and beam in the direction of the camera. Glowering, Wayne takes a few photos. "Now smile for real," I say, nudging her side.

Jordan rolls her eyes, but she obliges. When she smiles, I swear she glows brighter than all the Christmas lights twinkling around us.

Wayne and Jordan swap places. Now she's the photographer. I don't have to tell Wayne to smile. He beams like nothing's wrong.

We move away from the tree and shuffle down an alley where staple holiday tunes play. I can't quite believe Christmas is just around the corner. It's amazing how different things are from a year ago.

Last Christmas, I was still with Cara, but we spent the season apart. She was in Europe for a photoshoot, and I spent my down time watching Hallmark Christmas movies alone. I'd been miserable. I'm still a little miserable, but at least I have things to look forward to this season.

I'm excited to give Jordan her gift. I bought it last weekend. It's wrapped and hidden on the top shelf in my closet. I know Jordan's going to freak when she sees it—a brand-new motorcycle helmet. She's constantly complaining about the one she has. The shield is all scratched up and the chin strap is frayed. It can't be safe.

Since I'll be taking off for the chalet before Christmas, I won't be around when she opens it. But maybe I'll insist on her unwrapping her gift before I go. I want to see her smile when she sees the flashy Shoei label. The store representative assured me that it was the best helmet they had.

I also purchased Wayne's gift, but if he keeps bugging me, I might reconsider joining him on the spa retreat.

The Distillery District is an overcrowded pot. It's annoying how often my Prada boots get stepped on. A vendor stall catches my eye; I navigate us towards it. Rows of rings, necklaces, and earrings line the pale-blue tablecloth. I doubt anything on the spread is real gold.

Wayne picks up a pair of snowflake dangle hook earrings with inlaid white and blue stones. "These are giving Elsa in her frozen castle realness." He flips over the price tag and dramatically rolls his eyes. "I will have to hold off on my *Frozen* fantasy until I'm rich."

"I can get them for you, if you want," I say, thinking the offering might get him off my back.

"Thanks, but I will pass on that offer."

I give him a dose of side eye. If he keeps giving me the cold shoulder, Jordan's bound to ask what's up. And who knows where that conversation will lead.

"Oh look, they're giving out free samples," I say, snatching Wayne's hand. I pull him away from the table—away from Jordan. We dart through the thick of people, towards a woman holding a tray of miniature s'mores.

I don't want s'mores. I want to talk to Wayne. Jordan

doesn't follow us, and I'm glad for it. She must realize that I want a moment alone with him.

When we're far enough, I drop his hand and glare at him. "Can you quit it?"

"Quit what?"

"You're acting all bratty."

"You need to talk to Jordan," he says flatly. "She likes you. I'm sure of it, and it feels wrong lying to her."

I bite my lip. "I know she's attracted to me, and maybe she likes me, but … she's not over her ex."

"Did she tell you that?"

"Pretty much—I told you this already," I say. "They hooked up on Thanksgiving."

"Did they though?"

"Yup, I'd fucking bet on it." I recall how Samira righted her dress and grit my teeth.

Wayne shakes his head. "I still think you should tell her."

I groan. "So I tell her that I like her, and then what happens when she gets all weirded out?"

"She won't."

"You don't sound sure about that."

Wayne shrugs. "She might get a little weirded out, but what does that matter?"

"We live together," I say. "If she doesn't feel the same way about me, it'll just make things very awkward. She might have to find somewhere else to live."

Wayne sighs. His expression tells me that he finally gets it. "Fuck, this is so messy," he whines, rubbing his eyes. "Shit! Did I mess up my mascara?"

"Nope, it's fine," I say.

"Is that you, Noémie?"

Both Wayne and I turn towards the voice. It's Felix! I didn't know he was back in Toronto.

My smile is immediate. Beside me, Wayne goes completely still. His eyes appraise my best friend appreciatively. "Noémie, who is this?" he whispers in my ear.

I do quick introductions. Wayne gets quieter than I've ever seen him. His cheeks redden, and I don't think it has anything to do with the cold.

My gaze flits between them, analyzing their compatibility. I think Wayne is Felix's type. My best friend is into twinks, but I've only seen him show interest in white or black men. Wayne's Filipino, or at least his mother is. Should that even matter though? Wayne is prettier than me.

It's hard to get a read on whether Felix is down. He barely registers Wayne. Instead, I'm the focus of his blue eyes. "So what were you two arguing about?" he asks.

I frown. "We weren't arguing."

"Not buying it," Felix says. "So what's up?"

"Noémie likes my friend, and I'm pretty sure my friend likes her back," Wayne pipes in, cocking his head towards the vendor stall. "But Noémie's too chicken shit to say anything, so I'm stuck in the middle of their tragic little rom-com."

"Ahhh … are we talking about Hot Barista?" Felix's gaze darts in the direction of the stall where Jordan stands, looking down at something on the table. "Wow, she is cute … but is she even your type?"

I roll my eyes at that. "You know nothing about my type."

"She's very different from Cara," Felix states.

I cross my arms. "Maybe that's why I like her."

"Oh, she's headed this way," Felix says. He grins mischievously. "Maybe we should test Wayne's theory?"

"What theory?" I ask.

Felix steps towards me and grabs my shoulders. I don't trust the glint in his eyes. I know that look. He's plotting something. "If she likes you. Let's see how she reacts to me kissing you."

"Ewww ... no," I say, shaking my head. I try to shove him away. He doesn't budge.

Felix leans in.

"Felix, no—"

He cuts my words off with a kiss. His hard lips on mine feel wrong. The grit of his stubble against my chin is abrasive. I hate it. But I guess we're doing this, so I should just go with it. And I'd be lying if I wasn't curious to test Wayne's theory. If Jordan does like me, she won't be happy seeing me kissing someone else.

I press into Felix and twine my hands around his neck. Merde, it feels wrong. Thankfully, he doesn't slip me some tongue. I'd probably gag if he did.

Finally, we split apart. I can't stop the nervous giggle from escaping my throat. "I can't believe we just did that," I say.

"Blame the mistletoe," Felix says despite there being no mistletoe anywhere near us.

My stomach knots as I turn. Jordan's expression is blank. She's totally unfazed, so I have my answer. No, she doesn't like me.

My heart dries up like a day-old baguette. Suddenly, I feel the chill of the weather more than ever. Part of me wants to say that I'm ready to go home, even if we just got here. My bed calls to me. I want to lick this new wound in solitude.

I clear my throat and force myself to smile. "This is Felix. He's an old … friend." I say. "Felix, this is Jordan, my roommate."

Felix extends a hand out to her. "Nice to meet you, Jordan."

"Same," she says, taking his hand.

Felix drills Jordan with a hard look. It's unwarranted. Why is he being a jerk to her? Sure, it sucks that she doesn't like me back, but it's not a crime.

"Did you guys really have to put on such a show?" Wayne grumbles.

I glare at him. "Shut up."

TWENTY-ONE

I'm not sure what Felix witnessed, but he somehow agrees with Wayne. He's convinced Jordan's really into me. Can't say what logic he used to come to that conclusion, but it's flawed. Yeah, sure, Jordan's mood shifted for the worse after Felix showed up, but that doesn't mean anything. Maybe she just doesn't like him—he can be quite pretentious. Anyways, he doesn't know Jordan like I do. Moody is her default.

When we get home from the market, Jordan doesn't say anything to me and takes off upstairs.

I decide that she must be pissed about something and worry that Wayne might have said something to her. Fuck, maybe that's exactly what happened. The sneaky bastard probably told her everything when I wasn't paying attention. Shit!

I shrug out of my jacket, hang it up in the closet, and dash up the stairs. My heart bangs against my chest as I knock on her door. "Hey, Jordan, do you have a sec?"

"Yeah, sure, come in," comes her muffled voice from behind the door.

All my thoughts liquify when I step into her room. My grip on the door handle tightens. Jordan lays on her bed. She's only got on a sports bra and a pair of tight Calvin Klein boxer briefs. Too much of her smooth brown skin is on display, and my eyes feast. I can't look away. And for once she's noticing.

If Wayne didn't say anything to her, it wouldn't matter. I'm sure as hell busted now. My face burns hotter than a whistling kettle. Every square inch of my body heats. All I can hear is the pounding in my chest.

"What did you want to talk about?" she asks. There's a snap to her tone.

Blinking, I bite my lip and divert my gaze. I stare at the pulled curtains. "I just wanted to check on you."

"Why?"

"You seemed off tonight," I reply.

There's a pause. Then she mutters, "I hate Christmas."

I wasn't expecting that response, and I'm back to staring at her. My lust tamps down when I notice the shimmer in her eyes. She's looking straight at me, but it feels like she's looking right through me. Physically, she's here in the room, but I can tell she's gone somewhere else—a dark place. I recall our conversation on Thanksgiving. She told me about her father and mentioned not being able to feel merry around the holidays. "Because of your dad?" I ask softly.

Jordan nods her confirmation but doesn't offer up much else.

Fuck, I'm an idiot. Her grumpy mood has nothing to do

with me at all. Maybe it was insensitive of me to urge her to come out today. She hates the holidays, and I dragged her to a fucking Christmas Market.

I wring my hands. "I'm so sorry. I guess it was inconsiderate of me to ask you to come out."

She shrugs. "It's okay."

"It really isn't." I shake my head.

"It is—I'm a big girl," she says. "Besides, my dad's passing is just one of the many reasons I hate the holidays."

I frown. "There are others?"

"Yeah, the holiday season has never been a merry time for me," she reveals with a sad chuckle.

I cross the room, approaching the bed. "Can I ask why?"

Jordan sighs with her whole body. She's quiet for so long that I decide that she's not going to tell me. It surprises me when she does. "My mother usually works during the holidays to get the pay bonus. And for the longest time, Amari and I celebrated Christmas with my dad's side," she starts to explain. She pauses and looks to be considering what she wants to reveal. "I think Amari and I were only ever tolerated—not ever really considered as family. We never had a seat at the main table. No one ever went out of their way to talk to us. And it was always so exhausting trying to pretend to want to be there. Of course, you know my sister—she never pretended. Maybe that's part of the reason the invitations stopped coming the moment my dad died."

My heart aches for her. Taking a seat beside her on the bed, I squeeze her hand. I hate seeing her so sad. I want to drop a ladder into the pit of her despair so she can climb out of it. But I don't know what I can say, and I know better than anyone how hard it can be to shake off the bad feelings.

What would Rebecca say in this situation? For me, keeping busy, having a schedule, and working out helps. But what would work for Jordan? Maybe a change of environment?

"You should come to the chalet," I say, making the offer before analyzing the risks—the main risk being my brother. I kind of don't want Claude and Jordan in the same room. My brother doesn't know how to keep his mouth shut.

"Huh?" She blinks her confusion.

I give her hand another squeeze. "For Christmas—come to the chalet with me. The change in scenery might be just what you need," I say, making the offer again because it's too late to take it back. Also, it really might be the best thing for her. I'll figure out how to deal with Claude. "The view is to die for. We can roast marshmallows by the fire pit. We can even go skiing or snowboarding. You'll have so much fun." I try to sound excited to sell the idea.

"I wouldn't want to intrude—"

"C'est tiguidou. You wouldn't be," I say with a wave of my hand. "It'll just be me, my brother, and his fiancée. There's plenty of space. You'd have your own room. And I know you've been looking for inspiration for your next graphic novel … maybe you can find that inspiration in Québec. You know I'm dying to read the next chapter, especially after that cliff-hanger." I'm not sure how I did it, but I managed to talk Jordan into letting me read her graphic novel series. She really is so talented. I couldn't put it down.

Jordan sighs and looks down at her lap. Deep in thought,

she goes still like a statue. Finally, she says, "I don't know … I become somewhat of a Grinch around Christmas. It … it's really a hard time for me. I don't want to ruin it for you." Biting her lower lip. She goes silent again and sniffs. Her back hits the mattress, and she covers her face.

"Jordan …"

Silence fills the space for more beats than I can count.

"You know, I … I was the one who found him," she whispers, so low I barely catch it. "The day after Christmas, and … he was gone. He had been gone for awhile. And I found him."

Her hands drop from her face, and she stares up at the ceiling, blinking away tears.

I wish I knew the words to make it all better, but none exist. Grief doesn't have a time limit. It flares like an old injury, bringing a fresh wave of pain. I understand her pain. I hate that there isn't a pill for it. I hate there's no pushing past it. I hate knowing she will carry the weight of it forever.

Our situations are different. I don't know what it's like to find someone I love dead, but I remember being in the hospital room the moment they told us Antoinette was gone.

I lay down beside Jordan and take her hand, lacing our fingers together. She doesn't look at me. She looks up at nothing. Misery never looked more beautiful.

TWENTY-TWO

Jordan sits up in her seat when the chalet comes into view. The way her mouth drops open makes me realize that it's probably not what she'd been expecting. She'd probably envisioned something quainter—cozier.

It used to be just that, but my father renovated the old structure years ago. The St. Pierre chalet sits perched on a snow-covered cliff, overlooking the lake. It's very off-the-grid, only accessible via a bumpy ride up a twisting gravel path flanked by a thick forest of tall maple, fir, and cedar trees.

I park the car and turn in my seat. "We're finally here," I say, stretching my arms over my head and yawning. Jordan yawns too. Dark circles rim underneath her eyes. I'm exhausted too. All I want is a hot shower and a glass of wine.

Including a stop to recharge the Tesla and another stop to use the restroom, the drive from Toronto to Québec's Laurentian Mountains took almost eight hours. We took turns at the wheel. Jordan did the first length of the trip, and I took over in Kingston.

Jordan clicks out of her seat belt. "I have to admit, this is not what I pictured when you said family chalet."

I'd been right, she'd been expecting something less flashy. "A few years ago, they added on to the place. It wasn't always this …" Maybe added on isn't the right word. Barely anything of the old cabin remains—bits and pieces of the old facade. Most of it was knocked down. From its ashes, Hugo erected a giant timber and glass mansion. I'd love to say that I miss the chalet from my childhood, but I'd be lying. I love all the modern luxuries—the grand open kitchen that seamlessly blends into the living room, the high vaulted ceilings, and the heated floors. The old place might have felt cozier, but cozy doesn't equal comfort.

"Over the top?" Jordan offers.

I nod.

We exit the car. As we are grabbing our bags from the trunk, another vehicle pulls in behind us. I recognize the silver Mercedes G-Class and tense.

"Câllisse!" I say. Why the fuck is Paul here? Claude better not have invited him to stay for the holidays. Merde, Paul knew about my relationship with Cara. What will he think when he sees me with Jordan?

"What's wrong?"

Exhaling a breath, I look at Jordan. "Seems like my brother extended invitations."

The driver's door to the G-Class swings open, and Paul hops out of it. With his red beard and flannel shirt, he's always looked like a jolly lumberjack. "Salut, Noémie, c'est bon de te voir," he greets with the largest smile. "Qui est ton ami?"

"Hey, Paul," I say flatly. It's hard to smile back. "This is my roommate, Jordan. She doesn't speak French."

"Very nice to meet you, Jordan," he says in English. His accent is thick.

The passenger door of the G-Class pops open, and a fashionable blond woman slips out into the cold. Seems my past really is trying to haunt me—Angel and I have history. We do not share the same friend circle, but over the years there have been a few times our two groups merged via mutual acquaintances.

Perhaps a week after my birthday trip in Vegas, I met Angel for the first time at a party in Montreal where DVBBS was performing. Still sulking over Tamara, I'd been in a foul mood. If possible, Angel seemed to be in an even darker disposition.

At one point of the night, everyone exited the booth to shove their way closer to the stage, but Angel and I hung back. She complimented my outfit, and when I returned a compliment, it hadn't been out of sheer politeness. I liked the way she looked in the loose-fitting Dior pantsuit. I'd liked the way she'd worn her blond hair slicked back—it'd been way shorter back then.

Conversation and alcohol flowed freely. I'm not sure how drunk Angel got, but I'd been plastered. To this day, things are a little hazy. I'm not quite sure why or how we ended up back at her city flat. But I subtly remember hooking up and that it'd been fun.

Apparently, Angel did not have fun. In the future, she

steered clear of me whenever our friends got together. I never cared enough to question her about it.

Seeing her now, with Paul, I'm quite confused. I thought she was gay, but maybe she's bi. I didn't know they knew each other. But I guess it isn't a coincidence. Paul works with Timothy, who is married to Angel's best friend, Maria.

Did Angel ever mention me to Paul? I hope she hasn't. The jolly lumberjack is smooth brained and yaps about anything and everything unless directed not to.

"Tabarnak! C'est froid," Angel says, hugging her thin arms around her torso.

"This is Angel, my girlfriend," Paul says. "Angel, rencontrez Noémie, la soeur de Claude et Jordan, son ami."

So it looks like I've never come up in casual conversation between the two of them. Good. I need to keep it that way.

"Salut," Angel says. Her blue eyes barely register me and go right to Jordan. When she smirks, my blood simmers. If she tries to make a pass at Jordan, I'm not sure how I'll react.

Jordan waves at the couple. "Hello, nice to meet you."

Not interested in prolonging this meeting, I tug on her arm. "It's cold. We'll continue this greeting inside, Paul," I call, pulling Jordan towards the entrance of the chalet.

"He seems nice," Jordan says as we climb the steps leading to the set of front doors. When I snort, she looks at me inquisitively. "I sense there's a story."

"Not now. I'll tell you later." I have no plans to tell her anything. I'm banking that she'll forget to ask me about it. Later, I will have to have a frank conversation with Paul, asking him not to say anything to Jordan about Cara.

Angel … I'm not sure how I'll manage her, but I'll think of something.

The last thing Jordan needs is to find out that I've been lying to her. Now is not the right time to tell her I'm not straight and get into why I didn't want to talk about it. The whole reason I invited her to the chalet was for a change in scenery—a chance for her to have a relaxing Christmas. I won't let anything get in the way of that.

I'm fiddling with the key when the door opens. Henri stands in the frame. For a brief moment, I forget about Paul and Angel and my lies. "Henri!" I drop my bags and embrace the butler.

"Bienvenue, Mademoiselle St. Pierre. Bienvenue, Mademoiselle Alexander," he says, taking a step away from me and bowing slightly.

He takes our things and ushers us inside.

I watch Jordan's gaze dart around the room. I try to see the space through her eyes. The way she's gawking tells me that she thinks it's grand. I guess it is. The foyer boasts soaring ceilings with exposed wooden beams. The stonework is intricate. But there are several design choices I'm not fond of. If I'd been included in the design process, I would have selected a lighter stone for the floors and perhaps darker wood for the panels. All the taxidermied animals would be gone.

I think Jordan's awe is cute. The part of me that isn't flooded with anxiety is glad that I invited her. I want Jordan to experience nice things.

"How did Claude manage to steal you away from our parents?" I ask Henri.

"Business sees Monsieur et Madame St. Pierre in the U.S.," he replies.

Nodding, I look at Jordan. "Henri is our butler—my parents' butler," I correct before directing my attention back to Henri. "That still doesn't explain why you are here. Didn't you want to take the holidays off?"

"There's no place I'd rather be than here with you and Claude," he says.

"Always the charmer." I shake my head. The man deserves a vacation. "Where is my brother?"

"I believe he is in the study."

"Of course, he is. Claude never knows when to give work a break."

"Follow me, I will show you both to your room," Henri says.

I freeze. I had to have heard him wrong. "You mean rooms?"

"Unfortunately not."

"Putain," I say, gritting my teeth. A headache blossoms out of nowhere. I rub my temples. "Don't tell me Claude invited all of his friends."

"He did," Henri confirms. "So you and Mademoiselle Alexander will be sharing your room."

My heart stops. A second later, it's pumping too fast. My thoughts go to wild places—Jordan holding me in her arms, our legs intertwined, her body pressed against mine in bed. Every inch of my skin grows hot. I could probably fry bacon on my forehead. Luckily, Jordan isn't looking at me. She doesn't see my blush.

If Jordan is disturbed by the news, I can't tell. She seems

unfazed. I hate her indifference. Like, I know she finds me attractive, but she's shoved me so far into the friend zone that sleeping in the same bed isn't a big deal to her.

I wish I felt the same way. I wish I didn't care. I wish there was a button to press and shut down all my feelings. I am going to kill Claude.

Henri escorts us down a hall, passing by the main living space. The room has even higher ceilings, and the entire back wall is glass with a view of the water.

Jordan's gaze zips around, processing her environment. She's an artist—what does she think of all the gaudy framed landscapes lining the walls? In my opinion, there are far too many. When it comes to decor, my strong belief is that less is more.

We climb a flight of stairs, and Henri stops at my bedroom door. He sets down our bags to open it and waves us through. He drops our luggage down next to the dresser and makes to leave.

"Thank you, Henri," I say.

"Thank you," Jordan parrots. She spins slowly. Her eyes grow wide as she digests the layout of the room.

"I'm so sorry about everything." I stare at the bed and swallow. In a few hours, I will have to sleep in it with Jordan beside me. The prospect is both heaven and hell blended in a Vitamix. The bed is a king, so it should allow enough space. The real problem is that I don't want space. I want to be close to her, and I've gotten in the bad habit of always pressing my luck with her. "Did you hear what I said?"

Blinking, Jordan shakes her pretty head. "Sorry, no."

"I was just apologizing. It was just supposed to be me,

you, my brother, and his fiancée. But Claude invited all his friends."

She shrugs. "It's okay."

"It really isn't," I say, spinning to head for the door. "I'm going to go and give my brother a piece of my mind."

"You really don't have to."

"I really, really want to though," I say. "Make yourself comfy, I'll be back in a bit."

TWENTY-THREE

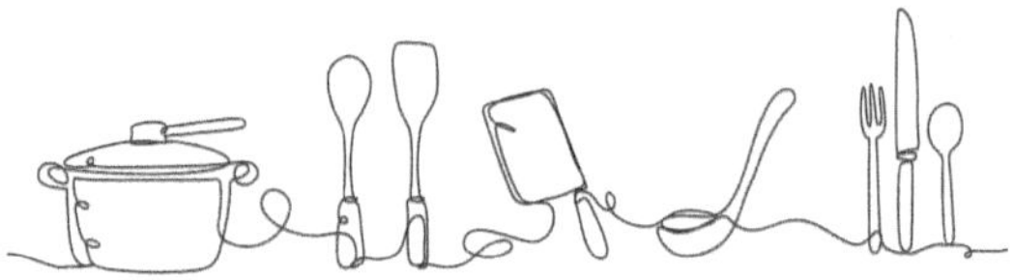

Claude sits up and rubs his eyes when I enter the office. He looks like shit. Our father works him too hard.

"Ah … Noémie!" My brother rises from his seat and moves around the large mahogany desk Hugo got custom built for the space. The room is large but too busy for my tastes. There are so many knickknacks—a large globe set on a wooden stand, a telescope that isn't even facing a window, an unfortunate collection of lacklustre oil paintings hung in goldleaf frames, and then there's the abstract blue-and-black rug that throws everything off. The designer my father hired should quit their day job. Nothing about the office reflects Hugo's tastes.

"Ça m'rend heureux que t'es arrivée en un seul morceau." Claude stops a couple of feet away from me. He smiles.

I fold my arms over my chest and answer back in French. "What were you thinking, inviting all your friends?"

My brother's bushy brows draw together. "I thought you

wanted your *roommate* to meet François? And you know how my friends are. If I only invited François over, it'd be this whole thing."

"Why did you say 'roommate' like that?"

"Like what?"

"With emphasis," I snap. "Like I'm lying to you."

"Are you lying to me?"

I snort. "About what?"

"Your relationship with her," Claude says. "You never introduced me to your ex, never brought Cara's name up in conversation. But now you're living with a woman you just met and asking favours for her. What am I supposed to believe? Especially when …"

"Especially when, what?"

"What do you even know about this woman?" he asks instead.

"Especially when, what?" I repeat, ignoring his question.

Claude sighs with his entire body and then looks over at the desk. "Come, let me show you something," he says, walking over to it. From the top drawer, he removes a manila folder stuffed with pages and slides it towards me. "I've done a little digging into Ms. Alexander. I've deduced that she's a deadbeat womanizer intent on weaselling her way into your good graces. She's taking advantage of—"

"Shut the fuck up, Claude!" My hands ball at my sides. Every nerve in my body vibrates with anger. "You investigated her? How dare you—"

"Can't you see that I'm looking out for you?" He shakes his head.

"I don't need you looking out for me," I shout.

Claude closes the distance between us. He takes me by the shoulders. "Noémie, I understand your anger, but try to see things from my side."

I brush his hands off me and pin him with a glare. "You had no right digging into Jordan's past."

"Well, I'm glad I did it. I will not apologize for doing what I feel is right." His voice thickens, breaking a bit, when he adds, "I've already lost one sister."

And just like that, I have nothing to say. He has nothing to say. Tears mist Claude's grey eyes, and my own tickle with heat. We stare at each other. My brother blinks first, but who will cleave the silence?

Seconds tick to a minute, and it gets a little easier to breathe. I sink down in a soft leather couch and cross my legs. "I want you to leave Jordan alone." When Claude opens his mouth to argue, I hold up a hand. "We are friends— nothing more. And frankly, that's why I'm pissed you invited everyone here. I don't want to share a room with her."

"Jordan can always room with Margot," Claude offers.

"No!"

My brother's eyes narrow on me. I was too quick to voice my objection. Whatever. I don't owe him an explanation, and he'll go on believing what he wants regardless.

To the best of my knowledge, Margot doesn't have any queer leanings, but she's too pretty, with her curly red hair and legs that go on for days. I kinda want to punch my brother for putting the image of Jordan and Margot sharing a bed in my head.

"I want you to leave Jordan alone," I say again.

Claude clucks his tongue. He leans against the desk and folds his arms. "Noémie—"

"I'm serious, Claude! I didn't invite her here to be cross-examined," I say, blowing out a breath. "Jordan's been through a lot, and I just want her to have a good time."

"I don't trust her."

"Why?" I ask, arching a brow. "Is what you dug up on her really that bad?" I know it can't be. Jordan has her faults, but at the end of the day she's a grumpy teddy bear. "If I had to guess, that file won't tell me anything I don't already know. Jordan parties quite a bit, and she sleeps around. That's not a crime."

"And how do you feel about that—her promiscuity?"

I grit my teeth. "It's none of my business."

"But you don't like it," he states.

"We aren't together." I roll my eyes. "Why should I care?"

"You care. A lot from what I can see," he says. "And I don't trust her. She has a cousin who is always in and out of jail. Her late father was an addict who overdosed. She wasn't raised in a good home—"

"Do you even hear yourself right now? Do you think we were raised in a good home?" I scoff. When Claude tries to speak, I don't let him. "Now, I'm only going to say this one more time—leave Jordan the fuck alone. If you do anything to ruin Christmas for her, you will have lost another sister."

Claude's whole demeanour collapses like an unset cheesecake.

Deciding that I'm done with the conversation, I rise from my seat.

I throw open the office door, stepping into the dimly lit

hall. Not far ahead, I see the back of Jordan's buzzed mid fade. Had she heard me and Claude arguing about her? A flash of worry follows the question. The feeling is short-lived. Jordan has the French comprehension of a kindergartener. Perhaps even worse. Even if she had overheard anything, there's no way she could've followed.

"Jordan," I say.

She stops walking and slowly turns to face me. She's changed out of her road clothes, swapping her sweats for a pair of loose-fitting jeans and a black-and-grey plaid shirt. I like the way the shirt showcases her broad shoulders. In the months we've lived together, I have seen Jordan make use of the basement gym only twice. Considering her healthy appetite, it's a miracle that she maintains an athlete's physique. I could never live such a sedentary lifestyle and expect not to blow up.

"Hey. I was looking for you," Jordan says, scratching the back of her neck. She strides up to me and frowns as she gets closer. "You okay?" She reaches out and squeezes my shoulder. Her eyes scan my face.

What must I look like to her? My whole face burns. I almost always leave encounters with my brother feeling hot, bothered, and untethered.

At that exact moment, Claude joins us in the corridor. "Salut, Jordan, very nice to see you again."

I drill him with a harsh look. He better not say anything to disrupt Jordan's peace.

"Good seeing you as well," Jordan says. She doesn't sound happy to see Claude. There's an edge to her tone.

Not trusting my brother, I grab Jordan's hand and tug her down the hall, away from him.

When we round the corner, she asks, "What was that about?"

"It's nothing."

"Your tight grip tells me that it is something."

"Oh, I'm sorry." I drop her hand and nervously comb a hand through my hair.

"It's okay," Jordan says lightly, before her expression sobers. "But I just want to let you know that you can talk to me. If you ever want to vent to me about your brother, I'm all ears."

"Thanks. I appreciate that. But seriously, it's nothing." It would be nice to talk to someone about Claude, but Jordan's not the right person since she's the reason we're quarrelling now. I should book another appointment with Rebecca or try to phone Felix. "I'm just irritated that he invited all his friends without giving me a heads up. Can you do something for me?" I ask, biting down on my lip.

"Yeah, sure. Anything."

"Try not to be alone with my brother."

She frowns. "Is he dangerous or something?"

"No, no, he's just a dick. And I don't want him upsetting you. I invited you here to get away from it all, not to suffer through his bullshit," I explain. "Anyways, have you had a chance to meet everyone yet?"

Jordan shakes her head.

I force myself to smile. "Let's get these introductions over and done with then."

"Hey, can I ask you something?"

I look up at her. "Sure."

"Ummm … so, I couldn't help but notice that everyone is calling you No-eh-mie."

"Yeah, that's my name," I say.

Jordan's mouth drops open. Her beautiful brown eyes go wide. "Oh shit! I'm so sorry. I've been saying it wrong this whole time."

"It's no big deal." I shrug. "Back in grade school I got so fed up with everyone mispronouncing it that I just told them to call me Naomi, like Naomi Campbell."

"Would you prefer No-eh-mi?"

"You can call me Naomi."

She chuckles. "My accent that bad?"

When I say, "Yeah." Her face falls into a sad puppy dog expression that plucks on my heart strings. Not thinking, I rise on my toes and kiss her cheek. Christ, her skin is so soft. The brief contact gives birth to flapping butterflies in my stomach. Flushing, I pull away.

Jordan clears her throat and looks down the hall.

"Come, let's introduce you to everyone," I say, hoping to God I sound normal.

TWENTY-FOUR

Dinner is a complete disaster. I should have known Claude was up to something when he insisted that Jordan sit beside François, forcing me to take a place across from her.

The food is catered. It's nothing special. I find the roast beef quite bland and dry, but at least the buns are soft and pillowy. And the butter is butter. I avoid the protein, settling for carbs and wine.

Earlier, I introduced Jordan to everyone. Amelia, my brother's fiancée. François Lafontaine, my brother's best friend and best man. Mathieu, my brother's friend from university. Margot, Amelia's maid of honour. I saw no reason to bring her around Angel and Paul again as they already met outside.

Conversation at the table is uninspiring—the men are yapping about hockey. I only tune in when Jordan mentions that Toronto recently got a professional women's hockey team. It's news to me, but I only care because she seems to care. Maybe I should buy us Sceptre tickets—that's the name of our newly minted team. What a horrible name. My interest in sports doesn't extend beyond Megan Rapinoe, but if going to a PWHL game would make Jordan smile, it'd be worth it.

The discussion drifts into unsafe territory when François starts talking about his latest project—a graphic novel that he's marketing as a cross between *Macbeth* and *Resident Evil*. I know what *Macbeth* is, but I haven't the slightest clue what *Resident Evil* is.

François thinks it will be his most successful release, which is saying a lot. My brother's best friend has made quite the name for himself over the years. There are even rumours swirling that his debut series is being picked up by Netflix, which is why I'd asked Claude if he could connect Jordan with François. I have the sense that she does want to publish her work, but I think she needs to be pushed a little. François could be that for her.

"You know, Jordan is also working on a graphic novel," Claude says.

Jordan nearly chokes on her wine. She recovers and glares at me.

I look away from her and pin Claude with a cutting look. My brother grins like the devil he is. In that moment, I realize that I should have approached François myself. It's just like my brother to put Jordan on the spot like this.

"Is that so?" François asks, turning in his seat to look at Jordan. Everyone at the table is suddenly looking at her. Jordan fiddles with the end of her knife. The attention is making her uncomfortable. My heart squeezes for her. Merde, I'm going to kill my brother.

"Ummm … yeah," Jordan says.

François doesn't take the hint that Jordan's not interested in talking about her work. "What's it about?" he probes.

Jordan doesn't say anything for several moments. I open my mouth to bail her out of the situation, but she clears her throat and speaks up before I can. "It's about a woman …who works as an accountant by day, but secretly she is one of the country's deadliest assassins. And … there's, like, a detective investigating her crimes, so the assassin snuggles up to the detective to sabotage the case." She clears her throat again. "Anyways, it's like my version of a queer *Death Note*, minus anything supernatural."

François claps his hands in delight. "You've sold me, I love *Death Note*."

"It's really, really good," I say, nodding and beaming at him like an idiot.

Jordan scowls at me. I choose to let her think that I don't notice. I reach for my wine.

Thankfully, the topic changes to the weather. Paul raises a good point about tomorrow being a perfect day for skiing. Both Mathieu and Amelia agree.

It's been ages since I've hit the slopes. A ski outing sounds amazing. Has Jordan ever been skiing? If she hasn't, I can teach her. I like the thought of introducing her to new things.

Across the table, François and Jordan have a quiet exchange that I don't catch. I see my brother's best man pull out a business card and hand it over to her. I take that as a good sign. I take it to mean that he wants to see her work. If that is what's happening, I feel less aggrieved about everything.

Jordan might be mad at me, but she doesn't know what's good for her. Dreams don't just drop into your lap. You have to work hard for them. I should really start working harder on mine. I've started a rebrand on my socials, uploading videos and pictures of the meals I'm cooking. A lot of people have stopped following me. They miss my fashion content, but I can already see I'm gaining a flood of new ones—new followers who might give me future leverage. Still, I need to plan more. I can't work at the coffee shop forever, but it's hard to know where to go from here.

Momentarily, I think about Hugo and the restaurant he promised me. Claude ruined everything for me. Draining my glass, I signal to Henri that I need to be topped up.

Jordan is the first person to leave the table. My eyes follow her as she leaves the room. I think about going after her, but then Mathieu fixes his attention on me.

Mathieu is a handsome man with thick black hair and icy-blue eyes. He had a thing for Antoinette. After she died, he started showering me with compliments. At first, I'd been kind of thrilled by his interest. Shortly after my break up with Travis, I went on a few dates with Mathieu. I don't think Claude knows.

Things with Mathieu burned out quickly. At least, for me it did. I didn't like his kisses or the feel of his rough hands on my body. I ended things before we got too serious. All these years later, Mathieu is still bitter about it. For the most part, he's made a point of ignoring me over the years, so it's odd that he's sparking a conversation with me now.

"What made you decide on getting a roommate?" Mathieu empathizes the word roommate. I know what he's insinuating. Did Claude tell him about Cara?

My brother might not have. It could be Jordan that's making him suspicious. Anyone with eyesight can clock that she's gay. And yes, I recognize how weird it is for me to have a roommate when there's no reason for me to have one.

I take a gulp of wine before answering. "Jordan was looking for a place, and I had a spare room," I reply in a matter of fact tone.

Mathieu seems to be weighing my response. He traces the rim of his wine glass with a finger. "That's very generous of you."

I shrug. "I'm a generous person."

"That hasn't been my experience," he mutters.

"What was that?" Claude asks, straightening in his seat.

Mathieu sighs and looks at my brother. "Do you have anymore of those cigars, Claude?"

My brother nods eagerly. "Yes, in the office."

"Good, I'm killing for one."

Amelia makes a face at Claude. "You know I don't like it when you smoke."

My brother leans over and kisses his fiancée on the cheek. "I only do it from time to time, and it's the holidays. Give me a break this once."

Amelia pouts as Claude rises from his seat and gestures for his friends to follow him. All the men leave the table and walk out of the main room. The moment they're gone,

Margot grins ear to ear and says to Amelia. "My gawd, isn't Mathieu the most handsome man you've ever seen?"

"I don't know about that. I think Jordan's got him beat," Angel says.

I spear her with a harsh look. "Jordan's not a man."

Angel sighs with exasperation. "I didn't mean it like that. I was just saying she's very handsome."

"I didn't know you were interested in women," Amelia says, eyeing Angel as if seeing her for the first time.

"I've had a few dalliances with women," she says. Her blue gaze falls on me, and it all feels so deliberate. After years of not acknowledging what happened between us, she's choosing now to covertly bring it up. What is her end game?

I don't like that she brought up Jordan. I don't like that she finds Jordan attractive. I don't want her to go anywhere near Jordan. My grip tightens on my wine glass as I bring it to my lips.

Margot changes the subject back to Mathieu. Amelia and her dive into a conversation about his interests. I tune them out and lock eyes with Angel, and for the first time that day, I really look at her.

Tonight she's dressed in a navy Chanel bouclé dress. It's vintage. I would push a nun down an escalator to have it. Her loose blond hair curls below her shoulders. Objectively, she's stunning, but I liked her better in the pantsuit. "I'd like to talk—privately."

Angel's lips quirk up. "Lead the way."

We walk onto the terrace. It's freezing outside. I hug my arms around my chest.

Angel lights a cigarette and leans her back against the

railing. She blows a cloud of smoke into the sky. "You wanted to talk, so talk."

"You're the one who started it," I say.

Angel's brows pinch together. "Started what."

Snorting, I roll my eyes. "For years, you ignore me after we hooked up, and now you're choosing to bring it up."

"I don't recall bringing it up." She brings the cigarette to her lips and sucks. The tip glows red in the night.

I groan. "Sure, whatever—what do you want, Angel?"

"I think you're reading too much into nothing." She flicks off some ash.

"No, I don't think I am."

For many moments, Angel is quiet. Then she asks, "Are you and Jordan together?"

I hesitate. "No … But what does that matter?"

"I think she's cute."

My jaw clenches. "You're with Paul."

"Because I'm choosing to be with him." She shrugs, like she really couldn't care about the man.

While I really couldn't care about their relationship, I do care about Jordan. I don't want Angel making any moves on her, especially not here—not now with Christmas right around the corner. I'd like to think that Jordan wouldn't be susceptible to Angel's advances, but Angel is a very beautiful woman. Just the possibility of something happening between them makes my temperature rise. Suddenly, my skin barely registers the chill of the night.

"Look, Angel, I don't know where things went wrong with us, but—"

"You really don't remember?" She stomps her cigarette into an astray.

"Remember what?"

Angel shakes her head. "Nothing, it doesn't matter."

"Clearly it does. So why don't you just tell me already? What did I do to piss you off?"

Angel pushes off the railing and crosses her arms. "So you really don't remember breaking into tears after we had sex?" She arches a brow at me. "I thought we were having a good time, but then you were crying and carrying on about a woman named Tamara for so long. I left you to go sleep on the couch."

Merde, did I really do that? "I'm sorry I did that," I say, meaning it. "And I'm not trying to make excuses, but I'm pretty sure I was borderline blackout drunk." Back then, I'd been such a fucking mess. Though crying about another woman is probably one of my less egregious offences.

Probably one of the dumbest things I did was dislocating my shoulder to dodge a hook up. A guy I met at a house party wanted to "show" me something up in the bedroom. When I clued into what was actually happening, drunk logic convinced me to throw myself down the stairs to avoid the situation. I remember screaming at Claude over the phone. I told him I was dying and that he needed to come get me immediately. I don't remember my brother picking me up. I don't remember him taking me to the hospital. But the next morning, I was wearing a sling and Claude was demanding I get help.

"It's fine," Angel says.

"I really am sorry," I apologize again.

She looks at me for a beat and then sighs. Turning, she stares out into the night. If it weren't so dark, she'd be met with a spectacular view of the water. "Paul is a good man. But I miss the intimacy of being with a woman," she admits.

I go to stand beside her. I don't say anything. I'm not sure what to say. It's been a long time since I've dated men. I can't relate to her predicament.

"I can tell there's something up with you and Jordan," she says.

"There's nothing—"

"Save your excuses for someone who will believe them. Don't worry, your secret is safe with me. I won't say anything."

"Thank you," I say, feeling a flood of relief. "But seriously, Jordan and I aren't together."

Angel looks at me. "You want to be with her though?"

"Is it that obvious?"

"Yes." Angel braces her arms on the rail and stares off into the darkness once more. "So why aren't you two together?"

"Jordan doesn't do relationships—she's hung up on her ex."

Angel cackles. "Isn't that always the case?"

I sigh. Why is that so true?

TWENTY-FIVE

I step into the bedroom. Jordan's gaze connects with mine, and my heart stutters. She's in bed. The sheets cover the lower half of her body. A tight ribbed tank top shows off her strong shoulders and the sharp lines of her collarbones. My mouth goes dry, and I clear my throat.

"Hey," I say, shutting the door softly. Anxiety bubbles in my veins. I don't know what I'm more nervous about—begging for Jordan's forgiveness or sharing the bed with her.

The look on Jordan's face makes it clear that she's pissed at me. She's got every right to be, but I only had her best interest at heart. Jordan's too talented to go unnoticed. Her art should be shared with the world, and I think it's what she wants. I'm trying to help her.

Jordan doesn't say anything.

I ask the obvious. "Are you mad at me?"

"No," she says flatly.

"Okay."

Jordan rolls over, giving me her back. I hate it when she gets like this. Instead of just saying what's on her mind, she shuts down. But I do the same sometimes—okay, all the time. Who am I to judge?

I get ready for bed in the bathroom. My hands shake as I clean off my makeup, wash my face, floss, and brush my teeth. I change out of my clothes and throw on pyjamas.

I stare at my reflection in the mirror and bite down on my lip. If I had known I'd be sharing a bed with Jordan, I would have opted to bring something less revealing. Then again, maybe I want her to see me in the sheer camisole night dress. It's been so long since she's looked at me with desire flashing in her eyes. Even if I know we can't be anything more than friends, I miss feeling wanted.

I hate, hate, hate that Jordan is still hung up on Samira, and I won't do casual with her. Angel is also in agreement that I should try to make it less obvious that I'm interested. Despite the cold, we spoke for longer than I would have expected.

I told Angel more about the situation than I think I wanted to. But I guess I'm glad I told her. I'm glad someone else sees the logic in me keeping silent. Wayne doesn't see my side. Wayne is still trying to convince me to come clean to Jordan about everything.

Releasing a trembling breath, I fuss with my hair a bit before exiting the safety of the bathroom. The bedroom is dark. When I shut off the bathroom light, I can't see anything and navigate my way to the bed from memory. I slip under the cool sheets.

"Jordan," I whisper, inching closer to her. "Are you awake?"

She must be asleep. No response is forthcoming. I make to retreat to my pillow, but Jordan's voice stops me. "Yes."

I close the gap between us. Jordan tenses when I hug her to me. Her body is warm. Holding her makes my insides buzz. She smells like vanilla and faintly of cigarettes. I thought she quit. Maybe she picked the habit back up because the holidays are so stressful for her.

"Don't be mad at me," I say.

"I'm not mad," she grumbles.

"You are, I can tell," I say against her neck. "I get that you have every right to be angry with me, but I was trying to help."

"I don't see how telling your brother helps anything."

"You underestimate your talent, Jordan. I couldn't put your graphic novel down, it's so good," I say. "And I'm not just saying that because Pamela is based off me."

"She's not. You're so conceited," she mutters. "You shouldn't have told Claude. I draw for myself. I make stories for myself."

"So you're really telling me that you never once thought about getting your work published?" Jordan's silence tells me everything I need to know. "You never once thought about putting your work out there?" I push.

"Why does it even matter?"

"Because it does. If it's what you want, you should do it."

She tries to pull away. I hold on to her tighter. If it was up to me, I'd never let her go. The way I want Jordan, I can't say I've felt this way about anyone else, and it sucks.

We can't be together, at least not now. All I can do is hope that things might change one day—that one day she might feel something deeper for me than attraction and friendship.

"I know it's scary, putting yourself out there," I say. "Especially when it's something you're so passionate about."

"I can't do it again." Jordan's voice catches, and she sniffs. "I can't put myself back out there."

I rub her arm. Her skin is so soft against my fingertips. "You can."

She shakes her head. "It's not so simple."

"It really is," I say, thinking about my own dreams. Opening a restaurant is still possible, but the road will be bumpier. At the end of the day, I know I can do it. "It won't be easy. Nothing worth having is ever easy. But if it's what you want, you need to go for it."

Jordan stays quiet for a beat. "I don't think I have it in me to …" She sighs. "It's just, like, I put so much of myself into my work. What if nobody wants to read it? What if people hate it? What if nobody cares about a story with a dyke for its main character?"

I stiffen. "Did somebody tell you that?"

"Pretty much."

"Whoever told you that is a homophobic asshole, and they're wrong. I loved it, and I'm sure François's going to love it too," I state, remembering how he'd handed her his business card.

If Jordan can just get her work in front of him, I'm sure things will start happening. François is one of the kindest human beings I know. It's a wonder he's hitched his wagon to Claude. François will see Jordan's talent, and he will want to help her. He's that kind of guy.

"Look, I didn't mean to say anything to Claude. But after I finished reading it, I just—je ne sais pas. I wanted to help, and François is literally my brother's best man, so I asked my brother if he could introduce you to François," I explain. "Of course, I never imagined that his idea for an introduction would be to invite François here for the holidays—merde."

"You shouldn't have underestimated him." Jordan chuckles, and I know I've gotten through to her. My heart sags with relief. "I really shouldn't forgive you—you're the absolute worst."

"Really, I'm the bad guy for pushing you to reach for your dreams?"

"Yes, yes, you are." She groans. "I kind of hate you for it."

"Shut up. You love me, and you know it." I say, curling up even closer so that the entire length of my body presses against hers. I suppress a moan. Fuck, she feels so right in my arms.

Jordan clears her throat. "Since you are forgiven, you can go to your side of the bed now."

"Is it okay if we stay like this?" I whisper, not ready to let go. Yes, I'm pushing my luck and playing with fire, but friends cuddle all the time. My request shouldn't register as abnormal.

When Jordan nods, I relax and savour the heat of her and the rhythm of her breaths. Her neck is an inch away from my lips. It would be so easy to kiss her, but I wouldn't dare. I wouldn't be able to explain that away.

TWENTY-SIX

Early on Christmas morning, I slip out of bed and do my best to get dressed quietly. There's a lot I need to get done. Dinner is my responsibility, and it needs to be perfect. I need it to be perfect for Jordan.

Down in the kitchen, I start pulling bowls and measuring cups from the cupboards. Consulting my list, I locate ingredients and arrange them in neat piles. The scheduled menu is maple-orange-glazed spatchcocked turkey, roasted Brussel sprouts with balsamic, fresh rolls, and Hugo's signature mashed potatoes. I'm still thinking about what kind of salad I'll make. For dessert, I'm making apple pie, because Jordan said it's her favourite, with homemade vanilla ice cream.

I fall into a flow prepping. The kitchen brightens as daylight streams through the windows with the rising sun.

At some point, I notice a figure watching me and jump. "Câlisse!"

It's Jordan. I tap on my phone, muting Tiësto. "I didn't expect anyone to be up yet."

"I thought I could help out," Jordan says. She's holding a large wrapped gift.

"That for me?" I ask, unable to hide the excitement in my voice. I love gifts. I love to give gifts. I can't wait for Jordan to see her helmet.

"Maybe." Jordan fidgets. Her nails pick at a corner of tape. The large rectangular box is covered by shiny red wrapping paper decorated with Santa hat–wearing Yorkshire terriers.

"We will be exchanging gifts after dinner," I say, wiping my hands off on the towel tucked in my apron. "You should put it under the tree."

Jordan shakes her head. "Yeah, I know, but I'd rather you open it now." She practically shoves the gift at me, like it's a hot coal burning her palms. She's acting weird. Her standard is cool and reserved—not anxious and jittery.

"This wrapping paper is great," I say.

"I thought you'd like it." She clears her throat. "Any Céline status updates from Wayne?"

Wayne offered to house sit and watch Céline over the holidays. My dog doesn't do well on road trips. She throws up, even if she's given a dose of Gravol. She also hates the chalet. The last time I brought her over, she barely slept a wink and barked at her shadow. Surprisingly, she's okay with planes. Animals can be so weird sometimes.

"She's doing good. Wayne sent me a video of her yipping in her sleep last night. I'll send it to you."

"You better," Jordan says with a chuckle. She's really grown to adore Céline. Sometimes, I get a little jealous of their bond. The way Céline follows Jordan everywhere, you'd think she was Jordan's dog and not mine. But there's also a part of me that warms when I see them together.

The gift-wrapping crinkles in my hands. I look down at the package. "Are you sure you want me to open it now?"

Jordan nods. "Yeah."

I bite my lip and slide a finger under the tape, careful to not rip the paper. When it's off, it takes me a moment to realize what I am holding. My grip tightens on the frame. For a micro second, everything slows down. And then, my heart starts racing.

"You don't like it." Jordan's brows crush together. Confusion and vulnerability muddle in her brown eyes.

I tell myself to stop frowning, but I'm trying to process what she's given me. My gaze drops to the canvas, and I bite my lip again. It's a portrait of my face set against an orange abstract background made up of newspaper clippings and hand cut images of cooking paraphernalia. It's a big deal. About a million times, Jordan told me that she only makes art for herself. And yet … she made this for me.

My throat tightens, and my lungs feel half their size. "No, I love it," I croak. I do love it, but I'm also very confused.

"Oh … awesome, great." Jordan scratches the back of her neck.

I take a few steps towards her. It's hard to think straight when my brain is so fuzzy. My chest feels stuffed with cotton candy.

We stare at each other, and I wonder if she can see the question in my eyes. More than anything, I'd love confirmation that my feelings aren't all one sided. Feelings that I've been trying to lock down for what seems like forever.

I want to think her gift means something, but I could be reading too much into it. Maybe it's just a thank-you for the cheap rent and all the free meals. After all, Jordan doesn't look at me the same way anymore. She doesn't devour me with her eyes like she used to, and a piece of her will always belong to Samira.

At the same time, she's standing so close—almost leaning in. Her expression is soft. The brown eyes that stare back at me are so tender.

Someone coughs. Jordan and I spring apart. I think I'm thankful for the interruption.

Claude stands by the fridge with his arms crossed. I don't know how long he's been standing there, but it must have been long enough for him to see … Well, I don't know what exactly he observed. The way his eyes glitter tells me that whatever he witnessed displeased him.

"Bonjour, Jordan. Noémie," he says curtly.

Jordan smiles, but it doesn't reach her eyes. "Merry Christmas, Claude."

My brother better keep his mouth shut. If he says anything to upset her, I will kill him in his sleep. The glare I send his way says as much.

Claude's lips curl up the slightest bit, and his gaze flits to Jordan for a moment before he yawns and turns towards the coffee station. "I need coffee."

My brother is up to something—I can tell. I hate him. Merde, he's such a bastard.

Not wanting to give him the chance to ruin the day, I

grab Jordan's hand and drag her out of the kitchen—away from him. There's no resistance on her end. She lets me guide her up the stairs and down the hall. It isn't until we are locked away in our room that I let go.

I pace, trying to untie the knot of unease in my stomach. The way Claude looked at us … not good. But will he really go against my wishes? I told him to leave Jordan alone, and so far, it seems like he's obeyed. Maybe I am worrying about nothing, but I need Jordan to stay away from him. My brother is just like Hugo—he does whatever he pleases. Claude thinks the worst of Jordan, and he wants her out of my life. If he's given the opportunity, he'll make sure that happens.

Sitting on the edge of the bed, I gently set the portrait down on the mattress. "I thought I told you to stay away from Claude," I say the first thing that comes to mind. I'm banking that she will stay away from him if I insist again that she should.

Jordan looks at me like I've grown a second head. "Besides saying hello, I've barely said a word to your brother."

I put on a performance, blinking confusion. "Oh, I thought …" I rub my eyes with my palms and sigh. "Sorry. Forget it."

"Sorry about what? What did you think happened?"

"It's nothing."

"It doesn't sound like it's nothing," she huffs, approaching the bed.

I wring my hands. "My brother is just very protective of me. He's never liked any of my friends," I explain. It's not a lie. Claude despises my old gang. He thinks Patrice is reckless. He thinks Claire is flaky. He thinks Sophie is an airhead who constantly put herself—and me by association—in danger. And I'm not sure why he hates Lily. I just know that he does. When I cut ties with the group, Claude was ecstatic. My brother likes to think I'm better than them. But I'm no saint. I'm just as bad. Probably worse.

Rebecca is right, coping is not my strength. If I hadn't bumped into Jordan that night, and if she hadn't walked me home, I'd probably be masking my pain behind a fog of pills, alcohol, and heavy bass. Claude should be grateful Jordan's in my life.

"I just don't want him upsetting you," I continue. "I invited you here to relax, and it just seems like the opposite is happening ..." *So stay away from him.*

Sighing, Jordan massages her temples. She's probably frustrated with me. She probably thinks I'm being a little crazy. Whatever. As long as she avoids Claude.

My gaze drops to the canvas—the portrait she made for me. My fingers glide over the painting's textured surface. In some sections, it's raised like waves. I change the topic. "How long did it take you to make this?" I remember how long Jordan took to carve her pumpkin. She's a perfectionist.

"Not long," she says.

I don't believe her, but a part of me deflates at her nonchalance. "I love it," I say softly, meaning it. The warm, fuzzy feeling comes over me again. "It's possibly the most beautiful thing I've ever seen."

"That's because it's your face, and you're full of yourself."

"Anyone who looks like me would be full of themselves," I shoot back.

Jordan chuckles. The sound acts like helium, filling me with lightness. I wish Jordan and I could just fly away together like two balloons drifting up into the sky. It's such a gay thought, and I fight the urge to shake myself. When did I become such a cheese ball?

I stand and head for the closet, deciding that I want to give Jordan her gift. "Close your eyes," I say.

"Why?" Jordan crosses her arms.

"Because I told you to."

She exaggerates rolling her eyes, but she obeys the order.

I grab the box and bring it over to her. "Okay, you can look now."

Jordan opens her eyes.

"Joyeux Noël," I say, holding out an exquisitely wrapped box with a large red bow. I'm no good at wrapping, but Wayne's got an unmatched talent with scissors and tape.

"I thought gifts were going to be exchanged after dinner?" Jordan says.

I shrug. "I got to open my gift, so you get to open yours early too."

She takes the box and sits on the floor. I kneel across from her. My heart bats with excitement against my rib cage as she carefully peels off the tape. I just know Jordan's going to love it.

Jordan goes very still when the Shoei logo is unveiled. She frowns and looks up at me.

This is not the reaction I anticipated. How did I get it

wrong? I know she wants a new helmet. She should be jumping for joy right now.

"Do you like it?" I ask, my tone coming out sharp. "It's the same size as your current helmet. I wasn't sure what colour to get, but since you always wear black, I got you black. But if you don't like it or if it doesn't fit, there's a gift receipt—you can exchange it."

Jordan shakes her head, sets the box down on the floor and pushes it towards me. "I can't accept this."

What? I push it back in her direction. "Why not? You've been complaining nonstop that you need a new helmet."

"I know, but …"

I grit my teeth. "If you don't like it, you can exchange it."

"It's not that. I love it. Like, this is possibly the nicest gift I've ever gotten. But it's too much."

"It really isn't." I wave away her concern. It's not too much. If Jordan only knew … I would give her anything. If we were together, I'd spoil her to no end. I'd love to take her shopping and deck her in finery. Sure, black looks good on her, but it isn't doing her any favours. She needs a little colour. She should have clothes tailored to fit her lean frame.

"It is," she argues. Her dark brown eyes narrow on me. "Can you even afford it?"

"Merde!" Sure, I know I told her that I was in a bind for cash, but the way she's been grilling me about my expenses lately is irritating. Also, it's none of her business. "Jordan, if I couldn't afford it, I wouldn't have bought it for you. Why are you so difficult? You're, like, one of my best friends. I hate knowing that you ride around on that death trap with that banged up helmet. Also, it's rude to turn away a gift."

Jordan goes quiet for several beats, and then she sighs. "Fine, I'll accept it."

"You say that like you have a choice," I say, leaning back on my hands. "Put it on. I want to see it on you."

"You're so bossy."

"You love it."

Jordan snorts and pulls out the sleek black helmet. She slides it over her head. Flipping up the visor, she asks, "How do I look?"

"Very cool." I snap a quick photo of her with my phone.

"Delete that."

"No, I don't think I will." I grin. "How's the fit?"

"Comfortable. Thank you."

"I'm glad you like it." My gaze drops to my watch, and I sigh. "I really need to get back to the kitchen. I'm on a strict schedule."

Jordan pulls off the helmet. "I'm happy to help."

Holding up a hand, I shake my head. The last thing I need is Jordan hovering around me—distracting me. I need some space to sort out my feelings. I'm still confused about everything, and I want to dissect what happened this morning under a mental microscope. Jordan painted for me, and I want to think that means something, but I'm not sure. "Nope. I appreciate the offer, but if I let you help then Amelia will also insist on helping, and my brother's fiancée should never be near anything edible." It's an embellished truth, but I'm not about to tell Jordan that I need space.

TWENTY-SEVEN

Dinner is just about ready. Feet aching from standing all day, I lean against the counter and survey the area beyond the kitchen. The main room buzzes with chatter. Angel is seated by the fire, sipping wine while her boyfriend Paul excitedly yaps her ear off. She isn't looking at him, and I doubt she's registering a word coming out his mouth. Claude is sitting at the large dining table. François is on his right. Mathieu and Margot are across from him. They are loud enough that I can catch that they're talking about stocks and crypto currencies. Felix would fit right in. These days, all he ever wants to yap about is blockchain technology. It's getting tiresome.

Jordan's nowhere to be seen. Introverted as she is, she's probably holed up in the bedroom where it is quiet. Maybe she's drawing. At least, I hope she's working on the next volume of her graphic novel series. I want to know what happens next.

Undoing the tie of my apron, I exit the kitchen and head upstairs to search for her. "Jordan, are you in here? Dinner's going to be ready in about fifteen minutes," I ask, pushing open the bedroom door. All the lights are off, but the light spilling in from the hallway illuminates the lump of her body under the sheets.

"I'm not feeling well. I think it's a stomach bug," Jordan says. "I won't be coming down for dinner." She drags the cover over her head.

A seed of disappointment roots in my stomach. My hand tightens on the door handle. "Oh … okay," I say. I want her at dinner. Merde, I kept her in mind for the entire menu. And it's Christmas; she shouldn't be alone.

Maybe, I can convince her to come down, even if it's for a little while. I make my way over to the bed. "Do you need anything? Tylenol? Advil? I can make you some soup …" I rub her shoulder over the blanket.

Her voice is fragile when she says, "I just—I just need to be alone."

My hand stills. Shit, she's been crying. The kernel of disappointment sprouts, blossoming into worry. I'm taken back to the conversation we had after our outing to the Christmas market. I recall how she just stared up at the ceiling, blinking away tears. Of course, she's thinking about her father right now. Christmas is her October 5.

"Jordan, I …"

"Please, leave me alone. I just need to be alone." She sniffles. "Please."

"Jordan—"

"Please go."

Although she clearly wants me to leave, I can't seem to move. It's Christmas. She shouldn't be isolated. I want to stay. I want to be here for her. I want to crawl under the blankets, hold her tightly and kiss her tears away. But I'm her friend—friends don't do that sort of thing.

Time floats as I wrestle with what to do. I keep hoping that Jordan will change her mind and talk to me. She doesn't though, and I can't blame her. On some level, I even understand.

When I'm deep in a funk, I hate company. There's refuge in solitude, and nothing is more annoying than someone trying to save you when all you want to do is sink.

Jordan's continued silence tells me that she wants to drown in whatever she's feeling. So I should let her. For now, she's not looking for a raft. Perhaps tomorrow she will want a lifejacket. Perhaps tomorrow we can talk.

With a sigh, I leave.

Claude notices my dark mood at dinner, but he doesn't comment for once. He's merry and in high spirits. Everyone is, but me.

Plates are piled high with cuts of turkey meat, roasted Brussel sprouts, mashed potatoes, salad, and rolls. I'm thanked for my efforts. Between mouthfuls, I'm told that I've outdone myself.

Only François asks after Jordan, and I tell him she's unwell. "J'espère qu'elle ira mieux bientôt," he says.

I nod and reach for my wine. I'm already on my second glass. It's the only thing I can stomach. The food on my plate is untouched.

Conversation at the table is in full swing. Crypto isn't the topic. They've moved on to talking about the U.S. election, and it grates on my nerves that Mathieu's stoked about Trump's second term. "He's pro business, and will put an end to all this wokeness," he says. When I snort, Mathieu's eyes narrow on me. "You disagree."

My answer is a roll of my eyes.

"Maybe, we don't talk about Trump," Claude says.

"So you don't agree that his presidency will be good for the stock market?" Mathieu asks.

"You know, money isn't everything," I snap.

Mathieu smirks. "That's rich coming from a nepo baby like you, and don't you drive a Tesla?"

"I got my car years before Elon's ketamine addiction melted his brain and morals," I say. "And I'm planning to sell it. Jaguar's going all in on EVs, maybe I'll buy one."

"Jaguar's new logo is tragically basic." Angel's face contorts with disgust.

"I'm not sure why Elon is rigging elections for Trump," Amelia says. "The people who buy Teslas are liberal leaning. It's like he's trying to tank Tesla shares. Claude, please tell me you've cashed in on your options?"

"Can we just stop." My brother shakes his head and raises both hands. "No more politics. It's Christmas, and many of us at the table are not happy with the decision by our neighbours to elect a homophobic criminal into the White House."

Chuckling, Mathieu leans back in his seat and folds his arms. "Okay bud, it really isn't that serious."

After dinner, we exchange gifts in the seating area where the large fir twinkles. Claude got me a gold Van Cleef & Arpels necklace set with a pearl and a matching set of earrings. I thank him demurely. Setting the box down by my side, I grab my wine. I'm on my fourth glass now, but the alcohol isn't helping to dull the ache of absence in my chest.

I'm drunk when I finally stumble up the stairs and into the dark bedroom. It's past one, and Jordan's dead to the world. She doesn't stir when I drop down into the bed beside her. The room spins. I close my eyes, and the next thing I know, sunlight is assaulting my face.

Rubbing my face, I sit up.

Jordan is dressed and standing by the window. She looks as tired as I feel. Her bags are all packed by the door.

I clear my throat. "Morning."

"Morning." She doesn't look at me.

I bite my lip. "So …"

"I have a headache," she says, moving away from the window and dropping into an armchair. Jordan massages her temples and closes her eyes. It's her way of telling me she doesn't want to talk.

Sensing her eagerness to leave, I rush to get ready and pack up. Barely anyone is up when we make our way down the stairs.

Henri helps us load the car. Jordan is smoking.

My brother and his fiancée have pulled on their coats to follow us out into the cold. I say my goodbyes to Claude and Amelia and ask them to pass on my message, wishing everyone a happy New Year.

Jordan slips into the passenger seat without saying a word to them. "She's not feeling well," I explain.

My brother nods.

"I hope she gets better soon," Amelia says.

"Me too." I look at my car, but my view of Jordan is obstructed by the sun's glare.

Claude wraps me in a final bear hug. No one gets on my nerves like he does, but I know he means well. He just wants the best for me, and I'm glad he followed my wishes to leave Jordan alone.

Waving goodbye, I head for the car and drop down into the driver's seat. Jordan's eyes are closed. Her forehead is pressed against the glass. So much for trying to get her to talk to me.

I pull out of the driveway and make for Toronto.

TWENTY-EIGHT

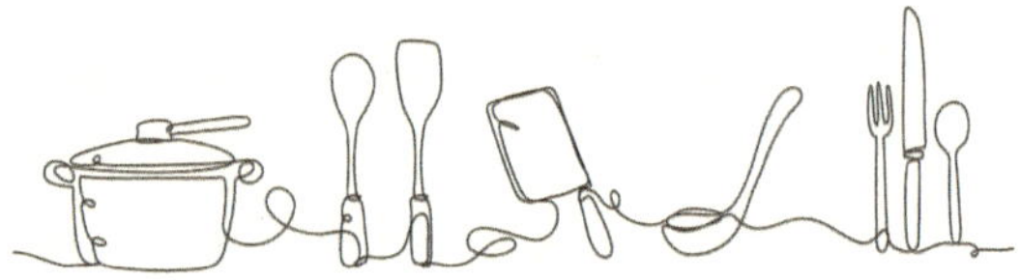

"It's been over a day, and she's barely said a word to me," I say, wringing my hands.

Wayne leans against the counter. "And you're sure you didn't say or do anything to upset her?"

I bite my lip. "I don't think so … but she was pretty weirded out about the motorcycle helmet."

"I told you not to get her that," Wayne says. "It's probably the most expensive thing she owns. Of course, she feels weird about it. Not everyone has millions stashed away to spend."

"Don't say that out loud," I snap. Worried, my gaze wanders to the entryway to the back room. Jordan's nowhere in sight. She didn't overhear. Good. I release a breath of relief. "And it's not millions," I whisper harshly. If I had millions, I'd be able to open my restaurant.

Wayne rolls his eyes. "Whatever."

"Can you talk to her? Find out what's eating at her? Because I've tried ..."

"Fine, I'll look into it," Wayne says with a sigh. "Be a doll, start the coffee and pop the croissants in the oven." He turns to head for the back office.

I start the coffee and then move on to shoving the pastries into the oven. I set the timer and move on to my next task, checking to see if the syrups and toppings need to be filled. I notice the ice box is empty and grab the plastic bucket. To reach the ice dispenser, I have to pass the office. The door is open. Jordan is slouched in a chair picking at the foam armrest. Wayne stands over her with his hands on his hips. "You need to tell Noémie," he says.

I go still. "Tell me what?"

Both of them stare at me. Jordan's mouth drops open, but only for a moment. She snaps it shut and frowns.

"Tell me what?" I ask again, stepping into the office. My gaze pinballs between them.

"I just remembered that I need to check the oven," Wayne announces. He pushes past me and shuts the door. I literally just put the croissants in. I know there's nothing to check on. If I had to guess, Wayne's probably at the door with his ear pressed against it. Nosy bastard.

Jordan stares at the floor and continues to pick at the armrest.

Annoyed, I drop the bucket. It clatters to the floor and almost falls onto its side. Frustration burns up my neck. "Jordan, is this about the helmet? Are you really that weirded out about it?"

She blinks up at me.

"The store opens in ten minutes, but I swear I won't let you leave this office until you tell me what's up." Crossing my arms, I press my back to the door. "I'm so fucking tired of tiptoeing around you. Just tell me what I did already."

Jordan exhales a deep breath and runs her hand through her hair. "You didn't do anything."

"Then why are you ignoring me?"

"You didn't do anything," she repeats. "But I don't know how to start to explain."

"You need to," I say. "This silent treatment is killing me." My eyes burn the slightest bit, so I rub them.

The chair screeches on the floor as Jordan rises. She comes to me and pulls me into her arms. A hug has never felt so good. Warmth buzzes in my chest. "Jordan …" I begin to say, not sure what words will follow.

Jordan lets me go too quickly. She takes a step back and rubs her jaw. "Your brother offered me money to stop being your friend," she says.

The buzzing stops. My heart stops. Everything stops. My tears are immediate. I already know what she is going to say next. Why should I be surprised? Jordan's just like Cara. Claude was right about her.

"How much?" I choke on the words. "And let me guess, you took the money, but now you regret it?"

Jordan drills me with a hard look. "Of course not. Our friendship doesn't come with a price tag," she says. "He offered me twenty-five thousand, but there's no amount of money I'd take."

What? I couldn't have heard her right. "You turned down the money?" I ask, needing to confirm I heard right.

"Of course, I turned down the money," Jordan says. Her brows squish together, and she shakes her head like I belched nonsense instead of asking a legitimate question. "Who the fuck wouldn't?"

"My ex," I reply on impulse. I hadn't meant to reveal that, but it's too late to take it back.

Jordan eyes go soft. It's the kind of expression my father wore when the knife slipped and I cut my hand. Her eyes tell me that she hates to see me in pain. I hug my arms around my stomach and stare down at my shoes.

"Your ex did what?" Now she's the one needing clarification.

A sad chuckle bursts out of me. "My father paid my ex to dump me," I say. Repeating what happened. Saying it out loud, makes it all feel real again. Cara's betrayal. Hugo's rage. I tremble.

I slide down the door until I'm seated on the floor. My body crumples. I squeeze in my knees to my chest, and my head drops. I start sobbing.

"Shit, I'm so sorry." Jordan's suddenly there, at my side. She rubs my back. "You're priceless. He's a fucking idiot."

I almost correct her. I almost say "she." I don't.

Jordan called me priceless. Lifting my head, I stare into her brown eyes. I hold my breath, waiting for her to say more. But she doesn't. She just sits with me in silence. I would eat pineapple on pizza to know her thoughts.

Wayne bangs on the door. He alerts us that we're late to open. There's a line forming outside of the shop.

Jordan sighs. "If you need the day off—"

"I don't," I say, wiping my eyes.

"Are you sure?"

I nod.

"Okay … but if you change your mind, it's okay to leave. We can manage."

"I won't. I'm fine." As if to prove my point, I stand up. "And I've seen what it's like when you're understaffed. Managing is not what I'd call it."

Jordan rolls her eyes and rises too.

We reach for the door handle at the same time. Our fingers brush, and the slight touch sends a jolt straight to my heart. Jordan smiles down at me, and my chest contracts almost painfully. It's a new, more intense feeling. I know what it means.

The morning rush is hectic, and I'm totally off my game. I can't do anything right. Oak milk gets used instead of whole milk. I forget an order is supposed to be a double shot of espresso. I keep spilling shit all over the counter.

Jordan doesn't acknowledge my blunders. She cleans up after me and keeps asking if I'm okay. I am not okay. The fever of limerence is familiar. Obsession, I can handle. But this? This is worse. Because it's real—realer than anything I've felt before. At the moment, standing beside Jordan, I feel drunk and starving at the same time. All my movements are impaired.

I am in love with her. And not the fantasy version that I

built up in my mind over the years. These new feelings terrify me. I am not sure I'll be able to hide them.

Around eleven, it's dead. I go on break. Exiting the coffee shop, I run to my car. I need privacy for the conversation I'm about to have with Claude. My brother picks up on the third ring. "Salut, Noémie."

"Fuck you, Claude," I shout into the receiver.

"Noémie—"

"Did you think I wouldn't find out? I told you to leave her the fuck alone. Instead, you try to fucking bribe her!"

"Merde, I was only doing what I thought was best for—"

"Claude, you are dead to me." I hang up. There's a storm in my mind, and the bad weather takes forever to clear. What was supposed to be a thirty-minute break turns into almost an hour away from the shop.

Jordan doesn't remark on my tardiness. She just asks if I'm okay. It's like the only phrase she knows. "Quit asking me that," I snap at her.

She flinches. "I'm sorry."

Wayne snorts, and I glare at him.

Jordan scratches the back of her neck and stares at the nearly empty seating area. "I've got a call with the owners," she says. "If things get busy, give me a shout."

"Sure thing, boss," Wayne says.

Jordan disappears in the back.

I take my place beside Wayne, who leans at the counter. Since there are no customers, and Jordan's gone, Kevin sees a chance to come talk to me. I'm not in the mood to deflect his advances. "Kevin, would you be a dear and wipe down the tables?"

A broad grin breaks over his face. He nods eagerly and rushes to grab the towel and spray bottle.

Wayne chuckles. "That boy's got it bad for you."

"I know, and it's kind of annoying," I say.

"So I thought you and Jay kissed and made up."

"If that's what you're calling it, we did."

Wayne arches one of his neat eyebrows. "Then why'd you bark at her?"

I grit my teeth. "Because she's annoying."

"I see annoying is your word of the day."

"Seriously, Wayne, can you quit being catty for once?"

"Girl, you know that's never gonna happen," he says. "How about you tell me what's wrong? You've been out of it all morning."

"You already know why—I don't buy for a second you weren't eavesdropping on my conversation with Jordan."

"Of course, I was," he confirms. "But I guess I pegged you as having more resilience."

"Well, I don't," I say, sighing. "And now ..."

"And now what?"

"Nothing."

Wayne frowns. "Don't leave me hanging, Noémie, you know I will just pester you until you cave."

My gaze travels over to the seating area, checking to make sure Kevin's out of hearing range. "I think ... I think I'm in love with Jordan," I admit.

"Ugh, that's your big reveal?" Wayne says. "Sorry, but that's old news."

I fold my arms over my chest. "Old news to who, because it's new to me."

"I clocked it weeks ago," he says. "When it comes to Jordan, you're worse than Kevin. The way you look at her sometimes, it's sickening. It's a good thing I have no gag reflex."

"TMI, I did not need to know that." My face scrunches in disgust. "And I am not as bad as Kevin."

"Are too," Wayne counters. "And where you're concerned, Jay's just as bad. As I've kept saying, she likes you. It's obvious."

"She likes me as a friend."

"A friend she wants to fuck," Wayne adds.

I don't argue that point. That Jordan is attracted to me is clear as crystal. "I'm not trying to be one of the many women Jordan hooks up with and ghosts," I say.

"Not sure how she'd ghost you when y'all live together."

"I don't want to ruin my friendship with Jordan for one night in her bed."

"And why are you so sure it'd be one night?" Wayne asks with a laugh. "Are you that bad of a lay?"

"I'm a great lay." I nudge him with my shoulder. "You really are the worst."

"I'm being serious though," he says, sobering. "Why are you so sure Jay's not going to want something more?"

I count off the reasons on my fingers. "She doesn't do relationships. She gets bored easily. She's a fuck boy. She's not over her ex."

"All I hear are excuses." Wayne snorts. "Honestly, Noémie, you know I'm dying to get my choice of purses from your closet, but by some miracle, I want you and Jay to work things out more. Look, maybe you are right—maybe you confess your feelings for her and it blows up in your face. But what if it doesn't? Nothing worth having is ever easy. A lot of the time, you have to risk being hurt to get what you want. If what you want is Jay, just go for it. You might save yourself a lot of grief by coming clean about everything and being honest for once."

Nothing worth having is ever easy. I told Jordan the same thing when we were in bed talking about her art. It's sound advice, but I'm not sure I have the balls to put it into practice. I'm not sure I want to risk it all. I'd rather have scraps of Jordan than nothing at all.

TWENTY-NINE

The New Year is four hours away. I stare at myself in the full-length mirror and question my choice of outfit. It's the strapless dress I wore the night I stumbled into Jordan on the street—the night she walked me home.

Now, the fit is perfect. My shoulders and arms are back to being toned, and the material of the garment accentuates my figure. By no measure is this dress one of my favourites. It's not even designer—I got it off the rack at some store in Italy that I can't remember. But I want to rewrite Jordan's memory of me in it. If there exists a reset button, I'm pressing it tonight.

I've decided to take the risk, and hopefully putting myself out there sparks a new beginning for me and Jordan.

My plan is simple, corner her when 2025 is only seconds away. And when the ball drops, when the fireworks start, when the confetti bursts into the air, and when the Champagne sprays, I will kiss her.

If Jordan kisses me back, I will come clean—okay, maybe not completely. But I will confess to liking her as more than a friend. I will tell her I don't do casual—that I don't share. From there, the menu will be in her hands, and she'll need to figure out the next course.

Rejection isn't my strong suit. I'm hoping Jordan picks me. If she does, there will be no hesitation on my end—I'm dragging her out of the club and into the first cab I flag down. More than anything, I just want to feel her arms around me without limitations and know they are there because she wants me too. I want to lose myself staring into her dark-brown eyes while tracing her jawline with my fingertips. I want to talk about a future together.

Sucking in a breath of courage, I look at Céline. She is curled up on my bed. "Est-ce que j'ai l'air bien?" My dog's response is a pathetic wag of her tail. She blinks slowly and closes her eyes.

I leave my bedroom and descend the two flights of stairs. Both Wayne and Jordan stand in the foyer. The way Jordan looks at me lifts my spirits. Merde, I hope tonight is a win for us.

Unsurprisingly, she's decked in black—a loose black blazer with a black tank beneath tucked into jeans. A thin silver chain dangles from her neck, and small cubic zirconia studs decorate her ears. She looks so good right now. She'll be devastating in clothes tailored to fit her.

I can't stop the smile from spreading across my face. "Ready to go?"

We're going to hit up a queer party in the Village. According to Jordan, the event mainly draws a Caribbeancentric crowd. Apparently, everyone is welcome. I've gone to raves and clubs all over the world, but I've never been to a Black party before. I'm a little worried about standing out.

"Yeah, I'm good to go," Wayne says.

Jordan nods. "Me too."

"I'll call the Uber then," I say. Reaching into my Chanel purse, I retrieve my phone and order the Uber.

Five minutes later, our trio steps out of my Yorkville residence and into the biting night air. The Uber is a black Honda Civic. Wayne takes shotgun. Jordan and I slip into the back.

The vehicle crawls. The closer we get to our destination, the tighter the knots in my stomach get. My heart races. I don't think I've ever been so nervous. The anticipation of what I'm about to do makes me want to bounce my knee and chew on my fingernails. But I'm not about to give myself away or ruin my manicure, so I try to keep completely still. I'll definitely need some liquid courage to execute my plan.

I look at Jordan. Almost as if sensing my gaze, she turns her head and smiles at me. The pounding mass in my chest squeezes.

"Excited?" I ask.

Jordan answers with a shrug. To be expected. Unlike me, she still parties a lot. Going out isn't a big deal to her.

Tonight, Toronto's city streets are alive. Rambunctious partygoers clog the sidewalks. There's a chaos of cars honking at drunk pedestrians stumbling onto the road.

Finally, we arrive at our destination and step out of the Uber. It's so cold that my exposed ears start to burn the moment the air touches them.

There's a line wrapping around the block to get into the venue. Lucky for us, Jordan's friends came earlier. They hold spots for us near the front of the queue.

Two of the three women are masculine presenting like Jordan. One is Black with dreadlocks and a pretty face that doesn't quite match her style. The other is a stout blond-haired woman. Not sure if it's bad to feel this way, but I'm a little relieved knowing I'm not the only white person in the group.

The last woman is a curvy goddess with long neat braids that touch her backside. The pink dress she wears barely reaches her knees. She must be freezing because her coat is one of those thin wool ones from Aritzia. But she looks amazing.

Jordan's friends all eye me like I'm the strangest specimen they've ever encountered.

"Everybody, this is Noémie," Jordan says. She nods at the dolled up woman. "Noémie, meet Corie, the resident femme of our group."

I move towards Corie, greeting her with a kiss on both cheeks. "Very nice to meet you. I love your outfit."

"I'm so glad to finally be meeting the infamous Poutine Princess," she says. "I've heard so much about you."

I drill Jordan with a hard look. "Poutine Princess?" I repeat the horrible moniker.

Jordan raises her hands in defence. "Hey, that was Wayne's nickname for you."

I direct my ire at Wayne.

He glares at Jordan. "Thanks for throwing me under the bus, Jay." He looks back at me. "I'll have you know that the nickname was retired the moment you started working with us when we realized you weren't the spawn of Coffee Satan."

"Spawn of Coffee Satan?" I chuckle and roll my eyes. "I wasn't that bad. It's not my fault that you guys kept messing up my order."

"Your order was fucking ridiculous," Jordan states. "Who the hell mixes whole milk and almond milk?"

"And exactly half a pump of vanilla syrup and hazelnut syrup," Wayne adds.

"Are you guys done?" The wind blows my hair into my face. I brush it back and then smile at the last two women. "I didn't catch your names."

The white woman speaks first, thrusting her hand out. "I'm Hailey, and this is my girlfriend, Kristen."

It kind of shocks me that they are together, and maybe that speaks to my ignorance. I've been to queer events before with Felix, but usually the places we go cater to a men-loving-men audience. And because of Cara, I'm well aware that a lot of feminine women aren't like me, preferring the company of other feminine women. But I never considered that two masculine-presenting women would want to be together.

I shake the outstretched hand. Kristen doesn't offer hers. Instead she sends her girlfriend a cryptic look. There's tension about the couple, like something's not quite right with them.

The line crawls forward. Wayne and Corie begin talking about sports. I didn't know Wayne liked basketball. I'm not sure what a shootout is, but Corie says something about Caitlin Clark being able to beat Steph Curry in one. Wayne shakes his head. "Gurrl, you've no idea what you're talking about."

There's a girl standing off to the side smoking. She's pretty but her hair extensions are atrocious, and her false eyelashes look like one harsh gust of wind will send them flying. The woman eyes Jordan a little too long for my liking.

I latch onto Jordan's arm, staking my claim. She's mine tonight. "This is so exciting," I say, trying to sound thrilled instead of nervous. "I haven't been out in ages."

Jordan grins down at me. "This your first queer party?"

"Nope," I reply, not offering up anything else.

Finally, we reach the front.

I detach from Jordan to be screened by security. A female bouncer beams a light into my purse after checking my licence. Then she opens the door for me, and I head inside. There's an ascending staircase a couple of feet away from the door. Not wanting to block it, I head up the stairs.

At the top, there is a ticket booth. After paying for my ticket and the fee to check my coat, a Southeast Asian woman with a wolf cut mullet stamps a blue star onto the inside of my wrist.

Jordan is the last from our group to make it up the stairs. Her gaze slides over the ticket seller with appreciation, and she smiles. To make things worse, Wolf Cut Mullet Girl smiles back. A bitter taste fills my mouth.

I hadn't noticed before, but the woman behind the booth is somewhat attractive—at least, if you're into grungy girls who wear way too much makeup and don't care about having chipped nail polish. She's wearing a name tag: *Sabrina.*

I decide I hate Sabrina when Jordan says, "I like your haircut."

When the ticket seller preens at the compliment and says, "I like your vibe," I wish I had the power to light her on fire.

Jordan is usually so quiet. I pegged her as an introvert. So it's kind of infuriating that she's able to flirt so easily with strangers. Jordan's never flirted with me. As a Grind That Bean customer, I only ever got tight grins or frowns whenever we interacted. Sure, her gaze hinted that she found me desirable, but I got no words of praise. I got no smiles. What is it about me that sets me apart from other women? I know Jordan finds me attractive. Like, who wouldn't? I'm hot—definitely way hotter than Sabrina. Why does Jordan become Casanova with everyone else? Am I really so unlovable?

I clench my jaw so tightly my teeth vibrate. Merde, I'm already so on edge tonight, freaking out about what I intend to do. And Jordan isn't helping.

I tug on Jordan's arm and drag her away from the ticket seller. If she's annoyed, she doesn't show it. She lets me pull her past the satin red curtain and into the club. I guide her over to the bar, and everyone from our group follows.

The club is all black—the walls, the sticky floors, the couches that rim the area. It's not the type of establishment I'm used to. It kind of reminds me of the drag bar Antoinette brought me to all those years ago—the night I first saw Jordan and discovered a new part of myself. I think I've had my heart set on Jordan ever since then. Tonight, maybe I can finally have her.

My irritation dissolves like sugar with the thought, and the nerves are back. Alcohol should help calm me down.

I order a round of tequila shots for everyone. The bartender lines up six shot glasses and fills them with a sloppy flourish. Each shot is topped with a lime wedge.

Jordan leans towards me. Her breath on my neck makes me tingle. "Tequila. I see you're looking to get wild tonight," she says in my ear.

Normal, try to act normal. Forcing a shot glass in her hand, I say, "Hell fucking yes!" I reach for the salt and perform the standard ritual. The liquor burns down my throat and fires up my insides.

Jordan downs her shot and winces.

"Not a fan of tequila?" I ask.

She shakes her head. "Nope."

"I am." Tequila and I have had some good and some rough times. I hated it the first time I drank it. I hated how my sister mocked me. But then she got hit by a car, and I began to drink and party in her memory or perhaps more to forget. I got acquainted with Clase Azul while sunbathing on a yacht floating in the Mediterranean. Before hitting up Tomorrowland, a bottle of Patrón was passed around with the molly. Tamara ordered me a paloma before she whisked me up to her hotel room. Tequila tastes like punishment. Maybe that's why I keep coming back to it.

Signalling for the bartender, I put in another order. Wayne and I clink glasses. I down my second shot.

Jordan orders a beer. I take note of the label—MGD. I didn't know she liked beer. I will stock our fridge with some.

Corie sets off for the middle of the dance floor and begins swaying to the music. Jordan's gaze wanders after her. "Let's dance with Corie," I suggest.

Jordan shakes her head and leans against the bar. "I don't feel like dancing yet. You go."

I don't want to go. I don't want to leave her side. But I also don't want it to look like I'm desperate or clingy. According to Wayne, Jordan doesn't like clingy women.

I decide some time away from Jordan might be good for my head, so I reach for Wayne. I pull him towards the dance floor. Corie smiles when she sees us drawing near. She's a very good dancer, but so am I, and Wayne's got moves too. The blasting music is foreign to me. I'm not even sure it's English, but the beat is great and easy to jam to.

I want Jordan's eyes on me. I want to put on a performance for her. I want to catch the moment her expression sparks with desire for me—only me. But she doesn't glance my way—she's engaged in a conversation with Kristen and Hailey.

"So what's the deal with you and Jordan?" Corie asks.

I play dumb. "Huh?"

"You guys sleeping together?"

"No."

"Interesting," Corie says.

Why is that interesting? I frown. "Why?"

Corie shrugs. "Jordan sleeps with everyone."

Her statement makes me freeze. Beside me, Wayne snickers.

"Have you slept with Jordan?" I ask, not sure I want to know the answer, but at the same time needing it.

"Hell fucking no," Corie says. "Jordan's hot, but not worth the drama. We're better as friends."

"Drama … what drama?"

"Let me break it down for you," Corrie says. "I used to date Paula. Have you met Paula yet?"

I shake my head.

"Well, Paula is very close with Sarah. You know who Sarah is right?"

I nod. While I haven't met or seen Sarah, I know she's Jordan's best friend and ex roommate—the one who relocated to Vancouver. Sarah's move is why Jordan needed to find a new place to rent.

"Okay, well, I'm pretty sure Paula has feelings for Sarah, which is part of the reason we broke up," Corie continues. "And Sarah and Jordan have been hooking up on and off for years—"

"Wait, Jordan was sleeping with Sarah?" I cut in.

"Yeah," Corie confirms. "My ex hated how Jordan strung Sarah along for years. So you can see how messy things are. There is no way I'm going to try to insert myself in that toxic love triangle."

Câlisse. I'm wishing I hadn't probed for details. I don't like knowing Jordan and Sarah were lovers. It changes things. It makes me want to abort my mission. My plans for the night seem doomed to fail. I don't want to be like Sarah. I don't want to be strung along.

THIRTY

The club is suddenly packed, and the foreign music feels louder. Wayne tells me it's called dancehall.

I break away from the group to search for Jordan, but it's like trying to find Waldo in a dark room with no lights. Panic claws my insides. Even though I'm sure I won't be going ahead with my plan, I still want to keep my options open. I don't want Jordan to be with anyone else.

Of course, it's when I'm thinking that exact thought that I finally see her. And she is with someone else. The tableau shatters me. Jordan locking lips with someone else. Jordan grinding on someone else. Jordan's hands on someone else.

I stumble into a stranger and almost fall. A grip on my elbow keeps me from going down. I thank the man in the neon-pink crop top who caught me. He nods with a smile and goes back to dancing with his circle of friends.

My whole body trembles, and the urge to abandon everybody overwhelms me. I just want to go home, crawl under my sheets and cry. It'll be me and my weighted blanket against the world, ringing in the New Year alone.

Because I love to torture myself, my gaze travels back over to Jordan. She's pulling away, but the woman is trying to reel her back in. They seem to be arguing.

I push through the dancers and step towards them. "There you are!" I say, a little too exuberantly. Internally, I cringe at the sound of my voice.

Jordan grins at me. The woman turns her head and scowls. I pretend she doesn't exist.

I go to Jordan, slip my hand into hers and thread our fingers. The woman can fuck off. Jordan is mine. "Wayne and I have been looking all over for you," I say.

"Jordan, who's this?" The woman hisses, crossing her arms.

I realize that I recognize her. Wayne had pointed her out to me before in a photo. This is the infamous Audrina. From Wayne, I understand that Jordan's interest in her doesn't extend past the bedroom. She's not a real threat. Just a road-block. I won't let Jordan leave with her. Not tonight.

Audrina is a beautiful woman. I can't pinpoint her ethnicity, but she's lighter in complexion than Jordan. She might be Black or she could be Latin American. I'm not impressed with her outfit; the loose jeans aren't doing her ass any favours. The cropped purple Raptors jersey is a size too big. She's got really nice dark hair though.

I beam her my most innocent smile. "I'm Noémie, Jordan's roommate. Nice to meet you." I hold out my free hand, banking that she'll ignore it. I don't want her to touch me.

Audrina does ignore my offered greeting. Her gaze bounces between me and Jordan. Her jaw clenches. "You never mentioned a roommate," she says, emphasizing roommate and sending me a dirty look. "Then again, we don't do too much talking when we're together."

My smile drops. I'm done playing nice with this bitch. "I need to go to the washroom," I say, squeezing Jordan's hand.

"And I'm going to get a drink," Audrina says, arching a brow. "Coming, Jordan?"

I hold my breath as I wait for Jordan's decision. She scratches the back of her ear. It's her tell. She's nervous about letting someone down, and I just hope it isn't me who gets left behind. "Maybe I'll catch you later," she says, diverting her eyes from Audrina's.

Having won the battle, I'm elated. It's a short-lived feeling. I know, where Jordan's concerned, there might always be a war. *She sleeps with everyone*, Corie had said.

Audrina's nostrils flare. "Don't bother." The woman forces her way through the web of dancers. Good riddance.

I don't actually have to pee, but I said I did, so I lead us off the dance floor and down a narrow staircase. The queue to use the toilet extends out of the washroom. We take our spot at the back of it. I'm still holding on to Jordan's hand. Unless she says something, I'm not letting go.

Down in the venue's dank basement, the music is drowned out, allowing for more practical conversation. Jordan keeps quiet. I do too. We shuffle forward as the line moves. Behind us someone says, "Gawd, you guys are too fucking cute."

The comment makes me blush because I just know

they're talking about us. Jordan and I look very good together. I look better on her arm than I ever looked on Cara's. Of course, back then I wouldn't have been caught dead holding Cara's hand, fearing someone might see and make assumptions.

The woman who made the comment matches my mental description for a queer individual. She's got pastel-pink hair and has the fashion sense of a unicorn on acid. No one should be wearing that many colours at one time.

"We aren't together," Jordan says. There's a bite to her words that makes me think she's annoyed with me. Perhaps she had wanted to be with Audrina tonight. I grit my teeth.

"Shame. You'd make the cutest babies," the pink-haired woman says.

"That's not even possible," I retort dryly, wishing she'd would go away or talk to anyone else. There is nowhere for her to go. Like us, she's trapped in line.

"Yes, it is. I read it somewhere …" Pink hair woman taps her chin and frowns. "I can't remember. Too drunk."

"Aren't we all," I mutter.

"How much have you had to drink?" Jordan looks down at me and arches a brow.

"I don't drink and tell," I say. The answer is exactly two tequila shots. I'm way too sober for New Year's Eve, but I'm not in the mood to drink anymore. At least, not here. I want to go home, grab a bottle of wine and drink it straight from the bottle while lying in bed, which is blasphemy. Wine is meant to be savoured, not devoured. But I want to drown in something other than the torrent of my feelings.

I can't stop replaying the scene I witnessed on the dance

floor. Jordan's hands gliding up Audrina's shirt—their lips locked. My jaw clenches.

Finally, we reach the front. A stall door opens and two women tumble out. One of them is Hailey, and the other is not her girlfriend.

"What the actual fuck?" Jordan rips away from me and storms into the washroom. All her cool is gone. I don't think I've actually seen her angry before. Jordan is grumpy, but she isn't violent. She's the kind of person who retreats when there's a hint of conflict. It's so odd seeing her like this—so enraged.

"You're fucking disgusting," she shouts, shoving Hailey.

The broad-shouldered woman trips into the garbage can. The grey plastic bin turns over with a thump, scattering crumpled and damp brown paper towels onto the stained concrete floor. "I'm not the one who's a homewrecker," Hailey claps back as she regains her footing.

I wonder what Hailey meant by that, but I'm not sure I want to know.

For a hot second, Jordan and Hailey square off. My heart jumps to my throat. It beats there, almost choking me. I'm scared for Jordan. She might be taller, but Kristen's girlfriend looks built to fight. She's security heavy.

Hailey snorts, grabs the woman from the stall by the elbow and takes off. My gaze goes back to Jordan. Every eye is focused on her. She droops like a willow under the scrutiny. Her brown eyes shimmer with embarrassment. She looks up at me and then bolts into the empty stall.

"Wow, that was intense," the pink-haired girl says behind me. "You should check to see if your girlfriend is okay."

Clearly, listening comprehension isn't for everyone—Jordan literally just told her we aren't together. I don't bother correcting her, but I do go to check on Jordan.

"Jordan, you okay?" I knock on the stall. There's no response. "Let me in," I say.

I'm not expecting her to actually open the door. Jordan is like me; she prefers to process her feelings alone. So I'm surprised to hear the lock turn over. When the door flaps inward, I squeeze through. We shut ourselves away from it all.

Jordan looks like a kicked puppy. Tears mist her eyes.

"Are you okay?" My hands go to her face. I try to comfort her. I stroke her cheeks with my thumbs, and it's hard not to register how soft her skin is—how full her lips are. Jordan turns her head and looks down at the floor.

She's trembling. My efforts to calm her down aren't working. If anything, her trembling worsens. If only I were a more nurturing person. But I think people learn that sort of thing from their mother. The last word I'd ever use to describe Hélène is nurturing.

"Jordan, please talk to me," I whisper. "You're worrying me."

Jordan doesn't say anything, but she does lift her head. And when our eyes lock, I gasp because the way she's staring at me ... she's never looked at me like this.

The kicked puppy is gone. In its place is a Doberman. Her gaze sears. Friends do not look at friends this way. Friends do not look at friends like they're a prime cut of meat just off the grill. And I don't need a mirror to know that my eyes are begging her to devour me.

Mon Dieu, this wasn't the plan. I never prepared for this. Suddenly, I miss the counter that once separated us. Our bodies are way too close. Almost touching. I don't want to be strung along. I don't want to be like Sarah. I don't want to be like every other woman Jordan has taken to bed who wasn't Samira. I want her to love me back, but I don't have the will to fight what's happening.

I lick my lips. Jordan licks her own and stares down at my chest. Her gaze lingers, branding me. I love it. This is what I've wanted all night—her eyes on me. Just me. Only me.

My breath catches. "Jordan …" I start to say. I lean in—not all the way, but enough to spur her forward.

She presses into me, flattening my back against the stall. Pleasure missiles to every point of my body. It's never felt like this before. With Cara, it always took some time to get me going. Jordan hasn't even really touched me yet, and I'm so wet for her.

I want her to rip down my thong and push her fingers inside me. I don't need foreplay or porn or dirty talk to coax me. I just want her to fuck me. One finger. Two. More. I don't care. I just need it. Right here. Right now. I don't care who hears, and the irony is not lost on me.

Jordan's hands skim over my body, filling me with sensation. Her fingers bite into my ass, and she rocks into me. My eyes squeeze shut. *Fuck, she feels so good.*

We stare at each other. A silent understanding passes between us. Jordan bends her head. My lips part, anticipating her kiss.

Someone bangs forcefully on the washroom stall. The door rattles against the frame. Jordan and I spring apart.

"Get the fuck out." There's more banging. "People out here have to piss!"

I don't know if I'm relieved or frustrated by the interruption. What I do know is that I need away from Jordan. I need to get my head straight. The fog of lust is thick in my brain. I need it to clear. Because this—this is dangerous territory.

Jordan is a threat to my heart. She's a complete fuck boy, flirting with and kissing on everybody. And I don't do casual. I don't share. And yet … I would have totally let her fuck me —in a filthy washroom stall. What the fuck is wrong with me?

Anger floods my system, and I welcome it because it's better than shame. I scramble for the lock and dart out of the washroom without another look spared at her.

"Noémie!" Jordan calls. She's chasing after me.

I quicken my pace, needing to get away. I push past a group of women coming down the steps and hurry up them.

It's when I reach the rim of the dance floor that I feel Jordan's hand on my wrist. I yank it back and glare at her.

Jordan's face falls, and for a moment she seems to space out. I don't know what she's thinking about, but in seconds, she snaps out of it. "Noémie, I'm—"

"There you two are," Wayne exclaims, rushing over to us. "We need to go. There's an emergency."

THIRTY-ONE

It's one hour into the New Year, and I'm already over 2025.

I take a long swig from the wine bottle and lean back against my pillows. I press the spacebar, and the pet grooming video begins to play. Sparing Céline, who's balled up beside me, a quick look, I wonder if she'd look cute with her paws dyed blue. I decide that it'd look weird. She looks better natural.

Everyone is downstairs consoling Kristen, who's crying about her recent break up with Hailey. Apparently, the two women got into a shouting match in the club and were kicked out by security. That was the emergency. Not wanting to be alone with Jordan, I extended an invitation to the group to crash at my home.

Disaster doesn't even begin to explain tonight. If we hadn't been interrupted, Jordan and I would have hooked up in a public washroom stall. It wouldn't have meant anything to her, and I'd be just like Sarah.

A knock on my door makes me jump. "Noémie, you up?"

It's Wayne. I hit pause on the video. If I don't say anything, will he go away?

I have no such luck. "Girl, I know you're up. I don't hear you snoring in there. Let me in."

Rolling my eyes, I say, "Come in."

The door clicks open, and Wayne shuffles inside. He looks exhausted. Dark circles peek out from under his concealer. "So … Jordan told me what happened."

Of course, she went and blabbed to Wayne. "What did she say?"

"That you two almost kissed," he replies, crossing the room and sitting on the edge of the mattress. "Funny thing is … she's still under the impression that you don't like her like that."

I don't say anything.

"I thought you were going to tell her about your feelings tonight? Wasn't that the plan?"

"Plans change," I snap, reaching for the wine bottle. I swallow the last of it.

Wayne's eyes grow wide. "Don't tell me you drank that whole thing."

I wipe my mouth. "So what if I did?"

"Girl, I think you have a problem."

"And … and I think you should go away."

"Why didn't you tell Jordan?"

"It's obvious why," I say.

Wayne blinks at me, waiting for me to expand.

"Criss, she fucks anything with two legs and boobs," I say.

"You heard Corie, she was fucking her last roommate—her best friend—for years."

"Yeah, definitely not one of her finer moments." Wayne sighs. "I told those two to quit fucking around. But I really think it's different with you."

A cold chuckle erupts from my mouth. "Willing to bet on it?"

"We already have a bet," he reminds me. "But I'm so over this game, Noémie. You need to come clean and tell her you're gay already."

I snort. "I'm not gay."

"Sorry for not being more specific—a lesbian."

"I'm not a fucking lesbian."

"So, bisexual," he huffs.

"I'm not a bisexual. I don't like men."

He throws up his hands. "Then what fucking letter of the alphabet are you?"

A headache builds behind my eyes. They also burn the slightest bit. I'm so done with this conversation. I rub my temples. "Can you go away? I'm tired."

Wayne's expression goes empathetic. "Noémie," he whispers.

"Can you just go?" I grab one of the extra pillows and cover my face because the tears are coming, and I don't want him to see them. If I press down hard enough, I wonder if I can put myself out of my misery. I wish there was a way to suffocate love—starve it of oxygen and put out its fire. I fear sometimes that my feelings for Jordan will consume me, burning me to a crisp. She probably wouldn't care. The tears come.

"Noémie," Wayne says my name again. He rests his hand on my leg. "I know it's hard to say it out loud, but trust me, it gets easier."

Wayne doesn't know what the hell he's talking about. There's nothing that needs to be said. "I … I want to go to sleep."

He gives my leg another squeeze. For once, he listens to me. Wayne rises from the bed and leaves.

I wake up the next morning with a migraine the size of Everest. Around 10:00 a.m., Jordan knocks on my door to check on me. I tell her to go away. I shutter my curtains. I don't leave my room except to feed and take the dog out.

Around 5:00 p.m., I call Kevin and ask him to take my day shift. He eagerly agrees. The following day, I call up a different colleague and talk them into switching shifts. The next few days, Ellis is going to work days, and I will take his nights.

I'm being immature. I don't care. I'm in self-preservation mode. Right now, I can't face Jordan. I'm worried my body will betray me if we get too close. The memory of her pressed against me and her lips hovering over my own is way too fresh. I need it to rot. I need it to degrade to a point where it no longer seems palatable. I need to get my head straight.

While Jordan is at the coffee shop, I don't do much. I try

to workout, but I just don't have it in me. Mainly, I spend my time on the couch, watching Netflix and eating junk. It worries me that the calories are going to go right to my thighs, but not enough to stop me from shoving more Miss Vickie's chips in my mouth.

On Friday night, I'm on my break at the coffee shop when I get a call from Felix. "Hey," I answer.

"Salut, Noémie."

My body stiffens. It's Claude. He's been calling me non-stop since our last conversation. I've let every one go to voice mail. "Why do you have Felix's phone?" I demand.

"We bumped into each other at the bar, and we are catching up," my brother says. "When I told him you've been ignoring my calls, he suggested I try calling you on his phone."

Why the fuck would he do that? Felix is my best friend, which means he should be on *my* side. I told him what Claude did. This is a betrayal of the worst kind.

"Look … Noémie, I am sorry for what I did. It was wrong," Claude says. "I see that now. At the time, I thought I was doing the right thing. I want to apologize to Jordan too."

I shake my head, and then realize he can't see it. "No—no you're not talking to her," I snap. "You've done enough damage." He'd made Jordan cry. He'd ruined Christmas for her. I will never forgive him.

My brother sighs on his end of the phone. "I know, I know. I want to make things right."

I snort. "There's nothing you can do. I hate you."

"Merde, Noémie, don't say that."

"I hate you," I repeat.

"What if I helped you open that restaurant you've always wanted? Would you still hate me then?" he asks. "I've been thinking for a while now that I'd like to do something different. You know, branch out from Poutine Heaven."

I go still.

When I don't say anything, Claude says, "Are you still there?"

I blink. "Yes, but I don't think I heard you right."

"I want us to open a restaurant together—you and me," he says. "How about it?"

My grip tightens on my phone. "I have to think about it."

"What?" My brother's confusion is evident in his tone.

He's not alone, I'm confused too. Because what exactly is there to think about? Sure, Claude may not carry the same weight as my father, but my brother is connected. He's been working in the industry for years. Unlike me, he has enough money to invest in a restaurant. And yeah, I hate his guts right now, but he's offering me my dream. I should be jumping for joy. I should be hooting and hollering. I should feel something.

"I said that I have to think about it," I say again. "Give the phone to Felix."

"Noémie—"

"Give the phone to Felix!"

"Hello," my ex-best friend says over the receiver.

"You bastard. I told you what my brother did."

"Forgive me for thinking that you'd want to hear about his idea of opening a restaurant with you," Felix says. "Are we still on for tomorrow?"

Somehow, Felix convinced me into going to a speed

dating event. He thinks I need to get myself back out there and get laid. I think he's just fed up about me whining nonstop about Jordan. Frankly, I'm sick of hearing myself whine nonstop about Jordan.

It's probably a good idea, getting back on the dating circuit. Though I seriously have doubts that I'll meet anyone at the event, and speed dating just seems a little too desperate. But I am tragically desperate, so I should probably shut up and go.

"I should bail on you after what you did," I reply.

"You wouldn't dare," he says.

THIRTY-TWO

Turning, I look at myself in the mirror from all angles. There isn't any evidence that I skipped all my workouts last week while also gorging anything within reach. I look good in the dark-blue Free People jumpsuit. I've accessorized it with a gold chain belt from Gucci. The outfit is stylish, but isn't trying too hard. I've decided on the pair of gold teardrop earrings set with orange topaz gemstones. I haven't made a choice of bag yet, but I'm leaning towards the Saint Laurent.

The unexpected knock on my bedroom door makes me freeze. In all the months we've lived together, it's only the second time Jordan's knocked on my door. These last few days, she's been good about giving me space. But everyone has their limits—she's probably reached hers.

Am I ready to have this conversation? No. But if I want things to go back to normal between us, I can't go on ignoring her. I miss the crumbs of Jordan that I can have.

At least there's a timer on this discussion. If things go

south … Felix will be here any moment. I'm going to try to talk him out of going to the speed dating event. I'd rather go shopping. Nothing makes me feel better than trying on new clothes. I need a pick me up.

I tell Jordan to come in. She opens the door and hesitates in the frame.

"Hey, what's up?" I ask. To my ears, my voice sounds chipper. Like I couldn't be happier. Like my stomach isn't a nest of writhing snakes.

Jordan shuffles inside. She's wearing an oversized hoodie with the hood up and basketball shorts. Her eyes scan my room. They fall on the portrait she did of me for a beat. Does she think it's weird that I've got it mounted in my bedroom? It hangs beside the bookshelf packed with popular titles I've always intended to read but never did.

Stopping her visual sweep of the room, Jordan looks at me in a strange way. Unsettled, I turn away and reach for the first earring laid out on my dresser. "Jordan, I have somewhere to be, so—"

"Do you want me to move out?" she asks.

My grip on the earring goes slack for a moment, and I almost drop it. "What?" I spin towards her. My brows pinch together as my heart freefalls. "Why are you asking me this? Do you want to move out?"

She blinks like she's the one confused. "You've been ignoring me." She scratches the back of her neck. "I figured you were mad and avoiding me because of what happened on New Year's Eve. I … I don't know what I was thinking, and I'm so sorry, Noémie. What I did was not okay, and I …" Her voice cracks. She stares down at her socks.

She thinks she did something wrong? I almost laugh at the absurdity of it. It's a good thing I don't. I'm not sure how I'd explain it away without revealing too much. "Jordan, it's okay," I say. "We were both a little tipsy. It's really not that big of a deal."

"It really is though." She snaps her gaze back up to mine. Her dark eyes shine with raw, aching vulnerability.

Merde, my lies are catching up with me. Jordan wouldn't be beating herself up so hard if she knew I wasn't straight. I'm a piece of shit. I should have talked to her sooner.

I open my mouth to repeat my earlier words, but she speaks up first. "I know what it feels like to …" She doesn't need to complete the sentence for me to know where she was going with it.

Jordan's body sags. She turns to go. I don't let her. I grab her arm. "Jordan," I whisper. I'm not sure what else to say. What do you say to someone who confesses something like this?

Jordan tries to pull out of my grip, but her attempt is weak. I force her to face me, and she falls into my arms. She starts crying. I hold on to her tight. She shudders, and her tears soak through the shoulder of my outfit.

"Jordan, you didn't do anything wrong," I say firmly, needing her to know because it's the truth. *Criss*, if only she knew how much I wanted her. I've wanted her from the moment I first saw her. She's been my secret obsession for years. "And I'm sorry that I've been avoiding you, but I guess I was kind of freaking out and embarrassed. Like, you're one of my closest friends, and I just—I don't know. Things got kind of weird, and I panicked a bit. But I should have talked to you. I'm sorry too."

The words aren't enough. I'm the absolute worst kind of person. I'm not a good friend. I'm so fucking selfish. Over the last few days, I only thought about myself and what I needed. Not once did I stop to think about what Jordan might be feeling. My actions raised her past trauma, and I have no idea how to make things right. Wayne would tell me to come clean, but I don't see how the truth won't make things worse.

I'm ass deep in my lies. If I fessed up … if I told Jordan everything, she might want nothing to do with me. She might want to move out. But where would she even go? And fuck, I don't want to lose her as a friend. I love her. I want her in my life. Maybe that is me being selfish again. I don't want to think it, but Jordan might be better off without me.

Jordan pulls away. Unwillingly, I let her go. Sniffling, she wipes her eyes. "Yeah, communicating would've been good." She clears her throat. "But I'd rather walk into traffic than have a tough conversation sometimes."

"I guess we are the same in that sense," I say. My mind spins as I contemplate how to steer this conversation. I wring my hands. "Moving forward, let's make a promise to always be honest with each other. Maybe we can both try to communicate better instead of running away."

She nods. "Okay."

Now this is where I should tell her everything—confess my sins like the good Catholic girl I was raised to be. My mouth refuses to open. I stare at Jordan. She looks like a shell of herself, like a thin breeze will knock her down. The truth might knock her down.

"Noémie, I—" Jordan begins to say. Her words are cut off by the sound of the doorbell ringing. Felix is here. I'm not sure if I'm saved or condemned by his interruption.

Céline hops off the bed and begins to howl. She storms over to the bedroom door and claws at it.

My gaze drops to the wet spot on my shoulder. "I'm going to have to change," I say. "Jordan, can you please let Felix in?"

Jordan's posture goes rigid, and she makes a face. She's probably upset that our conversation got disrupted before we could really resolve anything. "Yeah, sure," she says. "You guys going out?"

"Yeah, for drinks," I lie, disappearing into my walk-in closet. Sure, Jordan and I just made a deal to be honest with each other, but there's no way in hell that I'm telling her that I'm going speed dating.

"Like a date?" she asks.

My hand skims over a few shirts, but I'm barely registering anything. I keep circling back to what Jordan revealed. Anger sizzles in my core. Someone hurt Jordan. Someone touched Jordan without her consent. "Yeah," I say absent-mindedly. "Like a date." I rip a random shirt off a hanger and then a pair of pants.

"You're wearing that?" Felix asks me the moment I meet him downstairs in the foyer. "It's like you aren't even trying."

The oversized Guns and Roses cropped T-shirt is faded and frayed. It belonged to Antoinette. I don't think I've ever worn it out of the house. The Diesel jeans I threw on aren't my favourite pair and are too loose in the back, but I just didn't have the brain space to put together another outfit. This will need to do.

I pull my coat out of the closet and do up the buttons. "Where's Jordan?" I'd expected her to be downstairs, but I don't see her.

"She took the dog out," Felix replies. He chuckles. "That girl hates me."

I shove my feet into a pair of Prada ankle boots. "What makes you think that?"

"She greeted me with a glare."

I shrug. "You kind of interrupted our conversation," I say. "She's probably just annoyed."

"Well, you know what I think."

I do. Felix thinks our stunt at the Christmas market worked. He thinks Jordan is jealous of him. But I know her better than he does—the woman hates Christmas. Even before Felix showed up, she'd been a total Grinch about taking photos in front of the tree in the square.

We step out into the cold and slip into his Mercedes. Felix starts up the car, and we head south, deeper into the city.

My best friend strikes up a conversation. He wants to know if I'm considering Claude's offer. I tell him that I haven't really thought about it.

"Really?"

I sigh. "I have a lot on my mind right now."

"Want to talk about it?" He turns his head and looks at me for a quick second before directing is attention back on the road. The city streets are clogged with cars and construction cones. Toronto is always in the state of being renovated. Every time I blink there's a new condo erected. Meanwhile, nothing gets done to fix the actual problems—transportation being the big one. It takes an hour to get to Toronto from Toronto. It's a fucking mess.

Jordan is always telling me that it's such a relief living in the city now, so close to work. Before she moved in with me, it took her over an hour and a half to commute by bus and then by subway. I'm glad she doesn't have to put up with that anymore.

"I already told you about New Year's Eve," I say. "And I'm not sure what to do. I feel like I owe it to Jordan to say something, and tell her how I really feel. But … I'm scared it won't go well."

"Makes sense," Felix says with a nod. "And while I told you this already, I'll say it again—love's a game. You need to treat it like one. You can't let your opponent see your cards until you're certain of the outcome."

I grit my teeth. "Jordan's not my opponent."

Felix snorts. "Yes, she is, and right now, she has all the cards," he says. "But I'm thinking you can get the upper hand if you're patient enough. Clearly, she's attracted to you. Use that to your advantage. From what you've told me about her, she's used to getting women she wants. The longer you deny her, the more she will want you. Trust me on this."

"Jordan's not a game to me."

"Okay, then tell her how you feel," Felix says. "See how well that works out for you."

Done with the conversation, I cross my arms and stare out the window.

Minutes later, Felix drives down a ramp, and the car's cabin darkens as we make our descent into the underground lot. He parks and cuts the ignition.

"Look, I'm sorry if that last remark didn't land well, but I've never seen you so hung up on someone," he explains. "And if I'm being completely honest, I don't think you and Jordan are a good match."

"You don't know anything about—"

"I've seen and heard enough to know that you're both very different," Felix says. "I get it, she's hot. Like, I'm not even interested in women, and I find her … alluring. But she's also way older than you and probably set in her ways. So the way I see it, you either find another girl to fancy or you play the slow game with Jordan until she makes it very clear that she wants something concrete with you."

"She's not way older," I mutter. Seven years isn't that much of an age gap. Tamara—now, she'd been way older than me.

Felix throws up his hands. "Is that all you heard?"

"No, I heard you."

"Good," he says. "So can you promise me that you'll keep an open mind and try to have fun today?"

"I make no promises."

THIRTY-THREE

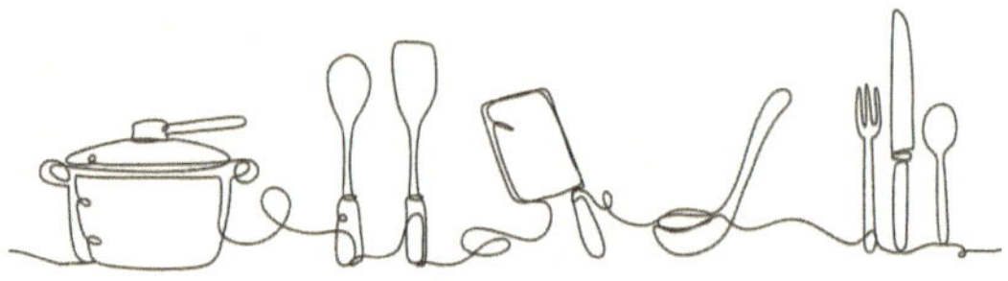

I didn't have fun at the speed dating event. Just as I knew it would be, it was a total waste of my time. Felix scolded me. He said that I wasn't being open minded, but I know what I am attracted to. No one there fit the bill. Okay, that is not entirely true. There was a woman named Marlo, who seemed okay. We even exchanged numbers. I don't think I'll be texting her anytime soon.

Marlo presented as a cute masc woman with wavy ash-blond hair. She dressed like a lumberjack, sporting a red-and-black flannel shirt, khakis, and a grey toque. Marlo's a mechanic, and her perfect date includes hiking, which I would probably get behind if Jordan wanted to do it. I don't see myself getting bitten to death by mosquitoes and wearing function over fashion brands, like Patagonia, for anyone else.

My read on Marlo is that she is maple syrup wholesome, uncomplicated, and probably never had a bad thought about anyone in her life. She smiled way too much, but her teeth were very white and straight. She was easy to talk to.

It's hard not to compare Marlo to Jordan. They are exact opposites in every way. Jordan is mysterious, complicated, and intense. Marlo's easier to read than a shopping list. Jordan is almost a full head taller than me, while Marlo is a couple inches shorter. Jordan is a woman of few words, whereas I don't think someone could pay Marlo to shut up.

When I get home, I find Jordan in the living room drawing on her tablet. Céline is asleep, curled up beside her. She looks up at me with the barest grin that makes my heart flip over.

Drawn to her, I cross the room and drop down onto the couch beside her. Our legs touch. Jordan shifts closer to the armrest, breaking the contact. I try not to let it get to me, but it does.

"I brought you something," I say, lifting up a plastic bag of takeout. "There was a popular Jamaican restaurant called Chubby's near the place Felix and I went to. I thought you might be hungry, so … here."

"Ahh … thanks," Jordan says, taking the bag and placing it down on her lap. She looks at her tablet. The screen is still on. There's a rough sketch of her main character, Zara Williams, aiming a gun.

"Working on the next volume?" I probe.

She nods and clicks the button on the device. The screen goes dark. "Yeah."

"How far are you into the story?"

"Not far."

From her curt responses, I can tell that Jordan's not in the talking mood. I should probably give her space, but I miss her. This morning was the first time in over a week that we spent more than five minutes alone together. I feel so bad for icing her out, and I just want things to go back to how they once were.

"Did you want to watch a movie or something?" I ask, leaning forward to touch her knee.

Jordan stands. My hand drops to the couch. "Ummm … actually, I'm tired," she says.

I watch her walk over to the fridge, where she drops off the takeout. She wishes me goodnight and leaves.

I would like to say that things get normal between us, but they don't. Jordan's back to treating me like I'm a piranha. If I get too close, she immediately has something else to do or somewhere else to go.

At work, she's all cool and polite. At home, things just feel off like the way milk tastes past its due date. The silence at dinner makes me uneasy, but I am sick of being the one constantly trying to drive the conversation. Whatever desire I had to be honest with her spirals down the drain, because I don't even see the point.

The few occasions Jordan does agree to watch Netflix or watch a movie with me, she picks up Céline and drops the dog down between us. I wonder if she even realizes that she's doing it, creating a barrier around herself.

A part of me wants to believe that Jordan is so infatuated by me that she can't suffer being close to me. That likely isn't the case, but a girl can dream. My fantasies about us get wilder.

For the longest time, I just thought about Jordan taking

me on the couch or on the kitchen island or up against the shower or on the stairs or in my car or basically anywhere in the house. Now, I think about her fucking me on the desk in the back office at the coffee shop, and for some strange reason Samira always walks in on us. Her ex screams and throws purple coffee cups, but Jordan doesn't react. She keeps fucking me, burying her fingers deeper and harder inside me. I stare into Samira's rage filled eyes as I come in my fantasy, and then in reality from my vibrator. Sometimes, my orgasm is so strong and so loud that I'm sure Jordan must hear. And the thought of Jordan hearing me, and getting turned on herself, makes me horny all over again.

I'll pick up the vibrator and get swept back to the office where she's fucking me, and I'm telling Samira with my eyes that Jordan's mine. It's a really fucked up cycle that I can't escape.

If I told Rebecca about it, she'd probably have a lot to say. So whenever she tries to get me to talk about my roommate, I change the topic. Rebecca calls me out on diverting the conversation away from Jordan. Each time, I tell her that I'm not ready to speak about it. My shrink doesn't press.

Out of boredom, I message Marlo one day. Her reply is instantaneous, which gives me the ick. I only keep the message thread going because she pumps up my ego, telling me how beautiful and amazing I am. It feels good to be wanted. Marlo keeps asking to meet up, and I keep making excuses. Time with her would be time away from Jordan. Doesn't seem worth it.

Felix is between contracts, so we get to hang out more. I believe him now when he says that Jordan hates him. The thought that she might be jealous tickles me, so I might get a little touchier with him when she's around. But seriously, she must know we aren't a thing. Felix might not be Wayne-level gay, but he clearly has gay accent.

Around February, Jordan becomes even more distant. When I ask her about it, she tells me that she's been working with François to publish her graphic novel. And I'm so happy that she's finally doing it—going after her dream. But now she's spending all her spare hours alone in her room, where she films and edits promotional videos she uploads to TikTok, YouTube, and Instagram.

The videos are not that good, but they're getting better. A micro influencer myself, I offer to help her. My altruism comes from a selfish place, but it doesn't matter. Jordan doesn't take me up on it. She tells me that she wants to develop her skills on her own, which I think is bullshit. A few times, I almost call her out on it.

The only time we really see each other is at work, but she doesn't talk to me. All she does is complain to Wayne about how long it takes to create content. Now that she's made the decision to work with François, everyone knows about her graphic novel. They've all asked to see it, but she won't let them. I feel special that she let me read them all.

"It's taking away from drawing time," she whines. "I hate it."

I hate it too. I miss her.

Cara gets a new number and messages me.

CARA, 5:52 P.M.

Nomi, I made a mistake. I will give the
money back. Please call me. I
love you.

The absolute nerve.

NOÉMIE, 6:00 P.M.

Fuck you! I never want to see you
again.

I block her new number instead of hurling my phone. I think that's growth.

Marlo and I text more frequently. The woman is obsessed with me. I both hate it and love it. One night, she tells me that she can't stop thinking about me. I ask her to tell me about it, and she proceeds to thumb type out a long-ass story. The girl goes into detail, describing how she'd undress me and worship my body with her tongue. It's quite vanilla, and she could have said the same thing with fewer words. Also, she uses the word *folds* to describe my vagina. Seeing the word on my phone's brightly lit screen makes me shudder, and not in a good way. My ick for Marlo intensifies. I leave her on read for a couple of days.

Jordan working so hard on her passion project reminds me of my brother's proposal, which I have yet to circle back on. I'm not sure when my dream of opening a restaurant got so sidelined. For the longest time, it was all I ever wanted. Now … all I want is Jordan. My obsession isn't healthy. Love is literally ruining me. It's worse than my pit of depression.

I call my brother. He picks up on the second ring. "Salut, Noémie."

"Hey," I say. "I thought about it … let's do it."

Considering that we argue more often than not, it's surprising how excited Claude is about the prospect of working together. He asks me to develop a business plan, and I tell him that I'll draft one up. When I hang up the phone, I realize that I have no idea what a business plan is.

Luckily, Felix is a business buff. He comes over a few nights to help me work on it. I'm so glad for his help. He walks me through terms I've never heard of before, like SWOT analysis, pricing strategy, and target customer demographics. A lot of it goes over my head. I don't know shit about numbers—my speciality is food. Claude could've pitched in, but maybe he's testing to see if I'm taking this endeavour seriously.

The business plan keeps me busy, and keeping busy makes me feel less hollow. If Jordan notices that Felix and I are working on something, she doesn't comment. She spends even more time holed up in her room. At work, she gets quieter. Instead of speaking to me, she will nod at items, expecting me to know what task she wants me to perform.

On a Tuesday, after the morning rush just ends, Jordan looks at me for a split second and cocks her head at the spray bottle. I lose my absolute shit. "I'm soooo sorry, but when I applied to work here, I didn't realize that I was supposed to be fluent in Head Bob, and I'm not planning on enrolling in Nod-Language Duolingo anytime soon. So quit with the head tilts and expecting me to read them like Morse code!" I regret snapping at her immediately.

Kevin's mouth gapes. Beside him, Wayne snickers.

Jordan frowns at me, but she doesn't say anything. She walks away, heading for the back office.

Because I genuinely feel bad, I chase after her. "I'm sorry, Jordan, I shouldn't have snapped at you," I say, stepping into the office. "But the silent treatment is killing me. Can you just tell me what I did already?"

Jordan sighs and scrubs her face with her palms. "You didn't do anything."

"Then why won't you talk to me?" My words come out soft and defeated.

Jordan's face falls. She closes the distance between us and pulls me into the warmth of her arms. My head falls to her chest. She smells like coffee and laundry detergent—earthy and clean. A hug has never felt so good. I want it to last forever. Every part of me aches for her. We are close now, but nowhere near close enough.

My gaze wanders to the desk. I recall all the times I fantasized about her fucking me on it. Heat burns my cheeks.

"You didn't do anything," Jordan repeats. Too soon, her hands drop to her sides. She clears her throat. "I have some work to do back here," she says, dismissing me.

After our shift, Jordan doesn't come home. She stays out all night, which makes me go a little feral.

If it weren't for Felix coming over to work on the business plan, I'd probably waste the evening drinking wine and crying into my pillow. So pathetic. My feelings for Jordan make me pathetic.

A few times, I think about telling Wayne about the restaurant, but the whole thing feels fragile. It's looking like it'll cost a fortune to start. Considering the thin margins and that fifty percent of restaurants don't make it to their fifth year, it's a risky investment. At any moment, Claude could change his mind. I don't want to jinx anything, so I keep quiet.

The night we finish the business plan and send it over for Claude's review, Felix and I decide to go out to celebrate. Felix throws himself down on my bed while I busy myself finding something to wear. "What do you think?" I step out of the closet holding up a checkered Louis Vuitton mini jacket dress.

Felix feigns a yawn. "How pedestrian."

Rolling my eyes, I head back into the closet and grab a strappy black dress from Dsquared2 that I haven't worn before. "What about this?"

"Yes, I like that," he says. "And put your hair down."

"No, I think I'll leave it up," I say, peeling off my top and then shimmying out of my jeans. I slide on the dress. "Can you help me with the zipper?"

Felix sighs exasperatingly as he hops off my bed. After fastening the dress, he tells me to spin for him. When I do, he whistles. "If I was straight, you could get it."

My face scrunches. "Ewww, never say that again."

He chuckles. "Want to invite Jordan?"

"I don't think she'll want to come," I say, picking up a tube of Rouge Dior lipstick. It's my favourite shade of red with its velvet matte finish.

"Because she hates me."

I don't respond as I apply the lipstick.

"Don't tell me you haven't noticed the way she glares at me," Felix says, collapsing back down on the mattress. "That girl wants me dead. Even if she hasn't realized it yet, she likes you. And despite not approving of this match, I'm glad you listened to me. Playing the slow game will work. You'll see."

My jaw clenches. "She doesn't like me," I say. "I don't know if you've noticed, but she pretty much ignores me lately."

Felix raises up on his elbows and eyes me. "And why do you think that is … hmmm?"

"I don't know—maybe she's on to me, and knows how I feel about her, and it weirds her out," I say. "Criss, whenever we sit together, she puts the dog between us."

Felix bursts into a fit of laughter. "Oh my god, she doesn't."

I don't know what he finds so funny. I cross my arms and drill my friend with a hard look.

When he sobers, he wipes his eyes. "That girl has it bad for you," he states.

"I don't get your logic."

"Let me spell it out for you: she hates me because she's jealous, and she's avoiding you because distance is probably easier than being close to you," he explains. "Trust me, it's only a matter of time before she breaks."

"Yeah, I think you're wrong about this," I say. "All Jordan cares about right now is her graphic novel. Yes, she hates you, but it's probably for something else totally unrelated to me."

"It's not—I know women."

I snort. "Do you now?"

"Yes," Felix says. "And I bet I know what might just break her."

Felix doesn't know what he's talking about. Still, I arch my brow and say, "Go on, I'm intrigued."

"Are you sure? Fair warning, you might not like it."

"Quit playing games, Felix, just tell me."

"Nah, I'm going to show you," he says, smirking. I'm about to ask how, when he rises to his feet and starts jumping on my bed like it's a fucking bouncy castle and he's a snot-nosed kid. First Claude and now Felix. What the hell is with grown-ass men in a designer suits jumping on my bed?

"Ahhhhh … Noémie," he groans out, so loud that I'm sure Jordan would hear it anywhere in the house.

I freeze. "Felix, stop it."

"Your … your boobs feel amazing!" he continues, ignoring me.

I launch myself at my best friend, tackling him. His back hits the mattress, the bed frame knocks against the wall. "Oh, wow! I knew you liked it rough," he shouts, wriggling under me. "But I never imagined …"

We wrestle a bit. He's so much stronger than he looks. "Felix," I warn.

He ignores me. "Oh yeah, that's my girl. Take it! Take this big, giant—"

I cut off his words, clapping my hand over his mouth. "What the actual fuck, Felix?"

My friend stares up at me with big blue eyes. He bats them innocently. I can't take him seriously and burst into laughter. I roll off of him, clutching my sides. "Seriously, what the actual fuck?" My ribs hurt. It's hard to breathe, I'm cracking up too hard. "My boobs are amazing. Merde, that's all you could think of?"

He sits up and runs a hand through his thick brown hair. "What can I say, they're your breast asset."

I double over again. It's been a long time since I've laughed so much. I didn't know how much I needed it.

When I finish my makeup, Felix and I exit my room. I knock on Jordan's door. There's no reply, and no light streams from the cracks, so I assume she's asleep.

The bar we check out is walking distance from my home. I'm not impressed with the wine list, but the ambiance is nice. Felix gets drunk, so I let him crash at my place. In the morning, I prepare a full breakfast for him—waffles, fresh fruit, and bacon—because he looks like he needs it, and I feel like waffles.

Céline starts barking all of a sudden. I realize why when Jordan stumbles into the kitchen in yesterday's clothes. Apparently, she went out last night too. She's just getting back home now. She looks like she woke up in a trash bin and smells like a brothel. My grip tightens on the ladle.

"Long night?" Felix says, grinning over the rim of his coffee cup. He sits at the island.

Jordan doesn't respond. She zombie walks to a cabinet and removes a glass. Her hand shakes as she flips on the faucet and fills it with water. I watch her gulp it all down and then refill the glass.

"Do you want waffles?" I ask.

Jordan winces. "No, no food. There's some Gravol in my room that's calling to me."

I've never heard of the anti-nausea drug being used as a hangover cure, but it makes sense that it'd work.

Felix chuckles. I glare at him and then snap my gaze back to Jordan. "Do you need help getting upstairs?"

"Nope." She shakes her head and leaves.

I smell something burning. Cursing, I bolt over to the waffle iron and lift the top. The waffle is dark brown and stuck to the iron plate. I peel it off and toss it in the bin. I lean against the counter and hold my head in my hands. My mind goes to what Jordan must've gotten up to last night. I wonder who she was with. Nobody ever talks about the horrors of being in love. My heart feels fried. I wish it could join the waffle in the trash.

"Not sure why you're so down," Felix chimes from his seat. "I think we did it—I think we broke her."

I lance him with a look that makes his smile falter.

THIRTY-FOUR

In a few hours, I'll be boarding a plane with Felix. A couple of weeks ago, he told me that I was due for a vacation. Agreeing, we decided to hit up the Four Seasons in Honolulu. What I need is time away from Jordan. Suntanning on the beach is the perfect getaway.

I'm in the process of confirming I've packed everything I'll need for the trip when the doorbell rings. Not giving it a thought, I throw open the door.

My guts twists like they're trying to crawl out of me. I freeze, but only for a moment. "What the fuck are you doing here?"

"We need to talk, Nomi." My ex stands at my doorstep. She holds a bouquet of roses.

"There's nothing to talk about," I snap, pointing at her car. "Leave."

"I don't care if I have to stand here all day," Cara says. "I'm not leaving until we talk."

My jaw clenches, and I think about Jordan. She's gone out, but who knows when she'll be back. I don't want them bumping into each other. I want to avoid the awkward conversation, or worse, the fallout. Cara is a woman. Jordan still thinks I'm straight, and things between us are rockier than finishing salt.

Everything I do rubs Jordan the wrong way. I don't know how to get through to her. Gifts don't even work. Gifts! Jordan is possibly the only person I know who hates getting nice things.

Just last week, at the coffee shop, Wayne was telling her how awesome *Elden Ring* is. "I wish I could play it," Jordan said, "but I don't have a PS5."

That night, I excitedly bought her the damned console and the blasted game. I thought it would make her happy. But when Amazon delivered it, she went berserk. Okay, berserk is not the best word—she was not happy though. Instead of thanking me she said, "What the fuck?" and narrowed her eyes on me. "Where'd you get the money for this?"

"It's seriously none of your business, Jordan," I replied, because it really isn't any of her business. She's always asking me about my financial situation. It's annoying.

"You shouldn't have bought this," she said, shaking her head.

"Why are you so difficult?" I snapped. "Seriously, you've been in such a shitty mood lately. I thought this would cheer you up ... I guess I was wrong."

Jordan stared down at the glossy white box and sighed the saddest sound. "Noémie ... it's just a lot."

It really isn't. I would give you anything. I had thought. "Whatever, if you don't want it, sell it. I don't care." I did care —a lot.

Ever since that incident, we're speaking even less to each other. Maybe it's a good thing we aren't dating. I would hate for us to get into a fight any time I wanted to splurge on her.

Felix says we broke her. He says that it's only a matter of time before she confesses to having feelings for me—real feelings, not just attraction. A girl can hope, but I also don't want it to be true.

Jordan hasn't had an easy life. Her sister and her have always been at odds. Her relationship with her mother is complicated. Her father overdosed, and she was the one who found him dead in his apartment. And someone touched her once, without her consent. My blood boils whenever I think about it. I hate that life's been so hard for her. The last thing I want to do is add to her pain. She's a person, not a shoe. I don't like the idea of breaking her in.

I decide to let Cara inside. If she wants to talk, we can talk—quickly. I need her gone.

Céline yips and whines as we walk to the main room. "You look good, Nomi," my ex says, running a nervous hand through her blond hair. It's shorter now. The style looks good on her, highlighting the sharpness of her jaw. She's sporting more masculine attire than I'm used to seeing her in —a Levi's Canadian tuxedo with the arms of the jean jacket rolled up to her elbows. I wonder if she's dressed this way to appeal to me. She knows I have a preference for butch women. I've never kept that a secret from her.

I keep waiting for Cara to say something. She doesn't. All

she does is stare. I toss the flowers on the couch and cross my arms. "You said you wanted to talk, so talk."

"I miss you, Nomi. I love you so much," she says, taking a step towards me. "We were so good together. You have to remember how good things were between us."

Cara's babble grates on my last nerve. I back away. "Merde, I told you that I never wanted to see you again! Decriss!" I point in the direction of the front door. "Leave—maintenant!"

"Nomi, let me explain. I know I fucked up, but I miss you," she pleads. Her tone is desperate, and I'm unmoved. "It was a mistake, and I knew it instantly. I'll give it back. I'll give it all back."

Every inch of my body burns. The absolute audacity. Cara just thought she could come here and I'd forgive her. Fuck her. "J'en ai rien à foutre! Leave!"

A whine from Céline makes me turn my head. Jordan stands in the entryway, holding the squirming dog who's bent on licking her face.

In an instant, all the rage drains out of me. My whole body stills. *Shit! This can't be happening. When the fuck did Jordan get back?*

Cara scowls when she spots Jordan. "What the fuck is Hot Barista doing here?"

Jordan frowns. Her gaze ping-pongs between me and my ex as she sets Céline down on the floor.

Panic fists my gut. "She's my roommate, but that doesn't matter," I say, trying to do damage control. "You need to go, Cara. Now!"

My ex doesn't budge. "Thought you were trying out men again—"

Who the fuck told her that? "Cara, shut up. I swear … if you don't get the fuck out of my house!"

"Trying out men again?" Jordan repeats. She stares at me, looking completely and utterly lost. I can't meet her eyes and look away. The timing couldn't be worse.

Cara chuckles coldly. "Why does Hot Barista seem so confused, like she doesn't know you're—"

"Cara, you need to go," I snap.

"What is she talking about?" Jordan asks.

Cara cocks her head to the side. "Nomi, don't tell me you followed your dad's orders and fell back into the closet." She fixes her eyes on Jordan. "I'm going to assume she never mentioned me to you. I'm Caralyn, Noémie's ex."

Jordan doesn't say anything. The look she sends my way tells me everything I need to know. She's shocked and hurt and confused. Jordan doesn't say anything else. She does what she always does when faced with a tough situation, she turns and leaves.

I glare at Cara. "I fucking hate you." I make to go after Jordan. Cara stops me, grabbing my arm.

"Nomi—"

I shove her away. "You shouldn't have come here. I have nothing to say to you. We are finished."

Cara winces like my words cut her. I really couldn't care less. I don't think I ever really cared about her. She was just one of many stops, and Jordan has always been my destination. There's no one else I want.

I chase after Jordan, catching up with her outside. She

ducks under the rising garage door and hops onto her motorcycle.

"Jordan, wait … let's talk," I say, gasping.

She doesn't look at me. She tugs on her helmet and slams down the visor. She shoves the key in the ignition. The bike purrs to life.

I grab at her arm, but Jordan bats my hand away and rolls the motorcycle backwards down the driveway and onto the street. She takes off down the road. I stare after her until the bright-green bike disappears from my view.

THIRTY-FIVE

Raindrops batter the windows like popcorn exploding in a pan. Jordan hasn't returned. I hoped she would before I left for the airport. We need to talk. I don't want to leave without trying to explain. She needs to know that it was never my intention to lie to her.

My UberX pulls into the driveway. It's barely visible in the torrent. I hate the idea of Jordan riding in the storm. I wonder where she is. What is she doing? Who is she with?

I get a call from an unknown number seconds before I'm about to reach for the door handle. The phone buzzes in my hand. I'm surprised when I hear Jordan's mother's voice on the other end. "Hello, Noémie," she says.

"Hi, Paulette," I reply. A bitter taste fills my mouth even before she says anything else. It's like I already know the bad news she's going to relay.

"Jordan's been in an accident," she tells me.

My breath catches. I swear my heart stops. *This is my fault.*

My brain jumps to the worst scenario. Jordan's been hit—run over. She's dead or worse … The doctor tells us she might push through. We're given hope that maybe she'll survive the surgery. But she doesn't. I will never be able to shake the memory of seeing Antoinette in her hospital bed—her face bruised and cut.

"She's been admitted at St. Joseph," Paulette says, pulling me from my thoughts. "I'm headed over there right now, but I just wanted to let you know."

Paulette doesn't drive. I don't know how I know this. Jordan must have mentioned it before. "Do you need a ride?" I ask. "I can bring you to the hospital."

Her mother is quiet for some time. Then, she says, "A ride would be nice, if it isn't too much."

"It isn't," I say. "I'm on my way right now."

"Thank you," she says. "Call me when you arrive."

I cancel my rideshare and let Céline out of her carrier before dashing out into the storm.

Usually, I'm a cautious driver. Driving in rain or snow always makes me uneasy, but the traffic isn't heavy for once, and I speed east towards Scarborough.

Jordan's mother and grandmother step out of the building minutes after my arrival. They both thank me.

"It's no problem," I tell them. "Any news about Jordan?"

Paulette sits in the front. She shakes her head. "No, no news." Her face is tense with worry.

My grip on the steering wheel tightens. The unknown

scares the shit out of me, but I tell myself that if Jordan's condition is critical, Paulette would know that. But … I bite my lip. What if we get there and I'm wrong?

The rain beats down on the car. Jordan's mother clears her throat. "Noémie?"

Her voice jerks me back to the present. Hospital—I have to get us to the hospital. I shift the car into drive and pull out of the complex. The westbound traffic is horrendous. There's a fender bender on the Don Valley Parkway. It takes us almost an hour to get to St. Joe's.

I drop Jordan's mother and grandmother off at the front entrance and then look for somewhere to park. The rain lets up a little when I exit my vehicle. I hurry into the hospital and rush up to the reception. "I'm looking for someone who was recently admitted," I tell the Filipino woman who sits at the desk behind the thick glass. I give her Jordan's name, and she gives me directions.

Like overworked dough, my muscles stiffen with every step bringing me closer to Jordan. My pounding heart drowns out the noise around me.

Soon, she comes into my line of sight. Relief rips through me. Other than the cast on her left arm, Jordan looks fine. It takes all my willpower not to run over to her. I come to a stop at the foot of the bed she lays on. Paulette stands over her. Grandma Janet sits in the chair at the corner of the curtain sectioned room. The old woman looks tired. Her eyes droop, and her head bobs towards her chest.

I try to smile, but my lips don't really cooperate. "Hey, Jordan," I say.

"Shouldn't you be flying to Honolulu right now?" she asks coldly.

Paulette stares at me and then frowns at her daughter. "Have you no manners?" She scolds.

A grunt is Jordan's response. Her gaze drops to her lap.

The awkward silence is suffocating. There's so much we need to talk about. There's so much I need to explain. But now is not the time.

"I'm glad you're all right," I say, wringing my hands.

When Jordan doesn't say anything, her mother's gaze narrows on us. "Is something wrong?"

"No," Jordan and I say at the same time.

"Everything is good," I add.

Paulette doesn't look convinced. Grandma Janet falls asleep in the chair.

Jordan's mother moves out of the room to find the washroom, and I go to stand where she once stood by Jordan's side.

"Jordan," I say, touching her shoulder. Jordan winces and moves so my hand drops.

The doctor walks in at that moment. He's a tall, balding man with bags the size of quarters under his eyes. He doesn't look up from his chart as he talks to Jordan. He tells her about the pain medication she will be getting and how to take it. He tells her that she will likely need to get her arm X-rayed in the future and advises that he will be providing a referral for her to see a physiotherapist. If Jordan is listening, I can't tell. Her mind seems galaxies away. I wonder what she's thinking about.

Jordan gets discharged, and we all head for the exit. It's still raining outside. Jordan sits in the back with her grandmother.

I drive us all to our home in Yorkville.

"Wow," Paulette says the moment we step into the foyer. "Amari told me that Jordan was living somewhere nice, but it's another thing to see it."

"Yes, your home is beautiful," Grandma Janet agrees.

"Thank you," I say, reaching down to pick up Céline, who's yipping like crazy. Both Jordan's mother and grandmother eye my dog warily.

"She doesn't bite. She's just very excitable," Jordan says. "Céline's a very sweet dog."

Her family doesn't look convinced. I remember how scared Jordan had been of Céline the first time they'd met. Now, they are as close as two peas in a pod.

Jordan makes for the stairs, and they follow her up. I'm not sure if it's okay to tag along too, but I go.

From the door, I watch them fawn over Jordan's room. They can't believe how large it is. They gawk at the size of her closet. They gasp upon sighting the ensuite.

Soon enough, their focus is back on Jordan. "You better get rid of that death trap," her mother states. "God spared your life. It's not wise to test your luck."

Jordan snorts.

I hope she listens to them. Motorcycles are dangerous. I don't like the idea of her riding around the city on it.

Deciding that I've overextended my stay, I make my way back downstairs. Half an hour later, I'm told Jordan's asleep, and I offer to take Paulette and Grandma Janet back to Scarborough.

It seems like the moment Grandma Janet settles into the back seat, she nods off again.

Minutes into the drive, Paulette asks, "What is going on between you and Jordan?"

I blink. "Huh? I mean … nothing is going on."

"You are not … together?"

"No, we are just friends," I reply.

"It is okay if you aren't," her mother says. "Of course, I can't say that I approve of Jordan's decision to date women, but I love my daughter. All I want is her happiness."

"It's not a decision," I say, gritting my teeth. "We can't choose who we're attracted to—it just is."

Jordan's mother doesn't say anything for a long time. I don't know if that's a good thing. I hope my tone didn't offend her. That's the last thing I need—her mother hating me.

"How do your parents feel about it?" she asks.

"My father cut me off when he found out." I curse internally. There were many ways I could've answered that question. I could have provided a more general response. Instead, I told the truth. Jordan's mother knows a fact her daughter doesn't yet know.

"I'm sorry," Paulette says. "That must have been very painful for you. I may not see eye to eye with Jordan's lifestyle—it doesn't align with my beliefs. But my God is a loving God. It's hard for me to understand how someone could disown their child."

"It's hard for me to understand too," I state. The words

come out soft, almost as a whisper. I think of how Hugo shouted and hurled the crystal glass at the fireplace. I think off how Hélène just sat there quietly watching. I think of how Antoinette fled the moment our father said, "Dégage d'ici câlisse!" He'd told her to leave, and she had. Now, she's lost to us forever, and he doesn't seem to care. Like he believes she's better off dead than being a lesbian. If I perished too, would he even care? I used to be his favourite. Now, I am dead to him too.

My eyes burn. Over and over, I blink until the feeling goes away.

I feel Paulette's eyes on me. "I'm glad you have Jordan," she says. "I can tell my daughter cares for you a lot."

That catches my attention. My gaze momentarily drifts from the road. I look at Paulette for a quick second. "Does Jordan talk about me?" I know I'm probably fishing for information that isn't there.

Paulette chuckles. "You know my daughter isn't much of a sharer," she replies. "But more than once she mentioned that you're the best cook she knows. She keeps telling me that I need to try duck." The way Paulette says duck, like it's a dirty word, leads me to think that she's frowning or making a disgusted face.

"Yeah, I made her a crispy duck breast once. She really liked it," I say, turning onto the off ramp. "Maybe one day you and Grandma Janet can come for dinner."

"If you will have us, we will not turn down the invitation," she says. "I'm glad you and Jordan have found each other. You treat her well."

From her words, I can tell she thinks me and Jordan are

together. I decide to correct her. "I'm glad too. She's become one of my closest friends."

"So you really are just friends?"

I nod. "Yes."

Paulette goes quiet again. The only sound that fills the cabin is Janet's soft snores and the car's blinking turn signal.

THIRTY-SIX

The door to Jordan's bedroom is wide open. She's asleep. I know I should leave her alone, but I step inside and walk to the edge of the bed.

Jordan looks younger with her eyes closed. Her face is relaxed. I stare at the cast and feel another wave of relief. Things could have been so much worse.

Guilt chews me up. She was riding in the storm because of me—because she was mad at me.

Biting my lip, I turn away from her. My gaze lands on the bookshelf. It's lined with comic books and graphic novels. I let my fingers trail down their spines.

After I tore through the three volumes of Jordan's graphic novel series, she'd insisted that I read the original *Teenage Mutant Ninja Turtles*. To be honest, I wasn't interested, but I couldn't say no to her. Jordan excitedly presented me with the first volume. The front cover was creased and wrinkled. She told me that it had belonged to her father and then proceeded to show me the rest of the collection she'd inherited. She told me that her father got her hooked on comics as a kid. She told me that she taught herself to draw because she dreamed of creating stories too. It's the most I've ever heard her talk. She'd been so animated. Just listening to her ramble brought me joy.

Moving away from the bookshelf, I wander over to Jordan's desk. There's a black hoodie neatly hanging over the back of the chair. I pick it up and hug it to my chest. It smells like her—a blend of detergent, vanilla, and notes of smoke. I hug it tighter and shiver. I pull the sweater on—not because I'm cold, but because I want to be surrounded by her scent. I get a thrill knowing only a day ago the fabric was on her body, touching her skin.

Not really sure what to do with myself, and not wanting to leave, I curl up on the cushioned bench beneath the window. It's raining again. The water splatters against the window, obscuring the view outside.

A ball of tangled emotions rolls around in my stomach, and it's hard to make sense of everything I'm feeling. Now that I find myself with nothing to do, it's like all I can focus on is the confusing jumble. Reflection has never been my strength. I've always preferred to ignore my emotions. More than a few times, Rebecca asked me to think about why that was. Once, I told her that I wasn't ready for the answers I might find.

For some reason, I think back on my conversation with Paulette in the car. "We can't choose who we're attracted to —it just is," I had told her. I'm still amazed I said that. Historically, I dance around questions about my sexuality, but in that moment I just spoke my truth without hesitation, without a single thought.

"I know it's hard to say it out loud, but trust me, it gets easier," Wayne had said. Is that what's happening? Is it getting easier to talk about?

Sighing, I rub my temples and then hug my knees.

Jordan stirs. She sits up and rubs her face.

Our eyes connect, and suddenly it feels like I'm breathing through a straw. I'm not getting enough oxygen, and the world grows fuzzy at the edges. My heart claws at my ribs like a lobster desperately trying to save itself from the boiling pot. I want to run, but running is what got us here. Jordan and I need to talk like the adults we are.

"I'm glad you're okay," I say.

Jordan lifts her left arm. "If you can call breaking my arm okay—sure."

"It could have been worse. You're lucky it wasn't worse. You shouldn't have been riding in that storm. What were you thinking?" When Jordan's nostrils flare, I realize that I probably shouldn't have said that. I should have started with an apology.

She stares at me for a long time. I can tell she's chasing her words. "This whole time … you lied to me," she says. "You let me and Wayne and everyone think you were straight. Why? I thought we were being honest with each other. You could've told me. I'm not your family, I would never judge you for—"

"It's my choice if I want to disclose my sexuality. It's my choice to come out when I'm ready." I don't know why I snap at her. She's got every reason to feel deceived and hurt by my omission. But what could I have said to her all those months ago when we sat across the table from each other at the coffee shop?

"And what do you think? Do you think the gays are confused?" she had asked.

That would have been the time to tell her, but what would I have said? If I told her that I'm not straight, Jordan would have probed, searching for a label I've yet to assign myself. Worse, it would have raised questions about why my father cut me off, and there was no way I was going to go into details.

I look away from Jordan and stare out the window. There's nothing to see. The dark and the rain hides everything.

When I was with Cara, I was in my comfy closet. Having a label didn't matter. I didn't have to think about it, and so I chose not to. Now the door is wide open, and I know what's on the other side, but for some reason I don't want to cross over. Maybe I should talk to Rebecca about it. Maybe it's about time I figure myself out.

Sighing, I run a hand through my hair. "I'm sorry if that came out harsh, but …" I swivel on the bench and face the bed, but my gaze drops to the floor. I think about what to say. I want to explain. I want Jordan to understand. "I guess I should have told you, but I didn't say anything the day you hired me, and then it just got harder and harder to tell you. There never seemed to be a good time." I look up at Jordan, and I hope she can see that I'm being sincere. I never went into this wanting to lie. Everything just sort of happened and snowballed to the point where telling the truth would have been worse than saying nothing. "There's so much that I need to tell you, but I … I don't want you to hate me."

"I could never hate you, Noémie," she says.

"You say that now." Holding back a cold chuckle, I lean back against the wall and stare up at the ceiling. My mind wanders to the night all my problems started, and I just start rambling. "The night my sister died was the night she came out to our parents. I've never seen my father so angry. He yelled and cursed and threw things. Antoinette ran away in tears, and my father just let her go …"

"Noémie …"

"The next morning we got the news that she got hit by a car," I tell her, hugging my arms around my stomach. It doesn't matter how much time has passed. It still hits like a blow beneath my ribs. "It's been hard for me—talking about my sexuality."

Jordan leaves her spot on the bed and comes to sit beside me. She squeezes my knee.

"Cara outed me to my brother," I continue, because now that I'm talking, it's best that I get the whole story out. But it's hard. Each word feels like a shard of glass in my mouth. A lump sits heavy in my throat. My eyes sting. "Then Claude outed me to my parents and …"

"Your father cut you off?" she finishes for me.

I nod. "And he paid Cara to … to break up with me. And she took … took the money."

Jordan puts her good arm around me and pulls me into her. My face buries in her chest. I cry for a long time, and she doesn't let go—as if she knows that I would fall apart if she did.

"None of them deserve you," she says, rubbing my back. I feel her hot breath on my ear. "You deserve the world. I would give it to you if I could."

Her words make me go still. I sniff and wipe my face with the sleeve of her sweater. Compassion wells in Jordan's dark-brown eyes. Her gaze is tender, filled with warmth and understanding. I love her so much.

My own gaze drops to her mouth. Her lips are full of promise and pleasure. I can't put a number to how many times I've thought about them grazing my skin and exploring my body.

I lick my lips and look back up. When our eyes meet again, I know Jordan knows what I want. There's no way she can't know now. All my defenses are down. My eyes silently plead for her to kiss me.

Jordan's brows furrow. She teeters an invisible line, still unsure.

Heart jackhammering, I decide for us both. Leaning in, I kiss her and groan when she kisses me back. A rush of pleasure pools to my core. My fantasies did not prepare me for how good it would feel. I never imagined how desperate and hungry her kiss would be, like she's also been dreaming of this and needs to make the most of it before waking up.

My lips part and her tongue slips in. I tug her closer. Needing her closer. My nails scratch down her neck. Jordan shudders and breaks away. "Noémie … we can't—"

I raise a finger to her mouth, hushing her protest and crawl into her lap. "I need this. I need you." It's the truth, and I'm done denying myself. If this is a mistake, I don't care. All that matters is now—this moment. I'm going to make it count. I'm going to fuck Jordan so good, she'll never think of anyone else.

"You don't know what you're saying—you're upset."

I press a kiss against her ear. "You don't know the first thing about what I want." If Jordan only knew how much I thought about her. What if I told her about my dreams? What if I told her that I get off almost every night thinking about her fucking me on the desk in the back office? What if I told her I wanted her from the moment I first laid eyes on her?

Jordan's hand slips under the sweater. Her fingers brush over my skin, making me ache for her to touch me.

I kiss her neck, and when I bite down on her earlobe, she gasps. "Fuck. If you keep this up, I won't be able to control myself."

"I have no plans of stopping," I say, pulling back just a bit. "Unless you want to stop. Tell me you don't want this."

Jordan's mouth falls open, but she doesn't say anything. I can tell she wants this too, her eyes betray her. Beneath me, her body hums like a plucked violin string. For whatever reason, she's still holding back.

Shifting forward in her lap, I kiss her again. "I can't stop thinking about the party," I murmur against her lips. "I wanted you to rip down my thong, push your fingers inside me, and fuck me in the washroom stall."

"You did?" I don't know why she sounds so confused. That night at the party, I couldn't have been more obvious. How she ever thought that she forced herself on me is unfathomable.

"Yes." I run my hand through her hair. It's even softer than I imagined. "You're such a distraction. It's annoying."

"You're the distraction," she shoots back. Her hand drops to my ass. She squeezes.

I suck in a breath and flip my hair over a shoulder. "I want you on the bed."

Jordan chuckles. The sound warms me from the inside out. "Is that an order?"

"If you're into that, then yes, it's an order." I wonder what Jordan's into. There's almost nothing I wouldn't let her do to me. Cara's kink had been spanking, but she lacked technique to smack me hard enough without a crop. I don't think Jordan would need a crop or a paddle. There's strength in her hands and body. A mental portrait fills my mind: Jordan bending me over her knee. She slaps my ass, and I cry out because the pain feels so good.

I realize that I don't really want to order her around. I want Jordan to dominate me. I want her to take control and tease and fuck me until I forget my name. I've always been a selfish lover, preferring to receive than give.

Slipping off her lap, I yank off her hoodie and the shirt beneath. My bra is sheer orange lace. Jordan stares at my tits. Her gaze smoulders, and I bask in the heat of it on my skin. This is what I need. What I've always needed. Jordan's eyes on me, praising me. Lusting for me.

I wish she would say something—give a voice to the desire reflected on her face. "Like what you see?" I ask, cupping my breasts and running my hands down my body.

Jordan bites her lower lip and nods. She sits up a little straighter when my fingers go to the button on my shorts.

She's eager for me to slide them down. I consider if I should make her wait, but decide not to. I'm too impatient. We can play games another day.

Merde, I'm already thinking of next time. Will there even be one?

According to Jordan, she gets bored easily and doesn't do relationships. Me, I'm not interested in being strung along. I don't want to be like Sarah—her ex-roommate and best friend. I don't want to be in Samira's shadow.

I'll just have to make it that good for Jordan. I need to get her hooked on me. I need to make her as obsessed with me as I am with her.

I undo the button. My gaze locks with Jordan's as I shimmy them slowly down my legs. She sucks in a visible breath. "I thought I told you that I wanted you on the bed," I say firmly.

"Noémie, I—"

"Why are you talking? Did I say you can talk?" I smile at her to mask the fact that I'm actually taking this seduction quite seriously. Yes, I want Jordan to take me every way possible, but before that, I will worship her body with my mouth. I will mess with her until she begs. I will fuck her so good that she wants me. Only me.

Hesitating, Jordan follows my directions. She gets on the bed. Her expression changes. Desire still lights her eyes, but she's frowning slightly. Maybe she doesn't like being ordered around.

"Noémie," she says. The crease between her brows deepens. "I don't like to be touched."

Well, that's a plot twist I wasn't expecting—Jordan's a

touch-me-not? Tamara had been one too. Anything below the neck had been off limits. For most of our encounter, she'd kept my hands tied. She'd taken her pleasure in giving pleasure, and I'd lived for every moment of it. If Jordan wants a pillow princess, I can be that for her. I can power bottom with the best of them. And if I am being completely honest with myself, it suits me better. I've always been a greedy lover, which often put me at odds with most of my partners who were switches. Cara had always been on my case about not touching her enough. Her constant complaints made sex feel like a chore.

"Okay," I say. "Do you not like to be touched everywhere or just …" I stare at Jordan's crotch.

"Just there," she says, scratching the back of her neck and diverting her gaze as if she's ashamed.

I want to tell her that there's nothing to be ashamed about. But that might ruin the mood, so I say instead, "Thanks for telling me." Remembering her earlier confession, I feel my anger flare. Does she not like to be touched because of what happened? If I ever find out who hurt her, I will put a hit on them.

"You're okay with that?" Jordan frowns at me.

I frown right back at her. "Why wouldn't I be okay with it?"

"Because it's weird."

"No, it isn't, and I hope no one ever made you feel like it is," I say a little too forcefully. It's hard not to be annoyed. There's nothing wrong with her. I hate that she thinks there is. I hate how vulnerable she looks. She's trying to take up less space in the room. Her shoulders hunch.

"It's why Samira and I broke up," she reveals, looking down at her lap.

Merde! I snort. Of course, it was Jordan's ex who filled her head with nonsense. "She's an idiot, and she knows it. She regrets letting you go. Her eyes give her away—the way she looks at you." I remember how Samira stared at Jordan on Thanksgiving. The woman hadn't tried to hide her desire, and the moment I had my back turned she cornered Jordan. I don't want to guess at what they'd gotten up to in the bathroom, but the images creep beyond the edges of my mind.

Pushing them away, I grit my teeth. "If we're done talking about your ex, I assume you have a strap. Where is it?"

Jordan's chin snaps up. That got her attention. The heat is back in her eyes. Good.

She clears her throat. "Top dresser drawer—in the closet."

I go to her closet and almost sigh at all the black clothing. When Jordan, and I are serious, the first thing I'm doing is taking her shopping. She needs at least a few pieces with colour.

I open the drawer. My eyes widen. There are ropes, and clamps and handcuffs. I see drip candles and gags and tape. There are a few vibrators, and anal plugs, and of course, there's a crop—no paddle though. Is this what she really gets up to with all the strays she's with? My hands tighten on the drawer.

Off to the side is a leather harness and three dildos. The smallest one in size and girth is black and made of a very firm material, so I write it off. The next size up is brown. It would be perfect if it didn't look so damn realistic. The largest is a fun hue of purple and curved at a slight angle.

The silicone is semi-hard. It's been awhile, but I think I can take it.

Closing the drawer, I return to Jordan with the purple toy and harness. My heart beats fast like a whisk whipping meringue. She doesn't take her eyes off me as I climb onto the mattress and crawl towards her. "Lie on your back."

Jordan complies. Her breaths come heavy.

I drop my loot, and my hands slide up her calves. Her skin is buttery smooth.

It's incredible that this is happening. For so many years, I could only fantasize about being with her in this way. Now it's happening. I tell myself not to overthink it. If I do, my nerves will ruin everything. So much is riding on this first time, and I need Jordan to leave this experience addicted.

I help her out of her basketball shorts. Beneath, she's wearing black Calvin Klein boxer briefs. Fuck, she's hot. My hands skim over the thick band. "Je veux tellement que tu me baises," I whisper in her ear.

"Hmmm?" She gives me a look, asking me to explain.

"I said, I want you to fuck me." I tear off her shirt and let my hands roam over her body—everywhere I've dreamt of touching but never could. She's got the most beautiful brown skin. I want to kiss every inch that she'll let me. Her shoulders are strong. Her stomach is flat. Her tits look so perfectly round in her sports bra. Never has a woman made me feel so much. We've barely done anything, and I'm soaked for her.

Jordan raises up on her good arm. "How do I say, I want you to come on my tongue in French?"

I shove her back down on the mattress. "Je veux que tu viennes sur ma langue."

Jordan tries to repeat. The attempt is egregious, but that doesn't matter. Her words undo me, making me shiver. It's hard to breathe. "Is that what you want?" My voice sounds foreign to me, husky and warm. "Do you want me to come on your face?"

"Fuck yes," Jordan says. She grabs my waist. I don't resist when she pulls me forward.

It takes a bit of manoeuvring to get in position without knocking her cast, but soon I'm straddling her face. Her breath tickles my skin in the most delicious way. I bite down on my lip in anticipation.

Jordan groans and nuzzles my thighs. "You're so wet for me." There's wonder in her voice, like she really can't believe it.

"I am … for you."

She makes a sound—a cross between a growl and a moan. Then her lips are on my skin, and she's kissing and nipping at my thighs, and it feels so good. My eyes shut. Needing support, I brace against the headboard.

Jordan teases me. Her fingers bite into my ass. She drives me insane with her mouth, applying pressure and heat everywhere but where I need it.

"I need your mouth on my clit," I tell her.

She rewards me. Her hot tongue licks down the length of my panties.

"Fuck!" I toss my head back as my body spasms.

Jordan slips my underwear down. Barrier removed, she has at me. Again and again. Her tongue glides over my pussy. My eyes roll into the back of my head when she falls into a rhythm. She's sucking and licking and circling my clit. The woman is driving me wild. It's almost too intense, and then it's not enough. I ride her face, needing more friction. Chasing that sensation.

Jordan sucks me harder. Licks me harder. "I'm … so close," I gasp. My grip tightens on the headboard. She doesn't falter. She keeps up her pace. Flicking, tugging, and making me crazy with her tongue.

Eyes clenching, I bite my lip. The feeling builds. I'm so … so close. It's Jordan's feral moan—her pleasure in giving me pleasure—that sends me over. I don't stop grinding, rubbing my wet pussy against her face as the heat washes over my body. All my muscles tense.

"Fuck!" I cry out. I come so hard that I swear I go deaf in one ear for a moment.

Every part of me is sensitive. I push Jordan's face away and collapse on the bed beside her. I squeeze my legs together and try to settle my breaths. My skin is sticky, red, and hot.

I'm barely recovered when Jordan shoves a hand down the waistband of her boxers. She's touching herself. My mouth goes dry. "Can I watch?"

Nodding, Jordan pushes down her boxers. My breath hitches. She's so fucking perfect. Jordan's not waxed like I am, but the hair is buzzed short. I'm not sure why I expected her to have an overgrown bush. Everything about Jordan is tidy. It makes sense that her need for order would extend to all her body hair.

Jordan touches herself, and for a few seconds, I just stare mesmerized. It doesn't matter that I just came. My desire flares back to life. I ache for more and drop my fingers to my clit. "You're so fucking hot," I say, rubbing myself.

Jordan's eyes narrow on me. "I want to watch you fuck yourself with your fingers."

Without delay, I push two fingers inside my pussy and moan. Jordan groans. Her head falls back on the pillow. I like that she likes watching me fuck myself.

I adjust my position, spreading my legs wide so she can see better. Jordan licks her lips. I lick mine. Our eyes connect as we fuck ourselves. That warming feeling builds again as I ram my fingers deeper and faster.

It's hard to imagine Jordan doing this with someone else. This chemistry between us, it has to be special. She must feel it too.

"Fuck!" Jordan's back arches. Her eyes clench shut. She's always so guarded. It's so hot to witness her breaking apart.

Not really interested in bringing myself to climax, I withdraw my fingers and turn on my side to look at her. Jordan's chest rapidly rises and falls as she comes down. She's so beautiful.

"You ... didn't come," she says, between breaths.

"I thought I was clear earlier." My gaze darts to the discarded strap. "I want you to fuck me."

Jordan reaches for it. I stop her with a hand on her shoulder. "Not yet." I move over, snuggling up beside her and dropping my head to her chest. Her skin is hot and coated in sweat. I think about wiping her down with my tongue. I think about taking the fingers she'd used to get off into my mouth and sucking them. I want to taste her, but I'm not sure if she'd be okay with that.

I lightly graze her cast. "How's your arm feeling?"

"I guess it hurts a bit." She shrugs. "It's bearable."

Her answer doesn't surprise me. Jordan tends to downplay everything. She's such a closed book, and I wish she would open up and let me read her pages. We are very much alike in that way. There's a lot more I could share with her. Maybe I can start to be more honest about my feelings and problems. Maybe she's the person who I'd feel comfortable revealing my secrets. Maybe the conversations I don't want to have with myself I can have with her. So many maybes.

Sighing, I trace the stitching on her sports bra. "When I got the call that you were in an accident, I … I just about lost my mind," I admit. "It was like reliving my worst memory."

"Your sister?"

I nod because I had thought about Antoinette. Mostly, I worried about Jordan. I'd been so worried about losing her. Even now, just remembering, overwhelms me.

"Hey, I'm okay," she whispers.

"I know. I'm being dumb." I sniff. "Sorry."

She wraps her arm around me, holding me like I'm precious. "Don't ever apologize for your feelings. They're valid," she says, brushing her lips against my forehead. I didn't realize that my eyes are watering until she wipes tears away with her thumb. Her touch is so gentle, it melts my heart.

Jordan lifts my chin. She kisses me slow and deliberately —like I matter to her, like she really cares for me. If this is how she kisses everyone, I can see why they stay stuck in her web. It scares me, not knowing where we stand. Not knowing if there's a chance for us.

My thoughts cut off when Jordan unclasps my bra. She dips her head and bathes my breasts with attention. I love the way her tongue swirls over my nipples. Pulling back a bit, she asks, "Do you want it now?"

Nodding eagerly, I swallow.

Jordan reaches for the harness and hops off the bed. I consider asking her if she needs help putting it on, but I'd probably just get in the way.

When it's on, I get on my knees and meet her at the edge of the bed. The dildo presses into my stomach. It looks a little intimidating from this viewpoint. Like, I'm sure I've taken bigger before, but I'm out of practice.

"Want me to get the lube?" Jordan asks.

"I don't think I need it," I lie. Wait? Why am I lying about this? Lube is my favourite thing in the world. I almost always needed it with Cara.

Merde, I can only imagine how Jordan will look at me when she tries to fuck me with that thing and she can't get it in because I'm too tight. And what will she think? She'll probably laugh at me for being so ambitious, and I'll be mortified. I'll be the worst lay that she's ever had, and she'll never want to do this again. I can't let that happen.

Needing to buy some time, I wrap a fist around the faux cock and begin stroking it.

Jordan draws in a sharp breath, and her lips part the slightest bit. She likes what I'm doing. Tamara had been really into it too.

"I'm so wet for you," I say, lowering my lips on the toy. Jordan's jaw drops, and she hisses like I've actually touched her when I take it in my mouth. I put on a show for her, licking the shaft and taking half of it down my throat. I flip my hair over my shoulder so she can get a better view. Her dark eyes sparkle as she looks down on me. I will do anything to bring her pleasure.

"Fuck, Noémie …"

"Do you like it when I suck you off?" I ask. The purple shaft glistens from my spit.

"Yes."

"I wish I could take all of you in my mouth, but you're so big."

"Fuck, your dirty talk is going to be the end of me," she says.

Merde, turning her on is turning me on. So much so that I'm suddenly aching to be filled. "Good, that's my goal," I say, smiling up at her.

I ease onto my back and spread my legs. I'm dripping for her. I really might not need the lube.

Jordan climbs on top of me. I love the weight of her and how our bodies fit together. She kisses me as she feeds the tip inside me.

I jerk, grabbing her shoulders.

"Too much?" She asks.

I shake my head. "No, it just feels so good. I need all of you. Please." It's not a complete lie. There's pain, but it's a drop in the bucket compared to the throb between my thighs.

I'm so tight, but Jordan takes her time with me. She works the cock in slowly. She slides it out and back in repeatedly, sinking a little deeper each time. It feels delicious.

I writhe beneath her. My fingers dig and scrape against her back as she stretches me.

It becomes impossible not to unlock the vault of my heart. I confess to everything I've been keeping from her. But knowing she won't understand, I say it all in French. I tell her that I've wanted her from the moment I first saw her. I tell her that she's all I ever think about. I tell her that I love her. Over and over.

When Jordan thrusts the shaft all the way inside me, my confessing stops because I forget how to speak. I'm so stretched, and it feels so good. Nothing has ever felt so good.

I grind beneath her, needing more. Jordan picks up the pace. She fucks me hard and fast, the tip hitting me deep. I never want her to stop. No one has ever made me feel this way. Sex with Tamara had been amazing, but it wasn't like this.

"Fuck, Jordan!" My legs wrap around her back. At the new angle, she's sinks even deeper. "You feel so good."

Jordan leans forward and captures my lips. Our tongues meet. She pumps her hips faster. I match her tempo, keeping up with her strokes. She's fucking me harder than I've ever been fucked. It's delicious. I never want her to stop. The tension builds and keeps building until I shatter.

I cry out, and my head slams back. Wave after wave of pleasure hits me. My legs lock Jordan in place. The contractions take forever to subside.

Jordan gently extracts the toy and rolls off me onto her back. She's breathing like she's just finished a marathon. A large smile breaks out over her face as she stares up at the ceiling.

My breaths are just as ragged. She's less than an arm's length away and that feels too far. I close the gap. Curling up next to her, I rest my head on her shoulder.

Still grinning, she tilts her head down to look at me. There's a tug on my heart.

I touch her face, brushing her cheek with my thumb. Her expression melts with tenderness, and I feel held by her soft gaze. The way she's looking at me now makes everything feel real. What's between us, it's more than just attraction. It's got to be. "I love you, Jordan," I hear myself say, the truth tumbling out. My heart freezes as my declaration hangs in the air, awaiting her reply.

Jordan responds with a frown. She doesn't say anything.

The quiet chisels a gulf between us, and the weight of nothing cracks me in two. Before I spoke, I was warm from afterglow. Now, I'm incredibly cold and heavy. The back of my eyes burn. A lump forms in my throat.

"I have to use the washroom," I manage to say coolly— like she didn't just pummel my heart. I bolt to the ensuite. There I break down wholly and completely in silence.

THIRTY-SEVEN

The plane is preparing to land. I stare out of the window. With every second, the tropical terrain below renders clearer.

For the duration of the flight, when I wasn't wiping tears back, I found myself thinking about Cara, of all people. We were together for two years. In the end, if it weren't for her betrayal and my father's role in it, I don't think I would have broken down so hard. If our relationship died of natural causes, there's a chance I wouldn't have mourned. I always knew we weren't meant for each other. She was always the safe option. She always cared more. She always loved more.

And now that I find myself in a similar position, I can understand how feeling more for someone can drive you to irrationality.

Felix was right, love is an arena. Cara probably took my father's money to regain some power in the game that was our relationship. Her move backfired though. Instead of checkmate, she lost me. In the end, I was hurt but not defeated.

I showed my cards way too soon with Jordan, and without uttering a single word, she dealt a critical hit. I've never played combat games, but I'm pretty sure my health bar is blinking near zero. The only thing I could think to do to recover after bawling my eyes out—for God only knows how long—was flee.

Jordan never came to check on me. When I exited the bathroom, she was asleep. Seeing her so at peace had me sobbing all over again.

I ran to my room and called Felix. I told him everything and then announced that I was grabbing the next flight I could get to Honolulu.

"If you're going to be heartbroken, better to be on a beach sipping sangria," had been his response.

I couldn't have agreed more.

Céline yawns when the plane lands with a thud. I scratch her head.

I move ghoulishly slow through customs until the lady at the desk asks me to remove my sunglasses. "Why?" I snap.

"I need to verify your identity," she says, tapping on the picture of me on my passport.

"Ostis de criss de tabernacle." I snatch off the sunglasses, the mask that made me appear somewhat normal. Now everyone can see my puffy red eyes. I glare at the woman.

She glances at me and then back down at my passport before nodding that I'm good to proceed.

I shove my sunglasses back on.

Felix arranged for the hotel limousine to pick me up from

the airport. The driver takes my bags, and I slip from the hot, humid air into the air-conditioned vehicle. I hold onto Céline like she's my lifeline.

It takes half an hour to get to the resort. It's just like every other luxurious hotel I've stayed at and doesn't leave an impression on me. In my dark mood, I could be walking through heaven's gates and not give a shit.

The concierge is way too happy and chatty. I couldn't care less about the catamaran or the Mauka and Makai Ritual spa treatment. All I want is a bed.

Finally, I'm being led to the suite Felix reserved for us.

The two-bedroom suite is on the seventeenth floor. Felix greets me with a flute of wine the moment I push through the door. "Glad you could finally make it," he says, smiling.

Setting Céline down, I grab the offering and drain its contents. Behind me, the hotel workers unpack my luggage from the trolley. Céline yips excitedly at them.

I follow my friend into the seating area. He drops down into the fluffy white sofa and sips from his own glass of wine. "How was your flight?"

"Turbulent." I reach for the opened bottle of Chardonnay and top my empty glass before taking a seat beside him.

The hotel workers leave after asking if there is anything we need. Felix answers for us, waving them away and telling them we are good. When they are gone, I remove my sunglasses, clipping them on the neck of my shirt.

"You look like shit," Felix comments.

"Think I don't know that?" I swallow a large mouthful of wine and lean back against the cushions. The suite is airy and bright, with beachy wood floors and white shiplap walls.

It's nothing spectacular, but the expansive private terrace that looks over the ocean is nice … I guess.

"I'm sorry about Jordan," he says.

I shrug. "It's not like I didn't know what would happen the moment we hooked up," I say, the words coming out choked. "You know … she called me right before I boarded the plane, and … she really doesn't care." I remember seeing her number light up my phone, and for a moment, I had hoped. But she had nothing to say to me and wished me a safe flight.

"Oh no … come here." Felix drapes an arm over my shoulder and pulls me close. He kisses my forehead. "I'm so sorry. Jordan sucks and you are incredible. She's a fucking idiot if she can't see that."

"I'm the idiot." I wipe my eyes and sniff. "I shouldn't have slept with her. Why did I have to tell her I loved her? How can I face her again? Merde, we live together. What am I going to do?"

Felix sighs. "You could always ask her to move out."

I move out of his embrace. "I can't do that."

He arches a brow. "Why's that?"

"She has nowhere to go."

"And how is that your fault? She's an adult. It's not your job to look after her."

Shaking my head, I look down at my wine glass. "I'm not going to ask her to move out," I say. "I will figure something out."

Felix snorts. "Figure something out," he repeats. "You mean you're going to torture yourself. Jordan's not worth it. There are other gorgeous studs out there."

I finish my wine. Setting the empty flute down on the coffee table, I stand. "I have a headache. Where's my room?"

Felix cocks his head at a set of doors. "I made us reservations for dinner," he says.

My hand pauses on the door handle. "Go without me. I don't think I'll be hungry." I push into the room and sink down on the mattress. I wish it could absorb me, swallow me up.

The next few days, I fall back into bad habits. I don't take my pills. I only leave the bed to use the washroom or attend to Céline. I guess my kink is self-inflicted suffering. When I'm not sleeping, I scroll through Jordan's Instagram timeline. I watch her not-so-good art videos repeatedly. I stare at picture after picture of her. There are so many of her at parties. There are so many different women, but there's a familiar woman who keeps making an appearance—the blond chick Jordan had been fucking in the washroom stall all those years ago. I grit my teeth whenever I see her. She's tagged as @musclemommy91. Her account is private, so I can't snoop further.

There aren't any posts of us together. Not a single one. I haven't made posts about Jordan either, but it's different. Jordan is obviously gay. I'm not sure how it would land with my following if I started posting photos of us. People would've speculated that we were together. They would've asked questions, demanding to know how I identified. So no, I haven't posted any photos of us. I never wanted the scrutiny.

But I have a whole album in my phone labelled Jordan. In it, most pictures are of her playing with or holding Céline. I love the picture of her scowling in her Mario costume on Halloween, but my favourite photo is the one Wayne took of us standing in front of the glittering tree at the Christmas market. We look like a couple. We look so perfect together. We look happy.

On Thursday, Wayne blows up my phone. The bright screen annoys me, so I shut it down and decide to go on a technology cleanse. I need to quit stalking Jordan's socials.

Felix keeps bugging me, but he's less persistent than my brother, and I'm pretty sure he's met someone who's keeping him busy. At least, I'm pretty sure I heard him bring some man over to the suite a few times.

On Saturday, Felix successfully talks me into leaving the bed to go down to the beach. The sun's rays are hot on my skin. The humidity is obscene and makes me want to take a cold shower. I order drink after drink. Men flex in their swim trunks to get my attention. Their preening is annoying, but it's easy enough to ignore. I close my eyes and bake in the heat.

I start feeling more like a person around Wednesday when Felix relays a call he had with Claude about a few venues he's been looking at.

"Why is Claude calling you?" I ask, sipping my coffee. My appetite is finally back, and we are eating breakfast at the hotel's main restaurant on the patio. "When did you two become so close?"

Felix rolls his eyes. "He's only calling me because you haven't been answering your phone. Did you lose it?"

I shake my head. "Nope, I've been trying out a technology detox."

Felix wipes his mouth with a napkin and drops it on the table. "Well, maybe it's time you got back online. Have a look at the locations Claude sent you."

Back in my hotel room, I grab my phone from off the nightstand and hold down the power button. It buzzes like crazy with notifications. None are from Jordan, not even a message checking to see how I'm doing. It hurts.

There are like a hundred messages from Wayne. He's demanding I respond to him. He says it's urgent. Curious, I call him.

He picks up immediately. "What do you mean you slept with Jay and then flew out to Hawaii?!" he screams in my ear. "You know she thinks you and Felix are a thing. What the absolute fuck, Noémie?"

Once again, Jordan blabbed to Wayne about us. "That's her fault," I say. "I never told Jordan that Felix and I are together."

"Not saying anything is still lying," he says. "And she swears she heard you and Felix hooking up—"

"Ewww, Felix and I would never." My nose scrunches.

"That's what I told her, but she was not buying it."

I pinch my forehead. "Why does any of this matter? So fucking what if she thinks I'm with Felix?"

"So fucking what?" He snorts. "So fucking what if my poor Jay had a tantrum about you ditching her to be with your supposed boyfriend?"

Tantrum? I go very still. "Jordan doesn't have tantrums."

"I thought so too," Wayne says. "Just the other day, we had a line out the fucking door, and she stomped off the floor to the back office. I've never seen her so distressed, crying and—"

"Jordan was crying?" Giddiness bubbles in my veins. I should probably tamp it down. What does it say about me as a person that Jordan's anguish breathes new life into me?

"Isn't that what I just said?" I can practically hear Wayne's eye roll. "I guess your pussy is magic, 'cause I never saw Jay getting so twisted like this. God, and now I'm going to have to run a stupid marathon."

"Technically, you won the bet. I slept with her." I say, playing with the ends of my hair. "She doesn't love me."

"Yes, she does. Did you not hear anything I just told you?"

"She doesn't love me," I say again. Sighing, I fall back onto the mattress and stare up at the spinning ceiling fan.

"You two are so fucking annoying," Wayne says. "Jay loves you. She told me so."

I almost lose my grip on the phone. My heart stops. "She told you what?"

"To quote her exactly, she said, 'I'm in love with Noémie.'"

My eyes squeeze shut. Wayne better not be lying to me. "Well, that's news to me," I say. "She didn't say anything when I told her how I felt."

"Y'all are hopeless," Waynes says.

"I'm going to call her right now."

"Yeah, maybe don't do that."

I frown. "Why not?"

"She's mad at you."

"I get that," I say. "But I'll explain everything." If Wayne isn't lying to me, I need to talk to her. I need to hear Jordan say the words to believe it.

"No, like, she's really mad at you. I've never seen her like this." Wayne goes quiet for a moment, and then adds, "She knows about the bet."

I bolt upright. "What? You told her!"

"I had no choice," Wayne says. "Fuck, I need blood pressure medication after being stuck in the middle of this for so long. Jay's my friend too, and she was hurting. I couldn't not tell her."

"Fuck, I need to talk to her." My hands shake. I breathe out an unsteady breath. "I'm going to call her now." I hang up on Wayne and tap on Jordan's number.

A picture of her lights up my screen as the phone rings. Each ring lands like a punch. I'm directed to voice mail. I call her again. Jordan doesn't answer. I call her again and again. She doesn't pick up. I revert to sending text messages. Hours later, she still hasn't read them.

THIRTY-EIGHT

An envelope with Jordan's key in it greets me when I get home, rolling my suitcase through the door. I run up the stairs to confirm what I already know: Jordan's moved out. The bookshelf is bare. The closet is empty. The bed is neatly made up. Everything looks the way it did on the day I first showed it to her.

Wayne told me she was mad, but I can't quite believe she's this pissed. I know her financial position isn't that great, and the renters market in Toronto is horrendous. Where did she go? How'd she find a place so soon?

I call her. Jordan doesn't pick up. I leave her a voice message. "Seriously, you just left? What the fuck Jordan?" Hanging up, I shoot her another text. Not sure why I bother. She hasn't read any of the million I sent her over the past forty-eight hours.

Felix was annoyed with me when I bought an earlier flight back to Toronto. "There's really no reason for you to jet out now," he said. I didn't listen to him and continued packing up my things.

"You know, I should have thought of this earlier," he said. "Sleeping with her and then making her think you chose me in the end. We could have broken her in earlier if we'd tried this tactic."

"Seriously, Felix, shut the fuck up."

"Isn't this what you wanted—confirmation of her feelings for you?"

"Yes, but not like this," I said. After that, I ignored my friend and he left our suite.

It's after six, so I can't just storm into Grind That Bean and insist that Jordan speak with me. Sensing my dark mood, Céline whines and scratches her nails on my calves. I pick her up and kiss her head.

I call Wayne. "Where's Jordan?" I demand when he answers.

"Hi to you too," he replies.

"Where is she? Why didn't you tell me she moved out?"

"Because it's news to me," he says. "You're not the only person she's ignoring. She's pissed at me too. It's been hell working with her."

"Any idea where she went?"

"Sarah moved back to Toronto," he offers. "My guess, she's camping out with her."

Sarah—Jordan's best friend, and the ex-roommate she's slept with God only knows how many times. *Merde.* I stab a hand through my hair and bite my lip. "Any idea where Sarah's living?"

"I might know."

"What's her address?"

"Maybe it's best for you to just drop it," Wayne says. "Give Jordan time to cool off."

"I swear I will make a scene when I come into the coffee shop on Monday if you don't tell me."

Wayne folds and tells me.

Deciding that I look a mess, I take a shower and wash my hair. I fret about what to wear for way too long, but land on an asymmetric sunset orange Versace mini dress that shows off my boobs. I do my makeup and decide it's not good enough. I wipe it all off and start over.

My reflection pleases me. The short time spent in Hawaii blessed my skin with a tasty tan. I'm banking that Jordan will not be able to stay mad at me when I look so delicious.

When I finally step outside, it's almost nine. I speed over to Sarah's place. She lives in Parkdale in an older brown brick building with long white balconies.

I park my car and wait in the lobby until someone exits to slip through the entrance. I'm not trying to buzz and alert Jordan that I'm here. Knowing her, she'll probably make an escape down the stairs rather than speak with me.

I ride the elevator up to the eleventh floor and knock on the door with the number Wayne gave me. My stomach ties into knots.

Finally, the knob turns. When the door is flung open, my jaw clenches. I'm staring down at the blond woman—@musclemommy91. Sarah's the woman Jordan had been hooking up with in the drag bar public washroom. The revelation makes the world swim. I hate how cute Sarah is, with her shiny blond hair and faultless skin. She wears a baggy white shirt and a pair of plaid boxers. Her feet are bare.

"Oh wow," she says, giving me a once over. She rubs a hand over her jaw. Her honey-brown eyes sparkle, and a large smile reveals dimples. "You must be Noémie. Gosh, you look even better than your photos."

Not interested in small talk, I don't return her smile. I fold my arms over my chest. "Where's Jordan?" I try to see past the woman and into the apartment.

"Out." Sarah chews on gum loudly.

"Where?"

"How about you come inside?" She takes a step back, making space for me. "I want to know your intentions."

Intentions. I glare at her. "Where is Jordan?"

Sarah doesn't answer me. Instead, she leaves the front door with the expectation that I follow her inside. Annoyed, I do. Bending down, I remove my strappy Gucci heels.

Sarah drops down into a futon that looks like it might collapse if more than three people sit on it. She props her feet up on a coffee table littered with cannabis paraphernalia. The whole apartment reeks of weed. It's sparsely furnished, with unadorned light-grey walls. I see boxes neatly stacked in a corner, which I guess belong to Jordan.

"Have a seat." Sarah waves at an arm chair across from her.

I don't sit. "Can you just tell me where she is?"

"Why?" Sarah reaches for a glass pipe and lighter. She sparks a flame under the transparent bowl and takes a deep pull. Smoke billows around her. "My girl doesn't want to see you."

Her girl? My nostrils flare. "I need to talk to her," I say. "I need to explain."

"Explain what?" Sarah leans back and takes another hit. "Why you lied to her about being into women and faked a relationship with a man to make her jelly? Do you even know how many levels of fucked up that is? No, I don't think Jay wants to hear it."

"I never faked a relationship with a man," I say. "Felix is my friend. Jordan came to that conclusion all on her own. I never told her that he was my boyfriend, and if she had asked, I would have told her."

"So you had no clue that she thought you and this guy were together?

"I knew." I grit my teeth. "But why was it up to me to say anything? Especially when she pretty much ignored me for weeks."

"Sounds to me like Jay had a good reason to ignore you," Sarah says. "Want some?" She holds out the pipe.

I shake my head. "Just tell me where she is … please."

"Tell me why you never told her that you're a lesbian."

"I'm not a lesbian."

Sarah's eyebrows lift. "Bisexual."

"I don't like men."

"So you're gay … a lesbian?"

"I'm not straight. That's what I am." Groaning, I decide that I do need to sit down.

Sarah chuckles and lights up again. "I think I get it now. You're still half in your closet, not ready to fully commit," she says. "If that's the case, you should just leave things with Jay as they stand. She will not be with someone who isn't out and proud. She's been there, done that before and has sworn never to hide a relationship again."

I cross my legs and cross my arms. "Jordan doesn't do relationships, so it's a shock to hear that she's ever hid one."

"You really don't know anything about her then."

Her words are a slap to the face. My cheeks burn. I've always known that there's so much more to Jordan than she's let me see, and it hurts to have someone point that out so clearly. "I want to know her," I whisper.

Sarah blinks. Her features soften. "Jay will kill me for saying this, but she only sleeps around because …"

"Because what?" My hands drop to the armrests, and I sit up in my seat.

"Never mind, it doesn't matter."

"It matters to me," I say. "You asked me why I didn't tell Jordan that I liked women. The answer is as simple as I was worried the moment I told her it would have signalled to her that I was interested."

Sarah frowns. "But weren't you interested in her?"

"Yes, but I don't do casual sex—at least, not with someone I have feelings for," I admit. "And I didn't want to be like every other woman Jordan strings along."

Sarah flinches like I struck a nerve. She diverts her gaze and sucks hard on the tip of her pipe. For a long time, she doesn't say anything.

I hope I didn't offend her—that wasn't my intention. She is, after all, Jordan's best friend. If she hates me, it will not bode well for any future together.

Sighing, Sarah drops her pipe back down on the coffee table and rubs her eyes. "Samira—Jay's ex—put a lot of stupid thoughts in her head," she finally says. "Jay likes to say that every relationship she's been in has taught her a lesson, and Samira taught her that she's not good enough for anyone."

"That's complete bullshit."

"It is, isn't it?" Sarah's back to chewing hard on her gum. Her feet drop to the floor. She leans forward to grab a piece of paper trapped under a Ziplock bag filled with dried green buds. It's a pamphlet to a party. "Jay's going to be at this event tonight," she says, holding out the flyer.

"Thanks." I take it and stand.

Sarah shrugs. "I'm only helping you out because it's been a long time since I've seen anyone get under Jay's skin the way you have." Sarah sighs with her whole body. "She … she really likes you, and in some ways, you've been a great influence on her. Like, I know what you did, getting her in touch with that bigshot artist with the YouTube channel. I've tried for years to get Jay to show off her work with no success. Now she's doing it. Because of you."

"You really care about her," I say.

Sarah nods slowly. "I do."

"Thanks again." I head for the door.

"Hey, one more thing."

I stop and turn to face her.

Sarah smiles, but the expression doesn't reach her eyes. "I get how scary it can be facing who you really are," she says. "For years, I told everyone that I was bisexual because I thought it'd be more palatable to my folks, but each time I brought over another girl, I could tell they wished it was a man, and deep down I knew that would never happen. So coming out as a lesbian was a freeing experience. Not just for me, but for my parents too. Like, now they know where I stand, and they're getting more and more used to it."

"That's good for you. My situation is … different."

"I wasn't implying that our situations are the same. But for real, if you're not willing to make peace with who you are, Jay won't want to be in a relationship that pushes her back in the closet, and she doesn't deserve that."

THIRTY-NINE

I'm parked across the street from the party, drumming my fingers on the steering wheel. The conversation with Sarah plays on repeat in my head. She told me not to bother going after Jordan if I can't make peace with myself, but I don't know what that looks like.

I never gave a second thought to holding Jordan's hand in public. If we became official, would that change? I like to think nothing would, but I remember how I flinched and moved away any time Cara touched me when we were out of the house. Of course, back then, I was worried about my father finding out about us. Now, Hugo knows that I'm not straight—not his perfect daughter.

I have doubts that I have the courage to be what Jordan needs in a girlfriend. While I've tried to emulate my sister in so many ways, I'm nothing like her. I'm a coward. Where she was able to stare our father in the eyes and say, "I'm a lesbian," I don't think I ever could.

I don't think I like men at all. The stubble on their chins, the way they smell, the thick hair on their chests. It's not for me. Is that knowledge enough to stake a claim to lesbianism? Don't I have to love and appreciate all female bodies to have a right to the label? Fact is, I'm not attracted to all women. I have a very specific type, and I don't know if that's because, on some subconscious level, I deduce that a masculine presenting woman is dominant. Experience tells me that how someone looks isn't a true indicator of dominance. My short relationship with Jess taught me that.

It dawns on me that I'm actually thinking about my sexuality—something I've avoided doing for years. Why does growth feel so miserable?

I slump back in my seat and stare at the busy venue. Dull pink and blue lights flash out of the frosted windows. Jordan is in there doing only God knows what with God knows who.

Gritting my teeth, I fling open the car door and step into the cool night air. I've made my decision—I want Jordan. I won't hide our relationship, and if I'm ever asked to explain what I identify as …

I swallow. Why is it so hard to say?

A painful memory dislodges from somewhere deep in my mind. Antoinette and I are in her bedroom. We were watching an *L Word* episode on her laptop. "Tasha's cute," I said, leaning back against the cushions on her bed.

Antoinette snorted. "Figures you'd only think a woman presenting like a man is cute. I'll never understand why some lesbians only date women who look like men. It's like, why not date a man if that's what you're into."

"Clothes are just clothes," I said. "Out of them, they're still women. I don't think it's right to make that judgement."

"You're not a lesbian, Noémie." Antoinette scowled at me. "Stay in your lane. Your opinion isn't needed."

Another recollection resurfaces. I'm telling Antoinette about Travis. "I think I want to break up with him," I said. "I want something real, like what you have with Arlene."

"Travis is as good as you're going to get. Be happy that you have a boyfriend who actually seems to care about making you happy," my sister replied. "It's different being with women. Your partner isn't just your partner, they're your best friend. Don't expect to find that with a man."

"Maybe I should try dating women," I said.

"Women aren't something you try," Antoinette barked at me. "Straight girls like you are such a problem. Lesbians don't need you testing them out like they're a fad."

Finally, I replay our last real conversation. "You're so pathetic. I like girls, so now you like them too? Give me a fucking break. Quit hanging out in my shadow and build your own life," Antoinette said. "You aren't a lesbian."

So many times, Antoinette shut me down. So many times, she told me I wasn't like her. My sister drilled in my head that I couldn't possibly be a lesbian, and I clung to her words. Or maybe, it's more that I've always felt like a fraud—never pretty enough, never courageous enough, never gay enough.

I tremble on the sidewalk as I wrestle with my thoughts. Sniffing, I wipe my eyes and turn my head towards the venue. Jordan's in there, but I don't think I can face her like this. My makeup is probably ruined. The whole point was to approach her looking hotter than ever and with determination to win her back. Now I just feel so beaten down.

Yes, Antoinette was right—in a lot of ways I am nothing like her. But she was wrong. My attraction to women is real. My love for Jordan is real. It's not an act or imitation. I am a lesbian.

The word lands in my chest like a chef's knife, and I don't feel free. I want to throw up and retreat, crawl into bed and just sleep until enough time passes, until the label doesn't itch like a cheap wool sweater.

Somehow, I find the will to cross the street. Somehow, I force a smile at the bouncer. Somehow, I strut into the party with my head high. I hand over my coat and pay the fee. And when I turn to face the bar, there she is.

I lock eyes with Jordan and time forgets how to move.

She's not alone. Some random sucks on her neck like a lamprey. I shouldn't be shocked. But my heart didn't get the memo. It frosts over, pumping ice through my veins. I shiver. My lips press together, and my fists ball at my sides.

Jordan smirks at me. Smirks! And I know what she's going to do before she does it. I watch her grab the woman by her hair, pulling her in for a hard kiss. It's a horror show she's putting on just for me—to hurt me. I want to look away, but it's like seeing a pan catch on fire. I'm mesmerized by the flames and forget extinguishers exist. I could look away, but I don't.

Someone rams into me. I almost fall, but I'm caught. "So sorry," a man says.

"Don't touch me." I yank my arm back and push into the crowd.

I sag against a wall. Jordan remains in my line of sight. She's still at it. My blood boils.

Stabbing a frustrated hand through my hair, I think that if she wants to play games, I can too. How would she like it if I started making out with the first stranger to flag interest in me? It wouldn't take long for me to find someone. I could do it—hurt her right back. But that wouldn't get me what I want. It would only continue this cycle of pain.

The crowd is thick and the electronic music vibrates against my skin. I'm reminded of my wild days—the days I thought I needed to live life to the fullest for both me and Antoinette. Merde, I didn't know shit about living. I still don't know shit about it.

Jordan extracts herself from the woman. They are still standing too close, bumping shoulders as they put in their orders at the bar. Jordan looks over her shoulder—my guess is that she's searching for me. I don't think she'll be able to find me. Bodies on bodies block me.

The bartender cracks open two beers. Jordan grabs one. She takes a very long swig. The woman stares hungrily at her. They move off to the side of the bar and exchange a few words. The girl nods. Jordan hands over her drink to the girl and kisses her on the cheek.

My jaw clenches.

Jordan moves away from her and heads for the exit. I take that as my cue and push off the wall. I start to follow Jordan outside. But before I do, I can't help myself.

I approach the bar. "Hey," I say, forcing myself to smile brightly.

The girl eyes me curiously. She's cute, I guess, with her

curly black hair and dimpled cheeks. But everything about her is off the rack—nothing special. Or maybe that's a lie I'm telling myself to feel better.

For a quick second, she looks at my tits. I know my boobs look great tonight. I wore my best push-up bra, and I chose this dress for a reason. It leaves nothing to the imagination.

"Hey," she returns.

"I couldn't help but notice that you were with Jordan," I say.

"Yeah, so?" She stiffens and folds her arms.

"She's not going home with you," I say, fixing her with a look as sharp as my favourite chef knife. The girl takes the hint. Her face falls. If I was a good person, maybe I would regret adding, "Oh, babe, you really thought you had a chance with her? That's kind of precious." But I'm not a good person, and there's an insufficient balance tonight on the fucks I have to give. I don't care.

If the girl has a comeback, I don't stick around long enough to hear it. I rush after Jordan.

Outside, I find her easily. Her back is against a brick wall. She's staring up at the night sky like it's glittering with stars. The cigarette in her hand is burned down to the filter.

"Jordan!"

She blinks slowly and turns her head slightly in my direction. She looks away from me. Reaching into her pocket, she withdraws a pack of cigarettes and smacks a new one out of the carton. She shoves it between her lips.

"Jordan," I say again.

Jordan doesn't respond. She lights her cigarette, inhales and blows out a large cloud of smoke.

"Jordan, can you look at me? I'm trying to talk to you."

She stares down at the glowing end of her cigarette. Her voice, when she finally speaks, is colder than I've ever heard it. "What's there to talk about?"

I swallow. "Us."

Jordan's head snaps up. Her dark eyes sparkle with rage. "There is no us."

I've only seen her so angry once before—when she shoved Hailey. I hate knowing that I made her like this. Jordan isn't an angry person. She isn't a cruel person. But her behaviour back at the party—putting on a performance to make me jealous—was meant to hurt me.

I think we broke her, Felix said. I really hope that isn't true.

Hesitantly, I step towards her. "Don't say that, Jordan. Don't be like this."

"Be like what?" she asks, tossing her cigarette on the ground and stomping it out with her foot. "I'm not a game. My feelings aren't a game."

I bite my lip. "You're not a game. You've never been a game to me—"

"You bet Wayne that you could tie me down. You paraded Felix around me to make me jealous. Sounds like all I ever was to you was a game," she says, pushing off the wall a little too quickly. Unbalanced, she reaches out to right herself with her injured hand. "Shit," she cries out, cradling her cast-bound arm.

I surge forward to her side, but she stops me with a scalding look. Jordan closes her eyes. She's breathing heavy. Her body sways. I wonder how much she's had to drink. "Fuck, I need to sit down," she mumbles, stumbling forward.

I grab her arm to steady her. She doesn't resist, which tells me she's in a bad state. "Look, I'm parked across the street. We can sit in my car while we talk. Is that okay?"

Squinting, Jordan nods. She leans on me as we cross the street, and I help her into the passenger seat. By the time I slip into the driver's side, she's already passed out. Her forehead squishes against the window.

I take us home. She's barely conscious, and it's a struggle to get her to walk up the short flight stairs. Luckily for her, I have loads of experience getting drunk friends to safety. Excited to see Jordan, Céline barks like crazy. I keep ordering my dog to be quiet as I guide Jordan down the hallway.

I lay Jordan in the recovery position on the couch and put an empty garbage bin on the floor in case she needs it. I only leave her side to change out of my dress, take off my makeup and brush my teeth. I sit on the opposite end of the couch and hug my knees. At some point, I fall asleep too, but I wake as soon as light starts dripping through the windows.

Hours later, Jordan stirs. Groaning, she sits up.

Hopping up to my feet, I grab the glass of water I set out for her. "Here, have some water."

Jordan doesn't argue. She takes the glass and chugs down its contents. When it's empty, I take the glass from her and place it back down on the coffee table with shaking hands. I'm wired with anxiety.

She rubs her eyes. "Why am I here?"

"You passed out," I explain. "I'm assuming you were drinking while on your painkillers, which is never a good idea. Don't ask me how I know."

"Thanks for taking care of me," she grumbles, staring down at her lap.

I kneel in front of her and squeeze her thigh. "Of course, I would never leave you like that."

She snorts.

"Jordan, we need to talk."

"I don't want to." She huffs. "Talking won't change things. It won't change what you did."

"What I did was wrong. I should never have made that bet with Wayne. It was stupid and inconsiderate, and I'm so sorry," I say, meaning it.

I will her to look at me, but she doesn't. She stares out the window. "Why did you do it?" She asks, her voice sounding so far away. "I know why Wayne thinks you did it, but I want you to tell me."

"Because I'm a horrible person. Because it was a challenge. Because I was trying to find a way to rebuild my pride after what happened with Cara." The last reason, I whisper. "Because I wanted you."

Jordan finally looks at me. Her sharp gaze skewers me. "Everything between us was a lie. You lied about everything. I thought we were friends. I told you things I never talk about. I trusted you." Jordan's voice breaks a little, and she clears her throat. "And for what—a place in my bed? I've been told that I fuck everyone. If you wanted me to fuck you, all you had to do was ask."

Her words connect like a slap to my face. I rise to my feet with hands balled. "I didn't want you to fuck me. I wanted to get to know you. I wanted to be in your life," I snap. "I didn't want to be another name added to the long list of women you fuck and ghost."

Jordan glowers. "And you think that justifies you seducing me—"

"Seducing you?" I roll my eyes. "Merde, I was not trying to seduce you. If I was trying to seduce you, I would have walked around the house in lingerie."

"I'm not buying that all those elaborate dinners weren't part of your greater scheme to lock me down," Jordan shoots back.

"Maybe at first." I drop down on the couch beside her and sigh. "But then, I just did it because I liked cooking for you. I liked getting you to try new things. I just liked being with you."

Our legs touch, and she's not moving away. It gives me hope.

"You know, I started falling for you around Halloween," she confesses. Halloween—months ago. Jordan started catching feelings for me months ago! Wayne told me as much, but I hadn't believed him. How aggravating. If only she had told me.

"But I thought you were straight, and I valued our friend-ship," she continues. "I loved you so much it hurts."

"Loved," I repeat. My eyes sting. "You don't love me anymore?"

Jordan shakes her head and stands. "I need to go."

"Really, you're not going to answer my question? You're just going to go?" I shout. "You're going to run away because of some stupid bet that I wasn't even taking all that seriously?"

Jordan doesn't say anything. She heads for the front door.

I go after her. "I love you, Jordan. I want to be with you, and I know you want to be with me too. Let's try to work this out. Please."

She stops walking and glares at me. "We can't be together."

"Why not?" I'm full blown crying now, and it's the ugly kind. I feel the snot dripping.

"Because I can't trust you," she says, blinking like she's on the verge of tears too. "And I don't think I ever can." She grabs her jacket and walks out the door.

FORTY

Patrice and I stumble into the booth. Giggling, we crash down on the white couch. She grabs the bottle of Grey Goose from the ice bucket and tips some in her mouth, then gestures for me to tilt my head back. I do, opening my mouth wide. The vodka slides down like embers and warms my stomach.

"I missed you so much, Nomi," Patrice says, hugging onto my arm.

I say, "I missed you too." I'm not sure I mean it, but my smile is so bright, no one could accuse me of lying.

Sophie, Claire, and Lily drop onto the opposite sofa. The whole gang is back, reunited for the VELD Music Festival. Our booth sits on a raised platform. We've got a great view of the main stage. The headliners are Cosmic Gate, Crankdat and Dana Vicci. I'm most excited for Tiësto though. Right now Loud Luxury is performing a mix of their hit "If Only I." I tune out the lyrics—they hit too close to home.

I'm trying to forget about Jordan. I'm trying to get over it. I'm trying to move on. And yet I've slipped back into old patterns. At least I'm not in bed. At least I'm outside. At least I'm not alone.

"Where are your boyfriends?" Patrice asks Sophie and Lily.

Sophie shrugs. "Probably somewhere near the main stage."

"I was just telling Noémie how much I missed her," Patrice says, squeezing my arm.

"Yeah, what's the deal with that, Nomi? Like, you just totally dropped off of the face of the planet," Lily says. She reaches into the bucket and grabs a can of tropical punch White Claw. Today she's dressed in a Y2K-inspired outfit—an off-the-rack mesh crop top bedazzled with rhinestones and faux butterflies, a neon-pink low-rise mini skirt, and chunky Jimmy Choo heels. It's not an outfit I'd wear, but she makes it work.

"I was in school," I reply. "And then I was working at that Michelin-star restaurant—Chez Avignon. It's on King."

"I know it. Adam took me once for my birthday. I had the lobster ravioli. It was good," Sophie says. She scrunches her nose. "Not sure why you want to work." Sophie's dressed the most conservative of our group, sporting a light-blue Versace floral-printed halter neck gown that I would trip a toddler for. I'm pretty sure it's vintage. It would look way better on me.

I don't reply to Sophie's last comment because it doesn't matter now. I was only working because Hugo demanded that I learned the trade before he invested in me. And now …

I've been radio silent with Claude. Surprisingly, he's been persistent, trying to meet up to go over the business plan. But I'm just not in the headspace for that kind of commitment right now. I should probably book an appointment with Rebecca soon. I should probably get back on my meds. I should probably find something to do with my life other than sleeping all day and binging Rupaul's *Drag Race*.

Right now, adulting isn't appealing, which is why I messaged Patrice when I saw that she was back in Toronto. She had an extra VIP wristband for the festival, and I jumped at the chance to come out. I needed a distraction.

Claude's wedding dinner rehearsal is tomorrow, and I'm kind of freaking out. Amelia consulted with me a bit about the wedding details, but my parents were never around for that. It's been almost a year since I've seen them. Will Hugo speak to me or pretend I don't exist?

Patrice and I almost match—we planned it that way. I'm wearing my tightest and shortest fringed jean shorts from Diesel and a suede tankini from Frankies Bikinis. My footwear is athletic—tan Nike Air Force 1's—because shuffling in heels is ridiculous. My hair is down, and I've applied a million layers of suntan lotion. No one would ever guess that I was a hobbit yesterday. Noémie's sexy today—I'm not into bratty femmes, and I'd do me sober.

The plan is to take a zillion photos of me looking hot and having fun. Even if Jordan is not following me anymore, I know Wayne is. And he's likely going to say something to her. Perhaps he'll even try to show her a picture of me. And maybe she will look. If she does, she will see how well I'm doing. And maybe she'll start having second thoughts. Maybe she will miss me.

Merde, why am I thinking about her? It's been months. I haven't seen or spoken to her in months. She is over us. I need to get that into my head.

I sniff.

"Hey, what's wrong?"

I look up at Patrice's concerned face. "Nothing, I'm good," I say, carefully wiping my eyes with the tip of my fingers. I really don't want to mess up my makeup.

"I know what will make everyone feel better," Sophie announces. Her gaze darts cautiously over her shoulder. When she's sure she's in the clear, she reaches into her bra and removes a bag of blue pills.

My eyes widen. Am I really getting back into this? Apparently, I am.

We each take a pill, chasing it back with a shot. Thirty minutes later, euphoria floods my veins. The music calls to me. It's a siren's call to all of us.

Each grabbing a can of White Claw, we exit our VIP booth and make for the stage, where we dance and dance and dance. And drink and drink and drink. I lose count.

The music thumps against my skin, and the bass becomes one with my pulse. Bright, colourful lasers entrance me. It's bliss being surrounded by the tight mob of sweaty bodies gathered around the stage. We're all strangers, but we're also one with the music.

Time dissolves and soon it's nighttime. Tiësto hits the stage. I lose my fucking mind. Patrice lights up a joint and hands it to me. I suck in the smoke, cough, and begin to giggle uncontrollably.

Patrice stands behind me and pulls me into her arms. "I really fucking missed you, Nomi."

I turn my head and smile at her. I think she's pretty. I think I like her shiny black hair. I think I want to touch it. So I do. "Your hair is like silk," I say.

Patrice combs a hand through my hair. "Your's is too."

We stare at each other. I think, fuck it. I kiss her. She kisses me back. I slip her some tongue. Somewhere someone hoots. Then there are a whole lot of hoots and hollers blending with the beats.

The world squishes together until all I see is black. And then someone is yelling. They are yelling so loud. Why are they yelling? "Noémie!"

Blinking hurts, like there's sand in my eyes. The world spins as I sit up. Patrice's arm falls off my naked chest. Both me and my friend aren't wearing anything under the sheets.

"Câlisse! Noémie cover yourself."

I look up and see Claude. He stands at the rim of my bed with his gaze diverted. Céline wriggles in his arms, trying to lick his face.

What is he doing here? Frowning, I pull the sheet up over my chest and lean my back against the headboard. "Why are you here?" I ask. One day I will need to change my lock.

"I should ask you the same thing," he says. His face is very red. All the veins in his face pop out. Why is he upset with me? Something tells me there's a reason, but it eludes me.

I just stare at him.

"The wedding rehearsal was today!"

Oh yeah … that. Fuck. I press a hand to my forehead. "I'm sorry."

Patrice stirs and lifts her chin. "Who's yelling?" She grabs a spare pillow and presses it over her head.

"You don't sound sorry," my brother snaps.

"Well, I am."

"Get dressed, and meet me downstairs," he says. "We need to have a talk—privately."

When he leaves, I drop back down on the mattress and stare up at the ceiling, trying to piece the night back together. It's all too blurry. I remember dancing. I remember kissing Patrice. And then … a cab. More kissing. We hooked up.

I should be more bothered by the indiscretion—she has a boyfriend. I can't find it in my heart to feel anything. Numb. Nothing. Space. My serotonin stores are depleted. There's nothing left.

I get up, and it's like the room is filled with water. There's so much resistance. Merde, I need an entire bottle of Tylenol to cure my headache. I find a discarded shirt on the floor and then shove my legs through the mini jean shorts I wore yesterday.

I have to lean on the banister as I take the stairs down. Claude's in the main room, seated on the couch. Céline's nestled in his lap. I shuffle towards him and sit on the coffee table.

"You missed the wedding rehearsal," he huffs.

"I'm sorry."

"You've said that already." His grey eyes glitter with a blend of fury, but something else … maybe disappointment.

"I know you hate me, but I thought you'd at least show up for Amelia."

I run a hand through my hair. "I don't hate you," I mumble. "I wanted to be there."

"Then why weren't you?" His voice cracks on the question.

"I blacked out," I admit. There's no point in lying.

"Merde." My brother rubs his face with both hands. "I thought you were done being so reckless," he whispers.

"I thought I was done too."

"I'm worried about you, Noémie, and I don't know what to do." His eyes are glassy when he looks up at me. "Tell me what I can do. I really don't want to lose you too."

I go to sit beside Claude on the couch. His head drops to my shoulder, and soon I feel something wet leaking through my sleeve. My brother is crying.

That does it. Something stirs inside me, and a lump forms in my throat. "I will get my shit together," I say. "I just can't say when that will be. But I can promise that I'll be on my best behaviour tomorrow. I'll be the perfect sister for your wedding."

Claude straightens and rubs his eyes. "I don't need you to be perfect," he whispers. "I just want to know you're okay."

I don't know what to say to that, so I keep quiet.

FORTY-ONE

My father is pretending I don't exist, but the moment Hélène sees me, she lights up with a smile and comes to kiss me on both my cheeks. "Ça fait tellement plaisir de te voir," she says.

I nod and break away from her orbit. I'm way too sober to be playing pretend that everything is all right between us. She also cut me out. Not once has she called me. On my birthday, I thought she would. She didn't.

I go to stand beside Amelia, who stands in front of a floor-length mirror, surrounded by her bridesmaids. She makes a stunning bride. I'm so happy for her. I'm so happy for Claude. He found himself a good one. Hopefully he's not like me and can figure out how to not fuck things up.

The wedding is taking place at Casa Loma, a famous castle in the heart of the city. My father spared no expense and bought out the entire building for the entire day, closing it to the public.

"Nervous?" I ask.

Amelia nods. "Yeah, just a little." She turns away from her reflection to look at me. "I'm so glad you could make it." There's no bite to her words. I would understand if she was bitter about me missing the rehearsal yesterday, but she isn't. I guess that shouldn't surprise me. Amelia's possibly the chillest woman I know.

"I wouldn't miss it for the world," I say. "I'm so sorry about—"

"It's really okay." Amelia smiles at me.

I smile back.

The wedding coordinator advises that it is time to leave, so we head for the waiting limo outside. The drive from my father's home in the Bridle Path to Casa Loma takes under thirty minutes.

In the morning light, the gothic castle looms ominously, with its ornate stone masonry and soaring turrets. It's a beautiful venue, but I wouldn't get married here. I want a destination wedding—perhaps at a vineyard in France.

We exit the limo, and the wedding coordinator fusses with Amelia's dress and hair a bit. I'm directed to stand beside Mathieu of all people. The bastard grins at me. I glare.

And then we are walking into the building. I loop my arm through Mathieu's and stare forward towards the conservatory. The buzz of conversation dies and guests stand as the wedding party makes its appearance.

The room is a lot nicer than I recall. Natural light streams in from the arched windows and the stained-glass ceiling. I remember wanting to throw up in my mouth a little when Amelia told me that the colour scheme was purple and orange. But by some miracle it isn't tacky at all; the flower arrangements are tasteful.

The bridesmaid dresses are orange—thank God. Purple isn't my colour. I'm also glad the style is a simple asymmetrical silhouette. I look good, which matters. The last thing I want is a million photos taken of me wearing something that makes me look hideous.

My gaze connects with Claude, who stands at the front of the altar. The smile that blossoms on my face is authentic. My brother cleaned up really well. The midnight-purple suit looks great on him. I'm so very happy for him. I might not be okay, but he's thriving. I love that for him. I love that he's moving towards something beautiful and meaningful. I love that he isn't a fuck up like me.

Finally, we make it down the aisle. I drop Mathieu's arm and slot myself in the first place I find. I'm not sure if I'm in the right position, but no one is glaring at me, so I take that as a win.

The music changes, slowing in tempo. Amelia is walked down the aisle by her father, and the ceremony is so heartfelt that it touches my soul. Tears prick my eyes when Claude slips the ring over Amelia's finger and kisses her. I'm bursting with love for them.

The guests cheer and applaud. My gaze strays from the newlyweds to the crowd. Hugo is grinning from ear to ear. Hélène demurely dabs her eyes. My parents are so thrilled, and it's hard not to feel the tug of sadness. I will never have this. They would never attend my wedding. They would never approve of their daughter marrying a woman.

I continue to vet the crowd, judging everyone's attire. I

see a face that doesn't belong, and my heart ceases for a moment. I blink because I must be seeing things—my mind's playing tricks on me. She can't be here.

But, the longer I stare, the more convinced I am that it isn't a mirage. Jordan's here—at Claude's wedding. My stomach turns over and my heart relearns to beat, but now it's thundering. I can't hear anything beyond it.

Someone nudges me, and I realize that I'm supposed to move. I leave the conservatory with the rest of the bridal party. I have to focus so hard on walking. My knees are fragile like an unset soufflé. The last thing I want to do is embarrass myself by falling.

I break off from the group when we're out of the room and lean against a wall. I tell myself to breathe. The task seems impossible.

Guests start to filter out of the conservatory to retreat to the garden for the reception. I make a concerted effort to straighten. I continue to tell myself to breathe.

Jordan is one of the last people to exit. Seeing her is like a punch to the gut. She's so fucking handsome in her perfectly tailored suit. And it's not black, but the lightest shade of lavender with white pinstripes.

When our eyes meet, a fire lights in me. Not the good kind, and I welcome the anger. How dare she show up here? Who the hell let her in? No one invited her.

I promised Claude that I would be on my best behaviour today, but my emotional stability is razor thin. Jordan's presence is sabotage.

I stomp over to her. "What are you doing here, Jordan?"

She does that annoying thing she does when she's

nervous—she scratches the back of her ear. "Claude invited me."

My brother did what? I shouldn't be surprised by this plot twist. Of course he did. Claude being Claude, he always thinks he's helping, but all he does is make things worse.

Truthfully, I don't know how to feel right now. I want to see Jordan, because I always want to see her. But I don't want to see her because it's too late. Months! It's been months. She's just like Hélène. And if she thinks it's just okay to pop back into my life after blocking me on every social media app … Fuck her.

I grit my teeth.

Not wanting to have this conversation in the open, I grab Jordan's hand and yank her towards the stairs. There's no resistance on her end. She lets me drag her up two flights and down a wide corridor. I spot a secluded stairwell and decide it's a good enough place to have it out with her.

"What are you doing here?" I ask again, putting some distance between us. I lean against a wall and cross my arms. The stone is cool against my back.

Jordan is quiet for a moment, and then she says softly, "I missed you."

My eyes roll to another dimension. "And it took you months to realize this?"

"Yes." She frowns. "I mean, no."

I stare at her, waiting for an explanation that I know won't come. Jordan's a woman of few words. I wonder if my brother had to bribe her to show up. It's not out of the realm of possibility.

Sighing, Jordan slumps on the opposite wall and runs a

hand through her short curly hair. "I've always missed you," she whispers. "Even when you were just an aggravating customer. When you stopped coming into the shop, I felt your absence like an ache, and I wondered about you."

My mouth drops open a bit. I wasn't expecting her to say that.

She looks up at me, and her dark eyes sparkle with feeling. "Noémie, for such a long time, you've preoccupied my mind. And after living with you, and getting to know you, and falling for you …" She breaks eye contact, stares down at the floor, and clears her throat. "I'm not good at this. The only thing I'm good at is running when things get hard or challenging, but I'm trying to change. I'm working on going after what I want, and I know that what I want is you. I'm not sure words exist to express just … just how much I miss you."

I swallow. This can't be real. I'm dreaming right? But even if I'm not, even if this is true … "Okay, but you missing me doesn't change anything," I say. "You made it very clear that you don't trust me, that you might never be able to."

Jordan pushes off the wall. She takes a step forward towards me. "Trust can be rebuilt."

She's saying all the right things, but it's been months. We can't just start over and pretend like everything didn't happen. Pretend like she didn't abandon me. Pretend she hasn't said a word to me for months. If she really cared about me, she would have contacted me sooner. She would have called me. She would have texted.

"Maybe, but I thought about it." I bite my lip. "We aren't

good for each other, Jordan. We hurt each other. We don't communicate well."

"Let's just be honest with each other from now on." She takes another step forward.

"Didn't we already try and fail at that?" I really wish she would stay on her side of the stairwell. It will be difficult to think straight if she gets too close. I want to stay angry at her. Anger makes the solution clearer. She has to go. That's the truth. There should be no goodbyes. No second thoughts. Just silence and the kind of forgetting that leave scars. Because it doesn't even matter that I love her. It doesn't matter that she's telling me what I want to hear.

She hurt me, and as it turns out, I'm a sadist. Right now, I want to turn her away because there's a high chance it'll hurt her back. Yes, I want her to hurt. I want her to lie awake crying and missing me. I want her to fall sick needing me. I want to get even. For too long Jordan's held all the cards. For once, it'd be nice to win, even if victory means being miserable forever.

What does that say about me as a person? I love Jordan. And even knowing all the shit she's been through, I want to destroy her.

"I don't think we actually tried," she says.

"You deserve to be with a good person, Jordan." Sighing, I shake my head. "I'm not a good person. There's a reason Cara took the money from my father—she was sick of my shit. You've no idea how vindictive I can be. You know I flirted with your cousin because I didn't like seeing you with your ex. You know I only brought Felix around so much because I knew it bothered you. You know I left for Hawaii because I knew you'd be pissed." Well, I wasn't sure of that, but I'd been hoping she'd care.

"I guessed as much, but …"

"But what? There's nothing you can say that can defend my behaviour." I chuckle coldly. "Want to know something else? I was ecstatic when Wayne told me you had a tantrum at work because you thought I chose Felix over you. Knowing all this, you still want to be with me?"

"I do," she says without hesitation. "Because you're telling me. We are talking about it."

I frown. I wasn't expecting that response, and my resolve melts like ice. But I'm so scared of giving my heart to her again. How can I be sure she won't jump ship the moment she finds out I'm everything she doesn't want in a partner? Maybe I just should put it all out there—all my crazy. She said she wanted honesty. I doubt she can handle it.

"I've heard you tell Wayne before that you hated how jealous and possessive Audrina was. I'm worse than her," I say. "Putain de merde. I wanted to kill that girl you brought over. I want to curse any woman that looks at you. On New Year's Eve, I just about lost my goddamn mind when you were dancing with Audrina."

Jordan's brows pinch together. "I didn't know you saw me with Audrina."

"I wouldn't have let you know, Jordan," I admit. "And that's my point. I lie. I lie a lot, especially when it comes to talking about my feelings."

Jordan isn't deterred. She closes the gap between us. She takes my hands in hers and stares into my eyes. The contact lights me up, filling up the empty space. Her vanilla-accented cologne overwhelms my senses. "You're doing a good job of talking about your feelings now," she says.

"That's because none of this matters."

"Don't say that." She squeezes my hands.

She's really making this so hard. I close my eyes and shake my head. "We aren't good for each other, Jordan."

"You don't know that. You can't know that. We haven't even tried." She drops my hands and holds my face. Her thumbs brush over my cheeks, and I get lost in her eyes. And if that isn't bad enough, she brushes my lips with her own. It's so gentle, but it makes me feel so much. Too much.

I tremble.

"You might be all those things, but you're also kind and thoughtful. When I got into my accident, you dropped everything and drove all the way to Scarborough to pick up my family," she whispers against my mouth. "You asked your brother to introduce me to François. You pushed me to go after my dream."

In a last ditch effort, I push weakly against her chest. "Jordan—no, we can't do this."

Jordan ignores my protest, and I'm torn between fury and relief. Her lips press against my neck, and I can't stifle my groan. Because, I do want this—even if I'm still so hurt.

Jordan sucks and nips my neck, and my traitorous body dissolves. My hands that were pushing on her chest now bunch her shirt, pulling her closer.

"I love you so much, Noémie," she breathes the words softly in my ear, and then draws back enough to meet my gaze.

Jordan still loves me. My heart clenches, and my lips part. All my defences crumble like shortbread.

Jordan stares down at my mouth and looks back up into my eyes. She's asking my permission. Where we go from here balances on my decision.

I'm scared, but maybe this could be the start of something new and beautiful. Happiness has always eluded me, but whenever Jordan and I were together—when we weren't fighting or ignoring each other—it seemed within reach.

Caught between pride and desire, I study Jordan's face and remember the first time I saw her. I remember how the world hit a red light and stopped. I don't think it flipped back to green until I saw her again years later. Jordan has always felt like my destination. I want to go to her.

I nod. Jordan smiles. I smile. She kisses me, and I feel it everywhere. I feel alive.

We grope hungrily at each other. Her fingers dig into my scalp. My nails rake down her back.

I fist her tie and jerk her to me. "I don't share," I murmur against her lips. "If we do this, you're mine. Only mine." Because that's the only way this has a chance of working. I won't be strung along.

"I wouldn't want it any other way," Jordan rasps, putting some of my concerns to rest. Her hands drop to my hips, and she presses into me.

I suck in a breath. "Mon dieu, you look so sexy. I think purple's your colour." My hands glide up her torso, fanning out over her chest. I'm aching so bad for her. "I need you to touch me."

Blinking, Jordan quickly looks over her shoulder. "Here?"

I arch a brow. "Problem?"

"No." Jordan chuckles and kisses me again, dipping her tongue in my mouth. She hikes up my dress. I feel the slide of her palm on my thigh. She's moving too slow for my liking. I don't want to be toyed with. I want to be fucked.

Grabbing her hand, I shove it between my legs where I need it. "You make me feel so much," I say, rolling my hips, grinding against her hand.

Jordan groans. She rubs me over my panties. "I love how wet you get for me." She nudges the fabric aside. Her fingers lightly graze over me. She's teasing me, and I hate it. I'm too impatient, and who knows when someone will come looking for me. The chance of being discovered thrills me, but it'd be a whole thing. So we can't get caught. We need to move fast.

"Stop playing with me and fuck me," I say.

"You're always so bossy."

"I'm needed at the reception. We don't have—" Jordan pushes her fingers inside me, and I see stars. "Fuck!" Squeezing my eyes shut, my head knocks the wall.

Jordan curls her fingers. She's hitting that spot and driving me insane. She fucks me hard and fast. Her firm grip locks me in place as I ride her fingers. She's stretching me three fingers deep. Her thumb rubs over my clit. With every stroke I'm brought one step closer.

Our eyes lock. "I want you to come for me," she says. Her expression is intense. It's the look in her eyes that sends me over. Jordan covers my mouth just as euphoria crashes over me. The feeling is better than any pill. I come so hard my legs buckle.

Jordan holds onto me, keeping me upright. My forehead drops to her chest.

She licks off her fingers and groans. "Fuck, you taste good." Her words make me shudder.

We stand like that for a while. Only the sound of my ragged breaths fill the space. Jordan kisses my forehead and smooths a hand over my hair. When she smiles at me, it's easy to forget all our problems. "I love you," she says.

I brush my lips against hers. "I love you too," I say back, because it's true. I just don't know if love is enough. I still have doubts. I'm still hurt.

We disentangle. I right my dress. "How do I look?"

"Perfect."

I roll my eyes. "I'm being serious. How's my makeup? I don't have my purse on me, and my compact mirror is in it."

Jordan gives me a once over. "Your makeup is fine. Not even your lipstick is smudged."

"Thank God for transfer-proof lipstick," I say, holding out my hand. "Let's go. I'm worried that someone's looking for me."

She frowns. "You want me to come?"

I frown right back. "Yes, you're my date."

"What about Hugo? I don't want to create a scene."

I sigh. "If my brother invited you, I think he's likely banking on us creating a scene. I think I told you that he tries to hurt my father any chance he gets."

"But what about you?" Jordan asks. "I have no problem leaving if it makes things easier."

"Fuck easier. If my father has a problem, we can leave

together," I say, and I mean it. "I'm done shoving who I am in a box just so he can sleep better."

She takes my hand, and we go.

FORTY-TWO

The reception is held in the glass pavilion. I guess the centrepieces are adequate—orange, purple, and cream flowers are positioned at the centre of white linen-covered tables. The blinking chandeliers above our head are a tad too gaudy.

Chatter fills the room. Claude and Amelia have their own table at the front of the space up on a dais. They look so happy and are laughing about something.

I hesitate. Maybe I should ask Jordan to leave. Who knows how my father will react to her presence at my side? Then again, Claude invited Jordan. He wouldn't have without clearing it with Amelia first. So they extended the invitation knowing the risks.

Hugo and Hélène are seated at a table near the front of the platform. Dread churns in my stomach. My grip on Jordan's hand tightens.

"I can always just go," she whispers in my ear. "You don't have to do this."

I give Jordan a look. Her words intensify my resolve. She's my date. We are together. Claude invited her.

When we reach the table, Claude is the first to notice us. He beams at us. "Salut, Jordan, I'm so glad you made it," he says.

My parents turn their heads to see who Claude is welcoming. Their scowls are immediate. They stare down at my fingers that are laced through Jordan's. My heart pounds in my head.

"Noémie, what is the meaning of this?" The chair scrapes along the floor as Hugo shoots to his feet.

"Jordan's my date," I say, managing to sound cool despite my racing pulse. Despite wanting to throw up.

My mother clutches the pearls at her throat. Her mouth hangs open. My father's face goes completely red. His fingers bite into the tablecloth. The glass of cognac is an inch away from his hand. I fear he might throw it at us.

"Your date?" he shouts.

"Not sure why you both seem so surprised," I say. "Didn't we go over this already? I'm a lesbian. I date women." We actually didn't go over anything, but I'm letting it be known now. I'm a lesbian, and I'm saying it out loud to others for the first time. I can't quite believe I said it. I feel so sick, but I can't let them see how much the confession took out of me.

Exhaling a deep breath, I tell myself that the hard part is over. All I have to do now is stand my ground. I can do that. And it helps that Jordan is with me. I know how much she hates conflict. It means so much that she's not backing out of this—that she's acting as my support.

"Tabarnak, you do not! You are not." Hugo's teeth mash together. The veins on his forehead protrude, threatening to burst.

"Pourquoi joues-tu avec nous?" my mother cries.

"I'm not playing games, Maman," I say.

"Whether this is a trick or not, she has to go," my father spits out, pointing a finger at Jordan. "And perhaps you should leave as well, Noémie."

"No one is going anywhere," Claude says, striding up to the table. I thank him with a look. He nods at me before fixing Hugo with a hard stare. "I invited Jordan, and if you have a problem with her being here then the two of you can go."

"You have some nerve, boy." Hugo's eyes narrow on Claude. "I paid for this wedding. And I—"

"And I'll pay you back, if that's what you want," my brother says, shrugging. "But what you won't do is tell me who I can and cannot have at my wedding. You have no right."

Things get worse from there. Every eye in the vicinity settles on us. Claude and Hugo shout insults at each other in French. My father tells my brother that he might reconsider Claude's role in the company. In response, my brother announces that he is quitting Poutine Heaven and that he and I will be branching off to start our own venture. I can't quite believe what I'm hearing.

"Tu es en train de déchirer notre famille," my mother says to me.

I am not the one who broke our family. Hugo broke us first. He thinks he can control us. He thinks he has a right to tell me who I can love. Shaking, I scream that at Hélène.

"I have every right!" My father breaks from speaking in French, I think he wants Jordan to understand his next words. "I am your father. It's my job to steer you two on the right path!"

"No, you cannot tell us what to do or who we can love," Claude screams back. "Your bigotry is disgusting, Father. The only path you are steering Noémie down is away. Is that what you want? Do you really want to lose a second daughter because of your hate?"

At the mention of Antoinette, our parents go very still. Seconds pass with them looking dazed, and then my father shakes his head. "Hélène, we are leaving," he announces, reaching for his walking stick. Then, to Claude, he says with a sneer, "I will have my secretary invoice you for the cost of the wedding."

My brother's jaw clenches. "I will pay it the moment it arrives."

Hélène rises from her seat, looping her arm through Hugo's. Without another word or glance, they leave. A few of my father's lackeys follow suit, exiting the reception.

Jordan looks down at me. "Are you okay?"

"No," I admit, offering her a shaky smile. I'm not sure if that went better or worse than I was expecting. Sure, my father didn't throw anything, but now Claude's out of a job, and he's been pinned with the bill for the wedding. My brother sacrificed so much for me. I don't deserve it.

Jordan pulls me into her arms and presses her lips to my forehead. "Anything I can do?"

"You're here. That's all I need," I say. It's a lie, but I can't say the truth. What I actually need is a quiet place to retreat to. I want to go home. I want to sleep off the events of the day. I want to hit reset and get back on track. I owe it to Claude. If he spoke truthfully, he really wants to open that restaurant with me. So I need to get my head back in order. I need to work harder than ever to prove to him that his investment in me and my dreams will pay off.

I stare at my brother with a promise in my eyes. Claude is grinning ear to ear. He looks like he couldn't be happier with how things played out.

Amelia comes to stand at his side looking quite unbothered. I don't know how she's so cool about everything. If all hell broke out at my wedding, heads would roll. She threads her fingers through Claude's. "It's good to see you again, Jordan. I know Claude was worried you wouldn't be able to make it."

"I'm so sorry about everything," Jordan says.

Amelia waves away her apology. "There's nothing to apologize for." She smiles at us. "But please, sit. I fear we need to get the speeches started soon before François gives himself an aneurism. Poor man, I don't think he even noticed what just happened."

Jordan pulls away from me to search for François. He's pacing in a back corner. Why is he so nervous about giving his speech? He runs a social media empire.

Claude chuckles. "I really don't get what he's so worried about."

My brother and his wife return to their table, and Jordan and I take a seat.

François is called up to take the microphone a minute later. He's sweating profusely. I tune him out. I tune everything out and replay the argument with my parents over and over. A heaviness falls over me.

Jordan's hand squeezes my knee under the table. Today was a complete shit show, but I guess something good came out of it. My gaze hovers over Jordan's face. I examine her profile—the fullness of her lips, the smoothness of her skin, the thickness of her lashes. I feel less overburdened. She grounds me. I really hope things work out between us.

François finishes speaking and everyone claps. It's my turn to take the mic. I rise from my chair. I'm not nervous about what I have to say, I'm just tired. Luckily, I'm a great actress. I know how to put on a smile and play a room. So I do that, and I can tell from the heartfelt expression in Claude's eyes that I'm doing a great job fooling everyone.

FORTY-THREE

Jordan leans against the side of the house. Her bright-green motorcycle sits in the driveway. I wish she would have gotten rid of the blasted thing after her accident. One day, I will figure out a way to convince her to stop riding.

I park my car in the garage and cut the engine. My hand hesitates on the door handle because I'm worried. Jordan and I just made up, which means we should have explosive makeup sex. That's how it's supposed to be right? But I'm not in the mood.

I've been off my anti-depressants for weeks, and after all the highs and the lows today, I just want to take a shower and sleep. I need to refuel to the point where I feel normal again, and I've always done that alone. But I also don't want to push Jordan away now that she's back in my life.

Pressing a hand to my forehead, I lean back in my seat and sigh.

There's a tap on my window. Looking up, I see Jordan.

"Everything all right?" she asks when I open the door.

"Yeah," I begin to lie, but then I shake my head. "Actually, no, I'm not okay." I slip out of the car and shut the door.

"Anything I can do?"

"I ... I don't know."

"Do you want to talk about it?" She asks.

I rub my eyes with my palms. Cara never wanted to hear about my problems. She always thought I was making excuses when I wasn't up for intimacy. While I know Jordan isn't Cara, I also don't know if turning her away tonight will ruin the little progress we've made.

Jordan doesn't wait for my response. She pulls me into a hug. "You were so brave today," she says. "I know it must have taken a lot out of you to face your father."

It's like she's reading my mind. I nod against her chest and wrap my arms around her waist. It feels good to be held. I realize that I don't just want to shower and sleep. I want Jordan to hold me. Is there a way to tell her that without it being a whole thing?

"Jordan ..."

"Yes?" She looks down at me.

I bite my lip. "I'm really tired."

"Me too. It's been a long day." She smiles, but it waivers. Her arms drop to her sides, and she takes a step back. "Did you want me to leave?" she asks softly.

I shake my head. "No, I want you to stay, but ..." My gaze drops to my wringing hands. "Is it okay if we just cuddle?"

"I would love that," she says. My eyes snap up to hers. The expression on her face seems earnest enough.

She arches a brow. "You thought I'd have a problem with that?"

"Yeah, maybe," I reply.

Jordan chuckles. "I know I have a reputation, but it kinda hurts that my girlfriend thinks I'm some kind of sex fiend."

Girlfriend? My heart melts into my stomach. "Did you just call me your girlfriend?"

Jordan blinks. "Too early to throw that word around?"

"Nope." Beaming at her, I rise on my toes and kiss her cheek. I thread our fingers together. "Let's go inside."

Céline's yapping greets us the moment we step through the door. When she notices Jordan, she begins to spin like crazy and whine.

Jordan scoops the dog up and scratches her head. "You bark way too loud for such a tiny thing."

"Finally, you're home," Wayne says, approaching the foyer. He stops walking when he sees Jordan. His mouth drops open, and he screeches. "Oh my gawd! You two made up? When the hell did this happen? Why wasn't I informed?"

Jordan rolls her eyes. "What the hell is he doing here?"

"He was dog sitting," I explain.

Wayne stomps his foot. "Don't ignore me! Answer my questions!"

"You need to chill, bro," Jordan says. "No one kept anything from you."

Wayne's face says he doesn't believe us.

"Claude invited Jordan to the wedding," I say with a shrug. "And Jordan grovelled, and now we're together."

"There was no grovelling," Jordan mutters, clearly amused. Céline wiggles in her arms and licks her chin.

"The way I remember things, there was grovelling."

"You need to get your memory chip upgraded," she teases, holding my gaze.

"Ewwww … and I thought you guys drooling over each other before was gross," Wayne says, reminding me we're not alone. "My eyes can only take so much. I will see myself out." He pushes past us and quickly exits through the front door.

Seconds later, my phone buzzes. When I pull it out, it doesn't surprise me to see a text from him.

WAYNE, 10:31 P.M.

OMFG!!! You get it girl!

I heart his message and put my phone away. The house is so quiet.

Jordan sets Céline down, and I take her hand and guide her upstairs. I steer her towards her old bedroom. "We're not going to your room?" she asks.

It's embarrassingly messy, and I don't want Jordan to think I'm a slob. Also, I haven't changed the sheets, and I won't have us cuddling on bedding with Patrice's lingering scent on them.

"Your shower is bigger," I say. I'm not lying, it's the truth.

Jordan's brows pinch together. "Not sure I follow."

"Don't tell me you're not dying for a shower too," I say, tugging her into the bedroom.

"I thought you just wanted to cuddle?"

"Yes, but I want to shower first," I say, giving her my back. "Unzip me."

The heat of her fingers brush against my skin as she undoes the zipper. I push the dress down my shoulders, and it pools on the floor. I'm feeling a little self-conscious about my body. For months, I've avoided the gym. My body isn't as snatched as it used to be, but the way Jordan's eyes feast on me at that moment puts me at ease.

Actually, it does more than that—something stirs. I'm still beyond exhausted, but now I'm thinking I might be up for more than just cuddling.

"You're so beautiful," she rasps.

"You're not too bad yourself." My hands go to her cream-coloured tie. I work to undo the knot and remove the silk fabric from around her neck. "Merde, I love this colour on you," I say, popping open the buttons of her jacket.

"Yeah, you've only told me, like, a million times today."

I choose to ignore her snarky comment and slide the jacket off her shoulders. It joins my dress on the floor. My hands fan out over Jordan's chest, revelling at the feel of her under the crisp collared shirt. "I can't quite believe that you're here with me now," I whisper.

"I'm here. I'm not going anywhere." Her hands encircle my waist.

I stare up and get lost in her eyes. "Kiss me."

Jordan bends her head. Our lips touch, and I get lost in the feeling. More and more, I'm thinking I've been too quick to write off having sex tonight. More and more, I'm thinking Jordan's wearing too many clothes. It takes a century to undo all the buttons of her shirt. She wears an undershirt beneath it—another barrier.

Jordan seems to sense my frustration. She breaks away from me and peels the stupid undershirt off in a fluid movement. Off goes her bra next.

It's the first time I'm seeing her bared breasts. They're smaller than mine and way perkier. They're perfect. She's perfect. Looking at her makes my mouth water.

She said she was okay with anything above the belt, but I decided to confirm. "Can I touch them?"

Jordan nods. She trembles when I do and groans when my thumbs brush over her nipples. "Fuck, you're making it hard not to want more. We should probably slow down Noémie."

I don't want to slow down. "I've changed my mind," I say. "I want you."

"Are you sure?" Her brows pinch together. "I know you're tired. I don't want you to feel pressured into—" Jordan gasps when I dip my head and suck on her nipple, swirling my tongue over it. The peak stiffens. Her reaction to my mouth on her skin delights me. Her fingers dig into my back as I nip and tug. Her breath hitches.

I unbuckle her belt, and she kicks her pants off. Jordan unpins my hair and unclasps my bra. When we're both naked, we stumble into the bathroom, kissing.

Jordan starts the shower, and the room fills with steam. We go under the spray. The water hits my back. Jordan grabs my face and kisses me deeply. She squirts some body wash onto her palms, working it into a lather. Then her hands are on me, moving over my body. "You make me feel so much," I say.

Jordan stares at me intensely. "The feeling's mutual." She spins me around and massages the soap onto my back. Her lips graze my nape.

I gasp when she nips the shell of my ear. "You said you

started falling for me over Halloween. What did it, the Princess Peach costume?"

Jordan chuckles. "No, not that. It was when we fell asleep together while watching that paint restorer's videos on YouTube," she says, kneeling in the tub to slather soap over my thighs and calves. "I woke up before you did, and you just felt so right in my arms. I didn't want you to wake up because I knew it'd mean I'd have to let you go."

Her confession makes my heart flutter. Jordan rises to her full height, and I turn around to face her. "You would have saved us a lot of grief if you'd just said something," I say.

"You could have said something."

"I couldn't," I say. "I wasn't lying, Jordan. I've had a hard time talking about my sexuality, but I realized I'm not a fraud. I've finally made peace with who I am, and I'm done hiding." I take her hand in mine and squeeze.

Jordan looks down at our interlaced fingers. "Why would you think you were a fraud?"

For a few moments, the only sound is the spray of the shower. "I told you that Antoinette was gay." A lump forms in my throat as the memory surfaces.

Jordan nods.

"My sister and I got into an argument the night she ... got into her accident," I say, my voice cracking. "She called me pathetic. She implied that I couldn't possibly be attracted to women too, and that I needed to quit hanging out in her shadow and build my own life. She told me that I'm not a lesbian, and it seems like I've held on to her words for years. I've ignored thinking about my sexuality, even when it became abundantly clear that men held no interest for me. Because in a lot of ways, Antoinette wasn't wrong. I've always stood in her shadow. I've tried to mimic her in so many ways. Some days, I'm not even sure who I am."

"I'm sorry your sister shot you down like that." Jordan pulls me into her arms and kisses my forehead. "But give yourself some slack. It's hard to figure things out."

"For some people it isn't. Antoinette always knew who she was." I stare up into Jordan's eyes. "I really never wanted to lie to you."

"I know that now," she says.

I sniff and reach for the body wash. "Now that I've told you my deepest darkest secret, tell me something I don't know." I want to change the subject.

Jordan shudders when I begin rubbing my soap slicked hands over her torso. "Pamela Cross was modelled after you."

My hands still on her body. "I knew it. Why didn't you tell me?" I go back to soaping her up.

"You already think you're hot stuff, I didn't want to add lighter fluid," she says. "And I was a little embarrassed. Like, it's kind of creepy when you think about it—designing a character off a customer."

"I'm not creeped out. I'm flattered that you were so obsessed with me," I say, pressing my lips to the hollow of her throat. I squat in the shower to clean her legs. I marvel at how smooth her skin is.

"I was a little too obsessed with you," Jordan admits. "And I hated it. You were such an annoying customer, but I … I always looked forward to seeing you. I anticipated seeing what outfit you'd pop in the coffee shop wearing."

"I only dressed up for you."

"What?"

I smile up at her, feeling the burn of embarrassment crawling up my neck. Since we're being honest with each other, why not lay everything out in the open. "I had a crush on you for longer than you can imagine. I first saw you ages ago at a drag bar where Rita Bitch was performing—I was smitten." Done with her legs, I stand.

Jordan squints like she's trying to remember something. "Did we meet?"

"No, not really." I bite my lip. "You stepped out of the washroom stall with Sarah, and I was washing my hands at the sink. I don't think you noticed me, but I … I noticed you. And then, years later, I saw you at Grind That Bean and I couldn't stay away."

Jordan grins. "Well, that's … wow."

"Wow indeed." I close the small gap between us. Our wet bodies press into each other. I kiss her neck and rake my nails down her sides. "I almost can't believe that we're together like this, after wanting you for so long."

"I'm yours now," Jordan says. She leans forward and shuts off the water. Tossing open the curtain, she lifts me into her arms and carries me over to the bed. The cool air makes my wet skin prickle. Water sprinkles on the floor.

I realize there are no towels down here. Before I can voice the thought, Jordan drops me onto the mattress and climbs on top of me. The weight of her is delicious.

She licks her tongue over my body until I'm squirming. "I

… I need you." I grab her hand and press it between my thighs. I'm aching for her touch.

"You're so impatient." She laughs and takes her hand away.

I'm about to whine when she shifts, raising my leg to get into the right position. I know what's she's about to do, but I can't quite believe it. Sparks of excitement shoot straight between my thighs. "I thought you don't like to be touched there."

"I don't count this as touching," she replies, shrugging. "Are you okay with it?"

"Fuck yes." I lick my lips. "There's almost nothing I wouldn't let you do to me."

Jordan raises a brow. "Is that so?"

"Yeah," I confirm, remembering her collection. "But maybe we buy new toys together. I allowed it that first time, but I'm not fond of having things that have been in other women inside me."

"Fair enough." Jordan chuckles. "If it helps, you're the only woman I've used the purple toy with. To be honest, I was a little shocked you chose that one … it's intimidating. Wayne bought it for me a couple of years ago as a gag gift. Ninety percent of anything you saw in that drawer are gifts from friends—it's a long-standing joke to buy me sex toys."

Her confession makes me laugh and feel a little relieved. I run a finger down her arm. "Enough talking," I say. She's still lifting my leg, and it's starting to get uncomfortable.

"Okay." Jordan does some more manoeuvring, searching for the right angle. She finds it and finally lowers herself, connecting our bodies in the most delectable way. She's so incredibly warm and wet. My breath catches as she grinds into me. "Does that feel good?"

I moan. "Yes, go faster."

Jordan picks up the pace. The friction of her clit rubbing against mine feels so good, but it's still not enough. I start to move under her, matching her tempo. That does it. I can feel it now—that building pressure. I chase the feeling. My hands dig into the bed sheets.

"Fuck, Noémie." Jordan's eyes squeeze shut, and she groans. She's getting close too. Her fingers bite into my hips. We fuck each other harder, driving towards that cliff.

Jordan falls off first. Her body tenses, and she throws back her head. Seconds later, I follow her over the edge.

"Oh fuck," I cry out. The world whites out as wave after wave of pleasure hits me. I have to blink several times before my surroundings come back into focus.

Jordan grins down at me. She leans forward, caging my head between her forearms. She kisses me, long and deep. "You're fucking amazing," she mutters against my lips before rolling onto her back.

I snuggle up to her, resting my head on her shoulder. Her breaths are as fast as my own. I hear her heart pounding. My fingers trace invisible patterns on her chest as we recover.

Jordan's hands comb through my hair, still wet from the shower. Her dark eyes glitter with emotion.

I raise a hand to her face and brush my thumb over her cheek. "I love you, Jordan," I say. "Now say it back."

I expect her to laugh at that. I expect her to call me bossy. She doesn't. Instead, she frowns the slightest bit. "I love you, Noémie," she says. "And I wanted to say it the first time we slept together, but I was scared you didn't mean it. I haven't had the best luck with love and relationships, but I really want this to work. I want us to work, even if that means working more on myself."

"I feel the same way," I say. "We can work on ourselves together."

FORTY-FOUR

Two Years Later

The day's finally arrived—Maison Antoinette is soft launching. My heart is in my throat, and I've probably gone over my list a million times, checking to make sure that I haven't missed anything.

My staff are probably super fed up with me consistently checking in on their stations, but I need today to be a success. I know Wayne is sick of me; he's calling me a micromanager. Whatever, I'm not nearly as bad a Chef Ricard.

I stole Wayne from Grind That Bean. About three months ago, I made him the offer to be my maître d', and he not so graciously accepted. My gut is telling me that Wayne is the right person for the job, even if he wasn't the most productive worker at the coffee shop, and even if his catty antics put him at odds with some staff. No one cares more about the customer experience than Wayne. No one can de-escalate a fuming customer like Wayne.

There's a lot of buzz online about the restaurant. Our table reservations for today booked up in under an hour, which amazed me, but Claude wasn't surprised at all. "It's all because of you. People are coming for you," he said.

I'm still grappling with my new fame—if you can even call it that. About a year ago, I began a new vlog cataloguing the entire process of designing the concept and menu for the restaurant. My followers have been taken on a journey where I covered everything from permits to whether the cost for designer ice is worth it. I determined it was, but Claude is still fighting me on the decision. The videos have raked in millions of views on YouTube, but what has really exploded my follower count to the stratosphere are the daily shorts and reels I post. I've flipped the script on the standard trad wife cooking video. Nara Smith is my main inspiration. I copy her ASMR calm and high-fashion flair, but my videos push the gay agenda instead of conservative values, and my voiceovers are filled with innuendos that would make a stripper blush. My viewers go crazy whenever Jordan does the rare cameo. They are obsessed with her and us as a couple, as they should be.

It's kind of wild, and it's more than I ever dreamed. Claude and I managed to pull it all off without seeing a dime from our father. I'm just a little bummed—okay, extremely bummed—that Jordan can't be with me here today.

Turns out a lot of people want to read a comic with a

dyke for its main character. *The Diaries of Zara Williams* really took off. Jordan's a big-shot artist now, and she's constantly being invited to expos and conventions. She's at a really large one in the U.K. right now. She's been gone for almost a week, and there's a hollowness to celebrating this milestone—opening my restaurant—without her.

"Gloom isn't on the menu the last time I checked," I hear Wayne say. "This is your big day, Noémie, what are you doing pouting in a corner?"

I look up from my list and sigh. "I'm not pouting."

"Do you need a receipt? I can bring you a mirror," he says, posting up on the wall beside me. "What's got you down?"

"I just sort of wish Jordan could be here."

"Y'all are too codependent for your own good." He folds his arms. "But I get it. She should have turned down that gig. I will give her a piece of my mind when she gets back."

I chuckle at that. "I'm not going to stop you. Go all out. Let her have it."

"Don't worry, I won't pull any punches," he states. "Anyways, I was coming to find you because there's a delivery out back that you need to sign for."

I frown. "I'm not expecting a delivery."

"Are you sure about that?" He raises a brow.

I confirm with my list. There's nothing about a delivery today. Fuck, what else did I forget about? Gritting my teeth, I rush out of the kitchen and push open the back door. There isn't a delivery truck parked outside. There isn't a package. The only item on my list that I was missing stands in the back alley holding a giant assorted bouquet of roses and Peruvian lilies.

Squealing, I lunge myself at Jordan. "Oh my God, you came!"

"Of course, I came," she says in a matter-of-fact tone, like I shouldn't have ever doubted it. "I think you're crushing the flowers."

I squeeze her tighter. "They'll survive." Pulling away, I wipe my eyes. The tears are happy tears. "Come." I take her hand and pull her through the door. My team yips their approval as I tow my girlfriend to the back office and lock us away.

Jordan looks yummier than an ice cream sundae dressed in Tom Ford. I remember when I bought her the ballet-pink button-down shirt. She'd made a face at the colour and then at the price when it flashed on the register.

When she hands me the flowers, I notice the forest-green Harrod's gift bag dangling at her side. "That for me?" I ask, setting the bouquet down on the desk.

"Who else would it be for?"

I hold out my hand expectantly.

Jordan shakes her head. "I'll give it to you later—after service."

Now I'm pouting. "I would think you'd know me well enough by now," I say. "You can't just show up here with a present and expect me to wait."

Jordan scratches the back of her neck. "Yeah, I guess I didn't think it through." She bites her lip. "Can you wait just this once?"

"Absolutely not. I'm curious."

"I think it's better to wait," she says. "It'll be something to look forward to after dinner service."

"I won't be able to focus on dinner service if my mind's preoccupied," I argue. "If I can't focus, dinner service might be a disaster, and if it's a disaster, I will blame you. If I blame you, I won't put out tonight. It's better for us all if you give it to me now."

Jordan sighs and holds out the bag. "Fine."

I snatch it from her and plunge my hand between the white tissue paper. What I remove confuses me. It's not jewellery. It's not a designer bag. It's not a Labubu. Jordan's gifted me a comic book.

My confusion morphs into a smile when I see the cover. "Oh my God, it's us!"

The smile Jordan sends back my way is tight. "Yeah, it's just something I've been working on. Put it back in the bag, you can read it later," she says, reaching to take it from me.

I hold up a hand. "No, I want to skim through it."

"Aren't you opening in like five minutes? You don't have time for this." She tries to take it from me, but I won't let her.

"We're opening in forty-five minutes. I can spare a couple minutes," I say, dropping down into the chair by the desk. I flip open the front cover, and the scene that greets me makes my chest get all warm. "Awww … it's our story. Here we are at the coffee shop. Why is my dialogue so bitchy? Seriously, I'm not that bad. But I'll give you a pass because I like my outfit. I look hot, and that's all that matters."

Jordan sighs a defeated kind of sigh. She leans against the desk and watches me flip through the pages. I'm going through it a little too fast, but I'll make a point to read the whole thing tonight. Outlined in a comic, I think our origin story registers as way more dramatic than it really is. Jordan plays up the drama of the night she walked my drunk ass home. She depicts herself as being perfectly cheery at the Christmas market. Somehow, my father's chalet looks even more over the top.

And then I get to the last page and my heart races. "Jordan?" I look up from the page in time to watch Jordan kneel. She reaches into her pocket and removes a blue Tiffany box. My eyes go wide. I stare down at the page again—Jordan's kneeling in the scene too. I look back up and meet her eyes. I forget how to breathe.

Jordan clears her throat. "Noémie, from the moment you strutted into my life, I dreamed of a universe existing where you saw me as something more than just a barista. And you make me better, braver, and happier than I have the right to be. I want to spend our lives together." She opens the box and a diamond ring sparkles back at me. "Will you marry me?"

Tears blur my vision. If the rock was a little bigger, I'd probably be ugly crying right now, but I can forgive Jordan since the ring is Tiffany & Co.

Nodding my head, I grab the back of Jordan's neck and force our lips together. "Yes, I'll marry you," I say when I break our kiss. I wipe my eyes. "But seriously, how am I going to manage to get through service now? All I want to do is rehearse for our honeymoon."

"I'm so sorry." Jordan deflates with a groan. "In my head, this played out differently."

Straightening in my seat, I sniff and extend my hand. "Slip it on my finger. I want to see how it looks."

"You're always so bossy."

"Shut up, you love me."

Jordan's gaze softens as she slides on the ring. "Always and forever."

THANK YOU FOR READING!

Thanks so much for reading *Slow Cooked Feelings* 😃 Every review helps, so please leave an honest review if you can.

Sign up for my newsletter if you want to keep up to date on what I'm working and for additional chapters (which I'm working on).

ALSO BY MC HUTSON

French Pressed Love

Born of Blood and Magic

MC HUTSON

M.C. Hutson is a booktoker, author and host of *A Very Sapphic Podcast*. She was born and raised in Toronto, Canada.

When M.C. isn't reading, reviewing, writing or talking about gay shit on her podcast, you can find her in the kitchen replicating recipes she finds on YouTube or trying to get her morkshire terrier to behave. Before M.C. was domesticated, she lived to party and lived for lesbian drama.

Follow MC on Social Media

tiktok.com/@mchutsonauthor
instagram.com/mchutsonwrites
threads.net/@mchutsonwrites